ROMAN
SHADOWS

Also by Ron Burns:

Roman Nights

ROMAN SHADOWS

A NOVEL

Ron Burns

ST. MARTIN'S PRESS
NEW YORK

Production Editor: David Stanford Burr

Design by Glen M. Edelstein

LIBRARY OF CONGRESS CATALOGING–IN–PUBLICATION DATA

Burns, Ron
      Roman shadows / Ron Burns.
          p.   cm.
      "A Thomas Dunne book."
      ISBN 0-312-08514-1
      I. Title.
PS3552.U73253R64   1992
813'.54—dc20   92-19662
                                        CIP

First Edition: September 1992

10 9 8 7 6 5 4 3 2 1

Once again, for M. J. F.

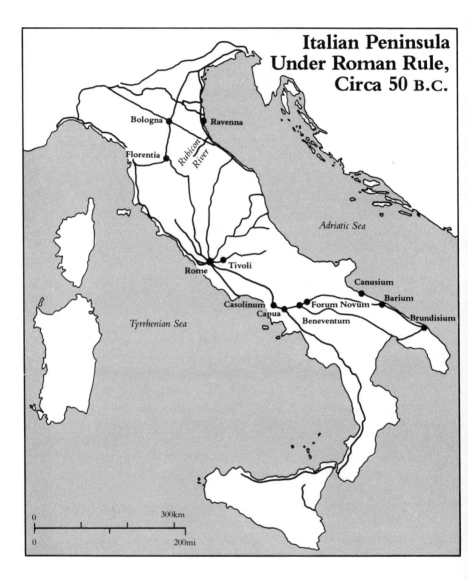

Italian Peninsula
Under Roman Rule,
Circa 50 B.C.

Bologna
Ravenna
Florentia
Rubicon River
Adriatic Sea
Rome
Tivoli
Canusium
Casolinum
Forum Novum
Barium
Capua
Brundisium
Beneventum
Tyrrhenian Sea

0
300km
0
200mi

INTRODUCTION

It is December in the ancient Roman year of 707—43 B.C. by the calendar of our day. Julius Caesar has been dead nine months. His great-nephew, Augustus, and his longtime deputy, Mark Antony, jockey for position and power.

Rome is in turmoil.

One Roman citizen, Gaius Livinius Severus, is able to explain this slide into chaos from the unique perspective of a truly inside observer. It is a role he stumbled into innocently enough more than nine years earlier: the role of detective.

Now it has landed him squarely in the midst of events that have become, quite literally, a matter of life and death—for Livinius and his family, and even for Rome itself.

ROMAN
SHADOWS

1

I expect to be murdered within the hour.

I expect Augustus to do it himself.

I've expected it, or at least half expected it, since dawn, when the guards came and took me from my house. But there's more certainty about it since a moment ago, when two men, apparently secretaries of some sort, walked past, looked at me sideways, laughed and whispered loudly to each other. And I distinctly heard one say, "That's the one. Another one gone. Be dead within the hour."

It was, I think you'll agree, convincing testimony.

★   ★   ★

The guards were quite polite when they came. After demanding, as a formality, to know if I was indeed Gaius Livinius Severus, which of course I am, one of them said, "Augustus wants to see you," in the mildest of tones.

They laid not a hand on me, and I made no move to resist. After all, there were four of them, all very large, suddenly standing around me in the atrium of my house. So what would have been the point?

I did hesitate for an instant: Looking around in surprise, past the large sweep of marble to the peaceful courtyard beyond, I saw my wife, Fulvia, stop to say something to the houseman. He smiled and bowed and said something in return, and she smiled and laughed that marvelously rich, throaty laugh of hers.

"My wife . . ." I said to the guards, gesturing toward her.

1

"She'll find out soon enough, sir," the polite one said, shaking his head, his tone almost sympathetic. "Best leave it, sir," another one put in, just as pleasantly. "You know how women are, they make such a fuss."

I had no argument for that. Naturally, she'd make a terrible scene, so perhaps it would be best to leave quietly. Best for me, to be sure, to remember her that way—smiling grandly, rather than in some panicky state. Indeed, these few hours away from her that smile of hers has done much to sustain me.

Once outside, the guards stayed close, but they did not bind or shackle me, and we strolled casually, with no great display of guards marching a prisoner through the streets.

Even so, the walk was not uneventful. Less than half a mile from my house, we encountered a small crowd gathered at the side of the street just at the end of an alleyway. As we approached, the people stepped aside (no doubt in deference to my imposing escort), and I could see a blood-spattered toga on the ground. Another instant, and I realized the toga covered a man's lifeless body.

"A thief, I'm sure," said one man in the crowd. "His money's gone, all right," said another, who was energetically rifling the dead man's clothing.

As the swelling crowd jammed the narrow walkway, we were forced to slow down, and for just a moment I was only a few feet from the body, near enough for a clear look at the man's face. With an awful start, I realized: It is my cousin, Claudius Barnabas.

Horrified, I stopped in my tracks. "Please move along, sir, let's have no trouble," one guard said.

"A cousin of mine," I blurted out, unable to take my eyes off the body. The guards seemed taken aback by that and allowed me a moment. I took a step closer and studied the sight. A patch of blood the size of a man's fist had spread to the outer toga over the left side of his chest. Seeing no other wounds, I thought: This was expertly executed by a man of great strength.

We had been quite close, cousin Claudius and I, and I stayed another minute, gazing at his face. It had been left unmarked by the bandit, and I could easily imagine him alive, full of his usual energy and wit.

What a waste, I thought, and felt my eyes water up and a tear

2

or two dribble down my face. And still young, I thought: a mere thirty, older than I am by just one year. And of course, with Augustus's guards standing beside me ready to take me away, I could not help wondering if I might soon be facing the same terrible end.

Suddenly one of the guards grabbed me roughly. "We must move on," he said in the tone of gruff impatience more typical of such men. I nodded and we continued our walk without further interruption.

★   ★   ★

"Augustus wants to see you," the guard had told me politely, as if he knew as well as anyone that the name was enough. For although it's been not even a year since the murder of his great-uncle, Julius Caesar, the name Augustus has become noticeably compelling. For Augustus rules here now, along with Mark Antony—with, I might add, no small amount of bloodshed dogging their footsteps since Caesar's famous assassination.

And still both men have their list.

And still the list keeps growing.

And still no one can be sure from day to day if his name is on it or not.

I was quite certain why Augustus wanted to see me, and indeed I hadn't been here a minute before he stormed into the waiting room and over to my side.

"No, no, no, this won't do at all," he said. He waved a long dagger vaguely in my direction, then used it as a pointer to indicate passages on a papyrus scroll. It was one of the scrolls I'd sent over to him a few days ago, the report he'd requested about an episode of some years earlier. I'd altered the facts in the report, given him what I thought he wanted to hear. After all, I thought, if he didn't know the true story, then so much the better. And if he did, he surely would not want it to be made part of the official record.

"You can do better, Gaius," he was saying. "You know what I want: the truth, or at least the truth as you know it. The report as you wrote it for Cicero."

We stood face to face, this Augustus and I, and I took new measure of him: Talk about young, Augustus is just nineteen, and believe me, he cuts no imposing Roman figure. He is slightly built

3

and not tall—I myself stand over him by three inches or more. And, as I say, the tales of his doings over the previous year are less than pretty.

Yet even at so tender an age and of such dubious disposition, he has become consul of Rome and now stands, with Antony, at the pinnacle of power over much of the world. I thought: Clearly I have miscalculated in some way. I had judged him to be a callous adventurer and something of a brat besides, and in my altered report, I gave him what people like that usually want—that is to say, something reasonable, something not too unpleasant, something to smooth everything back into place. Now here was the boy ruler suddenly voicing such interest in "the truth." It puzzled me, and I studied him a moment, staring straight into his eyes. Is there something more there? I wondered. Some depth, perhaps? Some trace of something solid?

I quickly sent for the "real" report, the one which, indeed, had been commissioned by no less than Cicero himself.

Ah, Cicero, I thought—now there's a statesman. As a matter of fact, we were in Cicero's old house, not far from the Forum, the house which had been appropriated by Mark Antony and, at the moment, was Augustus's temporary headquarters. It was in the small garden to the rear, not far from this very spot, where I and so many others had sat as pupils at Cicero's feet, enjoying the words of wisdom—

"Cicero!" Augustus fairly spat out the name. "What a fool that man is!"

A fool? How dare you say that! I wanted to snarl back. But naturally I held my tongue.

Augustus looked up abruptly as the timekeeper came in, then watched with uncommon interest as the old man and his helper lifted up the large hourglass in the middle of the room and artfully flipped it over. "Second hour, my lords," the timekeeper said, and walked off.

It was midday by the time the proper slaves of my household had been summoned, had finally found the proper scrolls in my most secret files and brought them to me here. Since then, they tell me, Augustus has been reading it all while, with guards just outside the door, I wait and think: about whether or not I'll be alive an hour from now, about the murder of my poor cousin, about my wife's laughter.

I think, also, about my report, the "real" one, that tells all about a series of events that began unfolding nearly nine years ago, and *about one person in particular who made so many of them happen.*

·   ·   ·   ·   ·   ·

The first time I met Gaius Scribonius Curio was at the theater one night. Plautus was on, or more specifically the play by Plautus called *Amphitryon,* which my parents and their friends found discomforting to watch, but which I and most of the younger crowd found thoroughly hilarious.

It was very early in the play. In fact, it was barely halfway through the prologue, even before Act One and the real beginning. As usual, most of the crowd were already in good humor. I remind you of the actor's opening lines, which are addressed directly to the audience:

> "Do you want me to be big-hearted and see that your business transactions, all your buying and selling, make money? Do you want me to expedite your business speculations and have them produce steady, fat profits? Well, my name is Mercury, my father is Jove, and the gods have assigned *me* the responsibility for handling all messages and profits. So, if you want me to aid and abet the pouring of perennial cash into your pockets, please, all of you, I have been ordered to ask a favor of you."

Even that quickly, many in the crowd, myself included, were bent with laughter at such bold irreverence.

> "The favor is simple and perfectly proper. I'm here as a proper person to put a proper request to proper people. After all, it's not proper to ask for improper things from proper people, and it's stupid to ask for proper things from improper people—they're a criminal bunch who don't know what right is and don't hold by it. As to the favor Jove has instructed me to ask of you: He wants detectives—"

At the mere mention of that word, I let loose a terrible, loud, embarrassed guffaw, and found that this Gaius Scribonius Curio,

5

who was seated just one row in front of me and one seat to the left—as it happened, quite by accident—turned fully around and looked me over. I'm sure I turned a deep shade of red, for in those days I blushed with humiliating frequency, and even now I have not yet learned to entirely control that habit.

"My father wants detectives," the actor was saying, "to go through every seat in every row of the house. If they spot a claque working for any actor, they're to strip each offender of his coat, right here in the house, and hold it as bail. And here's another order I've received: detectives are to be assigned to actors, too. Any actor who arranges for a claque to applaud for himself, or who arranges to cut down on a competitor's applause, is to get the whip till it makes tatters of his hide along with his costume."

Throughout all this, Curio kept looking at me with a broad, bemused smile, while my blush, I am certain, turned a deeper and deeper red. And all along, the laughter of the audience grew louder.

"You're not a detective, are you?" Curio finally asked, with a big, engaging grin and no hint whatever of any seriousness in his tone.

"No, no, nothing like it," I said, shaking my head. (And, of course, I had never thought of myself as a practitioner of anything so lowly as that until the instant the actor had said it. And I immediately thought: Well, in a way, I suppose I am. Then, a moment afterward, I'd found myself under Curio's penetrating gaze.) "It is only . . ." And I let my voice trail off, completing my remark with a gesture toward the stage.

"Yes, it *is* very funny," Curio said, still smiling at me in that charming way of his. And after an awkward moment I suddenly knew we were going to be great friends, though I wasn't at all sure it was such a good idea.

★　　★　　★

"You might want to meet this Scribonius Curio fellow," Cicero had said.

"Meet who?" I asked vaguely, for my mind that day would not stop wandering. We were in the garden of Cicero's Roman town house on a beautiful spring morning, and I savored the mixed scent of figs, olives and a pungent dash of mint. More to the point, however, I had first met the beautiful Fulvia just a few days before, and I could not get my mind off her. (Indeed, we were engaged a few weeks later and married a few months after that, and, to some extent, I suppose I still have that problem.)

"Gaius Scribonius Curio," Cicero said, sighing with exasperation and drawing out each syllable of the name. "I've mentioned him to you before, Livinius. He's only a few years older than you; he's just back from two years in Asia. He was quaestor out there, did an outstanding job managing the provincial treasury. And I told you: I think you would find him a useful and interesting companion."

I nodded, still struggling to focus my thoughts.

"Let me know what you think of him," Cicero went on.

"Yes, um . . . who? Curio?"

"Livinius, are you listening!" Cicero demanded with a sudden burst of intensity. Then he grabbed me roughly by the wrist, put his face close to mine and said with exaggerated slowness: "Let me know what you think of him, Livinius!"

And with the sudden force of a hammer blow, it finally sank in that my old friend and tutor was giving me something important to do. "Yes, master, I will," I said.

I nodded vigorously and met his stern gaze eyeball to eyeball, to let him know I understood both the import and the meaning of his request. Abruptly, he sat back, relaxed again, his eyes fairly twinkling.

"I hear she's very beautiful, this Fulvia," he said, smiling broadly. He leaned close to me, still grinning, and whispered, "And if you'll forgive an old man's cynicism, I also hear that she is very rich."

And there it was as usual—the hot flush of embarrassment across my face. "I might have known you'd already have heard," I said, trying not to laugh.

"I like to keep in touch with matters of importance," he said. "As you should know! Or, at least, as you're beginning to find out!"

I realized the connection he was making, and for some reason that only added to my discomfort. Indeed, at that moment, I felt as if my face might explode from the heat.

Cicero chuckled, tried to stop, then laughed out loud. "Forgive me, young Livinius, but watching you blush gives an old man great pleasure. Memories of the lost innocence of youth and all that."

"Yes, master," I said. I lowered my eyes and (what else?) blushed.

"Well, come into the house," he said. "Have some wine and some lunch, and perhaps we can recover ourselves sufficiently for talk of more serious matters." With that, he stood and I followed him inside.

•   •   •   •   •   •

(Of course, I did not know, then, that that was to be the last time I would ever visit him in this house. Even more unimaginable is the circumstance that has brought me back here nine years later.)

•   •   •   •   •   •

As it turned out, my chance meeting with Curio came on the evening of the very next day. The play was being held at the brand-new theater that Pompey had just built, and involved an innovation which the stage managers had tried only a few times before: performances after dark, by torchlight.

Curio and I introduced ourselves formally during the intermission and responded with identical gasps of recognition.

"Cicero mentioned—" we said in precise unison, then broke off with more laughter.

"So, you've been to Asia," I said. "I understand you were the provincial treasurer."

"The quaestor, yes."

"And were you a pupil of Cicero's before?"

"Oh, yes," he answered. "Those were wonderful times."

"He's a wonderful man," I said, to which Curio nodded agreeably.

There are people who feel comfortable with each other right off, and (even though, as a matter of fact, he turned out to be fully a dozen years my senior) Curio and I were two of them. We made plans to meet at the circus next day, then for the theater later in the week and for dinner a few days after that.

We drank wine late into the night, and I told him about Fulvia with a bit too much lilt and devotion in my voice than I suppose is proper for a manly conversation.

"So you're in love, eh?" Curio said with a kindly smile. "I suppose that means you've no interest in the parties I go to. There's one tonight at Hirtius Pansa's house. Dolabella will be there. Mark Antony. Everyone—"

"Mark Antony, eh?" I put in. "He's quite a scandalous fellow, I hear."

"Those stories . . ." Curio shook his head with mock concern. "I mean, what's so terrible? That is, if you don't count being a drunkard and a sex maniac." And with that, he burst into gales of laughter.

"Oh my," I said, laughing with him. Or trying to. There was an awkward moment between us, until finally I said, "Another night, perhaps; it's already late."

"Of course," he said.

His tone lacked conviction, so I said: "I trust you're not offended, Curio."

"No, no. It's as you say: some other night."

And then, after the brief formalities of departure, I made my way home.

2

Suddenly, Cicero was gone. Banished.

Sent into ignominious exile.

It happened one day just a few weeks after Curio and I had met—our beloved mentor and teacher disappeared from our midst. Let me briefly recount the events leading up to this infamy:

Two years before, an especially vile sort of Roman creature by the name of Clodius (Odious Clodius, I called him!) fell in love with Pompeia, the wife of Julius Caesar himself. He pursued her for months until one night, on the occasion of one of those mysterious ceremonies for women which men are not allowed to see, Clodius dressed in women's clothes and made his way into Caesar's house to meet her—as I say, at a time when no other men were there. Well, the idiot got lost in the corridors and was forced to ask directions. Naturally, whoever heard him ran off screaming that a man was in the house. The women closed all the doors, and eventually they found the hapless Clodius hiding in a closet.

Of course, there was a terrible scandal. Caesar divorced Pompeia and brought suit against Clodius for sacrilege. At his trial, Clodius insisted that he had not even been in Rome that night—that, in fact, he'd been staying with relatives far to the south.

Enter Cicero: Ever a man of truth, and in this case prodded by the nagging insistence of his wife (now ex-wife) Terentia, he testified that earlier that very day, Clodius had come to his house in Rome to consult with him on a variety of matters.

It was entirely true, of course, but even so, Clodius was outraged. At the trial, he threatened and bribed most of the jurors and won his acquittal by a narrow margin. Later, when he remarked that the jury had not believed Cicero's evidence, Cicero told Clodius to his face: "You will find that twenty-five of them trusted in my word since they voted against you, and that the other thirty did not trust yours, since they did not vote for your acquittal until they had actually got your money in their hands."

Biting remarks of that sort were not unusual for Cicero and helped make him many enemies in Rome, including a few of great wealth and power who were good friends to Clodius. So Clodius plotted his revenge. It was not a simple scheme; as I say, it took two years to execute.

His goal was to become a tribune. His reason was solely to gain the tribune's powers of exile, and only for the purpose of exiling one man. But Clodius was a patrician. Tribunes were, and are, from the lower class, the plebeians. What to do? Well, Clodius figured it out. He married into a wealthy plebeian family, adopted the demotion in rank for himself and had himself installed in his new job. After that, he wasted no time. In less than a week, the new-made tribune Clodius stood on the steps of the Forum and read the decree:

"By the powers vested in me, I hereby order the banishment to a distance of no less than five hundred miles from the city of Rome the senator and proconsul Marcus Tullius Cicero."

The notice was posted throughout the city. By the time of the reading, guards were already kicking down Cicero's door. Before anyone could move against it, he was escorted from the city and gone.

I was mortified—half the city was. But having schemed long and hard to get it, and, as I say, with the help of his rich friends, Clodius was allowed his revenge: Cicero fled south to Brundisium and then to Greece.

"This is terrible," I wailed again and again in the days right after.

"It's very sad," Curio answered calmly.

"He's a great man," I repeated, tears streaming down my face.

"Yes, he is," Curio quietly replied.

"But you don't seem to care much," I insisted, several days into my grieving.

11

He glared at me a moment, shaking his head. "Listen, young Livinius, I care as much as you do, all right! I just don't believe in blubbering over things you can't do anything about."

After some thought, I decided there was no sound argument to that, so I stopped my mourning. Or perhaps I only changed the form of it, for I then allowed Curio to take me along with him on his wild nights and show me a side of Rome I'd never even dreamed of. After all, I thought, it's as good a way as any to drown my sorrows.

So Cicero was gone and the parties were wild; and for a time I suppose I rather lost sight of things. In a way, the biggest surprise was how many homes of the most notable and noble Roman families were host to these affairs, so many, in fact, that it was hard to believe I had been so ignorant of their existence. The hilltop estate of the young senator Caelius, the garden villa of the astoundingly rich Trebatius, the charming little town house of the stylish and well-connected Dolabella—those and so many more saw gatherings of flowing wine and beautiful women. We lay back, caroused and drank all night long. We laughed and womanized and generally behaved badly: it was wonderful.

Actually, it was the wine, at least in such quantity, that was new to me. I had never imagined I could attain such a state of exhilaration—and foolishness—after a bit of excess. And, after several days of virtually nonstop indulging left me desperately ill for one full day and night, I quickly learned to moderate that habit.

As for women—well, that's another matter. In that, I confess, I was no baby. I don't mean to boast, but, truth be told, I'd long been hard pressed to avoid their attentions.

And, sure enough, at each new party, at least two or three would tell me, "You're so handsome." Or "You're pretty" or "gorgeous" or, worst of all, "adorable." Not that I'm complaining, mind you, for I cannot deny partaking of their favors, at least now and then, and even learning a few new tricks along the way.

One in particular stands out, a woman of thirty or so with enormous breasts and slightly plump, though very long, legs, who took me for a ride that left me dry as . . . Well, you get the idea.

As I say, it was nothing new to me: "You're so beautiful, Master Gaius," my mother's own personal maid had told me one quiet afternoon just a few days after my fourteenth birthday. And the next thing I knew—well, once again, details are unnecessary save to say that at that tender age it was quite an experience.

Situations of a similar sort arose more and more frequently after that, until, catching glimpses, I began to study myself in the reflections off the polished bronze and silver of our dining table, or even to sneak into my mother's private boudoir for a look into her shiny silver mirror.

What's all the fuss about? I'd ask myself, as I took those quick looks. True enough, my skin was clear, though perhaps I was a bit paler than most of my friends; my teeth were straight, my smile was pleasant enough. Well, so what—except . . . hmmm, something about my eyes, perhaps? Well, maybe not the eyes, exactly. But . . . ah, yes, the eye*lashes*. That was it! Dark and long and . . . in truth, well, my goodness: rather girlish, aren't they?

In any case, no need to dwell on such nonsense—although I have good reason for telling you all this, which you'll find out soon enough. For the moment, I am simply explaining how far from inexperienced I was in such matters as I embarked with Curio on our tour of Roman night life.

Thanks to the gods, my beloved Fulvia never heard so much as a whisper of any of this. But her father, the formidable Victorinus Avidius, did: Indeed, one bleary-eyed morning I awoke to a messenger in my bedroom presenting me with a most insistent invitation to meet Avidius for luncheon on that very day. Somehow, I pulled myself together and kept the appointment.

Being, as we Romans say, "rich as Crassus," Avidius owned what may have been the largest house in Rome at that time—or at least the second largest. He lived a twist or two of the road above my family on the hillside of the Quirinal in the exclusive north end of the city, and, in fact, after passing through the front gate of his property, my litter bearers still had quite a trek to go before finally reaching the house itself.

I was quickly escorted to an upstairs dining room, a lovely and quite intimate affair complete with frescoes of pastoral greenery and a grand view of the center of town.

Avidius greeted me graciously enough, and we quickly seated ourselves at the well-stocked table. He was an oddly proportioned man, with an enormous head perched atop a rather small and slender body. Standing up, one towered over him with seeming advantage. But seated at a table, listening to his deep, forceful voice and looking at his large, expressive face (dominated, I might add, by thick, grayish eyebrows that leapt up into his forehead at moments of agitation), one quickly forgot his diminutive stature and had the impression of addressing a very large and intimidating man.

"Where's Fulvia?" I asked, though in truth I would have been amazed to find her there. "She's well, I trust."

"She's fine," Avidius said pleasantly. "She may be along later," and went on to make the most charming small talk until well into the meal, when suddenly he said:

"So then, you *do* love my daughter? That is to say, you *will* make a good husband and father. That's right, isn't it, young Gaius?"

We had just been discussing some utterly inane subject, something about which team, the blues or the greens, had the best chance of winning the circus games that weekend. Indeed, at that precise instant, I had in my mouth a considerable spoonful of eggs and diced pork—I'm certain he had deliberately waited for such an opportunity. And, startled as I was, it naturally took me a long moment to swallow it all down and answer his question.

"With all my heart, your lordship," I said, still chewing the last of it. Then, my mouth free at last, I added: "Fulvia is everything to me."

"And to me, as well," he said, still in the most pleasant tone and manner. "It is only . . . well, let me put it to you this way, Gaius: there are Romans, and there are Romans. And, sad to say, in times such as these the differences grow more pronounced each day. Thus, it is more important than ever for a young man to understand those differences and to make the right choices."

He paused a moment, his great eyebrows calm, his eyes, it seemed to me, filled only with affection. "Remember," he said, with a little wag of his finger, "the company you keep, and all that . . ."

His voice trailed off and he stared at me another moment, then returned with silky smoothness to his pleasant manner and small talk. But I had listened carefully and understood his meaning. Even

14

so, it was not until after an episode one night about three weeks later that I felt compelled at last to alter my behavior.

We were at the estate of a certain Rufus Trebellenus: myself, Curio and the rest. I had eaten nothing since much earlier; also, instead of following the usual custom of diluting the wine with water, our hosts were serving it at full strength. Thus, even before finishing my second goblet, I was thoroughly tipsy.

As it happened, it was that particular occasion when Mark Antony decided to join us. Naturally, I'd seen him any number of times lately, and had even exchanged brief greetings with him at least twice before. But that time he sat down with our group, and after a few minutes I somehow found myself on the sofa right next to him.

"My lord Gaius Livinius," Antony said, by way of introduction, and we exchanged a vigorous handshake. "So, my young friend, just how are you finding our Roman night life?"

"Oh, very easily," I said, and noticed everyone around got a good laugh from that. "Oh, you mean . . ." I started to say, and felt the usual blush. ". . . that is, it's very enjoyable really, though a bit strenuous at times."

That drew even more laughter, and Mark Antony in particular turned red in the face and guffawed loudly.

"Very funny," he said, still chuckling.

After a short while, most of the others had drifted off to other parts of the house, except for Curio, who had sat down on the sofa at Antony's left.

"Our young friend is betrothed, you know," Curio said, nodding at me, though with no hint of derision in his tone.

"Ah, wonderful," Antony said. "And who's the lucky woman?"

Sipping yet another goblet of the powerful wine, I told him at great length about Fulvia and her family.

"Well, they're a fine old Roman house," Mark Antony said. Then, smiling his warm, wonderful smile and studying me with his large, expressive eyes, he urged me on, as if everything I had to say would no doubt be of immense importance. I obliged by talking shamelessly about my plans and hopes for the future: marriage, children, career.

"So you plan to read law, eh?" he said, and that set me off on a blazing new round of conversation, until, virtually enveloped by the cozy wine haze and Mark Antony's legendary dash and charm, I felt as beloved and respected as any young man could.

We talked a while longer—Curio had long since disappeared—until Antony said, "This house we're in is a wonderful old place in its own right, you know," and with that we were off on a tour.

A good deal of what happened after that is lost to me, I'm afraid, but I definitely recall finding myself alone with Antony in what must have been the master bedroom. It was, to say the least, an impressive chamber, with a marble mosaic of the founding of Rome by Romulus on the floor and several colorful frescoes of city and country life around the walls. Along one wall, on the far side of the handsomely covered bed, was an unusually large window facing north toward the Roman suburbs. I recall standing at that window admiring the view: hillsides covered with trees, all black in the pale moonlight.

I breathed in a bit of night air and listened to the summer breeze rustling through the empty darkness. And then Antony was beside me, his right arm around my shoulders, his left handing me yet another goblet.

"Beautiful, isn't it?" he said.

I nodded, drank down the wine and felt his right hand close with firm affection around my shoulder, then move with a caressing motion across the back of my neck and down . . .

And that, I swear, is all I have ever remembered of that time.

★　　★　　★

I woke up the next morning just as dawn broke. I was stretched out, toga askew, on a hard wooden bench. For a moment, I had no idea where I was, then quickly realized: I was in the rear courtyard of that very same house.

I sat up slowly, my head pounding like the inside of an iron forge, my mouth as dry and prickly as a wool blanket. Naturally, that much was to be expected, but that was only the beginning.

I'd already felt certain unusual pains, but I only understood the extent of them when I tried to stand. Even now, it is painful to think of—painful in the sense of humiliating. I will only say that I was sore in an area of my body that had no cause to be sore, or at least no cause that I could recall, and certainly no cause of which I approved.

In any case, it hurt even to sit up straight on that hard bench. To stand up, and then to walk, bordered on the excruciating. Being July and already uncomfortably warm for so early in the morning didn't help matters any, but somehow I made my way the mile or so through the deserted streets to my parents' hillside home. Fortunately, it was my mother, Cornelia, who saw me first, just outside the door to my bedroom.

"Where have you been!" she demanded, coming up behind me. Then, as I turned to face her, she gasped at my disheveled state. "Oh, my child, what has happened?"

We went into my room, and I barely managed the final few steps before collapsing across the bed.

Finding a nearby basin of water and a fresh cloth, my mother began gently sponging my face. "My poor baby," she went on, "your father is so angry with you." And just then we heard my father, Livinius Decius Severus himself, gruffly bellowing in the courtyard and coming steadily closer.

Abruptly, I sat up beside my mother and gently pushed her hands away, for I suddenly felt quite unfit for the privilege of receiving her touch.

"Oh, Mother," I said, and burst into tears. "Oh, Mother, I have made such a terrible mistake."

★ ★ ★

"I've had enough of this!" I heard my father shout. And then, barely an instant later, the bedroom door burst open and he charged inside.

"All night, every night! What in hell do you think you're doing, boy. Why, Avidius has sent me a note—"

"Decius," my mother hissed, which brought him up short. "Decius, not now!" And my father, always one to recognize a wrong moment (by then, having created so many of his own), made several harrumphing noises, then backed quietly out of the room.

"Please, Gaius, tell me what's happened," my mother said after a comforting pause. But I only shook my head, not knowing what to say. "It isn't Fulvia, is it?" she asked, clearly dreading the answer.

"Oh no," I said, facing her through my tears. "Fulvia is perfect."

She wet the rag and began sponging again. "Then what can be so terrible, eh?" she chirped.

For a moment I waited, savoring the touch of the cool cloth on my forehead. "Just some of these people I know," I sniffed. I paused again, then told her: "I met Mark Antony last night."

With that, she froze mid-dab, so to speak, and for a long moment neither spoke nor moved. "That terrible man," she said at last in a tired whisper.

Another pause and then: "Mark Antony, eh? Here, boy, let me look at you."

I turned away, but she reached her right hand to my face, squeezed it tightly over my jaw and pulled my head around to study me. As she did so, she shifted her weight so the bed linen pressed just a bit more firmly against that lower part of my body.

"Ow!" I said.

"What is it?" she demanded. "Tell me!" she insisted, when I didn't answer at once.

Finally, I said, "I hurt, Mother," and started to cry again.

There was a glimmer of comprehension in her eyes; then she set her jaw against trembling lips and sat like that for several minutes, willing herself not to cry with me. In the end, she won her little battle, and though her eyes might have misted up a bit, there were no tears.

"I've heard enough about Antony," she said in a shaky voice, "to surmise what has happened. But I also know enough about you to believe that there is no danger of it ever happening again." She leaned down and kissed me softly on the cheek. "So that's right, then, isn't it? And may I tell your father you'll be home early from now on? May I tell him he has his son back?"

"Yes, Mother," I said at once.

"I'll tell him you've learned your lesson," she said. "I'll tell him there's nothing at all to cause him worry."

3

The very next day, two months into his exile, I was honored to receive a brief letter from Cicero:

Dearest Gaius Livinius Severus,

In truth, it is not safe for me to write this letter, let alone to send it. Indeed, it is probably not safe for you to receive it or read it. Nevertheless, I must chance it to thank you for the splendid devotion and loyalty to me which I know you have shown during these perilous times. I must also remind you: Keep your own counsel, maintain correct and proper company, be wary of those around you, and continue to do what I asked at our last meeting in Rome. If the gods are willing, these terrible days shall pass and we will be together again. As always, with highest regards and affection, Cicero

I read the letter through a dozen times or more, even crying over it, until, indeed, much of the ink had smeared across the page. Then, recalling what Cicero himself had written about the dangers of such a communication, I tossed what was left of it into the fire. But one line, in particular, stayed with me:

". . . continue to do what I asked at our last meeting . . ."

Just what *had* he asked me to do? I wondered. Actually, nothing at all. Instead, he had merely suggested I meet Scribonius Curio. But I'd known what he meant: he wanted me to keep an eye on Curio, then write him letters describing what I'd seen, perhaps tossing in a line or two of my opinions along the way.

19

Well, suddenly Cicero had been sent into exile by the hateful Clodius, and somehow I'd found myself simply swept away by events: the powerful personalities of Curio and some others, the exotic settings, the indulgent behavior, all had compelled my curiosity.

Thus, I had failed in my little task. Not only had I not been watchful, I had participated to an extent and in a manner which quite certainly would have left Cicero appalled.

A few days later, when I was finally up and about, I made a decision: I would take on the role of detective and complete Cicero's mission. But I decided, as well, that I would need some help—someone to watch me (or, at least, watch *out* for me) while I watched Scribonius Curio: I called on my cousin, Lucius Flavius.

"Ah, Livinius," he said with a great smile as I arrived at the courtyard of his house just up the road from mine. "And the lovely Fulvia is well, I trust?" he said.

"Yes. Very," I said. I returned his amiable greeting, shaking hands with special vigor as much from relief as affection—thankful that the tales of my recent adventures (at least as far as I could discern) had not reached his ears.

After a few minutes of chitchat about family matters, I said: "I've recently made the acquaintance of this Scribonius Curio fellow. It was something Cicero suggested just before he left, something he especially wanted me to do."

At that, my cousin, who'd been only half focused on my words, suddenly widened his eyes and looked directly at me. "Oh, did he?" my cousin said.

I stared back at him, nodded and allowed myself a little smile, for I knew that Lucius Flavius had understood me at once. Though just eighteen years old at the time, two years my junior, my clever cousin was unusually sophisticated about such things. In truth, of my younger relatives, he was the truly remarkable one, and I frequently felt as if he were far older than I. Of course, when it came to women . . . well, all the younger fellows in our family deferred to me on that.

Later that day, Lucius and I called on Curio at his little town house near the center of Rome. To be sure, I was apprehensive about seeing him again. I wasn't at all certain he'd even receive me after the other night; if he did, I felt sure he'd treat me differently, possibly with some distance, or even derision.

"Gaius Livinius," he said, emerging from the inner rooms of the house. He hugged me warmly, and before I could say a word he went on: "I've been worried about you, my friend. If you hadn't called today, I would have called on you tomorrow, or at least sent a messenger. After the other night . . . well, I understand how you must have felt, and I wanted to wait a few days. But no longer than that. And, well, here you are, and I'm glad."

He paused briefly and smiled. "I must tell you: I made a mistake with you. I've made lots of mistakes lately. That kind of party life isn't for you, and it's not for me, either. Not anymore. And some of those people . . . Well, I'm sure you'll agree, it's not necessary to go into particulars or name names. In any case, too much is happening in Rome right now, events that need serious men willing to pay serious attention. There's a great deal of work to be done, and that will be my style from now on. And if it suits you I want you with me as much as possible."

All that came at a dizzying pace, completely the opposite of what I'd expected—and right there in the atrium, with slaves and servants milling about, and my cousin standing there, his mouth wide open.

"This is my cousin, Lucius Flavius," I said, able at last to get a word in. "Cousin, this is—"

"Gaius Scribonius Curio," Curio interrupted, shaking hands with a still dumbfounded Lucius. "And your cousin can work here, as well—if that's his desire."

A while later, as we were leaving, Curio pulled me aside for a word in private. "I must tell you, Livinius, I . . . well, I knew what was coming the other night. That is, I should have known. It's just . . . well, the way you look and all, the way women treat you, what they say, we've all seen it. And, well, Antony being what he is, he'd noticed you; he'd been asking about you. I thought, Well, you're old enough, you'll make your own decision. But later on, I realized that you . . . Well, I shouldn't have let it go so far, I should have intervened, and I simply wanted to tell you I'm sorry that I didn't."

I'd been standing there, staring at the floor, idiotically shuffling my feet, feeling as if my face were as red and hot as molten lava.

"It's all right," I said at last, in a raspy whisper. Then Curio shook my hand, I left with my cousin, and the subject never came up again.

★　★　★

Curio was true to his word. With Lucius and me assisting him, he set to work writing and delivering speeches, having leaflets inscribed and distributed, meeting late into the night with generals, senators, and other dignitaries.

"This Caesar is a growing danger to the republic," he told Lucius and me in private, "and the republic must be preserved."

He was a bit more cautious in public, though still fervent enough. "Our democracy is the hallmark of Rome," he said again and again. "We must preserve government of the people. We must avoid dictatorship at all costs."

Indeed, the work load quickly grew so large that, at my suggestion, Curio called in another of my cousins, one Junius Barnabas. Junius was two years older than I, and, to be frank, a bit of a windbag. But he was an intelligent and upright fellow who, incidentally, stood in great awe of me for some advice I'd once given him about . . . well, about a matter that involved my usual area of expertise.

"This is a most remarkable and efficacious opportunity with which you have presented me, Livinius, and I am now even more sincerely and deeply in your debt," Junius Barnabas said.

Lucius and I exchanged bemused glances, but somehow kept from laughing out loud.

★　★　★

Thus, my task of watching Curio put me squarely at the center of Roman politics—and in a perfect spot to watch everything else, as well. And, of course, Curio was right: they were tumultuous times.

Caesar and Pompey, always archrivals, had been accorded the joint consulship for several years in a row—far in excess of the constitutional limit. And that year, they jockeyed relentlessly for power.

More and more, the once illustrious Roman Senate seemed merely to cower before them—the senators bitterly divided between one man or the other, though some opted for a third wing:

22

the old-line aristocrats under the punctilious Cato. More and more, the Comitia Curiata, the assembly most nearly the voice of the common man, driveled at each session into unseemly chaos. "I hear thunder," some tribune would shout, invoking on even the sunniest days the old fear of that omen—thus bringing the government to a halt (as was the ancient custom) merely because he (or his clients!) didn't like the way a particular debate was going.

And that summer in particular, more and more the city fell victim to disruptions or riots led by rowdy street gangs. Yes, street gangs—composed of men no better than the lowest thugs, but run by, or in the pay of, some of Rome's most powerful men.

"We must maintain our constitution and the republic," Curio opined to the Senate, but with no noticeable effect.

Clodius himself ran the worst of the gangs, driving Cicero out, of course, and frequently posting his hoodlums at the very doors of the Senate building itself. No one had to say anything. Once Clodius spoke, or simply let word of his opinion get around, everyone knew which way to cast his vote.

"From what I hear, the republic is dead," Cicero wrote to his friend Atticus around that time. "And I understand only one man opens his mouth to defend it, and that is young Curio."

So Cicero has other sources of information, I thought to myself with amusement (after Atticus showed me the note), as I had still not sent off my own first letter. In any case, to help with Curio's work, I brought in yet another of my cousins, Junius's brother, Claudius Barnabas. They were opposite numbers, all right. "Yes" was all Claudius said, when I suggested the position. "Thanks" was his only word when, confirming the appointment, I introduced him to Curio. Once again, with great effort, Lucius and I kept silent.

"My dearest Cicero," I wrote soon after,

My cousins Lucius Flavius, Junius and Claudius Barnabas, and I, of course, have made the acquaintance of a former pupil of yours, the distinguished young politician Gaius Scribonius Curio. He speaks of you with great reverence and is a staunch defender of the republic. Indeed, he never ceases in his writings and speeches to fervently defend our democratic system and to condemn even the possibility

23

of dictatorial rule. He is an upright man of deep and sincere feelings, and Lucius, Junius, Claudius and I presently act as his confidential secretaries—helping a little with his writings and generally keeping track of his appointments. It is, we feel, work in a good cause. Cicero, my beloved master, I know that your forced absence must be causing you great pain, but I feel certain that these terrible times shall pass very soon, and I look forward to visiting with you in the near future. Please let me know how you are. Your affectionate friend, Gaius Livinius Severus.

Summer dragged into autumn, and the stench that made life in Rome nearly unlivable in hot weather gave way to brisk, cooling winds. People breathed more easily; the crowded Forum was bearable again. But the relief was all on the surface. Indeed, with new elections not far off, Clodius and his hooligans were demanding more brazenly than ever the promise of votes from ordinary citizens and senators alike.

Around that time, however, a powerful new gang arose, led by the formidable Annius Milo, who, rumor had it, was in the pay of some of those supposedly virtuous old-line senators. The inevitable clash came soon enough: It was a chilly October afternoon; the sky was magnificent—cerulean; the air smelled of sweet wine and ripe olives; banners, and even men's togas, snapped in the wind.

It all took place just a street or two from the Forum itself. The two gangs happened upon each other, each heavily armed, with sixty or seventy men on either side. The violence erupted at once: a great, quick clash of metal slashing on metal—daggers, swords, and a few long spears; one man even had the large net of a gladiator. Word spread quickly, and my cousins and I all dashed to the scene, but too late to make a difference. In the little street where the fighting took place, you could hardly walk without stepping on a body. The pavement was covered with blood, and the walls of the buildings on either side were spattered with it. And there, after a bit of looking, we found Clodius himself, his throat slit ear to ear—apparently one of the first to fall, or so some witnesses told us later on.

Well, soon afterward public outcry greatly diminished the gang influence—good news, I suppose you could call it, after such a bloodbath. Also, Cicero's banishment was soon revoked and he was recalled to Rome.

Scribonius Curio had helped to lead the campaign—both against the gangs and for Cicero. The day after Cicero's recall, Curio, my cousins and I celebrated our victories in the grand manner. With my parents away at their country villa near Tivoli, I invited them all to my house and set out the finest table, and we drank and ate till dawn.

"The republic lives," I shouted more than once during that long evening.

"One little sore has been removed, that's all," Lucius Flavius said. But though his words were solemn, even a bit reproachful, his tone was quiet and kindly, and he even smiled as he spoke.

"Not so little," I replied, standing up and reeling toward him. "A big sore. Big and bulbous and pus-ridden and—"

"Oh do shut up, you're drunk," Lucius put in with a laugh.

"Yes," I said, and sank back onto the nearest sofa. "Drunk but happy," I giggled.

"We're all happy tonight," Curio said.

"Damn right," I said. "And you're the man who did it—cut out the awful sore and saved Rome." I vaguely recall trying to toast him, but found myself waving my empty right hand. Where in hell's my goblet? I wondered. "Long life to you, sir," I went on anyway. "Long live Gaius Scribonius Curio, the man who saved the republic."

And then, you might be relieved to know, the night, already blurred beyond any semblance of good sense, went, for me, quite suddenly and finally black.

4

And so I sit in the little atrium of what used to be Cicero's house in Rome and wait for Augustus to finish reading my report. As I wait, a servant comes by with a tray of figs and offers me one, but I refuse. Off in a corner, another slave polishes silver, while a third scrubs the floor. A normal Roman household, I think, on a normal weekday morning.

The illusion, however, is short-lived. For suddenly, there is a terrible commotion of shouting and shoving, which is coming, I realize, from a nearby anteroom. From my seat on the hard bench, I can just catch a glimpse of Augustus through an open doorway: His face is filled with the wild rage of an animal, and I see the flash of his dagger in the light. Then I see red—spurts of red blood spraying everywhere. The shouts turn to screams, and I see another face, or a little part of it. That face, it's . . . oh God, it's familiar to me, it's . . . And then my entire body begins to quiver, and for a moment it's as if I cannot get a breath. Somehow I stand up, and the next thing I know I am at the doorway looking into that chamber of horrors in the next room.

And it *is* him: the man down on his knees screaming with agony, begging for mercy, is my cousin, the windbag Junius Barnabas.

He is already bleeding from several places, my cousin. But now I see Augustus draw a long, curving slit across my cousin's stomach, which will be the fatal wound, though, naturally, it will take a while for him to die. Then—for, of course, that is not enough to satisfy him—Augustus reaches over with his blood-covered dagger and, one at a time, gouges out my cousin's eyes.

26

I have, by now, lost any ability to control myself, and I'm not sure what I will do next. But just now one of the guards appears and escorts me back to my little bench and sits me down—though I can still see what's happening in the next room, and I hear the moans.

After a while, Augustus actually comes through the doorway and walks over to me. His unsheathed dagger is still in his hand and there is blood everywhere—on the knife, of course, and his tunic and even some spots on his cheeks and forehead. When he speaks, I realize that even his lips are covered with it, lending the distinct impression that he has been drinking the stuff.

"I'm enjoying your report," he says. He laughs—cackles, really—and waves the knife around. "Very well written," he goes on, "very interesting. And that Mark Antony! He really is disgusting, isn't he?" He stares at me a moment, smiling, and I actually do see several tiny specks of blood on his front teeth. "Well, I must get back to it," he says. "Still a long ways to go."

And with that, the blood-covered boy ruler of Rome walks off, and I sit on the bench trembling uncontrollably, wondering if any *whipped dog has ever felt more defeated or frightened.*

•   •   •   •   •   •

Clodius was dead and the gangs were mostly gone, but, as my clever cousin Lucius Flavius had suggested, Rome's troubles were far from over.

Indeed, Caesar and Pompey were still very much in contention, and their rivalry simply moved from the streets into the corridors of the Forum and the Senate building. The threat to constitutional government remained very real. It had merely shifted to a stage that was much more complex, and, ultimately, much more dangerous, as well.

Scribonius Curio, having conducted himself with such aplomb in recent months, found himself trusted by all sides. He shuttled tirelessly from Senate to Pompey to Caesar (or, more frequently, to Caesar's emissaries in Rome), and back again. "The Senate rules Rome," Curio wrote in a new leaflet, "the Senate and the people. Nothing else can be considered."

★   ★   ★

Three weeks after the death of Clodius, another scandal shook the city: The body of a young noble by the name of Fabius Vibulanus was found in an alleyway a short distance up the slopes of the Cispius, a hill of modest houses not far from the center of town.

Eyewitness accounts of the aftermath (no one could be found who had actually observed the crime) said the young man's neck was blue with bruises—that the cause of death was almost certainly strangulation, even though they also found a stab wound straight through the heart. Besides all that—and this was where the scandal came in—there was what the doctors delicately called "a significant inflammation about the aperture of the buttocks."

"I knew him slightly, I believe," I told my cousin Lucius, as we walked home that evening from work at Curio's house.

"Yes, of course, we met him at parties several times," Lucius answered at once. "You remember: good-looking fellow, a little shorter than you. He was seen with that girl once or twice, after you broke it off with her. That tall, blue-eyed girl—what was her name?"

I stared at him a moment, trying to recall, then slowly said her name: "Avidia Crispina. And . . . oh, yes, I remember Fabius. Pleasant fellow. So . . . my God, we did know him."

After that, we were silent awhile, until I suddenly spoke up. "And, by the way, I didn't break it off: She did."

"Just being polite, cousin," Lucius replied. "And she didn't break it off—her mother did."

I shook my head and even smiled, despite the horror of the moment. "This is fine talk, indeed," I said, "with this poor fellow just murdered."

I said it with suitable solemnity, and meant it. And, I must say, Lucius nodded guiltily. "Sorry," he said, and for once we finished our walk home without a single additional word.

★　★　★

That might have been the end of it, as far as I was concerned, except for what happened the next morning: We were toiling away as usual, my cousins, Curio, and I, when the doorkeeper suddenly showed in a young woman dressed all in black.

She came straight to me, peeled back her shawl and veil, and looked at me with misty, beseeching eyes. It took me a moment, but I recognized her soon enough: it was Avidia Crispina, the young lady friend of the young man who'd been killed.

"Oh, Livinius," she cried, and fell sobbing into my arms.

Lucius quickly came up beside us, while Curio discreetly left the room. The two Barnabas brothers sat at their work tables, gawking and bewildered.

"I'm so sorry," I said more than once. "If there's anything—"

"There is," she said immediately. Her eyes were suddenly bright and blue and determined; with her left hand, she flicked back her spill of long blond hair. "What they're saying about Fabius, it can't be true. If you could . . ."

She broke off weeping, and it was a while before she could speak again. "If you could look into it for me, investigate the matter, find out who murdered him and why, I know it would prove that . . . that . . ."

Understandably, she let her unfinished request hang in the air. But naturally I knew what she meant: that the world should know for certain that poor Fabius Vibulanus had not willingly taken part in such peculiar sexual practices.

"I'd like to help," I said, "but I don't know—"

"Of course we will," Lucius put in insistently. I looked around at him, my eyes wide with amazement—and annoyance! But, ignoring me, he went right on.

"You're right! Fabius could not have taken part in anything like that," Lucius said, "so we'll find out what's behind it all and set the record straight."

"Oh, will you?" she gushed, looking at both of us, her eyes now desperate, begging.

"Yes," Lucius said. "Definitely."

"Well . . . yes," I said softly, with a nod of my head.

★   ★   ★

"How can we, Lucius!" I demanded, a few moments after she'd gone. "What can we do?"

"We'll talk later," he said with a soothing smile. But when I brought it up after work that evening, he said simply, "There are things we can look into," then brushed aside my further questions with a terse wave and a shake of his head.

29

In the days ahead, I noticed him prowling about in odd ways, and three or four times I lost track of his whereabouts entirely.

"Can I help?" I asked him, more than once.

"Just wait," he said quietly. "The time will come."

★   ★   ★

I looked forward all November to Cicero's return, but at the last minute, he was diverted by an order from the Senate appointing him to a one-year term as provincial governor of Cilicia in Asia Minor. Thus, in December, right in the midst of the festivities of Saturnalia, when I learned that he still would not be coming home, I arranged for Lucius Flavius and me to pay him a visit. We raced south by horseback to Brundisium, hired the fastest available boat and sailed for the coast of Macedonia, where Cicero had been living out the days of his exile. In truth, he'd been on the verge of leaving for his new post many hundreds of miles to the east, but delayed his departure on our account.

"My two fine young friends," he said, greeting us himself at the front door of his hillside villa. He hugged us each with a tenderness and longing that's only possible for a man who is truly homesick.

"You must tell me everything," he said, and we walked through the atrium and the main courtyard to the rear of the house, where a picnic was set out at the edge of a small vineyard under the branches of a sprawling old birch tree.

"Everything," he repeated. And we gladly obliged.

★   ★   ★

We stayed with him two weeks, and what a time it was! Never before had I been privileged to receive so much of Cicero's attention, or hear so much of his wisdom. Lucius Flavius, who had also studied with him before, was an ideal companion. He rarely faltered in his understanding of Cicero's words and stated his own thoughts without pomposity or pretension; his questions were unfailingly sensible and appropriate.

In a way, Cicero was in an unusual frame of mind. Our discussions centered, as they had in the past, on right and wrong, no easy subject. But, for once, instead of talking in the abstract, he seemed especially interested in applying his ideas to some sort of practical system for everyday life.

"The obligation to cherish what is right," he said, "is not solely

30

that of the wise man, who, of course, considers right in the full and ideal sense of the word. All of us, all ordinary men, are morally bound to cherish and observe whatever degree of right that comes within our understanding—because that is the only way in which we can maintain whatever progress we have made towards achieving goodness. Anyone who states otherwise subverts the whole foundation of the human community, and that means the annihilation of all kindness, generosity, goodness and justice.

"So everyone," he went on, "ought to have the same purpose: to identify the interest of each with the interest of all. Once men grab for themselves, human society will collapse completely."

"But master," my cousin began, first thing next morning, "how can you—"

"Tell right from wrong? Well, young man, that's a puzzle, all right. That's the big question. But we've discussed that before, and it always gets so lost in esoteric fine points." Cicero, still not quite awake, stopped at the nearest basin and splashed cold water on his face. "I admit," he went on, "that I'm trying to work out a different approach to all this, get it to work in a way that can help us all. So, if you'll indulge an old man . . . well, perhaps we can even make some progress on the point."

At that, Lucius Flavius turned a deep shade of red—the first time I'd ever seen him blush. (I had almost begun to think of it as a minor affliction peculiar to myself.)

"Must run in the family," Cicero muttered with a shake of his head. Then he walked off into the garden where his breakfast was waiting.

★   ★   ★

"Look, my friends, the trouble is that somewhere along the line, we've all got it in our heads that there are actions that are right and then there are actions that are advantageous. But, if carefully thought out and with the long view of things taken into consideration, it's easy to see that they're really the same; there's no difference. For instance, if nature prescribes—as I believe she does—that every human being must help every other human being, just precisely because they are all human beings, then, by the same authority, all men have identical interests. And if that's true, where's the

31

advantage in pushing your own interests at the expense of others? In the end, you're only hurting yourself. Right?

"I know, I know: you're thinking, 'Easier said than done.' Well, it's hard to argue against that. Indeed, great-heartedness, heroism, courtesy, justice, generosity—all these are far more in conformity with nature than self-indulgence, or wealth, or even life itself. But to despise this latter category of things, to attach no importance to them . . . well, that really does require a heroic and lofty heart."

Cicero paused a moment, stood up, walked over to a nearby tree and plucked several well-ripened figs. He munched on one, walked back over to us and put the others down for Lucius and me. "Even my own relative, Gratidianus," he continued, after another moment's thought, "once failed to act as a good man should. While he was praetor, the tribunes of the people invited the board of praetors to meet them in order to decide jointly on a standard for the currency—for at that time the value of money was so unstable that no one knew how much he was worth. So they drafted a joint declaration, then agreed to reassemble later that day on the official platform. Gratidianus, however, went straight from the tribunes' benches to the official platform and published their jointly drafted statement as if he were solely responsible. And I have to add that his action made him a very famous man! His statues were in every street—no one has ever been so popular.

"This is the sort of case which can sometimes be perplexing— when the lapse from integrity does not appear to be particularly serious, while the favorable consequences of the action look extremely significant. For Gratidianus's theft of popularity did not appear to him to be so terribly wrong; on the other hand, his election to the consulship—which was what he was aiming at— seemed greatly to his advantage.

"But that was a mere delusion, for there are no exceptions to our rule.

"Work the problem out! Examine your conclusions. Will a good man lie for his own profit, will he slander, will he grab, will he deceive? He will do nothing of the kind, for what appears advantageous can only be so if no wrong action is involved."

★   ★   ★

On the morning of the fifth day, Cicero changed the subject, briefly, to a matter much closer to hand. "Livinius, I have read your letters and reports on Gaius Scribonius Curio," he said (for, unwilling to risk sending too much by courier, I had held on to almost all of it and handed him a great sheaf of the stuff as soon as we'd arrived). "Impressively done, my boy, and, I might add, very heartening as well to learn he's doing such good work."

He sat back on the sofa, then, a bit of a mischievous twinkle in his eyes. I looked over to Lucius, but he seemed as puzzled as I by the sudden silence. Finally, Cicero said, "So, is he, Livinius?"

"My lord?"

"That is to say, is he doing good work?"

I opened my mouth and closed it. "Yes, master," I said. "Absolutely." Then I smiled. "I certainly hope so, because Lucius and I have worked very hard to help him."

"He's sincere?"

"Yes, master."

"And capable, of course."

"Definitely."

"But you're still . . . well, still keeping an eye on things."

I stared at him, puzzled and even a little annoyed. I wanted to say, "You mean keeping an eye on Curio, don't you? Well, don't worry, your little detective is still on the job." I might also have asked, at long last, just what it was I was supposed to be looking for. Because as far as I was concerned, I'd seen everything there was to see and told him every bit of it—that Gaius Scribonius Curio was a true friend and a true republican.

But, of course, I had no intention of getting so blunt and awkward with old Cicero, so I said none of it. "Oh yes, sir," was all I actually told him.

Even then an odd sense of doubt seemed to linger, and sure enough, Cicero finally looked over at my cousin and said, "What do you think?"

"Oh, I agree with all of it," Lucius said, with no hesitation whatever. He paused, looked at me for an instant, then went on: "Well, I hope you take no offense, master, but I've seen all the letters, the reports, and I endorse them all."

"Good," Cicero said, and finally relaxed a little. "Good to hear

33

it." And that was all he said; indeed, he did not bring up the subject again.

★   ★   ★

"Just when did you read all that stuff of mine?" I asked Lucius later that evening, after Cicero had gone to bed.

"Well, I didn't read all of it, exactly," he said.

"Any of it?" I asked.

"Most of it, yes."

"And what do you think? Do you agree?"

"Yes, completely."

"Good," I murmured, more to myself than to him. We were talking quietly in the outer garden, nursing a touch of wine. It was the first time in a while I'd had a relaxed moment with my clever cousin, and I had no intention of missing the opportunity.

"So, Lucius," I said with a big smile, "when are you going to tell me about our 'investigation'?"

"Hmm?"

"You know. Into Fabius Vibulanus's murder; Avidia Crispina asked us to help?"

He looked around and smiled back at me. "Not much to tell, cousin," he said with a shrug.

"Oh, come on, Lucius!" I snapped, then stopped and let my little half-spoken complaint hang in the evening air. I waited, but Lucius Flavius said nothing. "Is it . . ." I let that trail off, not knowing if I dared ask what was in my mind. "Is it the girl?" I finally inquired in a voice barely above a whisper.

Slowly, very slowly, my cousin turned and faced me directly. "Ah, cousin," my cousin said with a sad little grin and a bit of mist showing in his eyes.

So it is the girl, I thought: Or at least that's the message he's hoping to convey. Without another word, I finished my wine, left him there alone in Cicero's garden, and retired for the night.

A short while later, he followed me upstairs. I listened as he walked down the hallway, waiting to see if he'd stop in, if only to say good night. But though he moved slowly and even seemed to hesitate just outside my door, soon enough his footsteps came and went, and then I faintly heard his own door close behind him.

★   ★   ★

Our great days with Cicero continued, with my cousin and me finally doing little more than listening, almost enraptured by our master's words. Indulge me by taking in just a few more brief examples:

"It is contrary to nature for one man to prey upon another's ignorance. Indeed, trickery disguised as intelligence is life's greatest scourge, being the cause of innumerable illusions of conflict between advantage and right. For extremely few people will refrain from doing a wrong action if they have the assurance that this will be both undiscovered and unpunished!"

And: "All sharp practice must go, and so must every kind of trickery masquerading as intelligence. The function of intelligence is to distinguish between good and bad—whereas trickery takes sides between them, actually preferring what is bad and wrong."

And: "To take something away from someone else—to profit by another's loss—is more unnatural than death, or destitution, or pain, or any other physical or external blow."

And: "There is an ideal of human goodness which nature itself has stored and wrapped up inside our minds. Unfold this ideal, and you will straightaway identify the good man as the person who helps everybody he can and, unless wrongfully provoked, harms no one."

Thus, after two weeks, Lucius Flavius and I returned to Rome in a remarkable state—a bit too solemn, perhaps, but altogether uplifted, eager and sincere.

•   •   •   •   •   •

Now, sitting in an anteroom of what used to be Cicero's house in Rome, I can hear Augustus a few rooms away, shouting orders, raging at someone about who knows what. I think of the madness I've seen this day: the ruler of half the world covered with my cousin's blood. I think of poor Junius Barnabas, the second of my cousins (and, I might add, the last of their line) to die by violence within just a few hours.

And then I recall Cicero's peaceful country garden and his famous words. I hope they will comfort me, but they only make things worse, and I begin to cry.

Where is Cicero now? I wonder. Somewhere in the South, I

suppose. In hiding. On the run. The desperadoes of the world are in control, and there is no place left for him, or those like him.

A fool, eh? I think that, and then I shout it out: "A fool, eh!" But my voice is so choked with tears, it comes out as muffled nonsense. The guard nearest me thinks he hears something, so he comes closer and looks me over. My face is soaked, and he can see that. He looks at me as if to say, What's wrong with you? But after staring another moment, he simply shakes his head and walks away.

And I sit and wait for Augustus to finish.

5

Three weeks and four days after my return from Macedonia, Fulvia and I were married.

Her parents gave a beautiful wedding. The atrium of their hill-top estate, already an imposing affair of fine marble—very much the latest fashion in Roman decor—was done up for the ceremony with garlands of flowers, long bands of brightly colored wool and several beautifully woven tapestries brought out just for the occasion. Indeed, the tapestries, my new father-in-law had told me, were part of Fulvia's considerable dowry.

Fulvia herself could not have been more magnificent: By ancient custom, her hair was coiled into six locks held together by pink ribbons; her straight white tunic was fastened at the waist with a band of wool tied in the ancient knot of Hercules—a knot which, once made, could only be undone by me. Finally, her face and shoulders were covered with a veil of bright orange—the color of flame.

The official "matron" of the wedding, a sister of Fulvia's mother, formally brought us together and joined our hands. Then, in a voice so soft and girlish it brought tears to my eyes and captivated us all, Fulvia spoke the ancient words of consent: "When and where you are, Gaius, I am then and there, as well."

Before an altar to the gods, she and I sat down on two small stools covered with the skin of a sheep that had been killed as a sacrifice. The high priest and the priest of Jupiter then made a bloodless offering in the form of a cake made from a special type of finely ground imported wheat. Fulvia and I each took a small bite of the cake, while the priests recited ancient prayers to Juno.

When all that was over, the crowd erupted joyfully in cheers and applause. "Felicitations," Avidius shouted over the noise. And everyone there echoed him—that, of course, being the word most particularly used to offer congratulations on a wedding day. My mother rushed forward and kissed the bride; mercifully, she refrained from kissing me. But then, a moment later, Fulvia's mother, Lucilla, ran up and kissed us both.

Suddenly the atrium was filled with servers handing out large goblets of wine. And then about a hundred of us adjourned to the main dining room for the formal dinner. It was a sumptuous feast—a boar's head, eyes and all, was the centerpiece of the table, while around it was a remarkable selection: goat, pork, oysters, baked thrush, mussels, raw sea urchin, jellyfish, ham, wild duck, hare and roast chicken, along with eggs, anchovies, olives, salted nuts, sausages . . . Well, it went on and on, and kept us there, along with the plentiful wine, until late in the afternoon, when finally it was time for the most important part of the day: the procession through the streets to our new home.

By the time we began, there was quite a crowd outside Avidius's estate, including many of considerable rank: Curio was there, smiling and waving, as well as at least a dozen senators, several praetors and a tribune or two. It was strong testimony to Avidius's great influence that so many of distinction, having not been invited to the wedding itself, would wait in the street for a mere glimpse of the bride—and also to show their respect for the bride's father.

When we all had gathered in front, a chorus sang one of the ancient marriage hymns. And then, with the customary show of force, I wrenched Fulvia from her mother's arms, followed, of course, by another great burst of applause. Fulvia then moved to her place in the procession, just behind the flute players at the very front, and began the walk; she was escorted by three young boys from the family, two of whom held her hands while the third walked just in front of her carrying the wedding torch. I, of course, was in my proper place a few paces behind.

All during the march, I could see Fulvia blushing with embarrassment as the crowd sang the usual songs, many of them quite bawdy, and, also as usual, spiced up with some decidedly personal comments. Meanwhile, according to the tradition, she carried three coins, one of which she dropped along the way as an offering to the gods of crossroads. Later, she would give one to me as a symbol of her dowry, while the third she would offer to the gods of my father's house.

All during the walk, I scattered nuts and sweet cakes among the crowd, many of whom slapped me on the back and leered mischievously. "You'll have fun tonight, eh, Gaius?" they cackled, while I could only smile and put up as best I could with that tradition of vulgarity.

We wound through the streets for nearly half an hour until we arrived at the front door of our new home. Fulvia tied bands of wool around the doorposts, a symbol, of course, of her work to come as mistress of the household, while I smeared oil and fat on the door itself, an emblem that this was, and would continue to be, a house of plenty.

With that chore done, I at last lifted Fulvia gently in my arms and carried her over the threshold.

"You're light as a feather," I told her softly as we stepped inside, and I stood like that for a long moment with her in my arms, for, of course, I did not want to put her down.

"You're blushing," she whispered with a smile, "as usual."

"You too," I replied.

Then, as the crowd quieted, she spoke the words of consent all over again, I put her down, and finally the door was closed to all but twenty or so close relatives.

We moved into the atrium where I presented Fulvia with fire and water, as you know, symbols of our future life together. But then, just as I was completing this ritual, there suddenly were angry shouts and a scuffling noise from a few feet away.

Then I distinctly heard, "Not my fault, damn it," and I knew it was my father.

He'd been so quiet all day, smiling pleasantly and speaking only a few polite words. But now, once again, a few too many sips of the grape had abruptly pushed him past his limit.

That had always been the way with him and drinking—quiet and sober one minute, sloshed the next. But ever since his troubles

39

of the last year or so, his tendency to get sloppy drunk had noticeably grown. "Doing the best I can," he was saying, referring, as usual, to his recent setbacks. "Can't help it if I can't afford better."

For, in truth, you see, during our long wedding procession, we had actually gone nowhere at all. We had turned and twisted our way through the streets, only to wind up at what in actuality was Avidius's back door.

Now this somewhat unusual arrangement had all been Avidius's idea, arising in the first place from his strong desire to keep his daughter close to home. But Fulvia and I were more than pleased about it: After all, the interior had been remodeled at great expense into lavish apartments.

Still, there was no escaping the fact that my wife and I were to be living in the back of her father's house. And at that moment, *my* father, unable to defeat the plan owing to his financial incapacities, was obviously feeling the sting of this not inconsiderable humiliation.

"No, you shut up," he was snarling to my mother.

She glared at him a moment, then, with a snap of her fingers, summoned a slave—a man so enormously tall and muscular that everyone there stopped and gasped as he appeared. In truth, I'd heard the rumor that she had borrowed the fellow on two or three recent occasions (parties, formal dinners and the like) from a rich cousin of hers for just such a purpose; now, to my astonishment, this giant of a man emerged from some shadowy corner of the room, came up behind my father, lifted him up (quite effortlessly, it seemed to me) and carried him out. His usual instructions, as I understood them, were to take him home and put him to bed.

"All right, children, do go ahead," my mother said, as cheerily as she could.

"Yes, please, let us go on," I said, and put on a determined smile, for I had no intention of letting this episode ruin the day. Indeed, I was deeply angered that even on so solemn an occasion as the wedding of his only surviving son, my father no longer seemed able to control himself at all.

★ ★ ★

We are speaking of my wife here, so I will not belabor the details. Suffice it to say that my wedding night was all any young man could hope for. Fulvia was delicate, soft and superbly proportioned, features, I admit, which I had dared to presume from the construction of her face: bright, twinkling eyes (her father's, it would seem, though inexplicably blue); soft, white skin; expressive mouth; regal cheekbones.

So how surprised could I be by the rest: the tiny waist; that wide expanse of arch across her back; those perfect breasts—smooth, luxuriant, of truly elegant size and texture.

Still, even considering all that, the best of Fulvia was her disposition, for she came to me that night at the tender age of seventeen with the easy confidence of a woman. There was no hint of fear and certainly no sign of brattiness, traits which would not have surprised me in the least. Instead, there was only a slight, beguiling, nervous flutter. Thus, so far as I could tell, she had slid from her sheltered little girl's life to the role of bride and wife without a noticeable ripple of uneasiness or complaint.

Indeed, it was Fulvia who got into bed first that night. Then, after I hesitated and fumbled for a while, not wishing to hurry or frighten her, she pulled back my side of the covers and said, "Please get into bed with me now, you beautiful man."

It was the first time I'd ever heard her speak in so frank a manner, and, startled, I stood absolutely motionless for a moment. After that, of course, I quickly climbed in beside her.

One real wonder of the evening was her laughter, which I realized I had not heard before: There was a throatiness about it, though naturally nothing loud or coarse; it was simply a richly engaging throb signifying depth and, perhaps, a tiny hint of arrogance. In fact, that laugh of hers is the only overt sign she's ever given of being a young woman of great wealth and position. It was a laugh which I at once found enchanting, and so far, I have found no reason to change my mind.

★   ★   ★

Two weeks after the wedding, I was inducted into the Roman Senate. Predictably enough, my sponsor was my father-in-law, the redoubtable Victorinus Avidius.

"A young man of great talent, good will, quick mind, honest heart, a pupil of no less than Cicero himself—" And here the senators broke into a great standing ovation, for Cicero still had several months to go at his post in Cilicia, he had not been back to Rome for eighteen months, and by that time everyone missed him terribly. "—yes, yes, that's good, that's right," Avidius went on, "and a *star* pupil, I might add," pointing to me, which set off a new round of cheers: "I give you my esteemed son-in-law, Gaius Livinius Severus."

After yet another burst of applause died down, I gave my own speech, a rambling, nervous little affair of thanks, which I won't bother to repeat here. Even so, there was more cheering, and then, that night, more banquets in my honor, and more of the same for several nights after—all much to my dismay, as I had barely recovered from a week of such dinners after the wedding.

"I feel fat," I told Fulvia after the last of them, but she only laughed and shook her head.

"I will never eat again," I said with mock seriousness, which for some reason sent her into absolute fits of giggling. Then she pulled me down beside her into bed, and we made the sort of passionate love which the gods mercifully reserve for those of us who bear that particular, once-in-a-lifetime designation:

We were newlyweds, of course!

6

So, why didn't I tell Cicero about the murder of Fabius Vibulanus? Or, for that matter, about Avidia Crispina asking me and my cousin to investigate his death?

Well, you might ask, why should I have? After all, what about that affair could be of interest to him? And what possible connection could it have to the more important matters at hand? Surely, I was not observing Curio on behalf of the illustrious Cicero to pass along mere innuendo, was I? But that was just it: if there was so clearly no connection, then what vague uneasiness in the back of my mind kept me from bringing up the matter in a casual way? Well, whatever it was, I said nothing about it to Cicero or anyone else, not even my cousin. And if my cousin felt any uneasiness of his own, he gave no hint of it to Cicero or me.

Nevertheless, my attitude changed, almost in spite of myself. I used my friendship with Curio now: it became more of a mask, a device—and far less real. And, with a lengthy interruption for travel, a wedding, Senate ceremonies and the like finally coming to a close, for the first time I really did begin to watch him, and almost at once I found myself both gratified and appalled.

It happened one morning just a few days after my return to work. Wanting to get an early start, I arrived at Curio's house at the crack of dawn. As I entered by the side door (my usual choice, as it led most directly to the study), who should I literally bump into on his way out but none other than Mark Antony.

"Hello," I said.

It was the first time I'd seen him, other than from a distance, since my "episode" with him of some months before. I looked him straight in the eye, but he gave me only the quickest sidelong glance and hurried off with a shake of his head, as if he could not possibly imagine who I was.

I turned back, heading for the study again, and there was Curio, lolling just out of the dim early light of the entranceway, looking alarmingly disheveled: his clothes a mess, his face flushed, his skin showing more than traces of perspiration.

I stopped and stared a moment, but he appeared so entirely oblivious to my presence that I didn't say a word. I simply walked past him, sat down at my usual place and went to work. Later, when he came in, his clothes immaculate and his manner crisp as usual—it was as if nothing had happened.

And all I could think of, all day long and for who knows what reason, was poor Fabius Vibulanus, so horribly murdered, and of Avidia Crispina, who so wanted our help.

And what was my cousin doing about it? And wasn't it time, by then, to take more action?

One evening just past sunset, a few days after my induction into the Senate, Lucius Flavius and I were on our way home from work when a man jumped out at us from an alleyway and blocked our path.

"You should stay out of this Fabius Vibulanus business," he told us.

"And why is that?" Lucius demanded at once in a cool tone of voice.

"Because . . . because I say so," he said, his tone less convincing with each passing word. "Because—"

"And just who are you," I asked, "to tell us what and what not to stay out of?"

We stepped up close to him and saw in the dim twilight that he was a young fellow, no older than I, and not big—no bigger than Lucius.

"I . . . I was a friend of Fabius's," he said. "I still am a friend of Avidia's."

"Then you should welcome our help," Lucius said. "You should want this murder solved and avenged."

"You . . . you don't know what you're up against," the young man said. "You'll get hurt. Avidia will get hurt."

He stepped sideways into a slightly better light and pulled back the hood that had been well down over his face. "My name is Flaccus Valerius," he said. "I know some things, too many things. You should get out of this while you can. Ask Avidia about me, ask her about Flaccus Valerius. She'll tell you how much I know. She'll tell you to take my advice and get out."

Then he suddenly turned and bolted down the street at a full run, leaving my cousin and me staring quietly into the empty twilight.

"Well!" I said to Lucius. "Anything to tell me?"

But he just shook his head and walked the rest of the way home in stubborn silence.

★   ★   ★

I tried more than once after that to pry something out of him, but it was no use. Besides, as before, there were other distractions that made it hard to focus on such matters—or at least that's what I told myself. Of course, there was some truth to that, for more than ever watching Curio put me and my cousins very much at the center of things, so indulge me while I backtrack briefly and bring you up to date:

The late Clodius had had a fair number of admirers among certain segments of the population, and after his death many of them erupted into sporadic rioting that continued for some time. Finally, the Senate conferred special powers on Pompey to raise an army, clear the streets and maintain order. By the time of my wedding, the job had essentially been completed. Rome was quiet again, but the subtle drift toward dictatorship had grown slightly more distinct.

This was nothing new, of course: For several years, most of the real power at Rome had been held by a loosely formed triumvirate consisting of Pompey, Julius Caesar and one Marcus Licinius Crassus, renowned as the richest man in Rome. (Word was that Crassus made most of his money by buying up properties cheaply just after they'd burned down; rumor was that Crassus started many of the fires.)

Now, two events took place in rapid succession that would each

45

have enormous impact: First, Crassus was killed in battle with the Parthians in the East. And without Crassus (or some other third party) to form a balance between Caesar and Pompey, it seemed to most of us inevitable that those two would wind up fighting each other.

Second, Pompey's young wife, Julia, died. Well, of course, that marriage had been purely political from the start, as Julia was Caesar's daughter. I would add that despite the huge age difference, Pompey had apparently taken good care of her, and she had worshiped him. In any case, her death broke a powerful bond that had kept the two rivals uneasily at peace.

Thus, like a terrible storm cloud, the possibility of one-man rule loomed larger than ever. And, as I say, it was just at that point that my cousins and I resumed our work in earnest for Gaius Scribonius Curio.

★　　★　　★

"I don't understand: You mean Pompey believes that he controls us, when actually we have the upper hand because—what is it again? Something about Caesar?"

We were in Cato's house at a private meeting of a dozen or so influential senators, all members of the old aristocracy trying to avoid dictatorship by either side. The fellow speaking was Lucius Domitius Ahenobarbus, one of Rome's most powerful men, and also, sad to say, one of the stupidest.

"Yes, old friend, that's right: 'Something about Caesar,' " Cato said, and then I heard one old proconsul behind me snort with derision.

Ahenobarbus clucked his tongue and stared at Cato, as if both dumbstruck and impatient at the same time—which, if you think about it, is a rather stupefying combination. "Well, what about Caesar!" he finally demanded.

"Oh listen, old man, and I'll tell you one more time!" It was a different voice—chilly, condescending, yet undeniably cultivated. I looked around the room: Of course! Appius Claudius Pulcher: long, aquiline, elegant, reptilian, moving upon his well-upholstered sofa with unstudied grace. He was the latest descendant of the Metellans and Servilians, two of Rome's most ancient families, between them the holders of dozens and dozens of consulships over the last several centuries. So, indeed, who but Pulcher could invoke such a tone of superiority by the mere utterance of a few words—and perhaps the barely perceptible arching of an eyebrow?

"Listen," Pulcher was saying, "our friend Pompey is playing a double game. He still cozies up to Caesar, while he secretly schemes to use us to destroy him—"

"But how!"

"Shut up and listen, damn it—"

"Wait," Cato said, and held up the palm of his right hand in a calming gesture. Pulcher quieted, and Cato made the point in his own way: "Pompey hopes, I believe, to maneuver us into using the constitution against Caesar, to unseat him from his command and dislodge him from his province. Undoubtedly, he feels this would clear the way for him to take power, though for whatever reason he doesn't seem to realize that we realize that. And, of course, that's his weak point. So far in our talks, I've pretended to sympathize with his cause."

"Which is what?" Ahenobarbus demanded yet again, and indeed he turned a little pink around the ears when the room erupted in a chorus of chuckles.

"Pompey's cause?" Appius Pulcher asked with a silky smile. "Why, it's liberty, of course." He paused and shook his head. "It's Caesar's, too, you know. It's ours, as well."

By then, the room positively resounded with laughter, and that touch of pink around the ears turned bright red and spread all across the broad, blank face of Lucius Domitius Ahenobarbus.

"But all that is beside the point—" Cato started to say.

"Oh, is it?" Curio insisted, suddenly daring to interject himself.

There were scattered sounds of unhappy grumbling around the room. "Now listen, young man—" one voice snapped. But Cato quickly held up his right hand again. "It's all right, gentlemen," he said.

He paused a moment, as if gathering his thoughts, then took an olive from a well-polished bronze tray being carried by an ancient slave, munched it, and said in a most congenial manner: "Young Curio, I don't believe I meant that quite the way it sounded. What I meant was that for the purposes of our discussion here tonight, Pompey's 'cause,' if you wish, has nothing to do with liberty, or anything else so high-flown. In truth, his 'cause,' quite simply and in point of fact, is his desire to become dictator of Rome. That, to clarify the point, is what I am pretending to be sympathetic to. Well, of course, not that exactly but, rather, sympathetic to how 'troubled' he says he is about the 'direction' our government has been taking of late.

"Now Pompey does claim that his underlying cause is liberty; so does Caesar. But how either man could become dictator and liberate us, both at the same time, is something my colleagues and I find quite puzzling, and, of course, in the larger sense, you are correct: it certainly is *not* beside the point; indeed, the matter of liberty and how to maintain it is something about which we are all deeply concerned. I point out its irrelevance only in terms of what we're talking about right this minute.

"As a matter of fact, just to finish up my answer to the question asked by our colleague, Ahenobarbus: I have been telling Pompey that I agree with him: that Caesar is evil incarnate, that Rome needs his strength to get rid of Caesar, and that the Senate is highly sympathetic to his concerns. I believe that he believes me. I also believe that having such clear knowledge of his thoughts and desires will allow us to anticipate him and gain a clear advantage when the time comes."

Cato looked over at Ahenobarbus, as if he were about to ask him if he understood. Then, apparently thinking better of it—dreading, I suppose, the posing of yet another half-witted question—Cato merely cleared his throat and smiled.

Just then the ancient slave who'd been making his way ever so slowly through the room finally came up beside me and held out his tray of olives. I was about to take one when I realized that strands from his beard were brushing over the tray and everything on it.

"No, thank you," I whispered, and the old man moved languidly off.

"And what of the Senate?" Curio was suddenly insisting. "Is liberty their 'underlying cause' as well?"

"Now that is quite enough, young man." Once again, it was the silken voice of the ancient aristocrat, Appius Pulcher. "It is not the Senate which foments revolution or civil war," Pulcher said. "It is not the Senate which seeks to consolidate all power in the hands of one or two men."

There was a smattering of applause and shouts of "Here, here" from the little group.

"We only desire a return to truly constitutional government," Cato put in, "under the rule of the Senate and the other duly authorized legislative and judicial bodies—the popular assembly, the board of tribunes, and the equestrian orders."

Cato looked slowly around the room, seemingly at each and every man there, then rested his gaze at last on Curio. "Liberty is indeed our cause," Cato said with finality, "and we have the only legitimate claim to it."

★   ★   ★

It occurred to me as soon as we left Cato's house: there was something odd about that meeting, something not quite right. Of course to me the oddest thing of all was that Curio had been invited in the first place. Had it all been staged for his benefit? I wondered.

"That's just what I was thinking," Lucius Flavius said when I raised the question first thing next morning, just after arriving for work in Curio's study. Of my other cousins, Junius Barnabas was doing an errand at the Forum, while his brother, Claudius, was at home with a cold. "Cato's answers were so set," Lucius was saying. "And Ahenobarbus—can he really be that dense? I mean, all of it had already been explained one way or another, and then he brings it all up again."

"W-e-e-l-l . . ." I said, drawing out the word. "As to that, they say he does the same thing in the Senate, asking questions again and again, though I haven't seen it yet myself. But I've heard Avidius remark on it. And even my father has noticed."

Lucius looked at me coolly, and I felt a small blush coming on. "You're so hard on your father," he said quietly, and my only response was to lower my eyes in embarrassment.

"Maybe Ahenobarbus just pretends to be that stupid all the time," Lucius said with a smile.

"Perhaps," I said. "Anyway, I agree about Cato. It was as if he'd been rehearsing. And that Appius Pulcher—as if he'd been practicing, too. Very peculiar."

49

"A little fresh blood's what Pulcher's family needs," Lucius said with a laugh. Then, abruptly silent for a moment, he scratched his head while I drummed my fingers on the table beside me.

"So what does it all mean?" my cousin said at last.

I shook my head and turned around to face Curio where he sat—in his work area just behind me. It was undoubtedly the most cluttered part of a well-cluttered room, stacked with scrolls of unused leaflets, discarded ideas and the like.

"I'd still like to know why you were invited to begin with," I asked, knowing of course that Lucius and I had been there only because Curio had brought us along. "What do you think, Curio?"

All during our chattering, he'd been quietly writing, not saying a word. Now he looked up with a heavy sigh and a thoughtful look in his eyes.

"Well, for one thing, from all I've seen or heard, poor Aheno-barbus is definitely as dumb as he seems," Curio said. "As for Cato and Pulcher, well, that's the way they are—well practiced and wordy, like actors who've been at center stage too long. Somehow, no matter what they say, it sounds so predictable that it's, well . . . unbelievable. It's as if some theater manager had miscast them for their parts. If, for example, old Cato came up to you and said, 'I've just raped your sister,'—why, you'd laugh in his face."

"Now, if *you* told me that . . ." Lucius said, looking at me with his most engaging smile. I stared at him through my customary blush, while Curio chuckled appreciatively. "I suspect you'd call out the legions, eh, Lucius?"

I stared from one to the other, shaking my head. "How amusing you both are this morning," was the only retort I could manage.

A bit later, when Curio was out of the room, my cousin quietly leaned over and apologized. "I really wanted to say it to Curio, but lost my nerve at the last instant," he said.

"Oh," was all I answered, then tried not to laugh too long or too loudly.

★　　★　　★

"But we didn't finish our talk," I complained later, over a lunch of oysters and olives in Curio's little courtyard. It was an unusually beautiful day: an early spring sun at perfect strength, a gentle wind rustling the trees, the sweet smell of figs in the air. "You still haven't answered me," I insisted. "Why were we there? What was Cato doing?"

"Cato's a blockhead," Curio snapped back with surprising finality. "He lacks the subtlety to 'stage' anything like last night's meeting—my 'actor' analogy notwithstanding." He took a bite or two of food, seemed to reflect a moment, then, while chewing some spinach, said almost casually: "And his commitment to 'liberty.' Well, it remains to be seen. In fact, I'd go so far as to say that our friends in the Senate are getting more impossible by the day. You know, of course, that they've voted down the latest road repair bill."

Having been there for the vote, I nodded quickly.

"I mean turning down road repairs! Can you believe it? And now you know what they're talking about? *Not* doing the intercalation next year—you know, inserting the extra month to keep the calendar in sync? And you know why? Just to make sure that Caesar gets stripped of his command as soon as possible. Can you imagine? By the time they're through we'll be celebrating Saturnalia in midsummer, just to get rid of Caesar a few weeks sooner."

I stared at him in amazement—I had not heard about the intercalation nonsense—and I was fascinated in a way by the absurdity of it all. But I was also determined not to let him change the subject.

I gave him a moment to swallow another oyster or two, then pressed the point again. "But why, Curio?" I asked. "Why invite *you*?"

He put down his fork, wiped his mouth off and stared at me for a long moment. "Because," he said at last, with an ominous shake of his head, "now the blockheads think that I've gone over to Pompey."

★   ★   ★

"Look in the middle drawer of the sideboard, then," Curio was yelling from the next room. Somehow, a key part of a Senate speech he was planning had slipped through the cracks, and we were all in a panic to find it.

"All right," I shouted back.

I pulled the drawer nearly all the way out and began rifling through it. "By the gods," I murmured, pushing my way with growing exasperation through the piles of discards and junk.

"This is a mess, eh, cousin?" Lucius said, coming over to help.

"It can't be in here," I growled.

Just then I spotted a page with writing in Curio's own hand across it. I grabbed it, but it turned out to be just a small scrap. Indeed, there were so few words on it, I couldn't help reading it at a glance, though from the bottom up. First came Curio's signature, then the note, saying, "Thanks for your fine work on that leaflet the other day." I nearly tossed it aside, then saw the top line, which told to whom the note was written. It said: "My dearest Fabius Vibulanus."

"Find it?" Lucius asked, as he noticed me standing dead still with the note in my hand.

I showed it to him, but he only looked at me with a puzzled face. Then I pointed to the name on top, and he gasped with recognition.

"My God," he whispered.

★ ★ ★

"So Fabius Vibulanus used to work for Curio?" Lucius insisted, as we strolled home that evening.

"I need a drink," I said.

"So what does it all mean?" he demanded.

By then we were in a second-floor sitting room of my house, finishing our second jug, and I could hear Fulvia, just down the hallway, chatting happily with the maids and quietly humming.

"What, indeed!" I said with a miserable shake of my head. "You're the clever one, cousin; you're the one who's been 'investigating' the murder; you tell me."

Lucius closed his eyes and leaned back on the sofa. "Too horrible to think about," he said.

"Damned horrible!" I said, a bit too loudly, as this was hardly the best place for such a discussion. Indeed, so far our talk had been most notable for what had *not* been said, especially by me. For instance, Lucius still had not told me what, if anything, he had learned in his "investigation." And I still had not told Lucius about seeing Mark Antony at Curio's house that morning. I had not told him because I doubted he would attach much importance to it, or at least that's what I told myself. In any case, I had no intention of telling him why it had special meaning and importance to me—at least, not while we sat just down the hall from my wife's bedroom. And, sure enough, Fulvia came in soon after.

"What *are* you boys doing?" she chirped, then walked up behind me and softly rubbed my neck.

"I'm sorry, darling, we're celebrating a bit," I lied. "Lucius here got big plaudits today for part of a speech he wrote."

"Oh, how wonderful," she said, in her inimitable way—throatily drawing out the words.

After another moment, she came around, sat down in my lap and said, "Can I join the fun?"

"Beautiful Fulvia, you can join us anytime and in any way you choose," Lucius burbled, for a change drunker than I was. I laughed out loud.

"Hmmm," Fulvia said, "you *are* celebrating." But though her words were a tad reproachful, her tone was soft and she smiled delightfully. Needless to say, she soon bundled me off to bed—though, thoughtful as always, not before arranging for a litter to carry poor Lucius safely home through the Roman night, with all our questions safely unanswered.

★   ★   ★

The next morning, they found the body of Flaccus Valerius. I rushed to the scene, only to find Lucius arriving a few steps ahead of me, for the corpse was almost exactly halfway between our two houses—hidden in some bushes by the side of the street that runs along the upper ridge of the Quirinal.

Once again there were the blue bruises on the neck, once again the fist-size bloodstain on the toga right over the heart. Once again there was the "inflammation" of the buttocks.

"By the gods, Lucius, you must tell me what's going on," I insisted.

We knelt down beside the body, and I watched Lucius staring at the victim's boyish face, struck, I imagine, by how young he was, by how easily this could have been one of us.

"He told us to get out," my cousin murmured, more to himself, it seemed, than to me.

"Lucius, please!" I said.

"Soon, cousin," my cousin said. "Very soon." But somehow I felt that he was only putting me off again.

53

7

Four days later events overtook us yet another time, as the Senate defeated a bill to award parcels of land to the legionary veterans of Pompey's campaigns against the Parthians. As before, the streets of the city erupted angrily; so did Gaius Scribonius Curio.

"The blockheaded, imbecilic fools!" he railed. "There's your Senate's version of liberty."

The vote against the bill was overwhelming, but only after two days of bitter debate. As a very junior backbencher, it would have been out of place for me to speak, but there was nothing to hold back Curio: "You cannot deny these brave men their just due," he insisted. "To do so would be to place a sword at our necks. Indeed, a thousand swords."

Even my father-in-law, the elegant Victorinus Avidius, voiced his own carefully phrased doubts. "It does not seem to me out of the ordinary to make these land grants. There is ample precedent going back several centuries. Indeed, even the ancient Law of the Twelve Tables indicates support."

"The Twelve Tables also imposed the death penalty for writing the wrong sort of song!" shouted Junius Silanus, a very senior member who, in fact, had been at that meeting at Cato's house. The remark drew raucous shouts and laughter from all around the Senate chamber.

But, indeed, it was Cato himself who led the assault: "What is the great rush of admiration for these so-called soldiers?" he demanded. "Who did they defeat in their so-called victories? The fierce legions of the Parthian kings?"

At that point, Cato shifted his weight back on his left leg, put his left hand on his hip, then held his right hand out in front of him and let it dangle limply from his wrist. A smattering of laughter began almost at once, as some in the room quickly realized what was coming.

"This," Cato went on, bouncing back and forth in his mimicry of an effeminate stance, "is your ferocious Parthian warrior. And what a struggle it is for him each morning: to decide how to color his hair, and what sort of paint to rub around his eyes, and whether to leave his lips shiny or dull"—all said in a mincing, womanish tone of voice. "In truth, half the time it's not possible to tell if these creatures are men or women—at least not without close inspection," Cato added, fluttering his eyelashes and swiveling his hips. "Perhaps, too close."

Of course, by then, the laughter was deafening, and it took a quarter hour or more for the room to settle down. Indeed, a few older men were so choked and red-faced that I feared for their health, though in the end, all recovered.

Naturally, Cato concluded his remarks on a more serious note. "I see no justification, based solely on the merits of their achievements, to award land to these veterans, land which I might point out, is already in short supply."

But it was with humor (grotesque and, I must say, inaccurate as it was) that Cato and his friends won the day.

As I say, riots broke out once again, and, of course, the question soon arose: Who can be called upon to stop them?

"Pompey, of course," Curio mused, after three days of violence. We were all there in his study, Lucius Flavius, the Barnabas brothers, and I, chewing over in our inimitable Roman manner every nuance of what had occurred.

"What game are they playing?" my cousin Junius Barnabas asked with refreshing brevity.

"I don't get it, either," Lucius said. "First, they slap Pompey down, or seem to. Then the veterans riot, which any moron could have predicted—"

"Thank you, Lucius," Curio interjected dryly.

55

Lucius brought himself up short, then laughed and apologized. "Well, you know what I mean. Anyway, now they're about to ask Pompey, the very man they're treating so shabbily, to use his influence—"

"And troops, if necessary," Claudius Barnabas put in.

"Yes, yes, and troops, if necessary," Lucius continued, "to clean up the mess which they created."

Curio, sitting with his elbow on his worktable and his chin propped on his right hand, shrugged and shook his head.

"So are they very stupid or very smart?" I finally asked of anyone who felt like answering.

"Precisely!" Lucius said, to my surprise and slight confusion. It was one of the highest words of praise my clever cousin bestowed, and I confess to being caught unaware that I had hit on a point which contained any notable insight.

"I sense a great, delicate web, brilliantly woven, ready to ensnare whoever takes the first false step," Lucius said. "On the other hand, what the hell is it? I mean, if it's so brilliant, shouldn't we be able to make *some* sense of it by now? Or has Roman politics become so obscure and cryptic that no one can figure out anything anymore—not even the plotters themselves?"

Curio laughed with real amusement in his tone, and his eyes suddenly twinkled with more life than I'd seen there in several days.

"You're probably not far wrong," he said.

Then, hesitating another moment, he cleared his throat and went on: "Cato and the others get these darling notions, as if through some nuance or other they can tilt the world this way or that. So that's exactly what they do, they weave webs and concoct plots that come to nothing. Of course, they're also simply trying to show they're still masters here, so they try to keep everybody else off balance—most particularly, Pompey and Caesar, of course.

"Also, they can't decide which one they hate more. In the end, it'll almost certainly be Caesar, because they know they can't control him. They still think they can control Pompey, and they may be right: Pompey keeps vacillating; he's alarmed by Caesar, but he's still not quite ready to dump him—as you'll see in the next few days.

56

"But remember this much: sometimes, these convoluted maneuvers of the Senate are just a smoke screen for what's actually going on. In this case, the land bill wasn't defeated just as a slap at Pompey; in fact, that was probably a very small part of the reason. Cato hinted at it himself when he said land is in short supply, and that's right. There's very little that's still left in the public domain, so where would all this land for veterans come from? Well, it can't come from the small landowners, because then we'd just be trading one set of malcontents for another. So it would have to come from the owners of the huge farms and estates—in other words, from all the rich friends of Cato and the other old-liners. And apparently, that isn't about to happen. In fact, I'd go so far as to say that we've all been sent a message: that the rich landholders of Italy are not about to part with anything."

★   ★   ★

The next day, Avidius summoned me to his house—or, rather, to his part of the house in which Fulvia and I lived. I was ushered into his study, previously a dark and dreary affair, and gasped at a new wall of gleaming white marble.

"Like it?" he said. "You wait. Twenty years from now, get rid of all this ramshackle old wood and brick. All Rome will shine— whole city: gleaming marble."

"It's beautiful," I said.

I sat down beside him on a large blue sofa and waited a moment while he finished a bite of fig. Then he smiled, or tried to, but I saw his great eyebrows nervously leaping.

"Something wrong, sir?" I asked. Of course, even to press him that much was taking something of a liberty, but, after all, I thought, I am his son-in-law now. Also, I had plenty of work of my own that morning and couldn't spend an hour while he built up to some dramatic surprise.

"How much," he said obligingly, and almost at once, "do you really know about this Scribonius Curio?"

"Well . . ." I said, admittedly taken by surprise at the cause of his concern. I hesitated: After all, I wondered, just what *did* I think of Curio now? Now I wasn't quite so certain—though, of course, that didn't necessarily have anything to do with what I might tell my father-in-law. "He's dedicated, quite intelligent," I said after

57

another moment and without a trace of uncertainty in my voice. "And he's very concerned about maintaining our liberty, hates even the prospect of one-man rule."

"I see," Avidius said, nodding his head thoughtfully. "It's only, well . . . these are tumultuous times, Livinius. Dangerous times. People will be taking sides. And which side they choose can mean a great deal." Again, he smiled feebly. "Even life or death."

He stopped and shook his head, silent for a long moment, as if to reflect on some ominous new possibility.

"What is it, Avidius?" I said, then dared to reach over and touch him affectionately on the shoulder. To my astonishment, he returned the gesture, reaching his right hand around and clasping it over mine.

"I just want you to be careful is all," he said. "I'm just worried about . . . well, about you and . . ."

"About Fulvia. Of course, sir."

He nodded, tight-lipped, his eyes a bit misty. Then he abruptly stood and began pacing in small circles. "Just how did you meet this Curio, anyway?" he demanded.

I looked up at him and blinked, as if to make sure I'd heard him correctly. "Why I thought you knew, sir. Cicero introduced us."

"Aaah," he said. "I see. Well, well." He walked off a few more circles, hands behind his back, eyebrows dancing. "But you believe him?"

"Sir?"

"That is to say, you believe that Curio is a sincere friend to the republic?"

"Oh yes, sir." And I thought: This is getting harder by the minute.

"You've heard nothing to the contrary?"

"Well . . ." I was about to say: Only what Curio himself has mentioned, that Cato and some others thought he'd gone over to Pompey. But, for one thing, we had all dismissed that with a laugh when he'd said it—it was that absurd; for another, to bring it up now would most likely force me to describe that meeting at Cato's house, a meeting which we had attended strictly in confidence—and breaking confidences was not something I did lightly, even to my own father-in-law.

58

"No, sir," I said finally. "Nothing at all."

Avidius smiled pleasantly, seemingly taking me at my word. Then, after a few moments of small talk and formalities, we ended our meeting amiably enough, and I went about my business.

8

The next day the Senate once again issued the formal call for Pompey to bring order to the streets of Rome: One day later, fresh troops moved into the city.

But this time there would be little of the relatively mild measures of the winter before; this operation would be carried out with merciless dispatch. Indeed, I had the misfortune to witness some of it myself: I saw soldiers cut men down where they stood; I saw them beat men's heads in, then carve up their bodies like so many sheep at slaughter. In one case, I saw two soldiers grab an old veteran and pin his arms back, while a third slit open the man's stomach and pulled out his insides. Then they simply let him fall to the street and die in slow agony.

Not surprisingly, by nightfall there were bodies piled high at every corner; little rivers of blood flowed down the gutters. One by one, the soldiers severed a hundred heads from their corpses, gathered them up, strung them together, and hung them across the main entrance to the Forum like some ghastly banner.

Rome reeled at the horror of it, but like some old man too worn out to yell, kept its voice of protest at the level of a soft murmur and went about its business. Within forty-eight hours, the rioters were crushed.

"I know, I know," Curio said, his voice filled with rare sympathy when he walked into his workroom that day and found Lucius and me in tears. "What a cranky old man that Pompey has become," he said, sounding as though he were trying to laugh. But

60

when Lucius and I looked up, we saw tears streaming down his face, as well; then he walked over and gave us each a long, comforting hug.

And I thought: Who else but a fine friend and a true Roman could act as Curio is acting now?

★　　★　　★

Events continued at a rapid pace: One week later, with Rome still in a state of postriot torpor, the great debate began at last over the command of Julius Caesar.

First, let me briefly remind you of the issues: Caesar lay not three hundred miles from Rome at his headquarters in the province of Cisalpine Gaul. He had been its governor nearly ten years and military commander of his ten legions for even longer. At the same time, he had also served several terms as consul, large parts of all of them in absentia; he'd also been sworn into office twice in absentia.

Any of these things alone would be regarded as an extraordinary and unconstitutional accumulation of power. All of them together amounted to a serious threat to the republic. In particular, it was the extreme length of his governorship that seemed to be the matter of gravest concern. Thus, the Senate considered a proposal to end Caesar's term in office and to abolish his military command.

"Does he want dictatorship?" asked Calpurnius Bibulus, in his slightly shrill manner. "We summon him to Rome, and he does not come. We suggest it's time that he relinquish his powers, or some of them, and he balks. What else can we imagine but that he wishes to subsume the state itself?"

"His manner is arrogant, his actions contumacious," said Quintus Metellus Scipio, one of the Senate's steadier voices and one of Rome's few men of truly impeccable reputation (and another who'd been at that secret meeting). Indeed, his uncharacteristically blunt words brought a rare hush to the chamber. "I'm sorry, but I find no other way of putting it," Scipio went on. "Caesar has become far too strong, the state far too weak. There must be a change, or everything we love, everything we value, even Rome itself, will perish."

"Impeach him!" came Cato's stern, familiar voice. "Impeach him for treason!"

I looked around and saw Curio roll his eyes and shake his head.

61

Once again, I thought, Cato pushes the argument to the limits of rhetorical grace. "His campaigns in the north have been brutal beyond need," Cato went on. "He has chopped off the hands of his captives, he has arrested chieftains who have visited his camp under flag of truce; he has massacred their tribes, including women and children, and burned their crops and homes. Perhaps he can be handed over to the barbarians as punishment." Cato paused for effect, and there was appreciative laughter. "But no!" Cato shouted. "With his added crimes against the state, we must deal with him. He must be removed from office and placed under arrest. He must surrender his arms. He must be made to face the enormity of his crimes and pay the penalty."

"Yes!" came a shout of several voices at once. There was a roar of applause, but there were shouts against it, too. For over the years Caesar had placed a good many of his loyal followers in the Senate—although more than a few were of clearly questionable qualifications and character.

"Why don't you arrest him yourself then, you old boob," came the voice of one such fellow, Livius Maecenas, a former slave and failed corn speculator. He was greeted with a great outburst of jeers and catcalls, but despite being a bit tipsy (or perhaps because of it), Maecenas stayed on his feet and went on: "I mean it, you old misery: Caesar won't come here and face your trumped-up charges. So go on up there and bring him back, if you can—or should I say, if you dare!"

By then, the whole room was in an uproar. "You sot," I heard one man shout at Maecenas. Shoving matches broke out as some of the senators tried to get at him. Order was finally restored only after several sympathizers escorted Maecenas from the chamber. "That," came the unmistakable voice of the ancients, "is the rabble we must contend with—thanks to the eminent Julius Caesar."

"Oh, God," I heard Curio moan from several rows away, and a few of those around him couldn't quite suppress a quiet snicker or two. Indeed, the new speaker was none other than Appius Claudius Pulcher.

"Lowlifes, scum, drunkards, who knows what," Pulcher was saying. His mellifluous tones, accompanied by the remarkably graceful movement of his hands—long, elegant, refined—fairly captivated the room, all despite the pretentious silliness of the words themselves. "Are we to have this Caesar and his bandit cronies at the head of Rome itself? I think not. I think such an eventuality would come over my dead body."

"That can be arranged!" came a shout from another of Caesar's followers.

"By the gods!" came Pulcher's indignant response. And then the chamber dissolved into chaos, with men shouting and shoving. After nearly an hour, with no hope of restoring order, I heard Cato finally call over the din for adjournment until the following day, and the senators slowly filed out.

★   ★   ★

"I was surprised you didn't speak today," I said.

I was alone with Curio in the little tavern up the street from his house, tired but too full of energy to sleep. The proprietor's son brought over a container of some cheap Italian red and plopped it down, leaving it for us to drink right out of the urn, with no goblets and nothing to dilute it.

"Were you?" Curio said, and took a great swig.

"Well . . ."

"It was best I kept my mouth shut," he said. "I had nothing to say today that they'd want to hear."

We each took another large gulp.

"Which was?"

"Look, the point is to find solutions, not create more problems," Curio answered. "Cato said, 'Impeach him. Arrest him.' So do you think Caesar will come to Rome for that? Of course not. No one would—not in his right mind. Not if he has, as Caesar does, the alternative of remaining in the safe haven of his legionary camp."

"So I suppose—"

"You suppose right, young Gaius. Caesar will not yield, and the crisis grows worse by the minute."

★   ★   ★

The next day's debate was not a half hour old before shouting and epithets took center stage again. I believe I heard the words "old fool" yelled more times in the following hour than in my whole life before that. Of course the insults rapidly grew far worse, until finally the Senate of Rome was nothing but a mob, first angry, then

63

laughing madly as two older members, gray-haired and well into their fifties, rolled about on the chamber floor in a preposterous simulation of a fight. Soon enough the ugly mood took a more serious turn, as first one fistfight broke out, then another, then still another after that.

I sat back on my bench and shook my head, too stunned by the spectacle, I suppose, to feel much of anything, even indignation. I looked around to see Curio give me a beckoning glance. I nodded; then, after a minute or two, I quietly followed him out the door to his town house a few streets away.

★ ★ ★

"You understand the other reason why I haven't spoken in the debate?" Curio said, as we took our customary places in his work-room.

"Yes, because no one could hear you anyway over the idiot shouting."

"Well, that, too," he said smiling. "But, really, what would I say? Essentially what I was telling you yesterday—to look for solutions, to seek compromise, to stop posturing and find real ways to preserve the republic. But any of that would only reinforce the feelings they already have about me."

I stared at him quizzically a moment, drumming my fingers on the table beside me. "Which is that you've uh, gone over?"

"Gone over to Pompey, yes."

I sat with my left elbow on the table and my chin propped in my left hand. "You know, my father-in-law—"

"Avidius?"

"He asked me the other day if I'd heard anything about that—anything about whether or not you'd 'gone over.' "

Curio started to say something, then stopped as an old slave, completely hairless (at least from the neck up), straggled in with a big dish of figs, set them down in front of us and left. Curio stuffed a couple in his mouth and offered the rest to me. I took one and chewed it slowly.

"You were saying," he said.

"Hmmm? Oh, about Avidius. He was asking—"

"Oh, yes, if I'd 'gone over.' And what did you tell him—if you don't mind such an impertinent question?"

64

"Not at all," I said. "I said I'd heard nothing of the sort, which is true, other than your own mention of it a week or so ago."

Curio nodded, munched some more figs, then shrugged and shook his head.

All the while, I mulled something over in my mind and finally decided it might be time for a touch of brashness. I waited another moment until Curio's mouth was especially full.

"So, have you?" I asked.

"What?"

"Gone over?" I said.

He carefully swallowed, then wiped his mouth and cleared his throat. "You must know how absurd that is," he said.

"Yes, I believe so."

"Well, it is. You of all people—you've been with me so much, helped with the work, with the speeches. You should know. Well . . . you want to hear me say it? Fine: I have not 'gone over to Pompey.' You have my word on that, Livinius. I always have been, am now and always will be a Roman patriot and an unswerving supporter of the republic."

★   ★   ★

The events of later that day came with the speed of a lightning flash, and, I might add, the force of a thunderbolt. We were napping, I on a bench in the courtyard, Curio in his upstairs bedroom, when a courier clomped noisily into the house. "Special session of the Senate in one hour," he shouted in a most officious tone, then swiftly clanked back out—even before I could wake up and shake off the feathery mist of sleep.

"Curio," I yelled, hoping to awaken him. "Hurry up, special session." Then, almost before I knew it, I had changed into fresh clothes.

"Curio," I yelled again.

After another moment, he came out onto the balcony. "You go on ahead," he shouted down. "I'll be right behind you."

★   ★   ★

There were soldiers posted outside the Senate chamber for that extraordinary session. I was vaguely glad about it till I saw some of my colleagues whiten with fear as they crossed the open plaza and first noticed the armed men. Naturally, some of that feeling was contagious: Just what are we in for? I wondered.

There were no soldiers inside, but it was enough to know they could quickly be summoned. As I say, it all happened so fast: Everyone was filing in, and some of the men had not even taken their seats yet, when suddenly we heard that familiar voice:

"Senate Fathers of Rome," Cato intoned from just inside the main entranceway, "allow me to present the esteemed Roman proconsul, conquering general of the renowned Parthian hordes of the East, Rome's legendary military commander, Pompeius Magnus." Indeed, right next to him, quite suddenly there was Pompey himself stepping into the chamber. He shook hands with Cato, seemed about to speak, then . . . wait a minute. Who is *that* coming up behind him, that much younger man? Pompey turns and even shakes hands with him, while I stare in speechless disbelief: For it is none other than Gaius Scribonius Curio.

By the gods, I thought: First comes Cato, one minute belittling the "womanish" Parthian troops, now praising Pompey's victories to the skies. Now here's Curio, seemingly in Pompey's camp after all. Can this be true? And . . . hold it, that's right, Curio knew days ago that something would happen to show . . . what was it again? Ah, yes, that Pompey still wasn't ready to break openly with Caesar. Would this be it? I wondered—whatever *this* was.

"Senate Fathers," came Pompey's unmistakably flat and reedy tone. We all looked straight at him, and even from a fair distance, I could see the craggy lines across his face and the tired eyes: Crinkly eyes, I thought; old man's eyes.

"Senate Fathers, I would like things to stay as they are for a while," Pompey said. "Perhaps another year . . ."

He let his voice hang for a moment. And I thought: Surely, he has something more to tell us; surely, this is worth an extra moment of his time, a few more words. But that was all he said. I blinked in confusion, but everyone else seemed to know exactly what he meant, for they all gave him a noisy cheer.

Then, after standing for just another instant in the doorway to the Senate chamber of Rome, Pompey the Great turned, walked off and was gone.

9

So just like that the long-awaited debate on Caesar's command was over—or at least put off a year. That was Pompey's message, and the Senate complied with the eager obedience of a lapdog.

"Well, yes, I had been privately in touch with Pompey's men for about two weeks beforehand," Curio admitted later. "I'm sorry I left you out of it, Livinius, but believe me it was for your own good. I couldn't tell how people might react if it got out that I was approaching Pompey. And, of course, it did leak out: After all, every time anybody sees him a dozen of his advisers know about it. And then word gets around. As it was, Cato found out almost immediately. I simply could not put you or your family at risk, and that might have been considerable if you had become openly involved in this particular matter." He stopped and smiled, clearly trying to smooth things over. "All right?" he said.

I nodded peevishly, for once again my doubts about this man had returned. "But what did you tell him?" I asked.

"Well, that's just it. I simply proposed some practical solutions. And I can tell you in all honesty that nothing I said was very well received. Until the Senate lapsed into chaos. Once again, the senators did it to themselves. When Pompey heard about their idiotic shoving matches, he was furious. And when he decided to make his move, he was good enough to call me in for a small share of the credit. Or, well . . . who knows?" He paused and laughed out loud. "Maybe clever enough to shift a little of the blame. After all, you can never be too sure in matters of this sort just how everything will turn out in the end."

★   ★   ★

With the big debate postponed, Rome, for me, was flat and lifeless that summer—like a man with the wind knocked out.

Thus, I was thrilled to receive word in June of a perfect chance to leave town for a while: It seemed that Cicero's term as Cilician governor was up, and my cousin Lucius and I were to be part of a big homecoming. We would meet him at the port of Brundisium, I was told, and accompany him by highway from there back to Rome. It would be, Cicero wrote to his friend Atticus, "a triumphal return to the capital." I wrote back at once that we'd be delighted to go, and the first week in July, Lucius Flavius and I set out on horseback for Brundisium in southern Italy.

We left with time to spare, so our families insisted on loading us up with a full-fledged caravan: several slaves, half a dozen mules and even a small supply wagon. Of course, they also packed some of our finest clothes, including one dashing blue silk toga that Fulvia had given me. As I say, with all that in tow, we made slow time, taking two days just to reach Capua, then turning due east onto the Via Minucia for the trip over the mountains.

"There's a good spot," Lucius said, as we emerged from a small arroyo at the end of our third full day of travel. He pointed to a well-cleared, flat area to the side of the road, which in turn looked out over a drop of two thousand feet or more and a vast expanse of sky beyond.

Behind us, the sun had not quite disappeared, and the sky, though darkening, still showed a deep shade of blue. Even so, dozens of stars were already twinkling, and the slim crescent of a new moon flickered. Indeed, on so beautiful an evening, it was a perfect place to stop and camp for the night.

"Not bad," I said with a smile.

We dismounted, and while the slaves tended the horses and set up the tents, Lucius and I scrambled partway up the hillside on the near side of the road, opened a pouch of wine and munched some dried meat and pickled eggs.

"You've seen better, I suppose, eh, cousin?" Lucius said with a sweeping motion of his right arm.

"No, in truth, I have not," I said. "You're quite right, Lucius, it's very beautiful."

We each took big swallows of wine, and my cousin stretched out on the ground beside me, smiling ear to ear.

I looked at him quizzically. "What!" I said.

But he simply rolled over on his stomach, looked back at me and kept grinning in his slightly off-center way. That, I had decided long ago, was his most engaging feature, that grin, for he was otherwise unextraordinary in appearance, much more typically Roman than I, with prominent nose, brownish skin, olive eyes.

No woman would ever call *him* beautiful, I thought. Then again, I had seen girls melt before that silly grin of his and those eyes—clever and captivating, wide with intelligence, radiating mischief, alertness and sympathy, all at the same time. Indeed, clever cousin Lucius had had his share.

He took another enormous swig of wine and kept smiling stupidly. "You drunk, already?" I said with mock irritation.

"Yes, cousin: drunk."

"Well, give me that wine, I won't have you drunker than—"

"I'm getting married," he said.

I stopped, blinked and shook my head. "You son of a whore," I said, laughing, and leaned over to embrace him. "Congratulations," I told him more than once.

"That's wonderful," I repeated, between swallows of the grape. "So, who is it?" I demanded. "Do I know her? Well, of course, I do; I must. Is it—"

"You better not 'know' her, cousin."

"Oh, shut up, cousin. I don't mean *know* her, in that way. I just mean, know her. Acquainted with her. You know."

"Hah! You're the drunk one now," Lucius said, and we both collapsed with laughter at what seemed at that moment to be utterly hilarious.

"Well, you remember last fall, that party at Hirtius Pansa's? Well, that's where we met. Beautiful little dark-haired girl."

I started to say, So it's not Avidia Crispina? But I gulped and held my tongue. "Was I at that party?" was all I finally asked him.

"Weren't you? I thought you were."

"Well, anyway, what's—"

"Her name's Matidia," Lucius said. "Matidia Gratus."

I ran the name through my mind, but could not place her. "By the gods, I don't think I do know her."

"No, I don't believe—"

"Oh, wait! Last summer. Well, that wasn't a party. That was that family outing thing that all the mothers put on. Yes, I did meet her. Beautiful girl. Very pretty smile."

Lucius looked at me then with as sad and suspicious a face as ever I'd seen. "Lucius, please! There were a hundred people there; we met for a moment; we exchanged maybe five words." He nodded, but remained noticeably more subdued. "Lucius, you're my most favorite and beloved cousin. I wouldn't lie to you about such a matter. Or let me put it this way: if there'd been anything more to it, I *would* lie to you; I would've denied ever having met her at all."

Slowly, Lucius sat up and really began to smile again. "Yes," he said with a laugh, "that's just the way you *would* handle it."

"Yes," I said, with a slight blush, allowing him his little victory, though honestly not at all sure what he really intended to say.

★　★　★

"You're also in a good mood," Lucius said.

By then, night had fallen in earnest, the mountain air had chilled down quite a bit, and we huddled in our tent beneath several blankets each.

"It will be good to see Cicero again," I said.

"Wonderful, yes."

"And it's so good to get out of Rome," I added.

Lucius looked over at me with unusual attention, as if he were studying me with his wide, knowing eyes. Suddenly, my cousin looked very sad; suddenly, as well, I felt for the second time that evening as though he had something especially important to tell me.

"Nothing's what it seems to be there, is it?" I said, in hopes of egging him on a little.

"Oh, cousin," he said with a shake of his head, as if quite suddenly he were on the verge of tears.

70

10

The crowd cheered and applauded Cicero so loudly and for so long, as he stepped off the boat at Brundisium, that for a moment I actually felt a kind of panic that they might never stop and we would all be there forever—or at least until our voices gave out and our hands were bloodied and calloused.

"My friends," Cicero said, when at last there was a moment of quiet. But then his voice choked and his eyes misted over, and then the cheering started all over again and he finally had to be escorted from the platform.

He was taken to the nearby home of the magistrate, where he was fairly smothered by hordes of fawning locals, all of whom wanted a word with the great man. Working our way through the layers of sycophants from the town bureaucracy, it took Lucius and me nearly an hour to reach him.

"Oh, my babies," he said with tears in his eyes, when finally we stood before him in his rooms.

"You're very popular, master," Lucius said dryly.

Cicero shrugged, then laughed out loud. "None of them wanted to be anywhere near me when I came through here two years ago. I was whisked to the docks and put on a boat that left with the tide that very evening."

He paced nervous circles and shook his head. "Now, well . . ." His voice trailed off, and he finished with a gesture of upturned palms that seemed to say he found it all quite mystifying—though he surely wasn't about to argue with such an outpouring of affection.

"Well, if nothing else, you look good by comparison," I said, "to everyone else in public life these days."

"There's no question!" Cicero snapped. "Should you expect anything less?" He pursed his lips and narrowed his eyes. "They'll all have to learn, won't they? Have to be reminded yet again of who saved them from destruction, of what Rome itself owes to me."

"Well . . . that is . . . yes sir . . ." I stammered, for it was hardly the reaction I'd expected. I suppose I'd anticipated some touch of irony. Even sarcasm would have done. But instead there was something close to bitterness as he harked back to the past (in particular, to events of his own consulship a dozen years before, when he had thwarted a conspiracy to overthrow the government by a man named Catiline).

"It's true," he said, his voice suddenly shaky and quiet. As he spoke, a tear or two rolled down his cheeks. "The savior of the state sent into exile . . ."

"Of course it's true," came a soothing voice from across the room. It was Cicero's old friend, the scholarly Atticus, who stepped over to him and held him in his arms, while I stood perfectly still, quite paralyzed from surprise. I stole a glance at Lucius, who for once looked thoroughly taken aback.

"It's all right," Atticus was saying, "you're home, you're safe, your friends are here . . ."

Just then Cicero's brother, Quintus, and his son, Marcus, who had both been with him on the last leg of the sea crossing from Macedonia, came into the room. At a glance, they seemed to size up the trouble, then walked over and helped the old master to the nearest sofa.

"Get some sleep," I heard his brother say. Atticus patted him on the wrist, and then his son leaned over and kissed him on the forehead.

"He'll rest now," Atticus said. And indeed he seemed to fall asleep almost at once.

But even as the others left the room, I waited a moment, wondering, What kind of sleep can it be? For watching his face—his eyes shut tightly, his neck throbbing—it suddenly struck me how much he had suffered, and I could not help crying for him a little.

Next morning, Cicero was his usual cheery self, or so it seemed. He even apologized to Lucius and me. "Too little sleep and too much to do for an old man," he said. Even so, starting at that moment and for the rest of the journey home, he was a whirlwind.

After meeting with every official of Brundisium all over again, he made three speeches in the town that very day, one down at the docks, one to the local assembly, and still another to an audience of the very rich at the house of the town's richest citizen, one Ampius Balbus.

"Do you know how much Rome owes me?" Cicero cheerfully insisted to throngs of adoring dock workers. "Only her life, that's all. Only her very existence."

"You all remember the evil Catiline?" Cicero asked the assembled officials of the town. "He thought he would overturn the Roman Senate, dismantle the state itself. Well, bad luck to him that your servant Cicero was consul then. And Catiline was squashed and eaten with no more effort than a frog would eat a fly."

"Cicero is back!" he told the rich men gathered in Balbus's enormous atrium. "Your savior is ready to save you again."

And so it went, all along the tour, from the coastal town of Barium and the foothill village of Canusium, to little Forum Novum and also Beneventum, built among the craggy hillsides of the Apennines.

At each place large crowds happily turned out to meet the renowned teacher, statesman, proconsul, philosopher. Each time, as Cicero mounted the platform, the crowds shouted and shrieked with joy. But soon enough Lucius and I could no longer deny that a curious phenomenon was dogging the journey: while the crowds started out frantically enthusiastic, by the end of each speech, applause erupted only sporadically, and the admiring followers departed, it seemed to us, with feelings more of confusion than inspiration showing on their faces. It was as if they were thinking, This is the great Cicero? If he's so great, why does he have to keep saying he's great? Why does he talk only about himself?

By Capua, where we would stay for several days, Lucius and I found ourselves truly cringing with embarrassment as he repeated the same self-laudatory pronouncements:

"*I* am the man Rome needs most."

"*I* will protect you from the bandits and pretenders."

"*I* will send the would-be dictators to oblivion."

"*I* will save the republic. *Again!*"

Remarkably enough, in private, he really was the same old Cicero: wise, bright, forthcoming. Indeed, at every stop he put aside at least a full hour each evening for my cousin and me, dwelling at length and with considerable insistence on the good to be found in every experience.

"Was it terrible for you, master, being away so long?" I asked, the first night after we had left Brundisium.

"In some ways, I suppose," he said with a shrug. "But remember this: one of man's distinctive faculties is his desire to investigate. Thus, we're eager to see or hear or learn new things, new ideas. Indeed, we don't feel entirely happy unless we study the mysteries and the marvels of the universe. Hence our fortitude, even our indifference, to the accidents of fortune."

"What do you think will happen now, master, between Caesar and Pompey?" Lucius asked a night or two later. "And what of the republic?"

But, unlike in public, Cicero (at least with us) avoided any specifics at all, instead talking only in handsome abstractions. "I've talked to you about the human instinct of curiosity; well, allied with that is the desire for independence. A well-constituted character will bow to no authority but that of a just and legitimate ruler who aims at the public good."

And so it went. A few evenings after that, when a similar question of politics came up, Cicero answered almost snappishly: "True law is reason—right and natural!" He shook his head as if to say, Isn't it obvious?—then went on: "Of course, its validity is universal; it is immutable, eternal. Any attempt to supersede or repeal any part of it is sinful; to cancel it entirely is impossible."

He sat back and stared off awhile; then, his tone more reflective, he added: "You know, man is the only living being that has a sense of order, as well as decorum and moderation, in word and deed. Indeed, I believe it's safe to say that no other creature is touched by the beauty, grace and symmetry of visible objects; and the human mind, transferring these concepts from what might be

74

called the material world to what could be described as the moral world, recognizes that this beauty, harmony and order must be maintained to an even greater extent in the sphere of direct and purposeful action." He paused a moment and smiled softly. "Reason shuns all that is unbecoming or unmanly, all that is wanton in thought or deed."

"How," I wondered aloud to Lucius our first night in Capua, "can he be so brilliant in private, and yet so . . . so . . ."

"Foolish in public?" Lucius said with a grin. "Well, I've always thought it possible for most men to be several things at once. Good, bad. Smart, stupid. Educated, ignorant. Even wise and foolish."

"Well, our old friend is certainly proving you right," I said.

My cousin shook his head and eyed me thoughtfully. "Except in your case, cousin," he said. "You're the exception to the rule."

"What?"

"It's just that quite often, Livinius, things happen which you don't see. For a long time, I thought you might be choosing to ignore them. But now, finally, I realize that you simply and sincerely do not notice."

I thought: I notice things, all right; I just don't necessarily tell you about them—that's all. But all I said was: "So what does that mean? I suppose I'm stupid, then?"

"Not at all, not stupid," Lucius insisted. "Just, well . . . good. Too good; almost entirely good. That's why you take everything at face value. You need to acquire some bad qualities, cousin, so you'll stop doing that."

"I don't think I'm so good."

"Oh, you've had your escapades, but even those were less from guile than from, well . . ." He broke off and was suddenly red-faced.

"What!" I demanded.

". . . unavoidable opportunities."

"Oh," I said, and felt myself blushing, as well.

I studied my cousin a moment. "Hmmm," I said and thoughtfully rubbed my hands together. This was not the first time lately, I decided, that Lucius had hinted at things he refused to talk about in more specific terms. Well, I thought, I still have time—though right now I could probably cajole him a little.

"You ever going to tell me," I asked, "what you were getting at the other night?"

"What—"

"I said that nothing in Rome's what it seems to be, and you said—"

"Oh, that again. I told you, Livinius, I wasn't getting at anything. I swear it."

"And what about our so-called 'investigation'?" I said. "I thought it was Avidia who kept you interested in that. But I guess not, since you're marrying someone else."

Lucius glared at me, his eyes fiery, his lower lip puffing out with disconsolate anger. "It might have happened," he said very softly. "With her, I mean."

I narrowed my eyes at him and decided to ignore his show of hurt feelings. "So then, Lucius, what are the results?" I asked with uncharacteristic bluntness. "Do you know who murdered Fabius Vibulanus? Or Flaccus Valerius?"

But he just shook his head and said nothing, and after a long moment I allowed myself a bit of a smirk. "You know, cousin, I could make you tell," I said in a teasing tone of voice.

I sat up suddenly on the edge of the sofa, as if I were about to spring across the room at him, and indeed my cousin flinched— quite the reaction I'd hoped for. The point was that although we were nearly equal in size, Lucius had always lost badly to me in wrestling—and for that matter in every other sport.

"It'll do no good because I have nothing to tell," Lucius said with a slight whine in his voice that made me smile.

I shrugged and lay back. "Whatever you say, cousin," I said. "Besides, baby that you are, you're too big now to have your face pinned to the floor and your right arm in a hammerlock for half an hour. Could be embarrassing, especially if Matidia found out. And anyway," I yawned, "I'm tired."

With that I rolled over and fell asleep, though not immediately—thanks once again to a most peculiar conversation with my clever cousin Lucius.

* * *

Our third day in Capua, Gaius Scribonius Curio arrived—with, I might add, considerable flourish. Decked out in fancy silks and accompanied by several dozen slaves, he bore gifts and greetings for Cicero from half the great men of Rome: from Caesar, a gorgeous silver stylus; from Pompey, a dozen gleaming bronze medallions, each inscribed with some famous line or utterance of Cicero himself; from the Senate, perhaps the best of all: unencumbered title to a fine new house, as his old one had been sacked long ago by Clodius's thugs.

"Friend and teacher," Curio said, as he embraced the old man. Cicero was clearly overwhelmed: Tears streaming down his face, it was several minutes before he could speak.

"My own student, eh?" Cicero said with a laugh, pointing at Curio in a manner that was plainly exaggerated for comic effect. "Taught him well, hmmm? He knows who to take care of in his old age."

It was all to the delight of the little crowd that had gathered, but a few minutes later, his face close to Curio's, I overheard him whisper: "Most will have to go back, you know. Yes, yes, no arguments. It's much too much. Of course, there are a few I don't dare return," he chuckled, raising his eyebrows, "and the house from the Senate, that one I'll have to take out of sheer necessity, I'm afraid. But most of the rest—well, it's all far too much for any man of ethics to accept. You know that, my boy; why, do you know what I'd owe down the road if I took all this?"

He let the question go unanswered, turning away with a smile to someone else (who knows which hanger-on!) demanding his attention.

★   ★   ★

"So how are you two, eh?" Curio asked Lucius and me a bit later that evening, when the clamor had finally died down. "Old Cicero seems fine enough."

"Oh, well—"

"Yes," I put in quickly. "He's fine. Definitely."

"Mmmm," Curio murmured. There was an odd silence after that, while he seemed to be thinking just what to say next, though it turned out it was not what to say, but how to say it.

"You know, fellows, he's always been vain," Curio said at last. He paused a moment, as if to let that much sink in, then went on: "I've heard about his speeches this trip, and, well . . . he did the exact same thing once before, right after that whole Catiline business. Went all around Italy proclaiming his own virtue, calling himself 'Rome's savior.' " Curio shook his head. "Nearly wrecked him politically. That's why his career . . . Well, you've seen some of the results. But don't let it bother you. He's still a great man, probably the greatest we have right now. It's only that he's a bit of a fool sometimes—just like the rest of us."

Later on, he gently pulled me aside for a word in private. "Livinius, you've forgiven me, I hope. About the business with Pompey."

I nodded and said "Yes," very softly.

"I hope so," Curio continued, "because I need you, Livinius, I need you with me—at my side. Once we get back to Rome, well . . . you'll see: I'll need you then, more than ever."

$$\star \quad \star \quad \star$$

"You all right, Lucius?" I said, as there in the darkened room which my cousin and I shared in some rich man's house in Capua I gently shook him awake. It was still hours till dawn—and the start of the last leg of our homeward journey; but he had been tossing and turning, even muttering fragments of words out loud—though nothing that made sense.

"Wha-a-a . . . wha-a-" he said, as if trying to wake up. Then, after a moment, he snapped out of his sleepy delirium. "Livinius?" he said, and sat upright with a jolt, breathing hard.

"Some dream, eh?" I said.

"Yes," he said slowly, then lay back down, his respiration calming a bit. "Some dream."

"Anything I can do?"

He took a heavy breath and shrugged. "Maybe," he said.

"Really?" I said. "Well, I won't divorce Fulvia and marry your girl. I'm sorry, but you're stuck with her."

"Stop it, Gaius, I'm serious. Come here and sit by me a minute."

"Now, Lucius, I've told you before; I don't do that sort of thing."

"I'm not joking, Gaius," he growled as I sat down next to him on the edge of the bed. "I want your promise on something, a promise on the heads of your wife and your family and your unborn children."

78

He stopped and I said, "Tell me, cousin."

He paused again, rubbed his eyes and cleared his throat. "I want you to stay alive," he said.

I flinched at the strangeness of his request, but after a moment of silence, I said, "That's all?"

"I really am serious, cousin: No matter what happens, I want your solemn promise to live a long, long time."

Sitting there in the darkness, I drew back from him and stared off into the blank void of my life to come. What do I know about the future? I thought. What do I know about surviving one day to the next, let alone a lifetime? "Well," I finally said. "Well, well."

"Promise," he said, his voice suddenly angry, commanding. "Please."

I shook my head and rubbed my own tired eyes. "All right," I said, "I promise."

"On the heads of—"

"Yes, yes. On the heads of all my family. I promise, I swear: I'll live forever if I can, just for you, cousin Lucius."

He let loose a great sigh of relief. "Good," he said. "Excellent. Now come and give your cousin a hug."

"Just a hug," I said. "Nothing else. No lips, nothing like that—right?"

And finally my cousin, whom I indeed loved very dearly, laughed out loud, apparently in spite of himself. And then I leaned close and embraced him.

"By the gods, your face is covered with sweat," I started to say, but caught myself just in time. For, at the very last instant, putting my arms around him, I knew it wasn't perspiration that had left him soaking wet, but a virtual waterfall of tears. Indeed, pouring down like a torrential rainstorm, they still had not stopped when I left him alone in his bed and told him good night.

11

Well, there were more towns to visit on our grand tour: first, heading due north, Casilinum, then Casinum, followed by Corfinium, and then Alba Fucens—a day and a night at each, the same speech, the same sort of crowds—cheering at first, then less certain of their enthusiasm.

Finally, nearly three weeks after Cicero had stepped off the boat at Brundisium, we were within thirty miles of Rome and expecting to arrive there by nightfall, when quite abruptly we diverted to the east by several miles.

For a moment, a peculiar panic, a fear of some sinister unknown, swept the entourage. But then I saw Curio smiling, and suddenly there was a festive new air afoot, as everyone but Cicero himself quickly learned the truth: that we were heading for an audience with no less than Pompey the Great at his estate in the fancy suburb of Tivoli.

We arrived at the town in late afternoon, and by the time we made our way through Pompey's main gate and up the three-mile-long entranceway to the house itself, the twilight sun bathed the scene in a delicate pink glow.

"Dear Cicero," Pompey said, as he greeted us personally at the front door. And poor Cicero practically fell into his arms, more overcome by emotion than I'd seen him yet during the long journey home.

"Dear, dear Pompey," he said, his voice choked, tears once again streaming down his face.

After a moment, as Pompey started to talk, Cicero tried to interrupt him. "No, no. I am Pompey, I will speak first," he said, with a forced smile that could not quite mask his actual irritation. Even so, the crowd laughed, Cicero kept quiet, and Pompey happily resumed. "Cicero, you are the wisest man in Rome," Pompey intoned, "and I hereby present you with this formal declaration of the Senate proclaiming you thus, now and forever."

Pompey handed Cicero the official scroll, bound with the Senate's own seal. Cicero stood there with an engagingly childlike expression on his face, crying and laughing at the same time. "Yes," was all he finally said, and the crowd clapped affectionately.

It was all very charming; indeed, it was as appealing a moment as anyone could hope to witness, and the crowd was swept away, crying and laughing right along with the great man.

Still, how odd, I thought, that no one seems to have noticed that Pompey has presented this declaration of the Senate—a truly extraordinary jurisdictional transgression. Taken it upon himself, has he? I thought. So who's really in charge now, eh? Indeed, just how much has Rome changed already during the brief few weeks of our absence?

★   ★   ★

The people lined the streets to see him, cheering and shouting all the way from the Salarian Gate, in the northern part of the city, to the steps of the Forum. Cato himself led a delegation of senators to escort him from the street into the Senate chamber.

As he had prepared himself for the ceremonies, his eyes were dry for a change, and his voice was clear as he began his momentous speech, his first to the Senate in more than two years:

"Senate Fathers," spoke Marcus Tullius Cicero, "you have my undying gratitude for the great welcome you have provided following my lengthy absence. I feel your deep affection and your unwavering loyalty, and, believe me, they are truly uplifting to the spirits of an old man. It is good to be home.

"Still, there are those who might say—indeed, there are those who do say—that coming home at a time of great trouble such as this has serious drawbacks. They would wring their hands, sniveling and cringing in their wives' boudoirs. They would bolt their doors; they would mask their faces from the very light of day. Even

81

I might feel the temptation, though only very slightly, I assure you, to return to some remote and placid place of some faraway province until all our troubles have been resolved. For we are, indeed, beset by difficulties—difficulties that will not easily be resolved.

"But what should a man do, if he is a good man, a man of ethics? Should such a man run off, hide himself away, ignore the turbulent events of the moment? Or, indeed, should he most definitely come home at such a time, put his best efforts forward and join the struggle to maintain the equilibrium of the state? Well, of course there is no choice in the matter—not, as I say, for a truly good and honorable man.

"So, Senate Fathers, now that there are problems to solve, disputes to settle, friendships to renew, tempers to soothe, wounds to heal—indeed, now, when it seems that all in the house is crashing down around us and there is no hope to be found save either to plunder or abandon it, I will gladly tell you that such a time as this is, indeed, the very, very best time to come home.

"So, as I have already said, I am happy to be here. Actually, even more than that, I am thrilled and proud to be here. And so, Senate Fathers, at long last let our work begin. It will be a grand work, a work of restoration. We know we will succeed, very simply because we have no choice. In success, and in success alone, lies life, dignity and honor. To fail, Senate Fathers, is suicide.

"Once again, noble Roman Senators, I humbly thank you, and I pray to the gods that I am worthy of your great trust and affection."

The entire Senate, each and every man there, had sat silently spellbound throughout the few minutes of the speech. At the end they stood and applauded without stopping for nearly one quarter of an hour. Thus, even as snickering rumors of the vain and silly speeches of his trip were reaching the capital, Cicero squashed them all with a few moments of eloquence: his reputation was restored.

★   ★   ★

With the summer nearly gone and Rome coming to life again, our work load with Curio rose to new heights. He brushed aside questions from my cousins and me about what seemed to be his newfound closeness to Pompey, tersely insisting that "in the long run it means nothing at all." Besides, he told us, he had a whole new approach—prepared, he said, with the approval (in a general way) of Cicero himself.

The centerpiece to the new campaign would be a grand new leaflet, which eventually would lead to a major new proposal in the Senate. It all involved considerable amounts of research and writing, enough, he said, to keep my three cousins and me busy for some time.

The theme of the leaflet—compromise—was old, Curio admitted. But the approach was new: it would entail what he called "a major reshaping of the opposing forces in the current turmoil, aimed at eliminating the dire threat which they pose to the very existence of Rome itself."

He divided the work: The Barnabas brothers, Junius and Claudius, were saddled with the lion's share of the research, including the tedious task of combing the ancient texts of the Twelve Tables, Rome's oldest written law. Lucius and I would do most of the writing, though we were also in overall charge of researching the much more recent adventures of Marius and the military dictatorship of Sulla, as well as the attempted revolt of Catiline and other recent cases, which naturally would involve the study of many of Cicero's own writings.

"The Twelve Tables," Junius Barnabas said after a few days, "don't deal much with grand affairs of state—of the military and so forth." (Indeed, as you well know, those ancient statutes dealt largely with the settlement of property disputes, theft, burglary, perjury, bribery, rights of inheritance, and so forth.) "So what's the point here?" he asked Curio. "What are we looking for?"

"Of course not, of course they don't," Curio snapped. "Just find anything on abuses of power. Too much given. Or too little. Something like 'Even the Twelve Tables said such and such . . .' That sort of thing."

Of course, the affairs of Marius and Sulla were more fruitful ground. "The end of the citizen-soldier, the start of the professional adventurer—more interested in loot than in principle, more loyal to one man than to the state," was a passage Lucius found one day and pointed out to me.

"The professional militarist indeed," I said, smiling. "That's good work, cousin."

"Thank you, cousin," Lucius replied.

So we toiled day after day, sometimes late into the night, until, with the leaves well off the trees and the air bracing, autumn was well upon us.

One especially chilly morning, with the wind rattling the windows and whistling through the cracks of the house, I awoke to find a messenger standing over me. The nighttime darkness was barely fading, and the predawn gray nestled in the room like a large, fluffy shroud. Needless to say, I was thoroughly startled.

"What!" I demanded, clumsily adjusting the bedding to make sure Fulvia was well covered. "Damn it, my wife's here," I yelled. "Now tell me and get out!"

"P-p-p-please, sir," he stammered, then handed me a sealed papyrus. I took it, still trying to focus my eyes. Finally, I realized it was stamped with the insignia of my cousin, Lucius Flavius, and I quickly tore it open.

"Please come at once," was the brief message written in his own hand, and I quickly sat up and swung my legs over the side of the bed.

"All right," I said more politely to the messenger, who had not moved. "Tell your master I'm coming now."

Still, he stood there (idiotlike, if you ask me!) until, yelling again, I said, "Go on, go tell him. Go on, do it now." At last he bolted from the room and clack-clacked noisily down the stairs and out through the courtyard.

★   ★   ★

"The honorable Gaius Livinius Severus for Master Lucius," boomed the doorman, Telephus, a great, tall, muscular fellow with a basso voice, a completely bald head and a particular flair for the formalities of life.

It was actually Lucius's parents who demanded such amenities on their old estate, where my cousin still lived. And in point of fact as I passed through the atrium, his mother, Hortensia, a short, dark woman of shrill tones and nervous, fluttery hands, emerged from a hallway and spotted me.

"Livinius," she cried, "it's been *ages.*" She rushed up and kissed me—as always, the ups and downs of her voice and hands working together with astonishing precision.

"Bit early for calling, isn't it?" she said, her gay mood suddenly suspicious.

"Lucius sent for me," I said. "Is he about?"

"Still in his room, I imagine." She abruptly turned and led the way down the corridor and up a darkened flight of interior stairs.

"*Lucius*," she called, as we approached his bedroom door. "Lucius!" she said again.

"Lucius," I called out, and knocked loudly. "He can't still be sleeping, he sent me a note just now," I said to my aunt, shaking my head. "You sure he's not having breakfast downstairs or something . . ." I banged on the door several more times. "Lucius!" I shouted.

"Should I—" I was about to say, Should I just go on in, when I realized my aunt was staring at me with considerable apprehension on her face. Then, before I could say another word, she opened the door herself and charged into the room.

"Lucius?" I said, stepping in right behind her. "Lucius?" His mother, still ten feet or more from the bed, stopped in her tracks so abruptly that I bumped into her.

Although the sun had risen by then, only scant, slender cracks of daylight seeped in through the shutters; mostly, a dreamy, predawn mist still filled the room. I sidestepped around my aunt and walked to the bedside, and there, despite the dimness, I could see my cousin easily enough, and then, after that, I saw the unmistakable patch of blood in the middle of his chest.

"Oh, Lucius," I whispered. "Oh, my cousin." Or at least that's what I remember saying.

I started to reach up and throw back the shutters, which would have flooded the room with sunshine, then caught sight of my aunt, standing precariously in that same spot a few feet away, staring at the bed.

"What . . . what is it?" she said in a voice so sweetly soft and frail that you knew that she knew whatever "it" was had to be terrible.

"Get Uncle Cornelius," I said gently, but she only stood there another moment, then darted around me, saw her dead son's body and threw herself down on the bed beside him, sobbing as deeply and unhappily as anyone could.

Then I began to cry, and then a servant happened in. And then, before I knew it, the whole household was in a mad, ghastly uproar.

· · · · · ·

I hear Augustus again, coming this way, and I start to tremble again; I can't help it; I can't get my cousin's murder out of my mind.

Augustus reads as he walks and munches fruit, a pear, I believe, and has his dagger tucked between the thumb and forefinger of his left hand. He finishes the fruit, tosses away the remains, then shifts the knife to his right hand, while still reading the scroll in his left.

Reaching me, he sits down just to my right on the bench in the little sitting room of Cicero's old house, still studying the words carefully and using his dagger to point. He is wearing the same toga as before, and there are still smudges of blood on the outer folds.

"You know—" he starts to say; then, as the timekeeper comes through to turn the hourglass, he stops and watches intently—just as he did this morning.

"Seventh hour," the timekeeper drones, for by now it is midafternoon; then he and his assistant expertly turn the glass and walk away.

Augustus watches in silence until they are well out of sight, then pulls another piece of fruit, this one an apple, out of some inner fold of his toga and begins eating and talking again.

"You know," he says, "this really is much better, this version of your report." He pauses, takes another bite, then, using the knife, searches through the last few turns of the scroll. "Yes, yes, interesting stuff, Livinius; long way to go yet, but so far, very good. And by the way, do you see what I mean about Cicero? What a fool he can be?"

Though I am still shaking and terrified, I turn my body entirely to the right, daring to look directly at the boy ruler. "No, I don't," I say in a wooden tone.

And then: "You murdered my cousin."

There is no reaction at first. Then, after a moment, he looks up and smiles, almost apologetically—much, it seems to me, in the manner that one might regret being, say, half an hour late to dinner. Then, still grinning, he cocks his head and shifts his eyes as if gesturing toward something of interest in the center of the room.

The hourglass!

I jerk my head around to look at it, then look back at him, my whole body suddenly numb with fear. "Be dead within the hour," I recall the secretary whispering not so long ago.

"You worry too much, Livinius," Augustus says, patting me on the shoulder while I try not to cringe. Then, with a shake of his head (is that truly a look of bemusement on his face?), he turns and walks back down the hallway to some other part of the house.

And I suddenly ask myself: Just why *did* he kill Junius Barnabas? And, come to think of it, what about the murder of Junius's brother, *Claudius? Was that really just a simple matter of a thief in the night?*

12

I am a detective now:

That was my instantaneous reaction.

Truly and honestly and in all actuality: a detective.

So: I will investigate; I will search; I will probe. I will learn the truth.

I will find the murderer.

Lucius's father, my uncle Cornelius Flavius, came breathlessly into the room. Then Lucius's little sister, Camilla, a child of nine, bounded in; then a slave ran in after to gather her up. Then came the house manager; then Cornelius's joke of a bodyguard—an antique of his old Iberian legion. Then the chief maid; then an aunt by marriage on Cornelius's side. And on it went—everyone crying, everyone shouting.

They all loved Lucius so much: He was the golden boy of that house, the brilliant youth with the blinding prospects. The lovable man-child. And, believe me, nobody loved him more than I did, and nobody cried more, either.

But I learned a new way of crying that day. It was something my clever cousin had taught me one strange night in Capua not so long before. Your eyes cloud over, of course, and there are tears. But somehow you can talk, and your tone of voice is natural—unaffected by the sobbing that fills your head and heart.

"Where is the messenger?" I said in a voice so clear and cool that it startled me most of all.

"The wha—"

"The messenger, Uncle. Lucius sent for me. That's why I'm here."

I pulled out the note and showed it to him.

"God," he said, swaying dangerously.

I caught and held him till two bearers stepped up and helped him to a chair. He sank down in it and held his head in his hands. "My poor, poor son," he said.

★   ★   ★

They all identified him as "that dolt Laertes"; indeed, he was Lucius's regular errand boy with—as one young servant so brightly put it—"cornmeal for brains."

"Find him," I said, and half the slaves in the room obligingly scattered.

I thought: Lucius knew he was in danger. I almost said it out loud, then looked around at the weeping household and thought better of it.

"So Lucius knew he was in danger, eh, Livinius?" my uncle promptly put in, and I thought: He's my father's brother, all right. And, of course, his idiot question was all my aunt needed.

"What!" she screamed and launched into fits of sobbing so shrill and crazy that they called the houseman back to give her a potion. Then three of the stronger young women carried her down the hall to her room and put her to bed.

And I suddenly asked myself: Where in the world did I get whatever brains I've got, let alone poor Lucius; where, indeed, did he ever get his? I almost said it; I wanted to very much. But then one doesn't always need to descend to the level of one's elders, does one?

★   ★   ★

It was nearly half an hour more till the doctor arrived. By then, there were only my uncle and I, alone in the room with the body.

"One forceful, plunging stab wound, straight to the heart," the doctor said, feeling, I suppose, that he could speak freely to us two Roman men. "A very powerful thrust, I must say," he went on, his back still to us, examining the remains—in a way, speaking more to himself than to either of us.

Indeed, he didn't notice at all as Cornelius's face turned bloodless white and he made a truly awful wheezing noise—so terrible

89

I feared for a moment that he might expire himself from the anguish of it all.

"Doctor . . ." I yelled, and he turned around at last.

"Oh my," he said—I must say, spotting the trouble at once. He walked nimbly over to my uncle slumping in his chair, patted his cheeks, looked into his eyes and took his pulse.

"It's all right, my lord," he said. "You just need rest for a while. Something like this, well, it takes it out of everybody."

I stood by, amazed and even a little impressed at how the doctor's wooden manner gave way so quickly to this oily smoothness. He opened his bag and poked around.

"I have something . . ." he was saying. "Oh, yes, just the thing." He pulled out a vial, removed the cork and handed it to my uncle. "Drink this, my lord," he said, and to my surprise Cornelius obligingly drank it down at once. Within moments, it seemed, there was color in his face and he appeared remarkably restored.

"Garlic and thyme, with a touch of cobra meat," the doctor smiled. "Always works."

★   ★   ★

About an hour later, having sent for the priests to prepare the body, Cornelius and I moved to his study on the far side of the house. He also had told the doctor to look in on my aunt before leaving, and on his way out the physician stopped by to see us, as well.

"Ah, young lord Gaius, there you are," he said, beckoning to me. "You can save me a trip by taking this new medication over to your mother. For her nerves and all; she's been in such a state."

"Her what?"

"Yes, yes, come out here, please, and I'll show you," he burbled on, waving me out to the corridor, and I followed him.

"What are you talking—"

"About your cousin, my lord," he quickly interjected in a quiet tone. "I didn't want to say this in front of your uncle, but, well . . . poor Lucius Flavius . . . he . . ."

"Yes?"

"There was an irritation, Master Gaius. A swelling, a redness. It was quite inflamed . . ."

"What the—"

"On the posterior, my lord. The buttocks. It had been abused,

90

I'm afraid. Damaged." The doctor stared at his shoes, his face flushed with embarrassment.

"Oh," was all I said after a lengthy silence. Then: "So you think . . ."

"Yes, my lord. I'm afraid so. I . . . well, I applied some ointment to ease the condition."

"What for, for God's sake?"

"For the priests, my lord. They gossip, you know."

"Oh," was all I managed once again, except for "Thank you." Then, after a long, awkward moment, the doctor assumed his more usual businesslike tone, wished me well and rushed off.

★　　★　　★

"Yes," I was telling my uncle, "I imagine Lucius knew there was some sort of danger afoot."

We were alone and undisturbed in his study at last, sipping wine and munching apples.

"But danger from what, Livinius? From whom?"

I thought: The shutters and windows of his room had been tightly closed and bolted. So obviously whoever it was had come and gone through the door. Had Lucius known the person? Was he caught by surprise? But how surprised could he have been, having sent me an urgent summons at the crack of dawn?

"I don't know, uncle," I said, "but I intend to find out." I hesitated a moment, then decided it would be best simply to plunge ahead with the next logical question. "Do you know," I asked, "if Lucius had a guest last night? Anyone you might have seen come and go, anyone he might have accommodated in a spare room someplace?"

"No one," he said with a somber shake of his head.

Just then there was a scream—faint in the distance but still plain enough for the terror in the voice to be heard.

"My God," I said.

"Now what!" Cornelius thundered.

I dashed into the hallway in time to hear one of the kitchen slaves shouting as he climbed the stairs and ran across the inner balcony. "O-o-o-h, master, come quick! It's . . . it's . . ."

"It's *what,* goddam it!" For, by then, my patience had truly run out.

"They found him, sir," the slave said, panting from his mad dash. He was covered with sweat and grease, and with each word came the powerful, breathy smell of onions and garlic.

"Who?" I said quietly, trying to keep myself calm.

"Laertes, sir. Master Lucius's messenger."

"Oh," I said, nodding. "Well, very good. Bring him up, then."

"Up here, sir? Oh, I don't think so."

The man was exhausting me and I gave up on words. I simply raised my eyebrows as if to say, Why not?

"Well . . . that is . . ."

"What, young man? Just spit it out."

"Laertes is dead, sir. Laertes carries messages no longer."

★   ★   ★

The body lay amid some piles of refuse in a dark corner of the lower pantry, not far from a freshly disemboweled sheep and a huge slab of pork loin. Examining the remains, I found that in this case the neck was not only bruised but broken; also, once again, there was the straight, strong knife wound through the heart.

I sent for the doctor, which raised some gasps among the kitchen help; normally, of course, no one would waste a physician's time to check on the body of a lowly courier—or of most any slave, for that matter. But naturally this case was special. Indeed, I knelt there beside the body for a long time, just staring and thinking, hoping some message, some clue, would reveal itself.

Later on, even the doctor had little to add besides the obvious.

"Anything on the . . . you know . . . the . . ."

"My lord?" he asked with a shake of his head.

"The posterior, doctor. The . . . buttocks."

"Oh no, sir. Nothing like that this time. You ask me, this was done much more quickly. The body left so carelessly like that. And the knife wound: well, it was pushed in much more strongly, more damagingly—but hastily, if you see what I mean. And the broken neck. The bruises so prominent. He must be a very strong man, sir, and I just wonder if he meant to go that far—that is, if he actually intended to break the neck. A man that strong, he might have done it by accident on account of being in such a hurry."

I wanted to tell him to shut up, for God's sake, but I just stared

92

at him wide-eyed, then thanked him again. And for the second time that morning the doctor left my uncle's house.

★ ★ ★

"Who found the body?" I asked of the dozen or so slaves gathered just outside the pantry door. *"Who?"* I called again when no one answered.

"Me, my lord," came a soft voice from the crowd, followed by a small-boned, pale young woman heavily smeared with dirt. "I'm Thespia, my lord."

"So, Thespia . . ." I said, clearing my throat and gathering my thoughts. "So, you work in the garden?"

She shook her head decisively and smiled. "Slaughter sheep," she said. She paused, and for a moment there was a surprising glimmer of brightness in her eyes. "It's not dirt, it's blood, sir," she went on, pointing at the dark smudges on her arms and face. "Dried sheep's blood."

"Aah," I said.

"I'm small but strong, sir," she said.

"You've got a big voice, too, for a little person, at least when you want to. That scream . . ."

"Oh no, sir, that was my mother," she said with a laugh. "She came in a step behind me, saw poor Laertes right when I did. Screamed to make the walls fall down, then fainted dead away."

Several of the others chuckled uneasily, and I barely kept a smile off my own lips. "And your mother? She's all right now? She's uh . . . here . . .?" I waved my arms vaguely at the little group, but no one came forward.

"I think she's . . . yes, sir, she's just outside," the girl said. "She won't come any closer, sir, not so long as . . . well, so long as the body's still here."

I stepped into the corridor, and there was a short, plump, trembling woman, ready to cry at the mere mention of the horror inside.

"You saw—"

"Horrible, my lord," she answered, and was suddenly wobbling on her feet.

"It's all right," I said quickly, then decided there was no point in questioning that old woman, at least not right now. "Thespia,

93

put your mother to bed for the day, then come back here, please."

Thespia smiled gratefully, and the old mother thanked me profusely as they led her away, bestowing upon me all the blessings she could think of for happiness and long life.

★   ★   ★

"So, did anyone see or hear of a guest Master Lucius might have had last night or early today?" I demanded. "And one other question: who saw Laertes last?"

I had assembled all two hundred slaves of the household in the main kitchen, save those who couldn't fit and spilled into the courtyard beyond.

"Anyone?" I asked again. "Oh come now, some of you must have seen something. Who saw Laertes leave when he brought a message to my house? Who saw him return?"

"Forgive me, my lord," came a man's voice, "but you see Laertes slept on a cot right next to Master Lucius's room. And it being so early when he left—"

"Who's speaking?" I put in, and a man in elegant livery raised his hand.

"I'm Calpius, chief footman, sir. I was saying it was so early and all, and Laertes in any case would have gone straight out the door with your message and then straight back to Master Lucius. So because of the hour, it might very well be that nobody did see him. Except for . . ." He stopped then, his voice trailing off.

"Except for?"

"Well, sir, except for Telephus, the doorman. He's up bright and early, all right, and that's his job, sir, watching that front door."

"Fine then. So, Telephus? Speak up, man. Did you see him?" I looked around for his unmistakable bald head, as did everyone else; after a moment or so, an uncomfortable murmur buzzed through the crowd: Clearly enough, Telephus wasn't there.

"I said everyone, didn't I?" I grumbled, fidgeting impatiently with the folds of my toga. "You there, footman. Go find Telephus; bring him here at once."

"My lord!" he said with a snappy salute, and took off toward the slave quarters at the rear of the house.

I waited around with the rest of them, shuffling my feet as I stood by the huge kitchen sink, my anger growing. Finally, after a few minutes had passed, it suddenly struck me with all certainty what the footman would say.

Sure enough, moments later, he came running in, breathless and flushed and a bit frightened-looking, as well. To make the point even plainer, he came right up to me and spoke in quiet tones.

"My lord, I beg to report that Telephus—"

"Is not in his room." I nodded. "And his clothes—"

"Are gone, sir."

"Anything left?"

He shook his head miserably. "Nothing, sir. All gone."

"It's all right," I said. "You've done well."

He bowed, smiled with obvious relief and backed away.

And there in my cousin's house, three hours after I'd found my cousin's body, for the first time I began to suspect the enormity of what I might be up against in my plan to solve my cousin's murder and bring his killer to justice.

For starters, there were now at least two murders to solve instead of one. For it was plain enough that without the one there would not have been the other.

13

My cousin's body lay in state for three days in the atrium of my uncle's house. He lay on a couch of silk and sheepskin, surrounded by a hundred bouquets of flowers in every color the world could provide; incense burned to give his soul everlasting life.

For three days, perhaps a thousand friends and relatives filed past, leaving flowers, wiping away tears, saying a prayer for my cousin's afterlife. His mother, my aunt Hortensia, and his fiance, the beautiful Matidia Gratus, never left his side.

For three days, the public criers went about the city, intoning the ancient call: "Ollus quiris Lucius Flavius leto datus. Exsequias, quibus est commodum, ire jam tempus est. Ollus ex aedibus effertur.—The citizen Lucius Flavius has been surrendered to death. For those who find it convenient, it is now time to attend the funeral. He is being brought from his house."

Then came the procession: First was a little band of musicians playing harps and lyres, followed by a chorus singing the traditional dirges. Then, by the ancient custom you know only too well, came the clowns and jesters to spread good cheer among the bystanders. After that, a troupe of nearly one hundred actors passed by, wearing the traditional masks of wax and crafted in the likeness of all my cousin's ancestors (and, of course, many of mine as well) stretching back, as legend would have it, to the god Jupiter himself. Following all that came Lucius's body, carried by special litter on the shoulders of a dozen slaves. Finally, there were all the relatives, and then, just behind us, a large crowd of my cousin's friends.

It was seven miles from my uncle's house to the site of the family burial ground—four miles to the Appian Gate at the southeast corner of the city, then another three down the highway. My aunt rode in her litter from the very start, and my Uncle Cornelius climbed into his a short while later. Even I took to mine not far outside the city gate.

The site of the tomb was just a few yards off the Via Appia in an elegant marble structure entered through a handsomely built archway. There was room for only thirty or so close relatives to descend the short flight of steps below ground into the sepulcrum, where the family dead had been interred for the last century or more. On the floor was a dazzling fresco that had been commissioned by my uncle: it showed himself, my aunt, Lucius, and the three younger children gathered happily around the dining table in the banquet hall of their house in Rome. Off to one side of the chamber, a bronze and marble sarcophagus sat already prepared on a raised platform. Once again, the priests said the ancient holy words to consecrate the resting place. Then the body was lowered into the casket and finally it was time for the funeral oration. I was the principal speaker.

"Beloved family," I began in the traditional way, "we come here to this hallowed place to lay to rest our estimable friend, beloved cousin, affectionate son, and loving husband-to-be, Lucius Decius Flavius Severus. How much we will miss him is beyond words: his charm, his good humor, his respectful ways, his loyalty, his wit, his brilliance of mind—these are all qualities that he possessed in abundance, qualities that will embody our recollections of him in the years to come. Of course, taken alone they are mere abstractions. Each of us will have a favorite few events or stories or episodes, small in themselves, that will form our memories: a boyish prank, a subject well learned, a debate well taken, a shared jug of wine, a kiss by moonlight, a pledge of matrimony. Hopefully, they will not be too painful to recall; hopefully, they will bring each of us a small measure of joy.

"So then let us pray that our beloved friend and relative finds the peace in the hereafter which he was so cruelly denied in this life. But let us also pledge that we shall have no peace for ourselves until we find the destroyers of *his* peace. For that is my promise; make no mistake: I *will* find the creators of this dastardly crime; I *will* give *them* no peace until they are brought to justice—and bring them to justice I will, or die trying."

Almost at once, I began to hear a chorus of uneasy mutterings and the clearing of throats from the little group. Of course it was partly because of the unusual nature of my speech, for such bold remarks are normally saved for later—not given at the funeral itself. Mostly, though, it was because they were all quite honestly afraid of what horrors my boldness might provoke, not only for myself, but for all of them as well.

Naturally I considered my pledge a brave one, but I also conceded its possible foolishness. Indeed, as I was soon to learn, some in my family thought it suicidal. Nonetheless, it was *my* pledge—and I planned to keep it, no matter what.

"But today," I went on, "let us focus our thoughts on our beloved. I myself recall so many things—a friendly gesture, a witty remark, an idea incisively expressed, a funny story. How much did I love my cousin? Words cannot describe it. So now, let us all pray for the soul of the departed," I concluded in the usual form. After a brief silence, my uncle Cornelius said a few standard words (with unusual brevity, it seemed to me), the priests placed a handful of dirt on the body, and after more prayers and songs for the dead the casket at last was closed and sealed.

★   ★   ★

I found Cicero sitting quietly in the little garden of his new house. I sat down beside him and told him everything.

"Poor, poor boy," he said when I finished. Then he stared off into space, and there were tears in his eyes.

"What do you think, master? What should I do?"

"Hmmph," he said, looking straight at me and smiling through the mist. "You always make your questions sound as if they should be so easy to answer; your poor cousin did that, too." He shook his head and stared off again. "And of course they are not."

He stood up, walked thirty feet or so to a pear tree, picked one and took a bite.

"I think you are in danger," he said, and I flinched. "I think you'll have to be on guard from now on. Don't trust anyone. Sleep with your knife at your side. And for God's sake, watch out for the food you eat."

"And the wine I drink?"

"That, too," he snapped. "Go ahead, make fun if you like—"

"I'm not."

"Oh, I know you think it's an old man's melodramatics—"

"No, not at—"

"—but believe me, I'm completely serious about all of it. And you should be, too—that is, if you want to stay alive for a while." He stopped and stared at me a moment. "I always hoped you might be one of the few good people of Rome who did that—who stayed alive awhile, lived a long time."

I flinched again as I suddenly recalled the curious promise which Lucius had extracted from me not so long ago. If Cicero noticed my reaction, he let it pass without a word: he simply ate the rest of the pear, tossed the stem away and returned to the bench.

"So who will you question next, eh?" he asked, rubbing his hands together and smiling.

"W-e-l-l . . ." I drew the word out and let my voice fade. "Well, I'm not sure I should tell you," I said, a teasing edge to my tone. "After all, you said—"

"Not to trust anyone—that's right," he said, clapping his hands in triumph.

I shook my head, smiled and felt a blush coming on. "Actually, I'm not certain right now," I confessed.

"I know," he said without batting an eye. "But you passed your first test; you understand—or at least you're starting to—what it means to be alert to everything around you."

"Yes," I said.

"And the closer the person is to you, the nearer he or she comes, the more normal and predictable he seems—the more alert, more careful and more on guard you must be."

14

Telephus the doorman was nowhere to be found.

I questioned Calpius the footman and Thespia the sheep slaugh-
teress and a few of the others who'd been there longest, but no one
had a clue to his whereabouts. No, he had no family that they knew
of. No wife, no mistress—for that matter, no romantic life of any
sort that any of them knew anything about. He'd never received
any letters, never written any, never spoken of anyone else. In
other words, there was nothing that might lead me to him in some
other part of the city, or anywhere at all throughout the whole of
the republic.

Even so, as you might imagine, I had my suspicions about where
to look. I kept thinking about how Lucius was killed and about the
condition of his body—so similar to that of young Fabius Vibulanus and Flaccus Valerius, murdered the year before. And, recalling
my own bizarre experience, I thought: Could I actually interrogate
him about this? He'd lie about everything anyway, so what would
be the point?

Could I search his house? I wondered. I'd love to, but how? Of
course, I could sneak in secretly, without warrant or sanction. The
trouble was there were always at least a few stray hangers-on
lounging about his digs. Could I disguise myself, perhaps, and
blend in with those dregs? It was possible, but risky. I suddenly
recalled Clodius in his woman's clothes and thought: No, no
disguises. Too idiotic to think about.

On the other hand, I could charge him publicly, which theoretically would clear the way for an authorized search. But that also seemed out of the question: Indeed, making an accusation of such magnitude against so powerful a person could easily result in my punishment instead of his.

Of course I had to wonder what his motive would be for such crimes. Unless he was mad, of course. He was crude and lewd and lazy and even a bit stupid at times. But he was sane enough—I felt reasonably sure of that much.

But dammit all, where is Telephus? I asked myself. And who put him up to all this? And who's he talking to now? And what does he know? Well, quite a bit, it would seem. And then it occurred to me: Maybe too much for his own good.

★　★　★

My aunt and uncle observed with meticulous care the traditional Nine Days of Sorrows after my cousin's funeral, not leaving their house, holding solemn dinners, wearing black. When the time of mourning was over, they were not yet ready to return to the world; instead, they clung to their grief like frightened children to a mother's breast. Day by day, they stretched out the somber rites, until, at day nineteen, with no end in sight, even I had had enough. I went back to work for Scribonius Curio.

In a way, my timing was good. After a short lull in politics, Rome was just beginning the most corrupt election campaign in all its history. And to my utter astonishment it was the old-line senators who once again seemed to be on the wrong side of the issue. For, as much as any man or group in Rome, they drove the corruption to unheard-of new depths.

As always, the jobs of most interest were the two consulships. The two men who won them would have enormous power; indeed, they would rule Rome (along with the Senate, of course) for the year to come.

With his group of senators behind him, Cato apparently decided that a man of his choosing would have one of the two jobs—no matter what. He chose as his candidate one Calpurnius Bibulus, an honest but artless politician, then flowed bribe money into the hands of the voters at a rate I can only compare to water flooding the banks of a rain-swollen river.

"So Cato has come down from the clouds," Curio said, smiling.

Bibulus won, of course, but Cato forgot to keep an eye on his flank. Indeed, Caesar himself wanted the other consulship; needless to say, he won it easily.

"They can't get anything right, can they?" Curio chuckled.

"It amazes me," opined my windbag cousin, Junius Barnabas, "that men of such apparent intelligence, avowed integrity and supposed devotion to the ideals of the republic could stoop to such low tactics, spend that enormous amount of money and still . . . well, still . . . that is, still . . ."

". . . mess it up," concluded my laconic cousin, Junius's younger brother, Claudius Barnabas.

"Indeed!" I said a bit too forcefully. Actually, I was trying somewhat clumsily to get a rise out of Curio, who always remained absolutely (and quite maddeningly!) expressionless during the brothers' peculiar exchanges. As usual, Curio did not bite, and I found myself wondering if I were the only man still alive who noticed the eccentricities of my two cousins.

★   ★   ★

"By the way," I said, "you never told me you knew Fabius Vibulanus."

I was speaking to my friend and mentor Gaius Scribonius Curio. I was sitting across from him at a quiet corner table in the little courtyard of a town house on the Cispius Hill not far from the center of Rome. The house belonged to Mark Antony.

The occasion was a birthday party for Hirtius Pansa, a deliciously decadent man in his early forties with an infectious laugh, a pleasingly corpulent physique that shook with his laughter, and a harmless liking for the pleasures of life—*all* the pleasures of life.

And, oh yes, one other point: it was a costume party.

Indeed, we all wore masks, and I had already been tricked several times as to who was who. In particular, my own cousins the Barnabas brothers had fooled me completely as a pair of mincing, overweight prostitutes.

"Who?" Curio answered.

I knew who Curio was because he and I had come to the party straight from his house. We had planned it that way because we'd known in advance that the day would be long and hectic. Thus, we had picked our costumes together and, later on, dressed hastily in his master bedroom. Fittingly enough, Curio was done up as an actor; he wore the comedy mask. Since, as I say, I'm not big on disguises anyway, I settled for dressing as his opposite number: I was tragedy.

"Fabius," I insisted. "Fabius Vibulanus. That boy who was murdered last year."

It didn't help matters any on such a busy day that Curio was rather drunk for most of it and in an odd frame of mind. Finally, by late afternoon, I succumbed and began indulging myself in a swallow or two of the grape. As we dressed, Curio's mood grew stranger, but I didn't catch why, precisely, until finally he touched me in a place he shouldn't. It was playful enough, or so he tried to make it seem, but the serious undercurrent was unmistakable. Even so, I simply smiled, shook my head and lightly wagged my finger at him, all as if to say, No, no, none of that.

"Fabius Vibulanus," I repeated, drawing out each syllable of the name. "Good-looking boy. He had an 'inflammation' when they found him."

You see, I was actually quite used to fending off such advances, for, in truth, Mark Antony was not my first time. Well, it was—in the sense that no one had ever gone so far with me before: nothing like it; not even close. But as you must know by now, I'm aware of my appearance—indeed, of my special charm in that area. And I admit that in the past, as a boy with a not so unusual craving for the experimental (and perhaps a touch of cruelty, as well), I took part in a bit of flirting now and then—or, more accurately put, a bit of egging on. I'd abandoned all that even before the episode with Antony, and of course I've avoided it ever more resolutely since my marriage. But now here was Curio in this unusual mood, and it occurred to me that allowing him a bit of leeway might work to my advantage.

"Fabius worked for you once, didn't he?" I asked. "I think I found a note one time—a note that you wrote to him."

Not that he needed any encouragement, you understand. Barely five minutes after his naughty touch, as we both stood bare-chested in our undergarments, Curio suddenly assumed a languorous pose, sidled up and gave me an affectionate hug. He pressed his cheek softly against mine, and I let that pass. (Maybe I even pressed back a little.) He kissed me lightly on the shoulder, and that was all right. I thought for an instant of kissing him back, but was afraid the results could be unpredictable, to say the least. And sure enough, even without such prompting, a moment later he dared to kiss my lips and I pulled away, though I moved slowly, even gently. I even smiled; I even touched him softly on the side of his face. The touch, in particular, was calculated to be exquisitely ambiguous. An expression of affection, perhaps? Or was it more like regret? Whatever, by the time we reached the party, Curio was stinking drunk and coiled around me like a slum whore at Saturnalia.

At first, we went our separate ways, mingling among the guests awhile, but soon enough he found me again. Then, jug of wine and two goblets in hand, he dragged me along behind him; I believe he was hoping to get me inside to some private room or other, but at the last moment I managed to steer him to our courtyard table, which at least was in plain view and safe enough on that account.

"Yes, yes, it's coming back to me now," he said. "O-o-o-h, yes: Fabius. Nice boy. Good worker. In fact, you could say Fabius was . . . fabulous." He cackled idiotically at his own bad joke. "Get it, Gaius? Fabius? Fabulous?"

"Yes," I said, "I get it."

"Of course, he was more . . . well, willing to do certain things than you are. At least, so far." He cackled again. "But maybe tonight will change that, eh?"

"Maybe," I said with a smile, still trying to flirt a bit. But by then I was losing interest in my charade and Curio was so plastered that such subtleties were undoubtedly beyond him. In fact, by then I don't think it mattered what I said.

*　　*　　*

There was supposed to have been a grand unveiling of all the guests' faces at midnight, but with Curio and so many others long since passed out, the festivities had simply been forgotten in the mist. Indeed, it was dark and quiet as I made my way inside the house and up the stairs to Antony's study, which adjoined his master bedroom. As I went, I extinguished all fire in the hallway lamps behind me, until, in the study itself, the only light came from the candle I carried in my right hand.

Not surprisingly, I had no clear idea what to look for. Something, some document or other, with Fabius's name on it, I suppose. That was all I could think of.

I poked about through a large sideboard in the study, looking at the scrolls and papers. There was a great deal of Caesar's stuff—apparently a draft of a new history he was writing, but I'd heard about that; we all had. The next shelf up looked full of bills and plenty of them: wine maker, glass blower, tile man, bricklayer. My God, there was even five hundred owed to the neighborhood baker and another thousand to the butcher. Pay up, Antony—you slut! That's what I felt like shouting. But, of course, I stayed silent as a cat—or tried to.

I shuffled through the other scrolls and such on his work table, then through a smaller sideboard across the room. There was even a quaintly carved wooden box that looked as though it might contain a secret or two; inside, however, there was nothing but a musty smell and—I swear it!—the moldy, crumbly remains of a piece of yellow cheese!

On the far side of the room was a handsome double door, which I assumed led to the bedroom itself. Dare I? I asked myself. Why not? I answered. What's to lose? (Actually, quite a lot, if I'd stopped to think about it, which I didn't.)

Holding the candle out of sight in my left hand, I slowly opened the door with my right. That room also was dark and quiet, and looked empty as well, so with the candle in front of me again, I crept inside. The first big shock was the bed, or rather the bed-clothes covering it: they were all silk and fiery red, and I could not help gasping too loudly for my own good. The next shock was that Mark Antony was in the bed, or, I should say, on it—on top of the sheets and completely naked, snoring away. I stopped in my tracks and stood as still and quiet as any man could.

But I looked around: As far as I could tell from that spot, there was yet another small sideboard that looked promising. Unfortunately, it was across the room and uncomfortably near the bed. There was also, as luck would have it, a large window with the curtains wide open and a full moon shining in. I blew out the candle, then walked slowly and carefully toward the sideboard. I had just reached it and was about to pull open the door when Antony shifted in bed, rolled over and opened his eyes.

105

"You know, the Twelve Tables prescribed death for thieves who stole by night," he said.

My reaction was instantaneous: "Oh, I'm no thief, sir," I answered.

"Oh?" he said, and with that he leapt from the bed and fairly flew at me. It was a graceful enough move, all right. He was, after all, a famous athlete and a strong man—much stronger than I. But he was not quite awake yet and still at least a little drunk. And in any case I was quicker.

You see, I'd thought it all out ahead of time, what I'd do in case of trouble like this. And that's always the most important part, because that way you're ready in your mind to do what you have to. Of course, I'd decided not to let him get near me, not so he could get his hands on me anyway—not ever again. Because, as I say, he was much stronger. And there's also that other reason which I'm sure you can guess.

So fine wrestler that I was, I simply sidestepped him, as I knew I could, and he missed me by a mile. He caught himself nicely, though, barely bumping the sideboard behind me. Even so, by the time he turned around, I'd circled the bed and was just a few steps from the hallway door, in a good spot to escape.

"Well, well," he said, smiling—I suppose from surprise at seeing me still in the room. "So who are you, then, if you're no thief?"

"Why, I came to see you, Mark Antony. I'm a great admirer of yours, and I thought we might . . . well . . . you know . . ."

"Oh, really," he said, his tone a tight, mincing line between annoyance and amiability. "Say, just who *are* you? I feel like I know you . . ."

"A secret admirer, my lord."

He was edging closer, and I knew he'd lunge for me again in a minute. "Let's get a closer look," he was saying, then made his move, reaching for my mask as he came toward me.

This time, however, he was caught even more by surprise— because I doubt he expected me to sidestep him again. But I did, and he lost his footing entirely. Falling forward, he knocked his head solidly on the corner of a clothes closet behind me, then fell to the floor.

He moaned, barely conscious, and I stopped, concerned; after all, I didn't want him to die (not yet, anyway, and not with me anywhere near him). I knelt beside him: I could see the lump rising on his forehead, but his breathing seemed normal. He was sprawled on his stomach, his arms outstretched on the floor in front of him.

My eyes followed his reach, and there on the closet floor just beyond the tips of his fingers lay a bright, silver-colored piece of satin, which by color and design looked somewhat out of place among this fellow's dashing wardrobe. I picked it up and looked it over: it was part of a sash, all right, a gaudy sort that a servant in livery might wear. I stood up and tucked it away in an inner fold of my costume toga.

Antony was struggling up, but was still too dazed to make sense of what had happened. I had no intention of waiting till he could. Without another word, I turned and walked out of that room and that house.

15

How much have I seen since my cousin's murder? How old have I grown? How much more can I stand?

The day after the party at Mark Antony's house, Scribonius Curio, red-eyed and nursing a blinding headache, apologized for his behavior. It was an abject apology, complete with a tear or two and a promise to reform.

"No more wine for a while," he told me.

I'd expected it, of course. I'd honed my reaction: a fine line between peevishness and joy, between simple satisfaction and obsequious sincerity.

It had to be just right, I thought. For now, more than ever, I wanted Curio's unqualified trust. There could be no flicker of doubt in his mind about where I stood. He had to be certain of my unswerving loyalty and friendship.

Indeed, I was convinced it had to be that way if I were ever to get to the bottom of these murders.

"Of course; I understand; quite all right," I said with just the right flavor of haughtiness in my tone. And I thought to myself, I'm getting good at this. And it occurred to me with a bit of a shock how meticulously calculating I'd become in a very short space of time. Indeed, with each intake of breath I felt myself growing older, and with each exhale I felt the boy within me disappearing into the endless dust of the great beyond.

* * *

"Are you out of your mind, boy? Are you totally insane?"

It was my father (who else?) shouting at the top of his lungs, pounding his fist on the dinner table as he spoke. His face turned bright red, bits of drool came spitting out, and a stringy chunk of pork—caught for a while in his upper front teeth—finally flew out, as well.

"Don't smile like that when I'm telling you something. Fine, go ahead: mock me. You're no son of mine, then. No, no longer."

Already drunk (needless to say!), he took an enormous swig of wine—the cheap northern stuff he'd been drinking lately; I suppose, by then, it was the best he could afford.

"Don't you have *any* explanation for your behavior, goddam it!"

"Decius, please—" my mother began.

"No, no, you shut up," he said. "You just shut up right now."

For a moment, it looked as though he might move toward her, actually strike her. It was not unheard of for him to do that, though never in my presence. Almost involuntarily, I felt my body flinch into readiness, and I'm sure there was a forbidding expression on my face. Drunk as he was, my father seemed to catch the change in my bearing, and he quickly backed off—for, of course, I had no intention of letting him touch her, at least not while I was right there and could prevent it.

Actually, in that particular case I'm sure my mother agreed with him; she had hinted as much earlier on. You see, I'd been avoiding him for a while, and now he was venting his long-delayed complaints about my controversial funeral speech. He'd also heard plenty since then about my work as a detective, so he was taking the opportunity to let all his anger out at once.

"You . . . you pissant," he was saying. "How dare you subject your family to such obvious dangers? Myself, it's bad enough; but your poor mother—to place her at such risk! And your wife. Well, it's stupid and thoughtless and utterly inexcusable."

He sat back in his chair and took another huge gulp. I awaited his next round of insults, but he just muttered quietly, apparently out of wind, at last—if only for the moment.

"Father—"

"Oh, shut up. If you want to kill yourself, then kill yourself. But don't take half your family down with you."

I shook my head and waited, but only briefly, for, as I say, I was ready for him and had decided at long last to join them this particular evening only after Fulvia had become suddenly indisposed. It gave me the perfect excuse to leave her at home and avoid subjecting her to the expected outburst.

Thus, after a brief pause, I began again: "Look, Father, I don't blame you for being concerned, and I'm sorry if my funeral oration upset you. But I did that deliberately; it was a calculated risk. I want whoever's behind this to know I mean business; I want everyone to know. Now, if something happens to me, well, it will be that much harder to brush aside whatever . . . difficulties I might encounter. In any case, at least four people have been murdered so far—"

"Four?"

"Yes, Father. Three besides Lucius. But I'm sure they're all connected. And whatever it takes, I plan to solve the mystery behind them. My cousin alone makes it . . . Well, he was my best friend, Father, and I won't let his murderer go unpunished."

"But think of us; think of—"

"My mind is made up, Father. If you won't help me, fine. But you've told me your objections, and that's the end of it. I won't talk about it further—now, or ever again."

He glared at me a moment, then stood up, grabbed the jug of wine and stalked out of the room.

★ ★ ★

"Look familiar?" I asked Calpius, the footman at my uncle's estate.

I handed him the silvery scrap of material I'd found in Antony's bedroom a few nights before. Calpius looked it over, smiled and nodded vigorously.

"You must recognize it, too, sir," he said.

"Perhaps I do." I squinted at him in a way that let him know I thought he was being just a bit impertinent.

"Well, it could have been worn by Telephus," he said quickly. "Could have been part of his silver sash."

"Indeed."

I showed it to my uncle later, but not surprisingly he was somewhat more vague. I was certain my Aunt Hortensia would be more definite about it, but I was too afraid of shocking her, so I held on to the scrap for a later time. After all, I decided, there was nothing so urgent about it since all it showed was that Telephus had probably been in Antony's bedroom.

And what does that prove? I wondered. Nothing, really. For, I thought with a wicked smile, isn't everybody?

The point was, where was this investigation leading? Who else could I question? What clues were there to build on to make a real case and solve the crimes?

★   ★   ★

This will be difficult, I thought. But it hadn't sunk in how difficult until the doorkeeper at the Gratus estate announced me:

"His lordship Gaius Livinius Severus to see Miss Matidia," he said. And standing there in the atrium of her father's house, I thought: I'm not so sure I can do this, after all.

But in another moment, being ushered upstairs into a lady's small sitting room, it seemed to me that I had no further say in the matter.

Actually, the room was more for little girls than grown women, with dolls lined up on a shelf, trinkets on the walls and frilly silks draped over a small sideboard.

"Oh, Gaius," Matidia Gratus said in her little girl's voice, and hugged me. And I realized that, of course, she thought I was making yet another condolence call. "Whatever will we do without him?" she said, her eyes filled with tears.

And I knew for certain, then, that my task was impossible.

She poured some wine into tiny silver goblets and sat beside me on a bench by a window that overlooked the rear courtyard of the house.

"I miss him so much," she said.

"As do I," I said, and felt my own eyes misting over.

So, I asked myself, What next, Mister Detective? Do I just come right out and ask her? Just what do you know, Miss Matidia, about the murder of your fiance, my cousin Lucius Flavius? That was the key question, all right, but not likely to get much of an answer, eh? I smiled to myself and thought: No wonder people who do jobs like these are looked upon as the lowest forms of human life. Why no general presiding over a blood-soaked battlefield could carry out so intimate a cruelty as this.

111

Still, I thought, it has to be done, so I'll have a touch more wine and ask her.

"So," she asked, "what have you learned about the murder of my fiance?"

Oh merciful gods, I thought, to let Matidia pose the question! I was, to put it mildly, caught off guard. I looked over at her, my mouth, I'm quite certain, wide open with surprise, and saw her dark eyes glisten with unexpected determination.

"Well, I—"

"You know, you should have come to me sooner, Livinius. Lucius left me with some papers that he said were of vital importance. I imagine he'd want you to have them."

Smiling, she stood, walked over to the shelf of dolls, picked up the biggest one, pulled off the head and reached inside. Instantly, the smile was gone and so was most of the color in her face. She pushed her hand in farther, then pulled it out, turned the doll over and banged it hard against the sideboard.

She wobbled a bit, and I helped her back to the sofa. "They're gone!" she said and began to sob as deeply as she had on the day of the funeral.

★　★　★

What a remarkable turn of events, I thought, as I made my way up the hill next morning to Avidia Crispina's house. That was my next indelicate task, to question the betrothed of yet another dead man, in this case, Fabius Vibulanus.

But my mind was still on my meeting with Matidia the day before. A sudden moment of elation over some papers, which I had not even known existed until then, had vanished just as suddenly as the papers themselves. No, Matidia could not recall anyone entering that room except Lucius and herself (other than servants, of course). Yes, she was certain that that was the right doll. Even so, we had decapitated all the rest and looked through her other shelves and cabinets, as well. Needless to say, we found nothing.

I thought: The more I work at this, the more of a puzzle it becomes. Indeed, so deep was my preoccupation as I turned into Avidia Crispina's street that I was nearly upon the house before I noticed a virtual frenzy of activity, including a dozen guards keeping sharp lookout at the front door. Just behind them, just inside

112

the doorway, were a man and a woman, still in their breakfast robes, crying quietly in each other's arms. They looked vaguely familiar, and I was fairly certain they were Avidia's parents.

A few steps from the doorway, one of the guards stepped up aggressively to meet me. "Your business here, sir?"

"His lordship Gaius Livinius Severus to see Miss Avidia," I replied with a loud, pompous edge to my tone.

With that, the woman in the doorway shrieked, "Oh, no," and began sobbing loudly until a slave came up and helped her back inside.

"What's that? Who did you say you were?" the man said gruffly, and walked over to me.

"Livinius Severus," I said again. "I wish to see Avidia, sir. Avidia Crispina. She is your daughter, isn't that right?"

The man opened his mouth, then closed it without speaking. He stared at me for a long moment, then said, "Yes, she is," very quietly and sadly. After another long pause, he went on: "My daughter's dead, sir. Murdered. Dead in her bed, her pretty neck broken . . ."

With that, he trailed off into terrible sobs of his own, while I felt myself sway from the shock. "Dead," I murmured.

"So would you be so kind as to leave us alone," he managed between spasms of crying.

I stood there, and he said, "Please!" most insistently. I wanted to say: But I need to see the body. But how awkward and terrible that would have been.

"My condolences, sir, on this day of sorrow," was all I finally said. He nodded and walked off, and I was left alone in the little entranceway, with the guards glaring at me and my heart too filled with sadness to think or speak or move.

★   ★   ★

It was as if a wall had been dropped down in front of me: witnesses murdered, documents gone. With each half step forward, I seemed to slip back five more. And now where else was there to turn? Sisyphus pushing his rock uphill could not have been more frustrated than I.

Conveniently enough, I once again found myself distracted by work—only this time I fairly buried myself in it. Certainly, it was an appropriate time to do so (or at least that's what I told myself). For as I rejoined my cousins full time in the study of Scribonius Curio's house, Roman politics indeed came noisily to life.

Nine days after Hirtius Pansa's birthday party, one week after the two new consuls, Julius Caesar and Calpurnius Bibulus, took office, Rome was again in the throes of upheaval. But while it looked on the surface much like the chaos of old, it was, in point of fact, carefully and cleverly contrived. This time it was Caesar's fine hand behind the madness.

The issue, once again, was land reform. Once again, the old-line aristo senators opposed it. Caesar favored passage of the bill. Or, putting it more accurately, Caesar *demanded* passage. As usual, Pompey's position was unclear.

By then, Scribonius Curio had become enough of a force unto himself that the Senate awaited his views on the matter with considerable interest. And, indeed, those views were now a well-kept secret. Even I did not know them, and neither did my cousins. For, as I realized late in the game, he had kept us all so isolated from one another in our work—so busy with individual projects and research—that, in the larger sense, none of us really knew what we were doing.

Of course, there were many who thought: once we hear Curio, then we will know Pompey's view, as well. And, in light of past experience, that seemed reasonable to me.

Thus, when Curio, his manner typically steady and self-assured, rose to begin his big speech, an unusually respectful hush came over the Senate of Rome.

"Senate Fathers," he began, "we face today the issue of land reform. It is an issue that has troubled us for some years now. It has caused considerable discontent throughout Italy; indeed, it has provoked riots and bloodshed in the streets of Rome itself.

"Now, once again, the issue is upon us. Now, once again, we must decide what constitutes worthwhile service to the state, and decide, as well, what is a just reward for that service. We must also decide if the land of Italy must now and forever remain in the hands of a few rich, old families, or if, in a sense, that land belongs to the republic as a whole, and, hence, to all her citizens—most especially

114

to those who have braved the dangers of the battlefield in her defense.

"Isn't that the issue confronting us today?"

At this point, Curio stopped and looked around the chamber, as if he were actually expecting a reply.

"Well, isn't it, Senate Fathers?"

"Yes. Yes, it is," came a few scattered shouts.

"You don't sound too sure of it," Curio resumed. He stopped again and looked around, but there were no more answers. "As well you should not be," he went on, "because the real issues in this debate have about as much to do with land reform as the Roman navy has to do with cultivating crops. Alas, within this issue, there are other issues, well hidden from view. They are issues of politics and issues of power; they are issues of ambition and greed—indeed, issues that strike at the very heart of Rome.

"Alas, land reform is only the mask. Let me explain, briefly, how all this works." He paused again and smiled, and there was muffled laughter around the room, for, of course, no one there required any explanation.

"Yes, please do," came an earnest shout from across the chamber. Indeed, it was none other than the imbecile senator Lucius Domitius Ahenobarbus.

Well, almost no one, I thought.

"One faction," Curio resumed, "insists that the patience and benevolence of the state has long since been abused and worn out, that no more can be afforded for the rascals and fakers of the mob. The rich have the land because . . . well, because they are rich, these men say, and they will not bow to the threats or intimidation of the rabble—or to the threats of those who claim to represent the rabble but really only use them to further their own ambitious schemes. The strict processes of the law must be preserved, they say; the liberties of the republic must be maintained.

"Another faction says all that is a sham, that it is the rich aristocrats who are the charlatans here. They have the land, these men say, because they are greedy. And because they are greedy, they want to keep all of it for themselves. But land, these men claim, is our most fundamental resource and, as such, cannot be so exclusively held. The land must be redistributed from time to time for

115

the benefit of all deserving citizens. Indeed, this faction says, they will not bow to the entrenched and intimidating power of the old families. After all, these men insist, the strict processes of the law must be preserved; the liberties of the republic must be maintained.

"Yet another faction floats somewhere in the middle of this. Yes, they say, we support land reform. But Rome is in a precarious state; land is scarce; the treasury is nearly empty. So now is not the time. Try again in a year or two. Then again, maybe not; maybe four or five years would be better. Besides, these men insist, we cannot accommodate the thugs and rowdies of the street; we cannot submit to unruly demands and violence, no matter how just the cause; of course, these men claim, neither will we kowtow to the rich. After all, these men say, the strict processes of the law must be preserved; the liberties of the republic must be maintained."

Curio paused again and smiled artfully—with just the right touch of rueful mirth playing about his eyes and lips. Again, there was a ripple of laughter through the room, but nothing more—no vulgar shouts or interruptions. Truly, one could say, he had their attention. And they were even getting the point.

"These various factions and their views encompass what seem to be the real issues at stake here," he went on. "These are the hidden issues I spoke of before, the issues of power, control and the fate of Rome itself. But I have a surprise for you, Senate Fathers: It is my opinion that these factions and their so-called real issues of power and control are actually the distractions, and, Senate Fathers, I implore you to strip away these distractions and to focus on the only real issue at hand. And that issue is land reform. I urge you, Senators, to consider that issue and that issue alone, and to consider it solely on its merits. Should modest parcels of land be granted to legionary veterans and other deserving citizens of Rome? Standing alone, without intrigues, there is only one answer to that question, Senate Fathers. Standing alone, without intrigues, the answer is clear and pure and meritorious beyond words. Indeed, the right answer can debilitate our warring factions and provide a solid foundation on which to rebuild our troubled republic.

"Noble Fathers, on the question of the land reform bill now before the Senate of Rome, I will vote an absolute, unchangeable and emphatic . . . Yes. And I urge all of you to join me."

There were tears in my eyes by the end of the speech, and I roared my approval so loudly and for so long that I was hoarse that night and all next day.

At his town house that evening, Curio broke out a jug of wine and celebrated with my cousins and myself. We sat around the courtyard and drank and howled till all hours.

"To the one true statesman, Gaius Scribonius Curio," I toasted more than once, and each time I found myself sobbing a little. They were sobs of guilt, I suppose: How could I have doubted him? I kept asking myself. How could I have believed he was responsible for any acts of infamy?—as most definitely my mind had been running in that direction lately. So he has his little flaws, I thought. Who doesn't? So he fancies Mark Antony. There are many in Rome who do, men as well as women.

Now . . . as for Mark Antony, well, that's another story. That's the fellow who bears watching in all this, I decided.

"A wonderful speech," I said, raising my goblet yet again. "A noble speech."

"It was truly the finest oration of its kind I have ever heard: the arguments were well taken, the phrasing economical, the delivery smooth and beautifully understated," said my windbag cousin, Junius Barnabas.

"Excellent," said his opposite number, my cousin Claudius Barnabas.

At that, I began to laugh very loudly and freely and for what seemed like a very long time—indeed, until the stars had set and the predawn sky was dangerously black and forbidding.

"Oh, cousins," I finally remember saying, "oh, cousins, I miss my cousin so much." And then my eyes were wet again, and it was plain enough even to me that I wasn't laughing anymore.

★   ★   ★

Every senator cheered Curio's speech that day, but, of course, in the Roman Senate, that can be deceptive. What they cheered were the well-formed arguments—the rhetoric—of the speech, and in some cases the noble sentiments behind it. But that had nothing to do with whether they agreed with so much as a single word of it, or with what action they might take later on.

Indeed, the good feeling left behind by the speech was short-lived: the very next day the esteemed Senate of Rome degenerated once again into a vulgar spectacle of jeers, insults and fistfights.

"You will pass this bill," Julius Caesar told the Senate, "or there will be dire consequences!"

Many of my colleagues seemed to take his words in stride, but I was astonished. Is that a warning, I wondered, or a command? His tone and words, it seemed to me, sounded very much like one or the other. Or both.

"You will not threaten the Roman Senate," Cato shouted back.

"You do not rule here, the Senate rules here," Calpurnius Bibulus put in.

Mark Antony then dashed across the chamber to Bibulus, and I distinctly heard him say: "But not for much longer."

I hardly need tell you the words sent a shudder up my spine.

And so it went: the insults got nastier, the threats less veiled. Caesar and Cato in particular sniped away at each other all afternoon.

At one point, Caesar mimicked Cato's stern demeanor, and Cato, affecting a mincing little two-step, said, "Whose wife are you this week, Caesar?" though probably not quite loud enough for Caesar to hear.

A bit later, Caesar said Cato might see the need for land reform if he could learn to relax a little, and that somebody should help "by taking the pole out of your behind."

"I'd say you know a lot more about poles up your behind than I do, Caesar," Cato shot back to raucous laughter. At that, Caesar apparently decided he'd had enough. He motioned with his right hand and a moment later two roughnecks dashed inside, grabbed Cato, lifted him up and actually carried him from the room.

I was horrified, of course, and for a moment it looked as if the entire Senate would erupt in a huge, noisy brawl. But, as usual, the few fights that did break out acted as a peculiar sop to the others: they laughed, they jeered, they grumbled. And slowly, over a period of perhaps half an hour, they all simply drifted away, until finally the chamber of the Roman Senate achieved the weary desolation it deserved.

★　　★　　★

Cato was back the next morning, of course. Caesar was much too clever to risk so impetuous a move as the jailing of Rome's most respected senator, and he even offered a quiet apology, which Cato promptly accepted.

But then it began all over again: "You fathead." "You sot." "You drunkard." "You thief." "You pederast." These were just a few of the tastier insults I heard during that day's debate.

Finally, six days later, the other consul of Rome, Calpurnius Bibulus, seeing the Senate leaning in favor of Caesar and his bill, declared, "I hear thunder."

It was, in fact, a clear and sunny afternoon, and the thunder that erupted at once came not from the skies, of course, but from Caesar himself. "God damn you," he boomed from all the way across the chamber, in what, for him, was a truly uncharacteristic loss of temper. "Get out of here, you old fool," he shouted as he ran over to Bibulus. "You can't bring all Rome to a halt with this nonsense."

For a moment it appeared as though he himself would strike Bibulus. But at the last instant he summoned his henchmen again: this time, four enormous thugs trotted in, pushed Bibulus down and dragged him bump-bumping down the gallery steps, across the floor and out. From my seat, I could just see them as they reached the outer door. The men helped Bibulus roughly to his feet, but then another immediately stepped up and dumped a bucket of dung over his head. I flinched as I saw the stuff ooze down his face and toga. As I say, I could not quite see everything, and I assumed the man with the bucket was just another of Caesar's rowdies. But, to my amazement, a dozen good men assured me later that it was none other than Mark Antony himself.

★   ★   ★

Thus was the state of affairs in the capital of the Roman republic. The very next day, the Senate passed the land reform bill supported by Julius Caesar. As for Calpurnius Bibulus, he would lock himself in his house for the remainder of his term, nearly one full year, and "stare at the heavens," waiting for the "thunder" to end—and the true and legal business of Rome to resume.

16

Of course, we congratulated Curio on the passage of the bill. But it was perfunctory: all of us, even Curio, agreed it was not a time for celebration. Thus, the day after, I found myself with my cousins at a cafe on the Cispius Hill, not far from the Forum, less to celebrate than to commiserate.

"Land reform is wonderful," I said, "but getting it like this . . ." I trailed off, shook my head and turned my hands up in a gesture of helplessness.

"It appears that the forces of darkness are, indeed, gathering to crush out the good, put an end to our freedoms and replace our vaunted republic with a dictatorship," Junius Barnabas said.

"Trouble ahead," said Claudius Barnabas.

I slumped forward, put my hands over my eyes and tried to keep from laughing. I managed to let just one slight chuckle escape, but I could not hide my smile.

"Do you do that deliberately?" I asked.

"What?" they both said. I stared at them: they were grinning ear to ear.

" 'What!' " I repeated. "What do you mean, 'What'?"

"You mean when one of us always says about five times what's necessary," Claudius said, "and the other sums it up in a word or two?"

"Yes, that's what I mean," I said.

"Yes."

"Yes, what . . . ?"

"Yes, we do it deliberately," Junius said. "Lucius always knew that. We thought you knew it, too."

"Lucius always knew that," I said, drawing out the words.

I leaned back on the hard bench in the little tavern and had my first real laugh in a long while—in fact, probably my first since before Lucius died. I took a large gulp of wine and studied my two cousins—both of them, I might point out, with idiot grins still on their faces: Junius's dark, fleshy features, covered those days by a full beard; Claudius's hawklike angularity enhanced by a full-figured Roman nose and eyes so sharp they seemed at times to generate an eerie light of their own.

I wondered: Does the fact that their behavior is so calculated make them more or less eccentric than I had previously thought? Probably more, I decided, though also more intelligent—or, at least, more perceptive.

"Do you ever switch off?" I asked, smiling. "You know, change roles: one day one's the windbag, the next day the other."

"We used to," Claudius said, "but, really, Junius has become so entirely efficacious as the man who is garrulous to the point of long-windedness, his phrasing and timing so expert in drawing out his thoughts, that, well, no, we no longer switch."

"Right," Junius said.

I stared at them, grinning. "You just did it," I said. "You switched."

"Mmm-hmm," they both said.

"How clever," I said, and they both erupted with laughter at last. And I realized: polite titters aside, that was the first time I'd ever heard either of them do that.

★ ★ ★

"You miss Lucius, don't you?" Junius was saying.

It was late, and I was a little drunk. But I still didn't entirely trust my two peculiar cousins. Not that I would expect them to betray me; nothing of the sort. I simply felt a distance from them. Partly, it was because they seemed so walled off, so much in their own little world. But, I thought, perhaps it's also because I've never taken the trouble to scale the walls. After all, it's obvious enough that some people are harder to get to know than others.

"So do we," Claudius said without waiting for my answer.

121

"Mmmm," I said with a slight nod.

They both fidgeted, shifting in their chairs and running their hands over their goblets. "I hope you don't mind me asking," Junius Barnabas said, "but . . . well, we both were wondering how your investigation is going."

"The one into Lucius's death," Claudius added.

I shook my head and bit my lip: I was determined not to cry again. "Nothing much so far," I muttered.

"Can we . . ." Claudius began, but his voice trailed off.

". . . help?" Junius said, finishing the question.

"I'm sorry, I'm not following . . ."

"Is there some way we can help with your investigation?" Junius elaborated.

I looked at them again: I had not even told them I was conducting an investigation, though of course they could have heard that much by now from any number of people.

"Thank you," I said quietly. "For offering, I mean. It would be wonderful, of course." I realized I was biting my lip again, though somehow that time I knew it wouldn't help. "But I don't know," I stumbled on. "I'm at kind of an impasse right now . . ."

And then it came, a nasty little sob from deep inside me, though hearing it, it was as if it had come from someone or somewhere else—indeed, from anyone or anywhere else but me sitting in that little cafe.

"We should go," Claudius said promptly. "Most definitely," Junius agreed.

They both stood at once—though quietly, without the clumsy haste that might attract undue attention, reached over to me and gently made certain that I got properly to my feet. Then, with no small amount of patience, my two cousins guided me out of the cafe and home.

Oddly enough, despite my condition, or perhaps because of it, by the time we reached my front door and I told my cousins thanks and good night, yet another new plan was beginning to form in my mind.

★   ★   ★

Fulvia was waiting up for me, stretched out in bed and dressed only in a suitably scandalous nighttime garment. "Hello," she said with a grand smile, looking cheerful and beautiful as ever.

122

Or trying to.

On second glance, I noticed with a start that her eyes were sad and red and tired. "Have you been crying?" I asked at once.

"Have you?" she demanded.

"I asked you first."

She sighed and smiled and even laughed a little. "Well, it's just that I have been a bit worried about you lately," she said.

"Have you?" I answered, crawling into bed beside her. "I'm sorry to cause you concern. But you know how heavy a work load I've had, and I've got a lot on my mind, besides that."

"Mmmm," she said, studying me closely. "So . . . have you?"

I hesitated a moment, then realized what she meant. "Well, yes, I was," I admitted.

She snuggled up beside me, gave me a kiss, then turned over so her back was to me and guided my arms around her; then, after a moment, she placed my hands over her breasts. "I love you so much, Livinius," she said.

I could feel her breathing; I could feel the flutter of her heart, and I took a deep breath of my own: in and out. It was, I suppose, the sort of intoxicating breath possible only for a man who is still, at least in spirit, a newlywed.

Peace of mind, I thought: that's what she gives me. That, and patience, as well as all the other things the poets say women give men.

"I'd say the feeling is mutual," I said.

"Don't be flip," she scolded. "Our love is sacred."

"Yes, it is," I said. "I agree."

We lay like that a moment, in silent pleasure, until she turned over again and faced me. "So . . . well . . . is everything all right? I mean . . . I hope you don't mind my asking, but how is your investigation going?"

I wondered: Why is everyone so polite to me this evening? Indeed, I asked myself, is the subject *that* touchy? Or do I appear *that* delicate?

"Of course I don't mind you asking, Fulvia. If I haven't told you much, it's because I worry that anything you do know might put you in jeopardy."

She nodded understandingly, waited a moment, then said: "And?"

"And? Oh: And the investigation is not going too well right now, but I have—"

"Is that . . . well, I don't mean to pry, but is that why you were crying?"

"Well," I said, blushing, "in a way. Mostly, it was—"

"Lucius. Of course! I miss him, too, Livinius. I loved him very much."

"Yes, everyone did. But I have—"

"Well, I want his murder solved, too," she said earnestly. She paused a moment as if in thought. "Livinius, do you think . . . that is, is it possible that my father might be able to help?"

At that, I propped myself up on one elbow and smiled, a bit smugly, I suppose. "My dear wife," I said, "I've been trying to tell you for the past ten minutes that I have a new plan. And, yes, it very much involves getting help from your father."

★　★　★

Victorinus Avidius received me the very next morning. He was in his library, surrounded by a veritable mountain of unread scrolls and a gaggle of nagging advisers. Needless to say, he was very busy, but he quickly shooed the men away, and I got right to the point.

"As you may know, Avidius, I have been conducting an investigation into the murder of my cousin Lucius Flavius."

"Yes, my boy, and if you don't mind my asking, how has it—"

"It has not been going especially well, Avidius," I put in quickly, not wanting to hear that particular question again. "And that's precisely why I'm here. I am determined to bring the murderer to justice, and, reluctantly, I must ask your help."

I paused to let that much sink in, and he looked back at me across his cluttered worktable with his usual graceful self-assurance: the receptive, eager eyes, though tempered, as always, by those dark, forbidding eyebrows; the mouth noncommittal, but also set and steady, with no telltale twitchings of the lips or jaw. All in all, it was a relaxed face, even serene—a face that seemed to say, I am at peace with myself and the world (or, at least, with the part of the world that counts).

"Well, naturally I'm not unwilling, Livinius," he said, "though I don't quite see how . . ."

I waited for him to go on, but his eyes told me he was finished—that, indeed, he was waiting for me.

I said: "My lord, I want a quaestorship."

With a slight jerk of his head, he looked around and stared at me blankly, then opened his mouth and closed it without uttering a sound. For a moment, he seemed to lose himself in thought. And then: "Aaah, I see," he said, nodding slowly and drawing out the words. "At least, I think I see. You mean, in the ancient form."

"Yes," I said, smiling. "That's it."

His momentary confusion was entirely understandable, for in our time, of course, quaestors are government treasurers and financial managers. (In fact, just to remind you, that was the job that Curio held during his term in the province of Asia.) But long ago—four centuries, to be exact, when the laws of the Twelve Tables were first set down upon the ancient bronze tablets—a quaestor was an investigator, most particularly of murder.

Quaestor parricidi was the precise term they used.

And that job, that title, was what I wanted: It would, I believed, give me the power I needed to conduct a proper investigation. It was brash, of course, even impertinent, but also bold and innovative, and the ancient flavor of the title would only enhance my prestige. It was, I felt, the best plan I could devise; indeed, I had decided, it was the only meaningful path to solving my cousin's murder.

"Interesting," Avidius said, still mulling it over. "Of course, quaestors are normally elected to their jobs."

"I was hoping you could arrange a special appointment," I said. "An emergency posting. There are precedents, I believe."

"Yes," he said slowly, "I believe there are."

He looked at me thoughtfully, a little smile on his lips and a slight sheen over his eyes. "You're a brave and clever young man, Livinius," he said. He stopped and drummed the forefinger of his left hand on the table. "You know, of course, how dangerous this can be."

"Yes," I answered.

"And not just for you."

"Yes," I said, my voice suddenly a whisper.

Avidius abruptly leaned forward with an odd expression: serious, but with a strong hint of mischief in his eyes. His eyebrows danced their mysterious signal: trouble ahead, it meant. Then, without another hint of warning, my father-in-law raised his right arm and swept it clear across the table in front of him, sending scrolls, wax tablets, seals, a heavy old stylus holder—in other words, everything in sight—crashing to the floor.

"Junk," he said, nodding toward the pile he had suddenly created. "All of it junk."

Hearing the noise, one of his secretaries came running in, then pulled up short and stared open-mouthed at the mess. My own face, I'm certain, was wide-eyed with surprise. Indeed, I had never imagined my father-in-law would have such a flair for the dramatic.

"Piso, I have cleared my desk," he told the hapless assistant. "Livinius, I will look into this at once. Until it is completed, it will take up all my time. And if it is possible—I mean, even remotely possible to obtain by whatever means are required—believe me, you will have what you desire."

17

Avidius handled it perfectly: Two days later he discovered a vacancy in the appropriate department, and five days after that, in the little office of some obscure third-rank functionary, I was sworn in as interim quaestor for the City of Rome. Officially, I was assigned to the Treasury Ministry, but my powers were specifically defined: I was an emergency investigator with authority to interrogate and arrest all citizens within the walls of the city.

I was given a specially constructed fasces, the ancient symbol of authority made of an ax fastened with red leather straps to a bundle of birch rods. I was also permitted to appoint two special assistants, or lictors: I immediately named my cousins Junius and Claudius Barnabas.

"We're with you," Junius told me right afterward. "Very much so," Claudius put in.

It all happened so fast that no one had a chance to complain or raise questions. And that, I thought, was just how it should be: to have the power without the publicity, if you will.

One day later, I was at the front door of the house where Avidia Crispina had lived with her parents. And, yes, it was the very house where I'd arrived a week or so earlier, just after poor Avidia's body had been found, and where her father, in particular, had been so unwilling to talk.

"His lordship Gaius Livinius Severus to see Rufus Crispina Egnatius and the Lady Octavia," I announced.

"State your business," the doorkeeper growled.

Junius immediately stepped into view, carrying the fasces, with Claudius right behind him. "None of your concern, doorman," I said. "I must see the master of the house and his wife."

Needless to say, his officious manner gave way quickly to a much more obsequious tone. "Oh, of course, my lord, now I understand," he said, and immediately showed us in.

It was barely half an hour past daybreak, and Rufus Crispina and his wife were still a bit bleary-eyed and just sitting down to eat in their second-floor breakfast room. Even so, to my surprise they invited us to sit with them.

"Sorry for the intrusion," I said, "and once again my deepest regrets at the death of your daughter."

"And we apologize for the other day, my lord," Rufus said. "But the shock of it all . . . you understand."

"Of course," I said, and meant it.

I waited just to give them a moment and let them swallow another bite of food. Then I pressed on: "I don't wish to cause you more pain than you've already suffered," I said, "but I must question you about certain circumstances of your daughter's life. You see, I believe her death is connected to the death of Fabius Vibulanus. And I think both those deaths are somehow linked to the murder of my cousin Lucius Flavius."

As you might expect, they both stopped eating at once, then stared at me with an odd mixture of curiosity and dread.

"What do you mean?" Lady Octavia gasped.

"Go on," Rufus Crispina snarled.

"Immediately after the murder of Fabius Vibulanus, your daughter approached my cousin and myself. She asked for our help; she wanted us to find out who killed Fabius and bring him to justice. My cousin pursued the matter with some vigor, but I never learned what he found out. He was about to tell me, but was killed before I could speak to him.

"So, first of all, if I may be so bold, was your daughter actually betrothed to Fabius Vibulanus before his death?"

Rufus and his wife looked at each other, then at me, then off somewhere into space. "We didn't know . . ." Octavia began breathlessly, then trailed off.

"We . . . that is, well . . . we had no idea they were close at all,"

Rufus grumbled. "We knew they had seen a bit of each other here and there, but as far as we knew that was all of it. They most certainly were not betrothed."

Suddenly, I felt once again as if I were nearing some low rung of humanity. I briefly closed my eyes and thought: How much will I learn in the course of all this that is irrelevant to the case? How much more will I know when I'm finished than I need to, or want to? Most important, perhaps: how many times will I inadvertently shock the innocent with facts they did not know before—facts that would best have been left unrevealed?

I thought: I cannot let this interfere. The greater truth is more important than the petty irrelevance, no matter how painful. Isn't it?

"I understand your surprise," I went on, "but she did come to us with her request. So let me ask you this: Were you aware that Fabius Vibulanus had worked in the past for Gaius Scribonius Curio?"

"For Curio?" Octavia blurted out, then turned a dangerous shade of red.

Rufus seemed to hesitate for the briefest instant, then said, "We already told you: we barely knew this Fabius fellow. We certainly had no idea of his politics or of what positions he held in the past."

"But I believe you're acquainted with Curio, aren't you?" It was my cousin Junius, suddenly interjecting himself. Trying not to look too amazed, I turned around and stared at him standing behind me. I was certain he also had noticed the lady's reaction to the mere mention of Curio's name, so it was a good question. Indeed, I was pleased that he'd asked it, for I would never have had the nerve. Is this, I wondered, the other side of detective work? The cheap thrills, the petty bits of excitement and power?

"What do you mean, sir!" the husband demanded, and stood up.

Junius, who had lowered the fasces in deference to that house, raised it at once. "Let me caution you, my lord," I quickly put in, "that this is a murder investigation, and I have full authority to pursue whatever seems pertinent."

Open-mouthed with amazement and no small amount of fear, Rufus Crispina sat back down.

"Well?" Junius demanded, staring at Lady Octavia.

"I am slightly acquainted with Curio, yes," she answered.

Junius and Claudius both glared at me as if to say, If you won't do this, we will. "And in this, uh, acquaintanceship with Curio," I pushed on, "did he ever mention the name of Fabius Vibulanus?"

"Certainly not."

"He didn't say, 'I have this talented young man working for me named Fabius Vibulanus, who I'm sure you must know'?"

"Well . . . he might have—"

"He *might* have?" I blurted out.

"Didn't you, in fact, recommend Fabius to Curio, my lady?" Claudius put in.

"No, no, no," she insisted.

"Now that is enough!" Rufus Crispina shouted. "I will not—"

"He was already there," Octavia interrupted. "Curio simply asked me if I knew him, and what did I think of him. That was all. I didn't know it would lead to . . . to all this."

She waved her hands around as if in confusion, then suddenly broke down and began to cry. Her husband stared at her, red-faced and helpless, from across the table. Some facade or other had been stripped away, and all we could do was make the all-too-obvious guesses at what, precisely, it had been concealing.

After an awkward few moments, we asked for and received Rufus Crispina's permission to search his daughter's room. As expected, it plainly had not been touched or rearranged in any way; after all, at that point there was surely no hurry about redecorating. We went through every drawer and cabinet. We felt along the walls and floor for secret compartments. We searched her clothing and bed linen. But nothing was there. And after another hour we left that house, hopefully forever.

★ ★ ★

"What I'm telling you is that no one is truly innocent," my cousin Claudius opined over a bit of lunch at a nearby tavern.

"I know that, cousin," I growled. "The point is—"

"The point is they all have their guilty little secrets," Junius put in. "Most of them won't be relevant, but some will."

"And we end up knowing so much more than we need to," I sighed.

130

"Or want to—I agree," Claudius said. "But we have a murder to solve. Five murders, actually."

"Five, counting the slave Laertes," I said. And I thought, And then there's Telephus, the doorkeeper: whereabouts unknown.

"You're right," I said. "I have to harden myself."

"Not really," Claudius said. He leaned close to me and spoke in earnest tones. "It's not so much a matter of being hard or callous; that's not what you want. It's more a matter of keeping everything in perspective."

"And of blinding yourself," Junius put in, "or, at least, of blurring your vision; looking the other way, but just when you need to."

"And just while we're involved in this one case," Claudius said. "Nothing permanent, you understand. Just a temporary impairment that can be fixed later on."

"Yes, yes, when the time is right," Junius said, nodding with a smile. "You'll see: it will all work out perfectly in the end."

★　★　★

I dismissed my cousins for the day and paid a visit on my own to Matidia Gratus. After all, I hardly needed the intimidating panoply of my new office to talk with the woman who would have married my cousin. So technically my visit was unofficial, but I gently let her know it could easily be otherwise.

"A quaestorship? I didn't know you were so good with math or money," she said.

"No, no," I said, laughing. "I'm a special investigator."

"Aaah," she said, apparently grasping it.

"I'm looking into Lucius's murder," I said. "I have two lictors and a fasces, and all the authority I need."

"Well, well, that's wonderful," she said slowly. She stared at me, obviously impressed. "Congratulations," she added, "and good luck." She smiled and gave me a soft kiss on the forehead. "And if there's anything I can do . . ."

"Keep your eyes open," I said, "and your ears."

"Of course."

I gave her a moment, then said: "Have you seen anything? Anything at all that might be useful?"

She shook her head.

"No sign of those missing papers, I assume."

"No."

"Any thoughts on who might have taken them? Anyone in this house? The slaves and such?"

"I can't imagine," she said, "though you know, Livinius, it occurred to me the other day that Lucius did mention something a long time ago about a secret compartment he had somewhere in his bedroom."

I nodded slowly. "Yes, that's certainly possible," I said, "but I don't . . . that is, Lucius gave the papers to you."

"And maybe he took them back," she said. "Maybe he decided there *was* someone in this house he couldn't trust, or maybe he had second thoughts about putting me in even the slightest bit of danger."

"Interesting," I said, nodding slowly. "But did he ever actually say anything to give you that idea?"

"Well, that's just it; in a way, it seems like he did," she answered, "but I can't really remember what, exactly."

"And he didn't by any chance give you a hint of any sort about precisely where that secret compartment might be?" I asked. But once again she shook her head emphatically.

After that, we traded bits of small talk and gossip; then we traded affectionate hugs.

"As you say, Livinius, I'll keep my eyes open," she said.

"Yes," I said, "that's fine, but above all be very careful how you do it."

★ ★ ★

The next morning brought the first real test of my new authority. It was not quite daybreak when I knocked my loud detective's knock on the front door of a gaudy Roman town house which belonged to that gaudiest of Romans, Mark Antony.

After several minutes, the door was suddenly and angrily pulled back. "What the hell!" the doorkeeper grumbled, barely awake and more than a little disheveled. He looked us over, all of us, with our official epaulets on, and, of course, Junius behind me with the fasces.

"So!" he said with a shrug, letting us know that he wasn't impressed.

132

"Official business," I said. "Gaius Livinius Severus for Mark Antony. We must see him at once."

The doorman just stood there, and finally we began to squeeze past him into the house, but he wouldn't budge.

"You cannot pass, sir," he said. "I have strict instructions."

I shook my head and sighed with exasperation. I looked at my cousins, and they appeared as impatient as I felt. "Don't you understand the meaning of that symbol?" I said, gesturing at the fasces and speaking in what I hoped was a dark and serious tone. "Well, it is a symbol of great power, and I am here on a matter of great urgency; so either escort us to your master, or bring him down here. Otherwise, I will go up into the house anyway, find him and place him under arrest."

The man stared at me, eyes wide with amazement: Clearly, no one had spoken to Mark Antony's doorkeeper in so rude a fashion before.

"Yes, my lord," he said at last, drawing out the words in a mincing, sarcastic tone. Then he walked in a slow and sullen manner back into the house.

As you might imagine, it took a few more minutes, but finally there was Antony himself, also barely awake and a bit askew, though still undeniably imposing.

"So what's all this, eh?" he said, struggling to keep the anger out of his voice.

"I have some questions for you, my lord, about a—"

"Questions! For me?"

"May we come inside, sir," I began again; "it won't take long."

"No, you cannot; I won't have you in my house—"

"It's regarding a series of murders, sir." I looked around, startled: Once again, it was my cousin Junius, this time talking much too loudly. Indeed, a little crowd of passersby gathering near the doorstep could easily hear every word. "In each case, sir," Junius went on, even more loudly than before, "there was a curious inflammation in a certain area of the body . . ."

He trailed off, but it was enough to draw some gasps and even a chuckle or two.

"Come inside," Mark Antony hissed, and we promptly followed him into the atrium.

133

"What do you mean by talking to me—"

"My lord," I said, "I have some questions to ask you, and I have the authority to ask them. So if you don't mind—"

"This is outrageous; I won't—"

"Where is Telephus?" I put in quietly.

"Who?" he snapped with convincing lack of interest, but from the look on his face, he seemed brought up short.

"Telephus, sir: the doorkeeper at my uncle's estate. He's disappeared."

"I don't know anyone by that—"

"He's been in your house, sir; been in your bedroom."

"Why, that's absurd. And anyway, how would you know—"

"I know, sir," I said, smiling a little in spite of myself.

"Well, I tell you I don't know anybody by that name," Mark Antony insisted. "Your uncle's doorkeeper, indeed!"

I paused a moment and took a deep, calming breath. "My lord, we've already told you: this is a murder investigation. Let me add that Telephus disappeared right after one of the murders—the murder of my cousin Lucius Flavius. Now I have evidence that Telephus has been in this house, and even, as I say, in your private quarters. So, Mark Antony, tell me, please: Why was Telephus here, and where is Telephus now?"

I watched him carefully all the time I spoke, and . . . well, well, what's this? Is it possible? The great and famous Mark Antony turning just a little pink around the ears?

"I . . . meet so many people. That name . . . I don't recall it. Maybe he was here . . . I don't know."

"Did you hear that?" I said, turning to my cousins.

"Yes, my lord: he admits to the possibility," Claudius answered with snappish efficiency. "Junius, is there an hourglass?" he said, turning to his brother. "If so, note the time."

At that moment, I found it hard—very hard—to keep from smiling, and I wondered if they weren't laying it on a bit thick. But if facial expressions are any guide, Mark Antony was taking it all very seriously. And I asked myself: Am I the only one who finds my two cousins to be such obvious play-actors?

"Mark Antony, I am going to search your house," I said.

"You what?"

"You heard me, sir."

"You can't—"

"I can and I will, sir."

Right then, Antony literally stepped back from where I stood—for the first time, it seemed, considering me seriously enough to take a moment and compose his thoughts.

"Well, then, young Livinius Severus, if you insist," he said slowly, still formulating something in his mind. After another moment, he said: "But in that case I must also insist; I also will apply the ancient laws."

I suddenly knew exactly where he was going with his little injunction, and I rolled my eyes.

"How was it the Twelve Tables put it?" Antony went on. " '. . . with platter and loincloth . . .' "

He referred, of course, to the old dictum about searching the house of a suspected thief. The citizen who made the accusation could conduct the search only after stripping down to nothing more than a loincloth—to prevent him from carrying in the goods, planting them in the man's house and accusing him falsely. The man doing the search could also bring in a platter, if he wished, to carry out whatever goods he found that rightfully belonged to him.

"If you insist, that's fine with me," I said.

"Though I doubt his lordship is hiding Telephus in his toga," Junius suddenly put in. "But if it gives Mark Antony pleasure—"

"That will be enough, Junius," I growled.

"Of course, my lord," Junius said. "I was only going to say that if it gives Mark Antony pleasure to humiliate you in such a fashion, then . . . so be it."

"Yes, Junius," I said. "So be it."

Indeed, I had no particular objection to disrobing under such a circumstance, though I knew full well what Antony was trying to do: Either I would call off the search out of embarrassment, or, if I did as he wished, he would spread the story, twisting it just a little in hopes of causing me public humiliation. That was why I knew the sooner I did it and the more casually I behaved, the harder it would be for him to make something of it.

So right then and there I peeled off my outer toga, then my tunic and sandals, until it was just me and my loincloth. By that time, a good number of servants were up and about, including several women cleaners scrubbing away as well as a few kitchen workers who happened at that moment to be coming to the front of the house.

More than a few of them, I realized, were staring longer than they should have and turning slightly pink. Then it was my cousins who rolled their eyes and grinned. I even caught Antony looking oddly in my direction, and quite honestly I half expected him to say something like: Oh, *now* I remember you. But even he kept such crass comments to himself (or perhaps he was just dumber than I thought and really didn't recall).

In any case, Antony was about to join me in the search as I headed up the stairs, but I warned him off.

"You forget your law, sir," I said. "If witnesses come along, then the searcher stays fully dressed. Having disrobed, sir, it is now my privilege to conduct this search by myself—absolutely in private."

Antony wavered a moment, stuttering, as if groping for some retort. But apparently he realized I was right, for he soon backed off without a word, and I climbed the stairs alone.

★   ★   ★

I spent nearly three hours searching Mark Antony's study and bedroom. I went through everything I'd gone through before, but much more carefully: I examined every nook and cranny of both sideboards in the study; nothing was any cleaner than it had been, and none of the bills seemed to have been paid. I pulled everything out, including the drawers themselves, and felt for false bottoms. I felt as best I could (without putting everything in complete disarray) for secret compartments in the walls and floor.

I also went through the bedroom, of course—especially through that sideboard by the bed, where I'd been interrupted earlier. I even found a hidden compartment in the wall near the window, but there was nothing in it—not a scrap, which of course in itself seemed rather odd. At one spot, where a rather cheesy fresco of some battle or other was peeling from the wall, I reached behind it and felt around, but again found nothing at all.

Finally, going through his bedroom closet, I noticed a partly hidden cabinet along the rear wall. I opened the door and saw it at once. With a frustrated shake of my head, I thought: It's just more of the same. Indeed, it was a much smaller scrap of the same silvery satin material that I'd found there earlier.

I took a moment to look around and see if perhaps it really did come from something of Antony's, but naturally there was nothing else in the closet quite like it. Almost certainly, I decided, it must have been part of a sash or other garment worn by the missing Telephus.

I spent a few more minutes pacing between the two rooms, thinking and looking, wondering if I'd missed some crucial spot. But nothing jumped out at me; nothing occurred. And finally I stepped out into the corridor that overlooked a small rear courtyard. What would the other rooms in this house reveal? I wondered. Nothing much, I decided, though who could tell for sure. Still, thanks to being so skimpily dressed, I felt as if I were covered head to toe by a thin layer of dust; besides that, in the drafty rooms of that house, I felt chilled to my insides.

I returned to the atrium, one flight down, to find a goodly number of Antony's hangers-on in attendance, including one man with red-painted lips and dark lines drawn around his eyes who winked at me and smiled. Junius and Claudius were nowhere to be seen.

"Your lictors have withdrawn," Antony said, "outside to the street where they should be." The little group began to buzz and titter. "Your clothes are out there with them, and that's where you can dress."

There was a rude round of laughter. But if raw humor was to be the weapon, I was not to be easily outdone. "From what I hear, Mark Antony, you're used to dressing in the street, so if it doesn't bother you, it won't bother me." The group laughed very loudly, but just for an instant—as if they all were laughing in spite of themselves—and I dared to egg them on by swiveling my hips and affecting a mincing form of speech. "And your friend Telephus *was* here," I went on, handing him the little scrap of satin. "It's all right, boys, don't be jealous," I told the crowd. "He wasn't here long."

Impressively enough, Antony remained quite calm and even held on to a thin smile. Then he stepped right up to me and, through clenched teeth, said quietly, "Get out!" And I promptly obeyed.

If he had said one more word, I might have retorted with some wisecrack or other about his unpaid bills. But he said nothing else so I let it go, saving it for another time.

Outside, my two cousins were ready and waiting. Indeed, they artfully strapped on my tunic and wrapped my toga over me so quickly that in the eyes of any reasonable man I escaped (albeit narrowly) the shame of being nearly naked in a public street.

"Let's go home," I said, smiling. Then I slipped on my sandals, and we headed away from Mark Antony's house with as much speed and as little fuss as possible.

18

Cicero was horrified.

He was frightened by my appointment as quaestor; he was appalled by my search of Mark Antony's house; he was terrified by my confrontation right afterward.

"This is not a man with a sense of humor," Cicero warned (as if I had not already noticed as much). "Sooner or later, this is a man who will do his damnedest to get revenge."

"Yes, master," I said, and took another gulp of wine.

We were in his garden, just he and I, a jug of wine and two goblets. Truth be told, it was our second jug and we were both at least a little drunk; certainly I was lightheaded, and Cicero looked more than that to me. In point of fact, it was by far the drunkest I'd ever seen him.

"Anyway, as far as the rest goes, the die, as they say, is cast. The republic is on its last legs. What I'm telling you," Cicero said, "is that Mark Antony may be very powerful soon. And very dangerous. He's a terrible man who'll thrive in the terrible times ahead."

We each downed another gobletful and poured some more. I felt like crying again, though I wasn't sure why.

"I kept an eye on Curio, sir, just as you asked me."

"I know you did," Cicero answered with a wistful smile. "And a fine job you did, too—you and your cousin Lucius."

"He's flawed, master," I said, "but he's basically a good man with good intentions."

"I think you're right," he said. "I think Curio learned his lessons well."

A sudden late-winter gust of wind blew across the garden, the dust blew up, and old Cicero shivered in his toga.

"We should go inside, master," I said, "where it's warm."

He shook his head, smiled and took another sip. "Everyone tells me that nowadays," he said. " 'Stay inside,' they say, where it's warm and safe and comfortable. 'Don't do too much, or say too much,' they all tell me. 'You're old now. You've done your bit. Let younger heads put themselves in danger. It's all but hopeless anyway'—that's what they all say."

Cicero leaned back, took a deep breath and suddenly tears streamed down his face. I'd seen him choked up and misty before, mostly on his big homecoming trip of a few months back, but nothing like this. Indeed, the tears still coming, he leaned forward, put his head in his hands and wept.

"Be careful, my child," he said. Then he just shook his head again, and I helped him inside and put him to bed.

•   •   •   •   •   •

"That Cicero's a great man, eh, Gaius?" Augustus says as he sits down beside me in the waiting room of Cicero's old house in Rome.

It is evening, the oil lamps are lit and there is only a streak or two of gray left to brighten the dark December sky. Augustus, still reading, has a scroll in his left hand and, as before, a dagger in his right.

I watch him carefully, but I am not trembling—I stopped doing that a while ago; indeed, I look the boy ruler straight in the eye, but in truth he seems calmer now: his eyes subdued and a little tired, his voice soft, even soothing.

"You said before that Cicero is a fool," I remind him.

"That, too," Augustus says with a slow nod, and I can hardly believe it: his eyes actually mist over and a tear wells up.

He walks off and I gasp, then don't even try to conceal my *reaction; indeed, I cannot help myself: As Augustus leaves the room, I laugh out loud.*

•   •   •   •   •   •

"So," announced my cousin Claudius Barnabas, "they say Pompey is finally rousing himself."

We were all in Curio's workroom, Claudius, Junius, Curio and myself, attending to a variety of routine matters.

"Yes, his extended period of torpor, marked, I must say, by a shocking degree of indolence and indecisiveness, may at long last have been terminated in favor of some hard work and important action," Junius Barnabas said.

For once, even Curio reacted: he looked up with narrowed eyes and a trace of a smile, then shook his head as if to ask, What did he say?

Well, the plain fact was that Pompey had taken steps to consolidate his political ties, strengthen his military command and place his own legions in Italy at a high state of readiness. Pompey, it seemed, had finally given up on the idea of compromise with Caesar.

"He's still fearful of Caesar," Curio said, "but he's finally decided that Caesar has just as much to fear from him—if he's ready."

"And now he is?" I asked.

"And now he is," Curio answered. "Or close to it."

"I understand Caesar's back with his legions now," Claudius put in.

"In Ravenna, yes," Curio said, "just across the Rubicon."

We all sat quietly, thinking over what it meant. "So . . . now what?" I asked. "A big clash between them?"

And instantly I thought: What a silly question that was. I had made a try for irony and only wound up sounding foolish, even disingenuous. Indeed, they all stared at me so sadly, though without anger; instead, just a trace of condescension, even sweetness, settled in their eyes.

And for once there was silence in that room—and not only because there was no need to correct or clarify my absurd understatement. It was also because none of them wanted to; none of them could bring themselves to utter the terrible words. For we all knew that if Caesar and Pompey ever fought in earnest, it would be far more than a simple "clash." There would, in truth, be only one way to describe it:

Civil war.

And the fury of that would shake the world.

★   ★   ★

The fact that Mark Antony was suddenly "in charge" didn't worry me especially. After all, he was merely the acting co-consul, sitting in for Caesar at his request, with specific powers at hand and tasks to perform. In other words, we were not yet a dictatorship, and Antony could hardly rule by dictator's caprice. In truth, as consul, being so much in the public eye, he had to curb some of his more indulgent behavior. So, as things turned out, he was, in a way, less dangerous now than before.

But Cicero was right: Antony was hardly a man to forgive and forget, and I had to be careful. Besides, if the burdens of his office made him less dangerous to me, the protections he now had as consul made me less dangerous to him.

★　　★　　★

"Antony's surely the murderer," Claudius was saying. He, Junius and I were in my study, and for once we were discussing this grim subject without benefit of wine.

"I believe that, too," Junius added, though with a slight ring of hesitation in his tone.

"Yes, I feel he's involved," I said slowly. "But something about it . . . I don't know. I mean, what's his motive? He'd have to be insane."

"Not really," Claudius said. He furrowed his brow and drummed his fingers on a little table beside him. "Let's say he kills Fabius in a lover's quarrel, then Flaccus Valerius for knowing too much. Then Lucius and Avidia start to uncover the truth, so he kills them. Laertes just happens to be in the wrong place at the wrong time, so what's one more murder. Of course, in a sense it *is* crazy. But not the way you mean: not madness, not lunacy."

"Mmmm," I said, rubbing my hands over my eyelids. "But what about those papers? Why was Lucius hiding them? And where are they now? That's what I mean: there's got to be more to it."

"Perhaps," Claudius said slowly.

"Mmmm," I said again. But even as I gave voice to my needling questions, there was never a serious doubt in my mind that Mark Antony was the killer—that either he'd done them himself, or had arranged them. My doubts, my questions, were all about how to bring him to justice.

142

"We need wine," Junius put in, and we all smiled.

"Not me, not for a while," I said. They both stared at me, and I said, "I told you why."

"Ah, yes," Claudius said.

"Oh, because of your wife?" Junius said. "Livinius, you shouldn't let your wife tell you if you can drink or not."

"No, no, it's not that," Claudius put in. The brothers looked at each other. "You remember what the doctor said."

"Oh, that's right," Junius recalled at last. For a moment he looked at me, red-faced with embarrassment, then apologized profusely.

I nodded with a smile, and then we shook hands and left it at that.

★   ★   ★

Of course, I had searched Lucius's room on the day of the murder, but it was a glancing look compared to what really was needed. I knew the room had been sealed since then, and when I finally could face it I decided to search it again.

I went to the house alone, hoping to be inconspicuous about it—or perhaps even to slip in and out without being noticed at all. But as I came up the stairs to the second-floor balcony, there was my Aunt Hortensia—waiting, almost as if she'd been expecting me.

"I just want to look over a few things," I said, trying to sound casual and even smiling a little. She nodded without saying a word, but kept looking at me oddly as I continued down the corridor. Indeed, as I pulled back the heavy bar and opened the door, I looked back over my shoulder and there she was, still waiting and staring.

Inside, the room was predictably warm and musty. I threw back the shutters, but the bright light only showed off the swimming particles of dust and the stale odor hung on stubbornly, despite a cool breeze.

I decided to get the worst of it over with: Taking a deep breath, I pulled back the bed covering. Naturally, it had all been carefully cleaned, but somehow, almost at once, I noticed two small spots of blood on the fabric. For a moment my head swam, but I shook it

143

off, and I even poked at the bedding and pulled up the cushions. But there was nothing more to see.

The worktable appeared completely untouched: there was his handsome stylus holder—part of a silver set I'd given him for his birthday a few years before—precisely in its place. There were his prized scrolls, Plato, Aristotle, Zeno, Sophocles, Plautus, Cicero, and many others, neatly stacked in the cabinet above.

Oddly enough, for the first time I realized that the stylus holder sat on the desk right next to a closed wax tablet. Why hadn't I noticed that before? I wondered. Well, for one thing, the last time I was here I hadn't even opened the shutters, so I could have missed it in the dim light. But even now, why didn't it leap out at me at once? I suppose because it looked so . . . well, so natural, as if Lucius were still alive and working, as if he'd simply stepped out for a minute and would be right back.

Yet another deep breath was required; then I opened the tablet and looked at the wax: it was empty except for three letters in the upper left-hand corner. The letters were *L-i-v*.

I felt a bit dizzy again, and that time I had to get off my feet. I sat down on the hard wooden stool by the table—I couldn't bear to sit on the bed itself—and kept staring at the impressions in the wax. What last message was he trying to send me? I wondered. Why wasn't it finished? Was it the last thing he tried to do? Was he, in fact, murdered as he tried to write?

It took quite an effort, but I forced myself to finish the search. I went through the sideboard and closet (all his clothes were still there, dusty but otherwise impeccably arranged, as always), then began the tedious hunt for a concealed compartment in the walls or the floor. After two hours or more, I finally found it in the floor, in the corner between the bed and the window. Carefully, I pulled aside the tile, then reached in and felt around, but there was nothing. Another empty hole, I thought. Another blank.

I stared at the tablet again. Has anyone else has seen this? I asked myself. It was hard to do, but I picked up the stylus and used the broad, flat top end to smooth down the wax; in a moment, the letters *L-i-v* were gone forever.

★　★　★

For an instant, as I walked down the long balcony away from my cousin's room, I caught a glimpse of my aunt. She had, it seemed to me, been waiting outside the entire time of my search, and now did not want me to see her anywhere nearby.

It wasn't hard to decide what to do next: I ambled along the balcony toward the front of the house, then crossed over the courtyard to where she and my uncle shared their corner suite of rooms. I knocked twice, then, getting no answer, let myself in.

She was all the way across the room, standing with her back to me, facing the large front window that overlooked the hills of the city and the tumultuous, ramshackle center of town. It was a commanding view of Rome, far enough away to feel a little above it all, but close enough to see and smell the grime that rose on dusty days, and even to feel a bit of the energy and grit and greatness. It was a view I knew well, from a time when Lucius and I were little children discovering the secrets of that rambling old house. Indeed, how many times had we played in these very rooms?

"Aunt Hortensia," I said, by way of greeting. But she did not turn to face me; as far as I could tell, she did not move at all.

I walked over and stood behind and a little to one side of her, just enough to see her face, so dark and sad and set as she looked out the window.

"Auntie?" I said. I hadn't really meant to, but there it was, flown from my lips: my little boy's greeting of years gone by.

Whatever my intentions, it got a reaction, all right. She actually flinched, then glared at me angrily. "So you've finally come to see me," she said. "Sooner or later, I knew you would." She turned away from the window, walked over to a nearby sofa and stretched out across it. I studied her carefully: the lines around her eyes were deeper than before, and her forehead was furrowed with worry; suddenly, she looked very tired and old.

"A servant told you, I suppose," she went on, her hands, as always, fluttering with the rhythm of her words and the tone of her voice. "We kept it secret for a while, or at least I did. But he blabbed, I imagine; men always do."

For a moment, I thought she might cry till I realized that she hadn't even come close and that she wasn't going to and, as a matter of fact, that she probably hadn't in many years. Had she

145

cried at Lucius's funeral? I wondered. I tried to recall, but the day was such a jumble in my mind that, truth be told, I had no idea.

"So what else can I tell you?" she said. "You probably know most of it, except . . . well, there is one new bit: I actually saw him yesterday, and, yes, he wants to see you, says he has something for you." She laughed miserably. "He's really something, isn't he? The son of a bitch."

By then all I was thinking was, How should I handle this? I had no idea what she was talking about. But should I tell her that? No, I thought, I must start getting to the bottom of all this, no matter what. So: be calculating.

I sat down beside her on the edge of the sofa and took her left hand in mine. "I want to hear all of it from you," I said, "from the beginning."

She shook her head. "Too painful, Livinius," she said and pulled away.

I stood up and paced melodramatically around the room. "Aunt Hortensia, I'm your nephew," I said, letting my voice break with emotion at just the right point. "And I was your favorite child's closest friend." I paused and took a heavy breath. "You have to," I added.

At that she shrugged and almost smiled. And I wondered: Is she on to me? But then: "I suppose I do," she said with a deep, dramatic sigh of her own. "Well, there's not much to it, really. I didn't love him, of course. But it had been going on nearly three years, so somehow I must have needed him. He was very manly in his way. I mean . . . well, just look at your Uncle Cornelius, for God's sake. He's not the mess your father is, but still . . . Well, anyway, it gave me an outlet, a change. And that's all it was, until all this terrible business happened. First, poor Lucius. And then *he* ran off, the S.O.B., and I didn't know why—I still don't, really. I mean, is there a connection, Livinius? And, as I say, last night he shows up and says he has these papers that might interest you. And, well, that's all of it—or all I know, anyway."

It was all I could do to keep from shaking; that is, I *was* shaking, but managing to hide it. As calmly as I could, I said: "And where is Telephus now, Aunt Hortensia?"

It was the first time his name had been mentioned, but it was nothing for her. Indeed, she answered at once, something about him being in the southern part of the city—"of course, the worst part of town, some awful slum." And, yes, she had the name of the street and the block for me.

Needless to say, I could hardly believe it; needless to say, once again that day my head was swimming, and, in fact, I barely heard her last few words.

"Yes, Aunt, yes," I said, or that's what I remember saying. Then, somehow, I found some papyrus and a pen and some ink, and I wrote down the name of the street. And then, honestly feeling as though I might strangle her if I didn't leave at once, I got out of that house as quickly as I could.

19

The big question was how to approach Telephus: should all three of us go, in full regalia—complete with fasces, of course—and attract undue attention? Or should I go alone, plainly dressed to avoid being noticed, but quite possibly putting myself in danger?

In the end, Junius and Claudius adamantly insisted on accompanying me, while I, just as adamantly, said the high-profile, official approach was absurd—that it almost certainly would scare him off.

"All he'd need would be a moment's warning to dash out some rear door or window," I said.

So we compromised: all of us would go, but quietly, wearing simple clothes and without any insignias of power. And, at Junius's suggestion, we added a fourth person to our group: He was yet another of our cousins, though a few years older, a fellow by the name of Avitus Lollianus Fino, a tough-as-nails legionary veteran of the German campaigns, short and squat and powerfully built, with a head of rock for punishment and the heart of a lion for courage. Indeed, though sometimes rash and explosive and certainly no big brain, our cousin Lollianus was neatly tempered by a well-honed and substantial portion of common sense. He was also, by the way, great fun to share a jug of wine with. All in all, he was a favorite of mine and an ideal person for the task at hand.

It was early evening by the time we got started: The sun was already glowing soft pink in the late-spring twilight; a slight breeze blowing up from the river carried a cooling mist, and for once there was a truly fragrant aroma of flowers and even a touch of mint.

We rode by litter down the slopes of the Quirinal and all the way to the Forum in the center of town. We disembarked around the corner on a quiet street, then dismissed the slaves and went ahead on foot. As always, heading south from that point into the flatlands of the city the odors were far less pleasing: sewage, urine, rancid olive oil, rotting garbage, dust from brick kilns.

On it went, past the tenement blocks, the people packed in. Most, thank the gods, were already indoors or preoccupied at that hour, too busy to bother with us—hauling water and food up four, five, six flights of stairs, eating their pork and cornmeal, drinking their cheap, bitter-tasting wines.

The smells are so different down here, I thought, and so are the sounds—that predictable drunken chorus of shouted accusations and complaints. Why is that? I wondered. After all, rich people argue and fight, and rich men beat their wives and children and have terrible problems of their own. Maybe it's just that there's so much more of it down here, all the people packed together, spilling out their open doors and windows, telling everybody their troubles, whether they wanted to or not. It was different in the rarefied greenery of the Quirinal and the other northern hills, where, I imagined, a man could torture and kill off every last member of his household and, quite possibly, not be found out till morning.

We passed through the slums into a factory district: iron forges and jewelry makers and wheelhouses and cart manufacturers and bakers and potters and who knows what else. To my surprise, the area still bustled: At many plants, slave laborers toiled into the night, while in apartments behind or right next to them, factory owners or managers were just joining their families for wine and dinner.

We emerged abruptly from all that onto a little street just off the Via Ostiensis. It was a mean little stretch leading straight to the banks of the Tiber and filled with the worst sorts of cafes and little gaggles of obviously disreputable men—toothless and unwashed and drunk and passed out in the gutters. They argued over money, or women, or nothing at all, and threatened each other with knives—all, quite literally, in the few moments we stood there.

I began to walk on, but Claudius grabbed me and pointed to a huge, crumbling structure right in the midst of it all: indeed, it was the tenement block where Telephus was supposed to be waiting. We had, I realized, arrived at our destination.

Despite the unsavory nature of the street, we decided to stick to our original plan: With all of us trying to behave as nonchalantly as possible, though still staying on our guard, Junius and Claudius walked twenty or thirty feet ahead of me, while Lollianus, bringing up the rear, kept at least that far behind.

We crossed the street and headed past the front of the building. Then, just as Junius was about to turn into the entranceway, one of the local hoodlums stepped out of some shadowy corner, said something I couldn't quite hear (Junius said later the man told him, "You're in the wrong part of town, my lord"), and brandished a knife. Claudius, who had drifted a few steps ahead, turned around just in time to grab the man's hand. I dashed up to help, but Lollianus raced past me with impressive speed, reached the man before I did and knocked him over with one blow. He then dragged him out of sight, and I heard a moan or two. After a moment, Lollianus emerged from the shadows breathless and perspiring.

"He won't bother us again, cousins," he said matter-of-factly.

I gasped in spite of myself, then just as quickly let it go, put it out of my mind. And all of us, bunched together tightly now, climbed the stairs in search of Telephus's rooms.

★   ★   ★

We followed my aunt's directions to the letter: We turned left coming off the stairway on the third floor, then headed down the hallway to the fourth door on the right.

I didn't bother to knock; I just let myself in, with my cousins right behind me. As you might expect, the room was dim and bare and dirty; what little paint there was was peeling, and behind the paint the walls themselves were chipped and crumbling. There wasn't much to show that anyone lived there, except a few nondescript pieces of clothing and, unbelievably enough, Telephus's telltale silver sash, or what was left of it, lying across the little bed.

Suddenly, we all looked around as the bulky, blocky figure of a large man filled the doorway behind us. "I've been expecting you, my lords," the man said, and I knew from the basso voice alone that it was Telephus at last. Then he stepped inside and into the tiny, flickering bit of light provided by the one small oil lamp in the room.

"And I've been looking for you," I said.

He walked over and sat down on the edge of the bed, the pale light reflecting off his unmistakable hairless dome. After a moment, Junius and Claudius sat down on the floor, while I grabbed a small stool, the only other place to sit. Lollianus agreeably remained on his feet.

"Sorry, there's no wine, my lords," he said in a lifeless tone. "Sorry there's nothing at all here, really. Just a place to sleep is all it is."

He looked around at each of us, his face a blank. Then he shrugged and stared at the floor.

"Why did you run away?" I asked him.

"Well . . ." he said with a heavy sigh, then stopped.

"Yes?" I said.

"Go on," Junius ordered.

"Well, my lord," he said, looking straight at me, "your cousin, Lucius Flavius, gave me these scrolls. He told me to take them to you, but just as I was ready to leave, you arrived at your aunt's house. And with her standing right there and you about to see your cousin anyway, I certainly didn't see the need to make any big display of handing them to you then and there. Well, a little while later the place was in an uproar. And when I heard someone say Master Lucius was dead, I was terrified. I . . . I suppose I panicked. So I ran off."

"And?" It was Lollianus, joining in the interrogation. Arms folded, he stepped up to the side of the bed and glowered down at Telephus. "Couldn't you have gone back?"

Telephus shook his head miserably. "That day I could have, I suppose," he answered, "but it was at least a day later before I could think straight, and by then . . . Well, by then, my lord, I was just another runaway slave. To show my face would have been to invite my own execution."

I had to admit it: he was right, of course. In fact, chances are he would have been put to death on the spot, even before I could have reached the estate to question him. Indeed, even as we spoke, he was in mortal danger because of his crime.

"So," I said, "let me have the papers."

The muscles in his neck jumped, and he looked up at me, obviously startled. "Why, I don't have them, sir," he blurted out.

Instantly, without the slightest hesitation, Lollianus grabbed him by the throat, lifted him up and threw him back with enormous force across the bed and against the wall. It was an impressive display of strength, for Lollianus was plainly the much smaller man.

"You told my aunt you had them," I said, "and if you don't have them, then why are we here and what's this all about, and, besides all that, where in hell are they?"

Telephus looked around at us again. His head had taken a hard knock, and he seemed dazed and a bit frightened. Lollianus hovered over him, hands up, ready to throttle him again.

"Please, my lords, no more of that," Telephus whined.

At a tap on the shoulder from me, Lollianus backed off a bit, and Junius and Claudius both softened their angry expressions.

Telephus shook his head and whimpered incoherently. "I don't know, I don't know," he squealed, or at least that was all I could make of it.

I stood there calmly, not saying a word, waiting, and finally Telephus composed himself enough to go on: "I never told your aunt I had them, sir, I swear it. I didn't go to see her about any of that; I just went to . . . well, to apologize . . . that is, for disappearing like I did. And, well, she happened to mention that you were looking for these papers. And I thought that was . . . Well, I thought it was odd, sir, and all I said was if you were looking for them, you should come and see me."

He stopped again, shaking his head as if he truly had nothing more to say.

"Yes?" I snapped, but he only looked back at me with a bewildered expression that was so annoying I felt like throttling him myself.

"Go on, dammit," I yelled.

"You mean . . ."

"I mean, you idiot, where are those papers?"

He stared at me, gulping air, and for the first time it seemed to me there was real fear in his eyes.

"What's wrong with you, man?" Claudius demanded.

152

"Come on, tell us," Lollianus snarled.

Telephus's mouth trembled, and once again he looked directly at me. "Oh, my lord," he said, then shook his head, gulped again and finally spat it out. "When I ran away, my one thought was what to do about those papers. So I marked them for you and took them to your house. I gave them to the man that greeted me."

"To . . . to whom . . . ?" I said, suddenly quite certain of the answer.

"Why, to your father, sir. I left the papers with him."

★   ★   ★

I felt the ground shake beneath me; I felt as if a hole in the earth would swallow me up; I felt as if I wanted to die.

"You're lying," Lollianus said, and began pummeling him again, enough to bloody his nose before all three of us jumped in and pulled him off. It was, I suppose, a tacit admission that I felt there was at least a little truth in the story.

Nevertheless, at Lollianus's insistence, we searched the room. We also, again at Lollianus's demand, stripped Telephus naked and searched his clothing and his person, but the papers were not to be found.

"He's lying, they could be anywhere," Lollianus insisted. "This man risks his life to bring us here; then it turns out he doesn't even have what we want. I mean, what's the point of it all? What's he up to?"

I nodded and turned to Telephus with a wicked little smile. "Why *did* you send for me, Telephus?"

"I . . . I thought to ask you for money, sir. Then, with all four of you . . . well, I . . ."

"You thought to rob my cousin if he came alone," Lollianus said disgustedly.

No doubt true, I thought, but I only sighed and shook my head wearily. "Enough," I said.

A moment later, as we finally left the room, Lollianus turned back and said, "Get out of Rome, Telephus! I see you again, I'll kill you!"

At that, I stopped, turned back myself and told him, "Good idea, Telephus. Leave Rome tonight. Don't let me see your face again."

153

20

Two days later my mother, my mother-in-law, my Aunt Hortensia and my wife Fulvia departed on their annual three-week sojourn to the waters of Aquileia in the north of Italy. One day after they left, I took the opportunity to invite my father to dine with me in the private dining room of my house high on the green slopes of the Quirinal Hill.

"Father," I said, and greeted him with an affectionate hug.

"Good to see you, boy," he answered.

It was to be a simple meal of roast beef, fish, pork, bread, broccoli and oysters, and, just after he arrived, I dismissed the servants for the night so we could help ourselves in private.

"We do this much too seldom nowadays," he said (as if we had dined together so frequently in the past!), and slapped me convivially on the back. "Father and son, happily together; no women around: Perfect!"

As usual, he had already reached that very pleasant place between sobriety and drunkenness which every true drinker knows so well and craves so dearly: his eyes warm, his smile serene, he fairly glowed with happiness—or what he took to be happiness.

Nevertheless, I had laid on plenty more for him, of course, and I poured him a gobletful even before he sat down.

"Yes, Father, I agree; we should do this more often," I said, and smiled my best. Needless to say, my little touch of irony escaped him completely.

★　　★　　★

"Do you remember," he was saying, "the time at Tivoli? Your mother was so angry with me. She thought I had taken up with the housekeeper, or some maid or other." He downed the remains of yet another goblet—his sixth, I think, but who was counting—and laughed uproariously. "Ridiculous, of course."

By that time quite drunk despite a fair-sized dinner in his belly, he slapped me on the back again and gave my shoulder a friendly squeeze. "Wonderful wine, Gaius," he burbled, and poured himself a refill.

"And then . . . well, there've been so many upsets with her: like when she thought I was sleeping with that fat senator's wife in Capua; and the time she nagged so much I got too drunk to attend that dinner . . . What was it? Oh, yes, the Lawyers' Guild banquet." He paused, literally out of breath from laughing, and wiped the jolly tears from his eyes.

"Women!" he said. "Always taking nothing and making it into something. An extra drink or two; an innocent smile at a pretty girl. The next thing you know, the end of the world: accusations, recriminations. Scandal, divorce."

He stopped and shook his head, then sighed with exasperation. "All so unnecessary, I don't know why we put up—"

"But you did fuck that maid at Tivoli," I interrupted. And, of course, he stopped dead in his tracks. He looked at me with the expected expression of shock and outrage on his face (if for no other reason, because of my coarse language), then spoke with such tiresome predictability:

"How . . . how can you say that, Livinius? Why, I never—"

"I saw you, Father," I said, and that time his jaw honestly trembled with surprise. "I was eleven years old, and I was exploring that house, and I stumbled into the wrong room, and there you were—"

"Well, what in hell were you doing there!" he fairly exploded, then glared at me with self-righteous anger. And it was all I could do to keep from grabbing him by the throat.

"I saw you, Father," I said quietly, and after a moment, even deep in his alcoholic haze, he backed down and said nothing; even he had finally gotten the point.

But he was far from beaten; oh, no. After a moment to recover, he raised his eyes, shed a tear or two and said, "So, this is why you called me here: to humiliate your own father, eh? Well, all I can say is, it's a pretty pass, indeed, to be turned on by your own son."

I looked at him with a bit of a smile on my face, but there was nothing to say. Well, there were things I could have said, of course, but none of that really was the point, after all. None of that really had anything to do with why I had asked him to dinner at my house.

"You have something that belongs to me, Father," I said.

He narrowed his eyes at me and slowly shook his head. "I don't know what you mean . . ."

"Some papers someone left with you about three months ago."

He opened his mouth and closed it, then as always recovered himself and forged on. "Look: First, you start making wild accusations about some whore I supposedly 'fucked,' as you put it, ten years ago in Tivoli; now you say I'm stealing documents of yours? Well, I'm not going to stay here and be insulted all night."

He stood up and turned to leave, but I grabbed his toga before he'd gone half a step and pulled him firmly down on the sofa beside me.

"Remain seated, Father," I said in a tone that was just above a whisper; indeed, I was hoping to achieve a kind of quiet menace that would get results without shouting. But it didn't work.

"Take your hands off me, you—"

He struggled to squirm away, but I clamped my left hand around his right wrist and actually put my other hand over his throat. "Remain seated!" I said at the top of my voice. And then, at last, he drew back quietly.

It was, of course, a horrible moment for me, to physically interfere with him in that way. True enough, it had been a long time since I'd felt any real respect for him, and I didn't even like him anymore. Nonetheless, there was still a powerful bond.

"I know you have them," I said, still shouting, "but *I* have to have them. They belong to me, and—"

"But I tell you, I don't. I mean, who told you such a thing?"

"Father . . . please?" I shook my head wearily. "The man who left them with you. Uncle Cornelius's doorkeeper: Telephus."

"Ah," he said, and that was all he said. Except he suddenly cast his eyes downward, and the muscles in his neck pulsed in silent embarrassment.

"Hmph," he said after a very long pause. Then: "Can I have another wine, Gaius?"

"Oh certainly, Father," I said, my voice slow and syrupy.

"Now don't get sarcastic with me, boy—"

"Shut up!" I said. And, to my great surprise and satisfaction, he did so at once.

★　　★　　★

". . . and anyway, Telephus didn't *leave* them with me, the scoundrel," my father was saying. "He *sold* them to me. A thousand sesterces—that's what I had to pay."

I was freely feeding him wine, indulging his thirst and egging on his sanctimonious blathering.

"Can you imagine? This doorman; this slave. Thinks he has something of value, and right off he's demanding money. Well, I told him a thing or two, I can tell you." Another big gulp; another refill. "Of course, I paid him in the end. Had to, you know. But nothing like what he wanted. I talked him down and talked him down till he begged for mercy. No wretch of a slave ever saw the day he could get the best of old Livinius Decius Severus. Eh, boy?"

It was entirely beside the point, but somehow I couldn't resist asking: "How much did he want at first?"

"Oh . . . well . . . I can't recall, really." He cleared his throat several times, shifted in his seat and finally answered: "Thirteen, fourteen hundred, I suppose."

And I thought: Talked him down a whole four hundred, eh, Father? Well, you're some bargainer; yes, you are.

"That's right: got his price down where it should be. I mean, I told him, 'These papers belong to my son, Livinius. And you'd just better hand them over, or you're in serious trouble.' So he listened to reason."

He smiled in my general direction and swallowed several more times, until yet another goblet was drained.

"Do you know what's in the papers?" I asked, my tone as soothing as a summer breeze.

He looked at me oddly as I offered another refill. "Oh, Livinius," he said with a shake of his head. "What do you take me for? I didn't read them; I wouldn't do that. So of course I don't know what's in them."

I waited awhile, actually taking some pleasure in this unusual form of interrogation, which, it seemed to me, consisted mostly of keeping your mouth shut while the other fellow talked. It also helped me ignore the pathetic parts and focus on the funny stuff, of which there was a considerable amount (all of which, I'm certain you have noticed).

"I knew they belonged to you," he continued. "I assumed they were important. As far as I was concerned, that was all that mattered."

Oh, of course it was, Father, I thought. But all I said was, "I need to see them, Father. I need to see them now—tonight."

"Mmmm," he said, and grabbed the nearest jug of wine. I waited again, and he began humming some tune or other. I waited longer, and after a while he started to hum something else.

"Father, I'd like to start getting ready. I know it's late, but I'll summon a carriage, and we'll go over to the old house—"

He looked at me with a cockeyed expression and even a bit of a smirk. "What for?" he asked, with a shrug.

"Why . . . to get them," I said. "To get the papers."

"Mmmm, yes, it would be nice."

As you can imagine, it was a struggle to maintain the calm demeanor which I had played so hard at all evening (or, at least, since my blow-up much earlier). "Father, it's so important. We really must get those papers as soon as we can—right now, if possible."

"Fine, Livinius, fine," he growled, and glared at me with implacable fatherly irritation. "Keep interrupting our evening together. 'The papers, the papers.' That's all I've heard all night long. Yes, they're important; I know that. Yes, you should have them, I agree. But for God's sake, I can't help you: I don't have them anymore."

★ ★ ★

I poured him wine till he passed out dead drunk, then had two slaves carry him down the hall to a small guest room with orders not to let him leave for any reason; I also gave instructions to wake me at dawn.

As soon as I was up, I sent messengers to my two lictors, Junius and Claudius Barnabas, as well as to my other cousin, Avitus Lollianus Fino. By the time I was dressed and bathed, they had arrived at my quarters; we then woke my father up, dragged him from his bed and, with all official sanctions at my command, proceeded with him as our virtual prisoner down the slope of the hill half a mile to our old house—the house of my childhood.

My father kept babbling his objections until finally, my patience running low, I made a fist and punched him quite hard in the forehead, and he shut up at once. Then, with Junius carrying the fasces, we entered the house and began the search.

We planted my father in silent humiliation on a hard, wooden stool, then literally tore the living quarters apart: his bedroom, my mother's room; his study, their sitting room. We pulled out drawers, tore open cabinets, stripped frescoes away, pried up tiles, scraped the floor for secret holes. I even sliced open sofa cushions and punched holes in the walls of his water closet. All the while, he sat silent and downcast, and in the end we found nothing.

Exhausted, I took a moment to catch my breath, but it did nothing to calm me down. To the contrary, my rage seemed about to boil over, and, true to form, my father picked that very moment to turn up the heat. "How much more of this am I supposed to put up with?" he suddenly demanded. "A son dragging his father through the streets, searching his father's house. Oh, the shame of it all, too horrible to—"

At precisely that instant, I'd had enough: Horrible though it was, in a moment of blind fury, I flew at him, knocking him off his stool, pinning him to the floor and placing both my hands firmly around his throat.

"Where-are-they-you-son-of-a-bitch!" I yelled, banging his head against the hard tile in time with my words.

"Aaagh," was all I heard him say, and then I felt my cousins pulling me off. "By the gods, Uncle Decius: tell us where the papers are!" Claudius insisted as he and the others held me back.

"Crazy . . ." my father panted, struggling for breath. Then he slowly gathered himself together and struggled up from the floor. "All of you—crazy," he said, leaning against the sideboard behind him.

While Lollianus held on to me, Junius and Claudius gently took my father by the arms, led him across the room and sat him down on the edge of the sofa.

"Please, Uncle Decius," Junius said, with a real quality of entreatment in his voice that I'd never heard from him before.

I studied my windbag cousin a moment and thought: Maybe it's only the way he looks nowadays that makes his tone *seem* more enveloping: his beard dark and thick and full, and those broad, bushy eyebrows, which suddenly seemed so endearing. In fact all that growth helped soften the somewhat hard, even pompous, jawline for which he'd been famous. Now, in truth, it was his eyes that dominated, glowing warm amidst the shrubbery. Yes, I thought, it is a hairy face, but also a friendly one.

In point of fact, even my father seemed taken by it. He stared up at Junius, especially at those eyes, as if he would find redemption in them, while the rest of us, knowing better, merely waited for him to speak at last.

"I sold them," he said.

"What?" I said. But, of course, I'd heard him; we all had. It was simply that words of such import, spoken so simply and softly after such a long wait, usually need to be said more than once.

"Back to the same man," my father said. "To Telephus."

He slumped forward a bit, his face in his hands. And I thought: If it were anyone else he'd be weeping by now, but not my father. He'd forgotten how long ago; I knew that well enough—except when he was very drunk and could still manage an alcoholic tear or two.

"When?" Junius asked.

"Day before yesterday, it was. Early morning. Telephus showed up, said he finally had—"

He cut himself short and gazed downward, clearly hoping no one had caught the blunder.

"He finally had what?" I asked him from across the room. Then I walked slowly over and stood above him. "Finally had a buyer? Is that it? Naturally, you'd been trying to sell them all along; naturally, you never intended to give them to me. Papers from your own nephew addressed to your only son."

I started to say something else, but for some reason couldn't; I

160

tried again, but still the words wouldn't come. And finally I realized my face was wet with tears and my voice choked and I stormed wildly out.

★ ★ ★

Of course Telephus was no longer in his tenement rooms. I made it all the way there on foot, starting out alone from my father's house—though I soon noticed my cousins trailing behind me.

We pounded on his door, then kicked it in, but the rooms were empty, stripped even of the few possessions that had been there before. We raged up and down the corridor, banging on all the doors: People filed out, angry and defiant at first, then scared and submissive after a glimpse of the fasces.

"Gone, my lords," said one old woman who lived in the room right next door. "No idea," she said when we asked where.

Everyone had the same answers: they barely knew Telephus—he'd only been there a few weeks. Indeed, they had no idea where he'd come from in the first place, let alone why he'd left so suddenly, or where he was now.

"People come and go down here," the old woman said with a grim smile, and a few others chuckled nervously.

We fanned out through the building. Lollianus took the floor below, and Claudius the one above, while Junius and I, staying on the same floor, knocked on the long row of doors on the other side of the entranceway.

We returned a few minutes later, frustrated at finding nothing again. We came across the narrow connecting walkway that led over the stairwell to the side of the building where Telephus had stayed, then turned down the corridor, heading toward his former room. And there to my amazement, just a few steps beyond it, stood a dozen heavily armed men in full battle regalia. With them and definitely in command of the squad, complete with his tribune's brown sash across his chest, was Mark Antony himself.

As we walked toward them, I saw Junius straighten himself and check the fasces to make sure it was prominently displayed. Just then, Lollianus, having finished his own inquiries, came stepping up beside me.

"Greetings, my lord Livinius Severus," Antony said with exaggerated formality.

"Yes," I said, nodding my head slowly for effect. "Greetings."

"I understand," Antony continued, "that you have been questioning the people of my district—these people"—and with that, he waved his arm grandly to indicate the score or more who now stood about gaping at us with wide, curious eyes—"regarding the whereabouts of a certain . . . Telephus? Is that his name?"

"Quite so," I said. "Telephus."

We had continued walking toward the room, and by then stood only a few feet from Antony and his thugs.

"You remember him, don't you?" I said. "The man with the silver sash, the man you liked so much. Or, at least, you liked him in your bedroom."

"Surely, my lord, you must know it is unlawful," Antony went on, smoothly ignoring my little jab, "to question anyone of the plebeian class without first consulting the tribune for their district."

"Telephus was hardly plebeian," I said. "Plebeians are free men and worthy citizens of Rome. Telephus was a runaway slave, and in the matter of a runaway, the rule you quote does not apply."

Antony nodded and worked his jaw in obvious annoyance; then, to my surprise, he slammed his fist very hard against the nearest wall. "My lord Livinius, spare me the technicalities: your inquiry is over."

"Antony—" Lollianus started to say. He stepped in front of me, and somehow I knew instantly what he was going to tell him: He would actually have challenged Mark Antony to a fistfight ("Just the two of us," he would have said, which, indeed, he admitted to me later on). I watched the men around Antony pull themselves to the ready—indeed, I saw the little smirks on their faces. So I quickly put a calming hand on my cousin's shoulder and, thank the gods, he stopped and took half a step back.

Antony and I stared at each other in silence a moment. Then I said: "Mark Antony, you cannot impede this investigation."

"Think not?" He laughed, and his men chuckled appreciatively.

"Your office can only immunize you from so much," I went on. "There are things so terrible that even a tribune can be brought to justice."

"Are you talking about me?" Antony said, laughing again.

Just then, Claudius came running up, leaned close and whispered breathlessly, "I've just bribed someone: they told me where Telephus has gone."

"Where?" I asked, and he whispered the answer.

"Ravenna?" I blurted out, and looked up quickly enough to see Mark Antony turn dangerously red. "That's where—"

But Claudius wisely squeezed my shoulder as a warning to keep quiet, and I stopped short before I yelled that out as well. For, of course, Ravenna was where Caesar waited with his legions of men.

★   ★   ★

By the time we all reached my house, it could fairly be said that I had unraveled a little.

Actually, it was more than a little. Actually, I was crying and shouting to the effect that nothing ever worked out right, and now how would I ever avenge my cousin, and, besides that, why in the world had Telephus gone to Ravenna, of all places?

My cousins helped put me to bed, but I kept on ranting, and they finally insisted that, as a start, I abandon the doctor's recommendation at once.

"That doctor's mad, I tell you," Junius insisted. "Believe me, nobody ever got his wife with child by *not* drinking. If anything, it's the other way around."

"You'll have some wine, by Jupiter," Claudius put in.

A minute later there was Lollianus handing me a full goblet. And with that my experiment in abstinence came finally and abruptly to an end.

★   ★   ★

I don't know how much I drank that evening, though I know it was a lot. I also know it didn't help much: Rather than getting quieter, I simply grew less coherent, and, through most of it, I still felt tears in my eyes.

"The nerve of Antony," I babbled for the fiftieth time. "And that no-good Telephus . . ."

I raved about them and whined about the lack of progress in the case. But not once did I mention my father and his role—which, almost certainly, was what had sent me over the edge.

"You need Fulvia," Claudius said suddenly. "We'll send a courier for her. We'll have her back in no time."

"No!" I shouted drunkenly, though it was the most sensible

163

thing I'd said in a while. After all, she wasn't due to be gone that long anyway, and sending a courier now would shorten the time by only a few days. Besides, the urgent call would terrify them, and then they'd all come rushing back—Fulvia, my mother and the rest—to a situation which, in any case, they were powerless to ease in the slightest.

"No," I said again more calmly. And then I turned over on my stomach and settled my mind enough for sleep with thoughts of Fulvia, who, of course, I needed at that moment more than anyone in the world.

★　★　★

"Hello, my child" came the sweet, unmistakable tones.

For an instant I thought I was dreaming. Then I looked around, and there he was, sitting on the edge of the bed: Cicero, in the flesh and smiling.

"Praise the gods," I said. Then I sat up beside him and put my head on his shoulder while he held me in his arms. "Beloved master," I sobbed.

"I understand," he said more than once, "how hard it's been."

"My own father . . ." I hiccuped.

"Yes," Cicero said. "They told me."

We sat like that a long while, he and I alone (as my cousins had gracefully withdrawn), until finally I calmed myself and the weeping subsided.

"Enough," Cicero said, gently pushing me to arm's length. "Time to harden yourself to the world."

I thought: You're hardly one to talk, Cicero, as delicate and sensitized as you are to every shifting breeze.

"Though I'm hardly one to talk," he said, "as sensitive as I am to every little change around me."

"Is there anything you don't know?" I gasped. And then we both smiled and even laughed a little.

★　★　★

"You have forgotten your mission," he said in a teasing manner.

"What's that?" I said. I grinned back at him, feeling almost my usual self.

"I told you a long time ago upon whom to keep an eye," he said

164

with ludicrous formality. And in spite of everything I laughed out loud.

"You mean Curio? It's been almost three years, for God's sake. And really," I said, "he's not *that* interesting."

"Oh?" Cicero said, and wagged his right forefinger at me.

"But master," I said, my tone suddenly quite serious, "I must find out who murdered my cousin, Lucius Flavius. And now," I went on, "I'm more certain than ever that it was Mark Antony."

Cicero rubbed his chin and nodded slowly. "That could well be," he said. "Antony's certainly . . . well, he's not a nice man." He stared off a moment, apparently mulling over an idea. "What about this Telephus—he's gone to Ravenna, eh?"

"Yes," I nodded.

"Well, who knows?" he said slowly. "Maybe there's something to it." Then, with the unmistakable air of a man who is both exhausted and resigned, he shook his head and clasped his hands together. "Look, Livinius: both camps are armed to the teeth—Pompey on one side, Caesar on the other. And Rome, the republic, caught in the middle." He paused and rubbed the fingertips of his right hand along his forehead. "And of course there's this investigation of yours: I don't mean to make light of it; I know you loved your cousin, and I know there've been other murders, besides. But somehow . . ."

He trailed off, looked at me, then held his hands over his eyes, and for the first time that evening, I was able to study him a moment. Truth be told, he looked terrible: old and tired and sick, with hollow spots in his cheeks and circles under his eyes and wrinkles everywhere.

In a way, it was no surprise: I knew—everyone in Rome knew—that our descent toward tyranny was sucking away the very lifeblood of his being.

". . . somehow, there is . . . well, I hesitate to use so strong a word as 'connection.' But I have a feeling—and I don't know why, so don't ask me to explain it—but once again I urge you to keep watch over Gaius Scribonius Curio."

I shook my head and thought it over. "Curio," I mused. "I've watched him so carefully for so long. He's hardly pure, master, hardly an innocent, as I've told you before. But an involvement with all this? A connection? To me, quite frankly, it seems absurd."

Cicero smiled—a great, deep, wide smile from the depths of his heart—and hugged me again. "Of course," he said. "Absurd. I'm an old man now, and I only suggest; I only indicate. Orders and commands, even recommendations, are beyond my feeble jurisdiction. But I can remind you, and that much I do: the republic is in danger; you are in danger. And Curio, as always, is your best and easiest access to the heart of it all."

He looked me over carefully through misty eyes. Then, once again with fatherly affection, he took me in his arms. "I love you very much," he said. Then he let me go, stood up and walked quietly out.

21

Cicero was right about one thing, of course: the breaking point was near. Pompey had agents everywhere, trying by whatever means possible to build up the number of troops under his command; what's more, he held two legions loaned to him by Caesar the year before, and now contemptuously refused to send them back. As for Caesar, his agents made much of his claim that he waited at Ravenna with just one paltry legion, but fresh reports, almost by the hour, said two more were on the march from Gaul and would join him shortly.

So where would all this leave our exhausted republic? What would become of elections and free speech? What about fair play and equality before the law? And, oh yes, foremost in my mind: What fate awaited that legendary hallmark of Rome—the swift and merciless rewards of justice?

*   *   *

I slept soundly and awoke feeling thoroughly recovered. I fairly leapt from bed, hungry as a bear, and found my cousins lounging in the breakfast room over eggs, oysters and fresh cakes.

"You look rested," Claudius Barnabas said with a teasing wink.

"Yes, very much so," I said.

They all glanced at one another, then at me, smirking. "You should," Junius said. "It's just at midday."

I opened my mouth and closed it, then felt a blush coming on; indeed, it was the latest I'd slept in years. "Well . . . you know . . . the benefits of rest and all." Then I served myself a heaping plate of eggs and sat down with them.

"Don't you believe it," Claudius put in. "Nothing like a little exhaustion to reveal your innermost soul, eh?"

"Oh, shut up," I said over a mouthful of food, and they all laughed. "Besides, I've had enough meaningful talk and deep thoughts to last quite a long time. From now on, I'm strictly superficial."

"Shallow, through and through, eh, Gaius?" Junius said, and we laughed again, except for Lollianus Fino who suddenly looked deadly serious.

"Well, I don't believe that, Gaius—not about you," he said.

And I thought: By the gods, I love this man for his sincerity. "I don't believe it either, cousin," I answered at once and looked him straight in the eye, for I never played games of that sort with Lollianus. For one thing, he didn't understand them too well, or at least he didn't appreciate them. For another, his straightforwardness was too rare and precious to toy with. And, if all that weren't enough, just remember this: my idiotic contention about turning over a new leaf was, of course, entirely untrue.

As you might expect, the Barnabas brothers were never so quick about knowing when to stop, and now their eyes were glinting with some clever new trifle.

"So enough silliness," I snapped before they could say another word and take things a step too far. And then they took the hint and kept quiet while I ate.

★　★　★

All that week Scribonius Curio had been asking us to come back to work for him. "Crisis imminent; need you now," he'd written in one urgent message. "Big new speech in preparation; need your help," said another. And there were several more along similar lines.

"So while I finish up here, why don't you two go over to his house and see if he still needs us," I suggested with a smile to the two Barnabas brothers. They dutifully left at once, but came back in less than an hour.

"The house is closed," Junius said. "The doorkeeper says Curio's gone to Tivoli, supposedly for a rest."

"But naturally he's probably there to consult Pompey again," Claudius added.

"Naturally," I agreed.

I had just finished bathing and was stretched out on a long massage table that was covered with hot towels. As we talked, two slaves wiped me down and sprinkled me with oil.

"We should go, Livinius," Claudius said. "You heard what Cicero said, that Curio—"

"Yes," I interrupted. "I heard what he said; I didn't know everyone else heard it as well."

Claudius turned a little pink around the ears, and Junius nudged him with a hard elbow to the ribs. "Ouch!" Claudius said. "What in hell . . ." Then he punched Junius in the stomach.

I looked around in time to see Junius double over with pain, while at that very moment Lollianus Fino stared at them both with a look on his face somewhere between amusement and disbelief. And I thought: Junius and Claudius are certainly intelligent enough, they've been extraordinarily loyal to me and, in their own way, they are lovable. But then and there I knew once and for all that no matter how hard I tried I would never escape the fact that they were two of the most peculiar people I had ever known.

"Cousins!" I said, a bit too loudly, and they both stopped their antics and looked at me, blushing. "It's all right, cousins," I said more calmly, then waited a moment to let them settle down. Then: "As I was saying, I know what Cicero said, and I have immense respect for his opinions and his insights. Therefore, we are going to Tivoli for an appointment with Curio. Or at least some of us are."

All three of them stared at me then, as I paused to mull it over. You see, I actually had no interest at all in following Curio, but I suddenly realized that his trip was the perfect opportunity for me, at long last, to engage in a minor subterfuge of my own.

"I want the two of you to go," I told Claudius and Junius. "Of course, you should arrange to see him as quickly as possible and find out all you can about what he's thinking and doing—but of course you know all that. So here's the tricky part: when you reach him, tell him . . . let me see. Well, tell him this: tell him I got word at the last minute that my wife is ill, and that I rushed north to Aquileia to see her. Yes, yes, that's perfect. Tell him that. That Fulvia's ill, and I went north to see her."

They kept staring at me blankly, until Junius finally said, "But she's not ill, is she?"

"No, of course not."

"Well, then, where are you—"

"To Ravenna, of course; that's where I'm going."

And then, in an instant, it all came clear to them.

★   ★   ★

Junius and Claudius left for Tivoli that evening, while at my request my cousin Lollianus Fino joined me for the journey north.

We left the following dawn, and despite riding day and night on the fastest horses we could find, it took us five and a half days to reach the outskirts of town. We found an isolated spot with a nearby stream to bathe in and camped there for the night. Then, well washed and refreshed, we entered the city gates early next morning.

"Papers, my lords," a guard asked us. I flashed him a bit of my green senator's sash, while Lollianus pointed to his legionary epaulets, and the guard quickly waved us through with profuse apologies. Then we turned in our horses at the station just inside the walls and continued on foot.

Ravenna was bustling, all right, though not bristling—which surprised me. For I'd expected a veritable armed camp of a town, filled with soldiers and heavy arms and supply trains and checkpoints every street or so. Instead, there were only scattered handfuls of soldiers out and about—and that on market day when you might expect them to pack the town.

What there were were vendors—vendors on every side, with, I might add, a quite remarkable array of goods: There were litters (with accompanying slaves, of course) to rent by the hour or the day; there was a huge variety of food, most of it of surprisingly high quality, including olives from far-off Iberia, figs from Sicily, and several sides of beef that would be the envy of any butcher in Rome. There were silver trinkets from some remote place called Britain; there were silk gowns and lip rouge from the mysterious Orient; there were even stalls of local speculators offering land for sale or houses for rent.

One man—a land agent, I'm sure—looked straight at me with the eye of someone practiced in spotting strangers and shouted,

170

"Ravenna, city of the future." And at that particular moment, the point seemed hard to argue.

After asking around discreetly, we learned that Caesar's encampment was about a mile outside the town, and that he cleverly rotated leaves so that no more than a hundred or so of his soldiers were ever inside the city at any given time.

Thus, as it turned out, Ravenna was enjoying the best of all possible worlds: wartime prosperity without a war—and without even the inconvenience of having large numbers of loutish soldiers set loose among them. It had been more or less that way, a few men told us, for a solid year or more. So I suppose it was understandable if just about everybody in town had reached the same conclusion: that their decidedly temporary way of life had somehow become permanent. Or at least that impression of permanence was what they seemed to be trying to sell to unsuspecting visitors.

Once done with our initial inquiries, we adopted an even more discreet posture, for we certainly didn't want to alert Telephus (or anyone else, for that matter) to our presence. Of course, we had an advantage: we were on the lookout, whereas he would probably feel safe enough and not be quite so alert.

Lollianus and I moved through the market; then, as that thinned out, we walked the streets with our eyes peeled. As we neared the fringes of the town center, we came upon a short block of unsavory-looking inns and cafes, and decided that could very well be the right place to look.

While I stayed out of sight as best I could (without looking too ridiculously suspicious), Lollianus prowled the area, wandering into the likely spots, until an hour or so later he returned to find me languishing near the side entrance of some especially filthy hotel.

"I've seen him, cousin; I couldn't miss that big bald dome of his," he said, smiling with relief. "He was in that tavern . . ." He pointed across and down the street a ways to a place with a bright yellow door that was on the ground floor of an inn. "Yes, that one, Livinius. He was in there with some people—I didn't recognize any of them. He was drinking, of course, and I overheard him make an appointment for this evening, at a place outside the town, out by the army camp, where all the soldiers go. Then he left the bar and went to his room. He looked drunk and tired, as if he'd been up all night. My guess is he'll sleep awhile now, then go out to the encampment later on."

I nodded slowly, rubbed my chin and grinned back at him. "I see," I said, then added: "Well, that's excellent work, cousin." For I knew how much Lollianus appreciated a little praise when it was deserved. And indeed this was—for he'd accomplished a bit of spying that neither I nor my other two cousins could have managed. And it all had been done, I might add, without even having to ask for Telephus by name—an action that could have put both of us in grave danger. I also congratulated myself, as it confirmed my judgment that Lollianus was the best possible person to have taken along for this part of the investigation.

"So I gather you don't think we should question Telephus now," I said. "You think it best to follow him later and see what he does?"

"I do, indeed, Livinius," he asserted.

Again, I nodded slowly and smiled, for there was no longer any doubt in my mind. After all, I'd heard an authority in his tone that he generally saved for his time in the army, and I thought: If he's that sure about Telephus, then so am I. And with that, the matter was decided.

★   ★   ★

The saloon at the edge of Caesar's camp was pretty much what we expected: a large, noisy room filled with rowdy, drunken soldiers. The place stank of spoiled wine, vomit and urine, and most of the soldiers smelled the same way.

"Oops," said one stumbling legionary, just as we walked in, then fell face-first over a large, round table halfway across the room. The place erupted into jeers and laughter, which was perfect timing for us, as it caught everybody's attention right at the crucial moment of our entrance.

Lollianus went off to buy a cheap jug of red, while I looked around. By the time he rejoined me, I'd spotted Telephus with three other men on a long couch next to a food table.

"Now what?" Lollianus murmured.

I shrugged. "You know any of the men he's with?" I asked, but my cousin just shook his head in silence.

We found two seats just near enough to watch him and sipped our wine nervously. After a few minutes, while I still pondered what to do, Telephus began elaborate farewells to his companions, then slowly stood up and finally left by himself.

We followed at a discreet distance. He turned left out the front door, then left again and headed up a path that led in the direction of the camp itself a few hundred yards away. It was pitch-black out, with no moon or stars, which helped to conceal us, but also made it hard to keep Telephus in sight. It also slowed the pace, as we struggled to avoid stumbling in the ruts and holes along the way.

The torch lights of the camp were soon in sight, and then we were there, trailing Telephus through the squads of men, some already asleep in the open for the night, some still gathered at their fires. He made his way past the plain soldiers to the little tents of the junior officers, then on to the more elaborate affairs of the senior commanders. Finally, he turned into the fanciest of all, a large tent draped with some regal-looking banner that I couldn't make out in the dark. He nodded at the dozing sentry, then went inside, while Lollianus and I stopped a short distance off—again, not sure what came next.

After a moment, I gestured for Lollianus to follow me, and together we crept very carefully to the rear of the tent. It took a little while, but I finally spotted a half-open flap, just big enough to slip through. We both went in, me first, then him, very slowly, without noise, and found ourselves in a tiny, darkened alcove with the main part of the tent stretched tight in front of us and voices close by. Lollianus pointed to a small shaft of light along the bottom, and we both dropped quietly to the ground, then eased the bottom edge up just far enough to see inside.

There was Telephus, all right, talking to some man with his back to us whom I couldn't quite see. "This is excellent," I heard the man say after Telephus finished. Then the man stood up, walked over to a sideboard and poured himself some wine. When he turned around to retake his seat, I had, for a moment, a perfect view of his face:

It was Gaius Scribonius Curio.

22

Lying there still and breathless in the darkness on the ground, I suddenly felt my cousin's hand on my shoulder. It was of course meant to comfort me, to signal that he knew how I felt, and to be brave in the face of it. And I was grateful. But whether intentionally or not, his gesture of reassurance also told me how shocked, even frightened, he was himself at the sight of my old mentor in such an unexpected place.

What had Telephus just told Curio? I wondered. Or, perhaps more to the point, what precious papers had he just handed over? I listened as closely as I could, but heard only intermittent phrases, and from what I could tell their conversation had dribbled down to nothingness—the smallest of small talk. I heard Mark Antony's name two or three times, followed once by raucous laughter; I even heard my own name once, followed by a chuckle or two. But that was all of it.

I thought: This goes nowhere, and for us to stay here grows more dangerous by the minute. I was about to signal Lollianus that it was time to get out, but right then there was a sudden flurry of activity. I heard boots clomping on the ground, as if a squad of soldiers had just come up, and then some commander or other stepped inside the tent. He looked around, then pulled back the front flap to admit someone else. And in another moment, sweeping in and exchanging greetings all around, was none other than Julius Caesar himself.

Lollianus gasped, and then it was my turn to give a touch of reassurance. For my cousin had served under Caesar in the German campaigns, and from what I'd heard had been quite a favorite of his commander among the up-and-coming junior officers.

For my cousin's part, he fairly worshiped Caesar—though needless to say he did so without considering any of the political aspects. He worshiped him for his military prowess, though whether he knew it or not he was certainly swayed (as were so many others) by Caesar's remarkable personality.

Indeed, watching him now (ironically, more closely than I'd ever been able to before), I began to see why. There was, for instance, the way he looked: A figure of ramrod-straight posture standing a half head taller than most other men, he could be described as forbidding in appearance. Yet all that was softened just enough by a grand and amiable smile, and by clear, knowing eyes that were somehow more patient than probing, more enveloping than intimidating. There was also the way he moved—he seemed almost to glide into the tent; and the way he behaved—the easy, gentlemanly manner in which he addressed all the men with him, even the sleazy runaway Telephus.

I suppose it goes without saying that neither Lollianus nor I could take our eyes off the scene unfolding in front of us. Curio and Telephus both leapt to their feet as Caesar entered. Caesar embraced Curio as he would a long-lost friend and gave a courteous enough greeting to Telephus, who was then quickly ushered out.

"Old friend," Caesar said to Curio once they were alone, and he hugged him again.

"My lord and master," Curio said.

And with that I felt a jolt of what I can only call pain—actual, searing pain across my forehead and a peculiar constriction in my chest. I wanted to cry; in truth, I wanted to die. And not long after I realized that something had died inside me that night, some last shred of boyish trust, I suppose. And I decided I would never again allow myself to be completely won over by any one man.

After that greeting, their voices dropped again to a soft murmur, inaudible except for an occasional word or two: "speech"; "very important"; "too generous"; "old fool"; "Pompey." Who could tell what it meant?

175

We lay there, not daring to move, barely breathing, for hours longer. Indeed, Caesar and Curio were dozing on their sofas when there was a new rustle of activity, and then yet another figure of some importance was ushered very swiftly into the tent and through the main area—into a small side portion straight across from where we were.

An aide gently shook Caesar awake and led him into the next compartment, and I could hear the faintly muffled voices of Caesar and this other man, first exchanging greetings and then in animated conversation.

With Curio still dozing, I took the moment to gently squeeze my cousin's arm, and he moved slightly to show me he was still awake. Meanwhile, Caesar's discussion with this other man seemed to be taking forever, and I could feel a familiar predawn chill creeping into my bones. I shivered from the chill, but also from the knowledge that we had to make our escape soon or risk being spotted in broad daylight.

Finally I heard what sounded like muttered noises of farewell, and Caesar soon was edging his way out, then standing in the opening between the two divided areas of the tent. Then at long last he stepped out of the way and let the other man move into that opening so I could finally see his face, and it was another horrible surprise; in a way, I suppose it was probably the most horrible of all: it was my father-in-law, Victorinus Avidius.

"When is it, Curio—a week from tomorrow?" Avidius asked in a booming voice.

"Yes, sir," Curio replied at once.

"Well, make it a good one, young man," Avidius said. "It'll change the world, if it's right."

"I know, my lord," Curio said, and they all laughed. "I'm sorry, sir; I mean, I know how important it is. So don't worry: I promise it will be my best speech ever."

★   ★   ★

We gave Avidius time to get clear of the camp. Then, with Caesar and Curio finally asleep for the night, we crept out of there. We took the long way around the rear perimeter, somehow found the road and made our way back to Ravenna.

Dawn was just breaking as we reached the town center. We

found a respectable-looking inn, banged on the door till the owner awoke, then gladly paid him double rates for his best rooms. Moments later, we were in our beds and sound asleep.

We awoke in late afternoon, sent for a huge dinner and stuffed ourselves, then promptly fell asleep again and didn't wake up till dawn the next day. Besides the obvious, which was that we were both exhausted, it was a definite plan of mine to take our time leaving town. That way, I hoped, we would avoid any accidental meetings on the road with either Curio or Avidius, but would still get back to Rome in time.

That was my hope, anyway, and it worked rather well, though not without one close call. Lollianus and I were both on horseback, without insignias and in very inconspicuous clothes, at a highway horse station about a hundred miles from Rome when Curio pulled in amid a considerable fanfare of elaborate carriages and a train of slaves and supplies. Another similarly fancy setup was already waiting at the front of the changing station, and it turned out to be my father-in-law's. As he emerged from the little inn to resume his journey, Curio actually yelled out his name in greeting. Avidius flashed him a quick, dark-eyed look, then went on his way, ignoring him. To my considerable amusement, Curio simply had to endure it with the look of a man who'd just committed a faux pas, tasted dirt in the aftermath and didn't much like it. Meanwhile my cousin and I, sitting right there with our dark capes pulled around us, went completely unnoticed.

To that point I had studiously avoided burdening my mind with any of the obvious questions. But seeing that little exchange, I could no longer help myself. So, I wondered, what's Curio playing at, anyway? And what about Avidius? And what was behind that whole incredible rendezvous in Ravenna? Of course I didn't spend too much time mulling it over. After all, what was the point— especially with Rome so near. For in fact this time I felt quite certain that Rome for once would have all the answers.

★   ★   ★

We reached the city gates at noon on the day of the big speech and went straight to the Senate building at the south end of the Forum. Lollianus said he would wait outside for me, and I headed off, just in time to join my esteemed Senate colleagues as they filed inside with a rare air of urgency about them. I saw Junius and Claudius, also waiting in the outer plaza, and I waved and smiled at them.

The first news I heard as I entered the chamber was that two major bills had already been defeated. One, demanding that Caesar lay down his arms, had been passed by the Senate but vetoed by Mark Antony. The other, telling Pompey to do the same, had been voted down by the Senate itself. Now Curio was about to give his opinions on the topic, and in point of fact that is exactly who I bumped into next.

"Your wife is well, I trust," he said, greeting me warmly. "I heard she was ill."

"Yes, she's much better," I said, trying not to sound flustered or surprised, though naturally I was both. So let me see, I told myself: Curio's probably been back a full day, so . . . of course—that's it! He's had plenty of time to talk to my cousins, or, for that matter, to talk to anyone they talked to at Tivoli.

"Well, exciting times coming," Curio said. "Today will be my most important speech of all."

"That's wonderful," I said with a smile.

Then we both took our seats, and the Senate quickly came to order. Curio was recognized soon after, and at last the time had come for him to tell us all what was really on his mind.

Or so it seemed.

* * *

"Most revered Senate Fathers," began Gaius Scribonius Curio, "I speak today amid the greatest crisis to afflict Rome in many centuries. All our freedoms, all our grand institutions, are in grave danger of being overwhelmed by a rising tide of rivalries among our most powerful men, and by their flagrant use and abuse of unlawful force and violence. This has come in many forms: gangs of thugs; armed sentries; the call for more and more legions and legionary veterans to join one side or the other. And now even praetors and other officials of the highest ranks have been seen moving through the streets of this city wearing the military cloak—in defiance of the constitution, the Twelve Tables and all known ancient practice.

"I say 'rivalries among our most powerful men,' but with apologies to my esteemed Senate colleagues—to Cato and to many others who are here today, there are really only two men to seriously consider, only two men who count:

"On the one side we have Pompey, the veteran of our eastern triumphs, encamped in the Roman suburbs amid a growing military force. And what does Pompey want? Well, he says he wants the Senate and the people to rule. But each day his words and the words of so many of our senators are increasingly so similar that it is harder and harder to tell where his rule ends and the Senate's begins. Pompey says he wants to be fair to his rival, but he won't send back two legions which he 'borrowed' from him more than a year ago. And each day he issues new calls for this rival of his to disband his armies and return to Rome as a private citizen.

"Pompey says that he is not ambitious, that he does not crave power, that he does not desire to assume the role of dictator or king. But each day he levies more soldiers to fill out the ranks of his legions, and each day he issues some new decree, legally or otherwise, to enhance the limits of his own discretionary powers at the expense of senatorial prerogatives.

"So much for Pompey.

"On the other side, we have Caesar, Pompey's rival and the veteran of our northern triumphs, encamped at Ravenna in his province of Cisalpine Gaul three hundred miles to the north, and also among a growing military escort.

"And what does Caesar want? Well, of course he also says he wants the Senate and the people to rule. He also denies that he is ambitious, or that he wants to be king. Of course, Caesar also contrives the words of a few senators now and then, and he also has more troops of his own on the march to join him at Ravenna.

"But in all this, what has Caesar demanded? Well, if he is not demanding, it has been argued, he is certainly defiant. He defies the Senate's demand, or is it . . . well, whosoever's demand it is . . . to return to Rome without escort or insignias or official status of any sort. That particular action, or inaction, of his is unlawful—there's no doubt of that. But as a practical matter we can clearly imagine him frightened by just the faint possibility that he might face unlawful actions of another sort should he agree to that demand. Certainly he has not demanded the presence of any of us at Ravenna, and certainly not as private citizens. Certainly, should he issue such a demand, none of us would go. If we did, the courts would no doubt judge us to be lunatics and hold us in stocks for our own protection.

"So, to get back to my question, What has Caesar demanded? Well . . . nothing. At least, *not until now.*"

Curio stopped then, deliberately and for effect, and the senators, who had already been paying very close attention, found themselves with that last remark fully riveted upon Curio and his words.

"Yes, yes. I have it on good authority. And I offer the proposal now, and it is simply this: that Pompey stop levying new troops, *and* that Caesar send his legions back to the northern frontiers where they belong. In other words, Senators, *both sides* must disband their armies at once! Senate Fathers, it is just that simple, for it is our only hope. It is the only way in which our freedoms can be saved and the only way that the Senate and the people can remain in control of their own affairs and destiny. Thus I urge you to approve this bill with all possible speed."

The senators' reactions began even before Curio could finish his last few words. There were what sounded like groans of protest at first, but those were soon drowned out by a round of applause and then a veritable eruption of approving cheers and shouts.

I joined the throng, clapping with the best of them, though even in that din I could hear lonely Cato raving: "How can you promise that? It's a fraud, I tell you. A sham and a fraud!"

Even so, within minutes the Senate had overwhelmingly passed the bill and issued the call for both sides either to disband their legions, or to move them to less threatening ground.

"Rome is saved!" many of the senators kept shouting, even as they filed out into the Forum and the nearby streets. And I thought: Why not? Why can't it happen? Why shouldn't it come true?

★　★　★

By the time the Senate adjourned, the Forum was filled with a multitude of cheering Romans from all parts of the city. I looked for my cousins but couldn't find them right away, so I simply walked off by myself toward home.

I made my way unmolested through the northern parts of the city and soon found myself puffing up the last few yards of the

Quirinal Hill. I walked through the outer gates and the courtyard of my house, then pushed open the front door without waiting for the footman. But the moment I stepped inside I knew with a start that something was different—something was out of place. I looked around: all the baggage scattered about, all the women's clothes. Then, an instant later, even before I clearly understood what had happened, there was Fulvia coming toward me across the atrium . . .

"I missed you so . . . much . . ." "And I missed you . . ." "Oh, my beautiful, beautiful . . ." "And you, my handsome darling . . ."

And there we stood, in front of a dozen slaves, wrapped in each other's arms, smothering each other with countless kisses and caresses. Oh, the smile on her face; oh, the glow in her eyes; oh, the magical softness of her skin. I felt the touch of her cheek—oh, how silken it was—and listened to the musical lilt of her voice. And I thought: Oh, the whole elegant, magnificent feeling of her softly, curvingly, perfectly shaped body melting into mine . . .

"We can never be apart again . . ." "No, never again, my sweet . . ." "I love you more than I can say . . ." "Yes, my dear, darling man . . ."

We walked with languid steps, half coiled around each other, to the master bedroom. I gave orders to close up the house for the day—indeed, that we were not to be disturbed for any reason. I had a bath drawn and some figs and other fruits stocked up for later. Then I bolted the door, and there I was at last, alone with my wife in my sealed bedroom.

"By the gods, you are wonderful," I said.

I took her face and held it gently between my hands, then kissed her softly—first on the forehead, then on the tip of her nose, then once on each cheek, then on the lips. Those lips! Pale, fluttering, voluptuous. I ran the tip of my right forefinger over them, then kissed them again. And again.

By that time she was nearly undressed, and I knew if I got one look at those . . .

"Wait . . . *please* . . . I'm so dirty, Fulvia, just let me take a bath . . ."

"Impossible!" she giggled, then stripped off the last of her undergarments and lay face down on top of me, and there were those firm, delicate, perfectly proportioned breasts. I softly pressed my mouth over one, then the other, kissing the nipples, licking them. A moment later I carefully rolled over to my right so we were more nearly side by side. Then, like so many times before, we coupled with such natural ease of movement that it was as if the gods had placed us in the world to love each other like this forever.

As always, it was a grand finale; as always, I felt that a dozen of Caesar's legions could not shake the world in quite the way that Fulvia did for me.

We lay there, gazing into each other's eyes, giggling like children. *"Now,"* she said with a burst of her famous laughter. "We bathe."

"We?" I said.

So, I thought: yet another surprise in a week of surprises. And for a change it's a very fine one, at that.

★　　★　　★

The warm water crept over us like velvet as we sank slowly into the tub together. Sitting opposite, we wrapped our legs around one another; we played and kissed and splashed, and, oh, yes, even washed each other.

After a while, Fulvia turned her back to me and pushed softly against me. I put my arms around her waist, put my legs around her legs, and we leaned back in the water, feeling clean and rested and very much at peace.

"I love your long arms," she said, rubbing her hands over my wrists and forearms. "And I love your pale, beautiful chest," she said, turning her head briefly and running her tongue over my right nipple. "And your tiny waist, and those long, beautiful, muscular legs. But most of all, I love your enormous . . ."

And with that, she deftly turned over, slid down the length of my body and put her mouth over my most private part. And before I knew it I was stiff and wide and very, very long. (Yes, it's true: that is an asset of mine which I have modestly concealed until now.) And then there was the inevitable result. Even as that happened, Fulvia kept her mouth where it was much longer than I would have expected. But then again (as those few days kept proving over and over), what is life without surprises!

182

"By Jupiter, Fulvia," I said when I finally was able to say anything at all.

"Oh? Do I shock you, my husband?"

I shook my head and smiled. "Well I suppose so, but pleasantly so. Very pleasantly."

"Yes, very pleasantly. That's what I thought."

We added fresh soap and washed again, and then at last we climbed from the tub, dried off and crawled into bed, clean and naked and wonderfully tired out.

Even so, we made love again, but still couldn't sleep, and it was then that I decided to tell her everything I'd been keeping back for so long—about the murders, about my investigation, about who was, or who might be, involved. Other than my embarrassing encounter with Mark Antony, I left nothing out: I told her all about Lucius and what he'd been doing, and about Telephus and my aunt, and about Fabius Vibulanus and Avidia Crispina and Flaccus Valerius, and about seeing Caesar and Curio during my trip to Ravenna, and about making up an illness for her as an excuse to leave Rome.

"I hope my father didn't hear that by accident; he'd be upset," she said, and I flinched. For that had never occurred to me, and I suddenly felt quite certain that by now he and Curio almost certainly had discussed it. Besides . . . well, as I'm sure you can guess, that was the one other item which I did not tell Fulvia—that I had seen her father with the others at Ravenna.

"We should send him a note right away, especially since I came back early," Fulvia insisted, but I managed to put her off.

"I'll . . . tell him all about it," I stammered. "I'll be seeing him soon enough. Tomorrow, I'm sure. I'll tell him it was nothing, a false alarm."

"Oh?" she said, and studied me a moment. "Won't you be telling him everything you told me?"

"Well . . . eventually, but I don't . . . need him to know I've been to Ravenna—not right now, anyway." Then it was my turn to study her, and when she stared off blankly, I asked: "Is that all right, Fulvia? You'll let me handle it, all right?"

Abruptly, she seemed to focus her thoughts anew and looked at me brightly. "Yes, of course," she said. "Whatever you think best."

"Good," I said with a smile. Then, a moment later, I had a sudden thought: "By the way, just why did you come back so soon?" I asked her. "I thought it would have been at least a few more days."

"We kept hearing rumors about all the troubles," she said quite matter-of-factly. "We didn't want to get stuck up there, get cut off from Rome. Besides, I'd had enough of healing waters for the year." She looked at me and laughed. "A bath with you, my husband—that's all the healing I need."

23

"What *is* this?" Fulvia insisted.

We'd slept awhile, then awoke and decided to munch on some fresh figs and peaches. We quietly ate two or three apiece. Then, still hungry, we brought over the whole bowlful, set it down between us and went on eating with long, slow bites. When the bowl was empty, Fulvia got up and carried it back to the food table, then, a moment later, crawled back into bed and suddenly began squirming.

"What in the world . . ." She reached around behind her. "It's like a . . ."

"What?"

". . . a lump. It's . . . crunchy."

Finally, she stood again, and I reached over and patted the cushion. "Hmmm, there *is* something . . ."

I reached across to her side of the bed and pulled back the covering, and there, just beneath the upholstery, I could definitely feel it. I looked closely at the spot and saw a neatly cut slit that had been hastily resewn in large stitches with thread that didn't match. I worked my fingers among the stitches, got enough of a grip and tore it open. Then I reached inside:

There was papyrus there, all right—in fact, what felt like quite a bulky roll of it, too big to pull through the slit without tearing the paper. I got up, walked over to my closet, took out a convenient dagger and brought it back to the bed. Then I carefully cut a much larger slit, reached inside again and finally eased the document out.

Actually, there were several scrolls, starting with a very short one: One glance told me who'd put them there.

"It's from Lucius," I said, and Fulvia jumped. "By the gods," she murmured.

And I thought: In my own bed—that's where he hid them, that idiot. But I simply shook my head and even smiled a little.

"To my beloved cousin, Gaius Livinius Severus," the first scroll began, but right then I was cut short by a sudden commotion in the outer corridor. I grabbed my knife and stepped between Fulvia and the door: There were great crashing and scuffling noises coming from outside. Then, a moment later, the unruly little crowd broke through the lock and burst in. It took a while, but I finally realized, to my considerable embarrassment, that the first two men were my cousins, Junius and Claudius Barnabas. An outraged footman came right on their heels, and a moment later four more burly slaves in various stages of undress rushed in, wrestled my cousins to the floor and pinned them. Both the cousins were screaming bloody murder, the servants were understandably breathless, and all at once my peaceful bedroom was a madhouse.

"It's all right," I shouted, then had to say it twice more just to get myself heard above the din. For the slaves were ready to throttle the cousins: one even had an ax at the ready.

"This looks familiar," I said, quietly taking the weapon in hand. "Isn't this . . ."

"They tried to kill us, my lord," one young slave insisted, nodding in the direction of the ax. "We told them you weren't to be bothered, and then they hurled it at us."

"From the fasces," Junius said with a gasp, for he was thoroughly winded and most likely a bit frightened, as well—or at least I hoped he was. "The birch rods weren't tied right," he went on. "We lowered it and it flew out."

"The ax itself?" I said. *"It flew out?"*

I put my upper teeth over my lower lip in a biting motion to try and keep from laughing. I turned and saw Fulvia doing the same thing, and when she saw me, it was too much for her: she fled at once to the water closet, where, I surmised, she would either calm herself or laugh to her heart's content.

"The birch rods weren't tied right?" I said with a shake of my head. "Is that what you're telling us, cousin Junius?"

"My lord, I think punishment is called for," another slave grumbled.

"Oh, by the gods, get them off me," Claudius whined.

I took a heavy, exasperated breath and rolled my eyes. "Well, we won't kill them—not now, anyway, not tonight." To my considerable satisfaction, the slaves all picked up on the spirit of the occasion and laughed wildly.

"You son of a bitch," Junius yelled.

"Shut up, Junius," I said. And he shut up—which, believe me, was the only thing for him to do at that particular moment.

Finally, I decided it would not be especially useful to drag things out any longer. "It's all right, let them go," I said. "They'll behave after this."

The slaves backed off, and I thanked them all profusely for a job well done. I also handed a gold talent to each and promised them a double ration of wine for the rest of the week, and they all smiled and bowed their way quickly and quietly out of the room.

"Kill my slaves with a defective fasces, will you?" I fairly bellowed, the instant the door was firmly shut. "You idiots," I yelled, then, at last, indulged myself and laughed out loud.

"Please, Livinius," Claudius began, "this is—"

"Oh, it better be," I cut in. "It better be *damned* important."

By then, Fulvia had come back into the room, dressed in a tasteful nightrobe. The two blockhead cousins, struggling up and still straightening themselves as best they could, smiled and greeted her with groveling politeness; she smiled back—though I could see she was still trying to be polite and not laugh.

In the meantime, I had sat down on the bed again and was holding the scrolls from Lucius in my right hand, glancing absently at the first page.

"So what is all this?" I insisted, then glared at them when neither of them answered. "Well!"

"We searched Curio's house," Junius finally said.

"Night before last," Claudius continued.

I looked at the pages in my hand, then looked up at my cousins, suddenly feeling terribly, terribly tired.

"And?" I said.

"We found it," Claudius said. "A big treasure chest filled with silver."

"And?" I said again.

"Best we could tell," Junius went on, "it was at least ten million sesterces worth."

"Oh," I said, then thought: Just ten million, eh? A paltry sum. Why, with prices what they are, you couldn't buy, say, more than the twenty biggest houses in Rome with ten million. Or maybe you could outfit one Roman legion. But what good is that? I mean, of what use is one lonely Roman legion nowadays?

Well, I just sat there and shook my head, too exhausted for the moment to absorb this stunning new bit of information brought to me so dramatically by my two silly cousins. So I simply went back to what I'd started to do before being so rudely interrupted. I started reading the scrolls from Lucius all over again, though this time I read them out loud:

" 'To my beloved cousin Gaius Livinius Severus," I began.

"In case something happens to me, I hope you won't have much trouble finding these. They contain what I believe is the entire and accurate story of who murdered Fabius Vibulanus. It turns out to be at least as important as either of us could have imagined, probably more so. Even I could not have foreseen all the entanglements that will be set in motion by the denunciation of the perpetrator of this crime—so you are herewith forgiven whatever lapses you may have shown."

Thinking of Lucius, I paused and felt a lump in my throat. Indeed, I trembled as it slowly sank in that I was holding in my hands the closest thing to him, to his being alive, that I would ever hold again. How odd, I thought, to be reading such things and thinking about how much you loved the person who wrote them—loved him enough not even to mind this written proof of his petty vanity. Then again, I asked myself, how could I mind when it was true: he had been smarter than all the rest of us put together.

"I believe this report [I read on] will answer all your questions, about the crime itself, of course, but also about why I did not keep you more fully informed of what I was doing and what I was learning along the way. As will be obvious enough by the time you finish, keeping you in the dark has turned out to be entirely point-less and is a decision I deeply regret. In any case, I trust it will not be necessary for you to be reading these without me—that, indeed, we will be working on all of it together before the day is out. So I remain your loving cousin, Lucius Flavius Severus."

That concluded the brief introductory scroll, and just as well, for we were already a bit misty-eyed and in need of a break. Besides that, the cousins were squirming in their seats, obviously bursting with some new tidbit.

"There's something else—" Claudius began.

"Oh, all right," I interrupted with a sigh. "Just what was it that made you search Curio's house?"

"There were rumors," Claudius said.

"Yes, we'd heard them all week," Junius added.

"Rumors?" I said.

"That Curio had taken a bribe," Junius said.

"So we decided to see for ourselves," Claudius added.

"Bribe from who?" I asked.

The Barnabas brothers looked at each other, then at me. "Why, from Caesar, Livinius," Claudius answered, as if all the world were well acquainted with this fact. Then, quite suddenly, he lowered his eyes and his tone grew soft and even a little ashamed. It was as if the enormity of what he was telling me had only just now occurred to him.

"So you got in there—into Curio's house?"

"Yes," they both said. "And we found the box," Junius went on, "behind a sealed-off partition in his bedroom."

"More silver in it than I've ever seen," Claudius said.

For a moment, they both sat silent—an unusual pose for them. And I knew that quite possibly for the first time in their lives they were really struck by the importance of something that was taking place outside their own little world.

"Well, you're both very brave to have done that," I said, "and I apologize for the trouble earlier. You were right to come."

I paused and rubbed the tips of my fingers over my forehead, trying to gather my thoughts. "You said there was something else, Claudius," I said at last.

He looked at me blankly a moment, then suddenly remembered. "Oh yes," he said. "Well . . . as I say, there'd been this rumor about the bribe. So taking Curio's disarmament proposal to be a trick to gain advantage for Caesar, Cato and the two consuls, Lentulus and Marcellus, led a deputation of old-liners straight out to Pompey's. They've given him a special mandate and the whole treasury of Rome if he needs it to levy all the troops he can all over Italy."

"By the gods," I muttered. "But that's—"

"Completely illegal and unconstitutional," Claudius put in. "Yes, we know."

Again there was a terrible moment of silence. "So that's it, then," I said with a defeated shrug. And I thought: So all our chances have run out, after all.

"Yes," Junius said. "It's war with Caesar."

"It's civil war," I said, and burst into tears.

★ ★ ★

The report from Lucius was contained in several long scrolls. Fulvia and I read them one by one, then, as we finished, passed them to the Barnabas brothers; it took us till dawn to read them all. And this, written in my cousin Lucius's own hand, is what they said:

From the moment Avidia Crispina approached us to investigate the murder of her friend, Fabius Vibulanus, I felt it was a matter I should handle without you. I hate to have to tell you this, but you see, I had already found out about your unfortunate encounter with Mark Antony. Even worse news, in a way: it was your father (who else?) who told me. He was drunk (naturally!) and—again this is painful to confess—there were several other people there, as well. Your mother was one, and there was my mother. There was also my friend (later my fiance) Matidia Gratus, along with our cousin Avitus Lollianus Fino, and a woman friend of his.

Luckily, *my* father wasn't there (though he was supposed to have been), or of course the episode would have been the talk of Rome.

So there were no real blabbermouths present, and everyone agreed wholeheartedly not to repeat a word. Needless to say, your mother was mortified at the disclosure, my own mother is generally discreet enough, Matidia certainly is, and Lollianus, I believe, is a basically closemouthed person (who, by the way, thinks the world of you) and is unlikely to talk out of turn. I know nothing about the woman who was with him; in fact, I can't even recall her name, but Lollianus assured me it would not be a problem, and as far as I know he was correct in that evaluation.

All that aside, I felt your 'encounter' with Antony could pose a problem for you in pursuing the investigation of the murder. First, I believed it might be hard for you to be objective—indeed, that you might quickly form unfortunate prejudices against a particular person or persons. Second, I felt your involvement could bring about an awkward, or even scandalous, situation for you, especially if word of your encounter suddenly (and, as always, inexplicably) spread through the city. And third, because of your experience I simply believed that it might be too painful for you to deal effectively and conscientiously with a matter of this sort.

So I handled it alone, and I don't mind telling you I missed you very much; I missed your wit, your directness and above all your common sense—your ability to cut to the heart of the matter. One more point: while it's probably unnecessary to mention it, let me assure you that there was never any romantic involvement between Avidia and me, and I apologize if I misled you into thinking there was. But obviously it was an easy excuse to keep you out of it.

Now to the crime itself. The story of what happened is based largely on statements by Avidia Crispina. But at my insistence we interviewed numerous people who could corroborate what she had told me. Of these people, only one, a childhood friend of Avidia's by the name of Annia Regilla, was of noble patrician birth, and was, therefore, easy enough to find.

All the others were disgraced freedmen, discharged servants, runaway slaves and the like. And the search for them took a long time and led us into contact with a number of noticeably disreputable people in some of the seediest districts of the city. Essentially all of them—the Regilla woman, the ex-slaves and all the others— were people who simply had overheard some or most of Fabius's conversations with Avidia, and therefore could support what she had told me.

Avidia herself, though she wanted the crime solved, gave her answers slowly—only after long and careful questioning.

"But it's so personal and so painful," she would say. Then she'd pout awhile and fidget with her long blond hair.

She's quite a pretty girl, and, true enough, I am fond of her, but, as I say, not in the way you imagined. In any case, she'd say, "Please don't make me tell you about that time, Lucius." But I'd coax and wheedle and cajole, and finally get it out of her.

"It all began soon after Fabius made the acquaintance of this Gaius Scribonius Curio," was how she put it. "Suddenly, I hardly saw him for weeks. He was out late every night, sleeping most of the day. When he did get up, he'd have a hangover and showed little enough interest in me. He'd tell me little bits here and there, about the big houses he went to and the famous people he met. He said Mark Antony was the most famous.

"This went on for several months," Avidia told me, "until one night he came home looking especially ragged. I asked him what was wrong, and he started to cry, which truly shocked me, because Fabius was a very cool and collected young man—that's one of the qualities I loved about him—and he wasn't much given to displays of emotion, like so many Roman men. I was very tender with him, and finally he told me. And oh, Lucius, it's so terrible. Do you really need to know?"

"Yes," I told her, most gravely, "I do."

"Well . . . it seems that he got especially drunk that night, and . . . well . . . he and Mark Antony had sex together. And he really couldn't believe he'd done it—he was so ashamed. Of course he could never face Curio again, that much was certain. Or at least that's what he insisted at the time.

"Anyway, Fabius survived the embarrassment—we both did. And after two or three weeks, suddenly one morning a messenger showed up at his house with an urgent call from Curio, of all people. So after talking about it with me and thinking about it most of the day, Fabius finally went to see him. Curio apologized profusely for involving him with Antony and said he needed a bright young fellow like Fabius to work for him, so would he please do so—and, by the way, there would be no more of those wild parties.

"So the next thing I knew, Fabius was working for Curio, helping with his speeches and pamphlets and such. Fabius said it was exciting work, that he thought Curio a fine man and a dedicated republican. And it all went on like that happily enough for three or four months, until one evening he came home looking white as a full moon in winter. Well of course something else had happened, and this time it was *really* terrible.

" 'I overheard a conversation, Avidia,' he told me, his hands trembling as he downed a full goblet of wine. For it seemed that quite by accident, he'd heard Curio and Mark Antony talking in the next room.

"According to Fabius, Curio was saying: 'Well, Fabius is the last; I won't send you another.'

" 'Oh, come now,' is how Fabius said Antony answered.

" 'No, I mean it,' Curio said. 'It's too embarrassing—too much potential for scandal. Besides, after what happened that other time, with that boy Silius. I mean, pederasty is one thing—'

" 'Hah!' Fabius heard Antony snort. 'You certainly should know.'

" 'Yes, well, all that aside, pederasty is one thing, but murder is quite another.'

" 'Murder!' Antony thundered. 'Why, you know damn well it was an accident.'

" 'Look, my friend,' Curio said, 'the boy was fifteen years old. He was found with a piece of glass up his—'

" 'All right, enough!' Antony said. 'I was drunk; things got out of hand. Besides, he was only the nephew of some ex-slave.'

" 'Yes, I'm aware of that; that's why we were able to hush it up so easily,' Fabius heard Curio answer. 'But I won't take any more chances. Things are getting too . . . critical. Too tense. A thing like this could bring down Caesar himself. Ruin everything we've worked for.'

" 'Hmph,' Antony snorted. 'Caesar, eh? You're suddenly so worried about Caesar. At least I don't need big bribes to buy my loyalty.'

" 'Oh, please. Caesar's been paying off your gambling for years.

193

And your other debts! Why, your butcher's bill alone is bigger than any so-called bribe I've ever seen. Don't tell me about bribes.'

"Well, at that point," Avidia told me, "Fabius said their voices were suddenly much louder. And then, the next thing he knew, they simply wandered into the workroom, where he'd been all along. Fabius said they both stopped and stared at him with amazed expressions on their faces.

" 'I thought you'd left for the day,' Curio told him.

" 'I just had a few more things . . . I'm leaving now,' Fabius said he managed to blurt out. Then he got out of there as quick as he could and never went back. A few weeks later, he was murdered in that terrible way."

And that, my beloved cousin Livinius, is the essence of Avidia's story. As I say, I confirmed it with a dozen others—piecing their accounts together, for nobody had heard it all in one lump, as she had.

I also checked the records and found an unsolved murder of a couple of years earlier, apparently before Curio had gone out to Asia. The victim was the son of a freedman with the name of Silius. And he was found in that same way, with that same sort of stab wound in the chest and that same inflammation.

Livinius, I spent a great deal of time and effort trying to find eyewitnesses to Fabius's murder, or to the aftermath—that is, someone who might have seen the body being left in the alley, or even the body being dragged toward the alley; anyone who actually saw anything. I even tried to find a witness to the rather long-ago murder of the Silius boy. But despite a very thorough and strenuous search, I never found anyone. Regarding Flaccus Valerius, all I ever learned was what Avidia told me: that Flaccus was a friend of Fabius who may have talked too much in the wrong places and got himself killed in the process.

Thus, what we can prove in the courts is one thing; what we can surmise is quite another. Of course, we have Antony's own testimony—although indirectly—about the murder of Silius (his claims of an accident being specious, I'm sure). And Avidia is eager to offer her own account. As for the murder of Fabius, as I say, we can offer only conjecture, though any reasonable man would agree that Antony is the prime suspect. And, ignoring for the moment the rigid legal standards of the courts, any reasonable man would pronounce him guilty on the spot.

In any case, that is *my* conclusion: that Mark Antony murdered Fabius Vibulanus.

Naturally, I'm expecting to talk with you about all this in person very soon—within a day or two, at most. In the meantime, I will look into just one or two more very minor loose ends, so I've hidden these papers in your bed (hah!) for safekeeping. (For a while, I had kept them in Matidia's room, but decided to move them just the other day.) When I'm finally ready to see you about all this, I'll probably send you another set by messenger—probably by my attendant Laertes, or by my father's doorman, that bald Telephus, just in case.

So be seeing you soon, and again please forgive me for keeping you in the dark for so long; I'm sure you understand, and I trust you agree that my intentions were the best.

Your most loving and affectionate cousin, Lucius Flavius Severus

Exhausted, I lay back across the bed, Fulvia beside me, and there was a long moment when I felt as if I might never move again; indeed, opening my eyes, gazing at the ceiling, the room spun and there was a pounding inside my head not unlike the beating of a drum.

"So terrible," Fulvia murmured, and wiped away a tear.

"Oh, Jupiter," I heard myself say, and then felt my own eyes misting over yet again.

The next thing I knew, Junius and Claudius were standing over me, each taking a hand of mine and gently pulling me up. "We need you, Livinius," Junius said. "Yes," Claudius added.

"We know we're foolish at times," Junius said, "but we want to help as best we can."

"But we need your strength," Claudius said. "And your clarity of vision," Junius went on.

"All right, all right," I said, sitting up on my own. "Don't lay it on too thick."

They both stared at me, mouths open. Then I laughed, and they laughed, too.

Just then another commotion erupted in the hallway, though

195

not nearly as noisily as before. That time, I was simply too tired to grab a knife or do anything at all, so I just sat there; of course, my cousins simply sat there, as well, following my lead.

After a moment, a footman entered the room and, though looking a bit frazzled at the edges, announced in his most formal manner: "My lord, your cousin, the honorable Avitus Lollianus Fino."

"That's fine," I said, even as Lollianus came in right behind him, followed in turn by two more of my men. "It's another cousin, so it's all right," I said, and they all withdrew.

"Lollianus," I said, standing to greet him, and he came over and embraced me.

"I came to say goodbye," he said, and actually kissed me lightly on my left cheek.

"Wha—?"

"I'm off to rejoin Caesar, Livinius."

I put my hands on his shoulders and held him away from me to study his face, his eyes. He smiled, but there was no bitterness about it, nor could I see any hint of mockery. It was simply the simple smile of a man who is happy to announce that he's doing what makes him happy—that he's doing what he thinks best.

"But you can't—" Junius started to say, but whatever the rest of it was was muffled by Claudius's hand over his brother's mouth. The two of them struggled, with Claudius trying to keep his brother quiet and wrestle him out of earshot to the other side of the room. But for an instant Junius managed to get free, and we all heard him blurt out: "It's a betrayal—"

All our eyes were suddenly upon him, and I saw Claudius shake his head with dismay. "Shut up, idiot," I yelled at once.

"Betrayal?" Lollianus gasped, and quickly turned to face the windbag Junius Barnabas.

"Ignore him," I said, grabbing Lollianus from behind, as he seemed ready to throttle him. Then, more softly: "You know Junius."

Indeed, Junius still struggled and shouted. "The murders—" we heard him say. But by then, Claudius had him firmly in tow and dragged him all the way across the room and into the water closet.

"Murders?" Lollianus demanded.

196

I looked past him and saw Fulvia curled up on the bed crying her eyes out. Lollianus looked from me to her and back again. While I still groped for words, he sat down beside her, took her hand in his and kissed it.

"My dear Lady Fulvia, what is it?" he said.

"We . . . found . . . the . . . papers . . ." she said, wrenching out each word between terrible sobs.

"What?"

"The papers from Lucius," I put in at last. "From what they say, it's clear that Mark Antony murdered Fabius Vibulanus, and therefore almost certainly murdered our cousin Lucius Flavius, as well as Avidia Crispina, Flaccus Valerius, and the slave Laertes, simply because they knew too much about the earlier murder—or Antony thought they did.

"Also," I said, "our old mentor Scribonius Curio has taken a bribe from Caesar of ten million sesterces. Claudius and Junius saw the money themselves. Curio, it seems, has been Caesar's agent all along. And his speech calling for both sides to disarm was meant only as a provocation—one which Cato and the others fell for only too easily."

"Ten million!" Lollianus whistled. Then he stood and stared at me in the oddest way for the longest moment. "I believe you," he said at last—though very quietly, just loudly enough for Fulvia and me to hear, then added, "but I love Caesar."

We stayed just like that, eyeball to eyeball, paralyzed by the awful turmoil of the moment—the sort of turmoil which, I suppose, is only too commonplace at the outbreak of civil war: father against son, brother against brother, cousin against cousin. It seems to leave everyone and everything in a state of confusion so agonizing as to be all but impossible to describe.

With his powerful grip, Lollianus suddenly pulled my head down to his and kissed me quite hard and very lovingly on the mouth. "Antony and the other tribunes have already fled the city," he whispered. "But if you hurry, I think you can still catch Curio."

Then he smiled and said: "You're my family, Livinius. I'll never do anything to hurt you."

197

And with that, he walked very rapidly out of my bedroom. I stood there, not knowing what to do next. I listened—we all did, I suppose—to his boots clomping down the stairs. Then, a moment later, I heard the front door close behind him.

24

We arrived at Curio's house just at daybreak and, I might add, with considerable commotion: on horseback at full gallop—a rare sight on the city streets of Rome.

While Junius and Claudius stayed on their horses, I dismounted, took the fasces (newly repaired and properly affixed!) and used its full weight to hammer on Curio's front door. A sleepy-eyed doorman finally answered, and I insisted he produce Curio at once.

While waiting, we all kept careful watch. Claudius rode nervously from one side of the house to the other, while Junius looked first up, then down the little street in front.

But there was no sign of trouble and even on a day as important as this, Curio had slept late. After ten minutes or more, he finally appeared, askew in his night robes and in foul humor.

"What is this, Livinius!" he demanded, but before he even reached the doorway, I stepped inside and blocked his way. Junius and Claudius dismounted and followed me in at once, and without actually touching him we forced him back into an interior room of the house; in fact, it turned out to be our old workroom.

"I asked what this is about, Livinius?" Curio repeated, though his tone was noticeably less insistent and his eyes were mostly on my two cousins standing behind me. Then, apparently for the first time, he saw the fasces in my right hand.

"Oh, Gaius, don't be absurd," he said. "All that's over and done with; your silly little quaestorship has expired, and your authority with it—such as it was, which never was much, believe me!"

199

Oddly enough, I'd been half expecting such a rebuke, and I wasn't the least taken aback. "Today I make my own authority," I answered smoothly. "Maybe I'll arrest you; maybe I'll try you, convict you and execute you—just me and my cousins: constables, judges, jurors and executioners." I paused, briefly closed my eyes and smiled with malicious playfulness.

"I . . . see," Curio said with a slow, heavy sigh. "Well, you must have a reason for being here, Livinius. Just tell me what it is. Perhaps, I can . . ."

His voice trailed off and he turned his palms up in a mincing gesture that made me want to smash his face in. When he didn't go on, I looked at him pointedly.

"What is it you can do?" I said. "Tell me."

"Well, you might want . . ."

"Yes?"

"That is, I could get you . . ."

I shook my head wearily. "What, damn it? Money, you mean?"

"Yes, well, if that's—"

"Some of the ten million?"

Curio turned very white, backed up a step and began groping beneath a cluster of papers on the table beside him.

"Get away from there!" Claudius yelled. We all grabbed him, and sure enough there was a long silver dagger hidden within easy reach.

"So it's robbery, is it," Curio said softly. "And murder, as well?"

I looked at my cousins, and we all smiled and rolled our eyes. "I don't suppose you can tell me why, can you?" I said.

There was a long silence while Curio looked at us not quite daringly, not quite with condescension in his eyes, but hardly with the shame I'd hoped to find there. There wasn't a trace of that, or even a shred of embarrassment.

"Why what?" he said at last.

"Why did you do it, for one?" I said. "And why did you lie, especially to us? And considering how ennobled I felt when I worked for you, why, thinking back on it now, do I feel so used up and dirty?"

Curio sat down on one of the workroom stools, rubbed the palms of his hands over his eyes and took a heavy breath. "I'm sorry

you feel that way, Livinius," he said, "though, of course, I understand your disappointment. But for what I was doing to work, it
had to be a secret—that much should be obvious. If it had become
known that I was Caesar's man all along, I couldn't have done what
I did. As it is, the maneuver worked perfectly. Most senators had
no idea of my true affiliation, so naturally they could be counted
on to give overwhelming approval to my disarmament proposal.
But Cato knew; so did Pompey. So did a few of their aristocrat
friends. And once again they reacted for all the right reasons in all
the wrong ways. They swore allegiance to Rome and faithfulness
to the republic. But to preserve it, they fell for my provocation and
gave Pompey his broad commission to raise an army—thereby
placing themselves squarely in the wrong with an unconstitutional
and illegal act. They did just what we thought they'd do: they
swallowed the bait. And in doing so they have brought Rome to
the brink of civil war."

"And I suppose the money played no part," I said.

"I didn't say that," Curio answered. "And, as I say, if you want
some . . ."

"We have money," Claudius said with perfectly honed aristo-
cratic timbre. It was obnoxious, but appropriate for the moment—
and I couldn't help smiling.

"So that's it? That's why you came here?" Curio asked. "To ask
my why?"

I exhaled heavily and closed my eyes a moment. "I don't know
why I came here," I said. I looked up and stared at him. "I wish
Mark Antony was sitting here now instead of you. I'd have words
to say to that man."

"There'd be more than words," Junius grumbled.

"He murdered our cousin Lucius Flavius," I said, "and several
others, including Fabius Vibulanus, who also used to work for
you." I nervously rubbed my hands together, then placed them on
top of my head and ran my fingers through my hair. "Damn it, I
should have arrested him when I had the chance!"

"Y-e-e-s," Curio said slowly, "I remember Fabius. Fine fellow;
good worker. Well, what can I say? Antony is . . . Antony."

What is it at this moment, I wondered, that makes it so hard to
keep myself from doing him serious violence? Is it the shallow look

201

in his eyes? Or the dismissive insolence of his tone and words? So with some effort he vaguely remembers Fabius, does he?—(except, it seems, when he's drunk). So he was a fine fellow and a good worker. So "Antony is . . . Antony." So much, I thought, for the trail of blood that man has left behind—at least in Curio's mind.

"And I have little doubt that what you say is true," Curio was saying. "But now, of course, he is beyond your reach."

"Or so it seems."

Curio looked at me and almost smiled a little. "You mean denounce him anyway?" He shook his head and actually laughed. "I don't know, Livinius. That could be risky."

And I thought: This is Curio at his beguiling best, but why's he bothering to play his little games now? I wondered. What's he up to? And it suddenly occurred to me that he might be happier if Antony weren't around. After all, with him out of the way, Curio would most likely become Caesar's most important adviser and confidant—a position which Antony now held with apparent invulnerability.

So, I thought, is it possible that Curio is trying to provoke me into taking some action against his more famous rival? But denouncing him now would be so rash—even suicidal if Caesar's side won the war. If that side lost, then Antony would most likely be killed anyway, and if by chance he weren't I could always denounce him later.

"Well, who knows," I said with a grand smile.

"Of course you won't," Curio went on with seamless self-confidence. "Much too dangerous. Though you could pursue him directly."

How idiotic that would be, I thought at once, to chase Antony straight into the protective arms of Caesar's encampment. But I simply smiled and said, "I doubt that would be wise."

"Of course," Curio said. He smiled pleasantly, waited a moment and said: "So . . . will you?"

"Will I what?" I asked.

"Denounce him."

I smiled back—mysteriously, I hoped—and shrugged. "You're leaving Rome soon, I imagine," I said. And he actually flinched at my unexpected change of subject. It was the first time I had ever seen him even the tiniest bit nonplussed.

"Yes. Very."

"I see," I said, affecting a thoughtful pose. "Well, that's wise, I think." I turned to my cousins. "Don't you think that's wise?"

"To leave Rome quickly? Yes, very wise," Claudius said, his tone dripping with sarcasm.

"Yes, yes, fine idea," Junius put in.

"All that money around the house," I said. "Rome's not safe these days for a man like you."

"Thieves everywhere," Junius said. "Thieves and cutthroats."

"I'll leave by dawn tomorrow," Curio said.

"Sooner," my cousins and I all said in unison. I kept a straight face, but naturally Claudius and Junius couldn't help snickering.

"I'll pack now," Curio said.

★ ★ ★

I sent Junius home with the horses while Claudius and I stayed behind to keep watch. We picked a spot two hundred feet or so up the street behind a large clump of wild brush, and sure enough there was an almost immediate eruption of activity at Curio's house. First, a team of couriers went dashing down the hill toward the center of town and quickly returned with a dozen thugs and gladiator types—presumably rejects left behind by Mark Antony. As the men took up their guard posts, we could already see and hear supplies being laid on, wagons being loaded, horses being readied, windows being boarded up—all the activity that is normally prelude to departure.

It was not a happy scene to watch: Obviously agitated, Curio (very uncharacteristically, I must say!) ran about, shouting orders. At one point, he slapped one slave very hard across the face; at another, he yelled so loudly we actually heard his word, "Imbecile!" as in fact, he lifted another slave up and threw him over the side of a high wagon. The man went down headfirst and landed on a rock; despite the distance, we saw the blood. We did *not* see the man get up—ever.

Finally at midmorning, probably the fourth hour after sunrise, the whole procession, with Curio in the lead, groaned slowly to life and rumbled away from the house and down the little hill.

203

"Well . . ." Claudius said.

"Mmmm," I said.

And that was all we said, either at that moment or during the whole long walk home.

25

For more than five centuries, since the people rose up and threw out the old kings, the Roman republic brought glory to itself and the world. Rome fostered democracy, championed free speech, extended the rule of law and protected the rights of all its citizens.

Precisely two weeks to the day after my cousin Claudius Barnabas and I watched Gaius Scribonius Curio leave his town house in Rome, Rome, the republic, ceased to exist.

Three weeks after that, I received from my cousin, Avitus Lollianus Fino, a firsthand account of that particular moment of extermination—as well as descriptions of what happened immediately before and after. Needless to say, I do not share whatever enthusiasm he may have had for the event, but occasional minor lapses in grammar aside, it is, I believe, a clear, truthful and, in a way, quite moving account of what transpired. I present it to you now, just as I received it:

My fine friend and cousin, Gaius Livinius Severus: I wish you were here, Livinius, and Lucius, too, if he were alive. You and he would have the proper words to describe what is happening here. I am a poor substitute, I know—but I will do my best:

I can't explain it, but somehow it is Caesar and Caesar alone who holds this together. Many of the men are not pleased about the likelihood of civil war, and I must admit even I have had dark thoughts since I saw you last. My trouble is I have no head for politics, and I hadn't thought it through; I just knew that Caesar was my general and my job was to follow him. Then I arrived at Ravenna and heard the talk among the men. They have misgivings and they're right: It's terrible to think of Romans killing Romans.

But then there's Caesar: his grand bearing; his easy manner of speech; his prowess as an athlete and soldier. Every man wants to be like him; every man wants to be his friend, to get to know him, to share a jug with him. And every man wants to follow him into battle, to mimic his heroics. To live and die for him.

How do you explain a man like that? I can't. Can you? I've fought by his side in battle, and that helps. I can tell you he is very brave; as far as I'm concerned, there are no words from anyone anywhere that can describe how brave he is. I've seen him plunge into a score of enemy troops, cut half of them down single-handed and get away without a scratch; I've seen him escape an ambush by diving off a hundred-foot cliff into a raging river; I've seen him charge up a hill at the head of a column of men and lead them to impossible victory—where other commanders would either have changed their minds halfway up and led a helter-skelter retreat, or gone on and been annihilated. Of course, most commanders would not have tried it in the first place.

And yet he's not a brutal man—at least, not in times of peace and not to fellow Romans. He is grand, but not fearsome; he smiles without fawning; he speaks with rare intelligence, but plainly—as if he's simply talking to you, not orating over your head. In another words, he's both endearing *and* inspiring.

When first Antony and then Curio arrived with word of the Senate's actions, the men grumbled, but Caesar quieted them with a speech that was simple and straightforward:

"They have seduced Pompey and led him astray," Caesar told us. "The decree calling upon the magistrates to act to save the state from harm, a decree by which the Senate called the Roman people to arms, was never passed before now except in the case of evil legislation or a mutiny of the people. But in the present instance, none of these things has taken place, or even been thought of; there has been no law proposed, no attempt to appeal to the people, no mutiny.

"I have been your commander for nine years; under my leadership, your efforts on Rome's behalf have been crowned with good fortune; you have won countless battles and have pacified the whole of Gaul and Germany. Now I ask you to defend my reputation and stand with me against the assaults of my enemies."

The men responded well enough, I thought. Many cheered and even the most reluctant applauded. Once again, Caesar saved the day. So, as I say, it is Caesar who keeps us going.

And now the moment is here—or it will be tonight. I will resume this letter tomorrow if I can (but no more than a few days from now, at most) to tell you everything.

*   *   *

At that point, there was a thick line drawn across the width of the scroll. Just below that, the letter resumed.

*   *   *

You won't believe it, Livinius: the most enthralling and frightening events I have ever witnessed. It is the very next day, though rather late, and if I get tired I may nap awhile. If I do, I will simply resume when I wake up; I will not interrupt the story again.

All day yesterday, Caesar kept me by his side. Partly, he said, it was because he enjoys my company; partly it's because he trusts me as a soldier, but also, as he put it, "as a bodyguard." But most important, he confided (and, again, it is candor like this that endears Caesar to us all), it is to keep enemy agents off guard. Thus, he told me, this day is to look as much as possible like any other—a casual day in which Caesar once again has decided to keep company with his young aide, Lollianus Fino, a promising but very junior member of Caesar's officer corps.

Early in the morning, Caesar placed his troops under the overall command of Hortensius. Then with just myself and two other juniors in tow, he spent much of the day casually strolling among the bustling streets and markets of Ravenna. We ate a light lunch and had just a touch of wine at a local magistrate's house, then took a nap.

In late afternoon, we luxuriated in the town's modest but well-scrubbed bathhouse. In the evening, Caesar allowed me to join him in his customary dinner at the encampment with a dozen or so local dignitaries. There was the banker Gallus, short, plump and albino, with his dark-eyed, brooding wife; there was a trade deputation of three men from Ariminum looking for a contract to manufacture

207

spearheads for Caesar's legions; there was the deputy quaestor of the province, one Marcus Norbanus, a nervous young man with darting brown eyes who kept winking at Caesar and making bad jokes and "inside" references—as if to display in public how close he was to the great man (when, in fact, Caesar hardly knows him at all); and there was the chief magistrate, Cornelius Gallus, a white-haired gentleman of such courtly manners and agreeably elegant conversation that his presence almost made the dinner bearable. Remember: I said "almost!"

After an hour or so, Caesar excused himself with a smile and a promise to "be right back." But that was a ruse; the whole day had been a ruse.

Outside, a hired carriage was waiting and off we went, while Antony, Curio and other commanders traveled by different routes in other carriages. The destination—actually rendezvous point is more accurate—was a few miles north of Ariminum, but we headed off at first in nearly the opposite direction. We wound our way around Ravenna and finally picked up the right road, only to get *really* lost after our lights were blown out by a high wind.

It was nearly dawn by the time we found it, a slight bend in the muddy little creek called the Rubicon that is the boundary between Caesar's province of Cisalpine Gaul and central Italy, which as you well know is forbidden ground to the legionary troops of any general.

Less than a mile from the spot, Caesar abruptly ordered the carriage to pull off the road and stop. Then he sat for half an hour or more holding his head in his hands, while a tear or two ran down his cheeks.

"I don't know," he whispered once. And that was all I heard him say.

Finally, he ordered the carriage to move ahead slowly. Then, within sight of the meeting place, we stopped again. Caesar looked pale and faint, and his eyes were wide and fiery, as if possessed by some demon. Later, he told me: "I had a vision, Lollianus, of our distressed country, her face captured by sorrow, her white hair streaming, her clothing and limbs torn, her speech broken by sobs. And this vision said, 'Where do you go from here, you warriors, and why do you carry my standards? If you come as law-abiding citizens, here you must stop.'" Caesar also told me—and I fear writing this down but I know you will keep it secret—that the previous night he had had a terrible dream in which he committed incest with his own mother.

Well, he ordered the carriage into the camp, disembarked, stood for a minute at the edge of the river and at last said: "Oh god of thunder who looks out over the walls of the great city; oh Rome, as sacred a name as any, smile on my enterprise. I do not attack you in frantic warfare; behold me here, Caesar, a conqueror by land and sea and everywhere your champion, as I would be now also, were it possible. His, *his* (meaning Pompey, I think) shall be the guilt, who has made me your enemy."

Caesar finally moved in on foot among the troops. Curio and Antony were already there, and Curio, studying Caesar carefully a moment in that clever way of his, apparently sensed his hesitation, rose up and spoke: "Caesar, law has been silenced by the constraint of war, and we have been driven from our country. We suffer exile willingly because your victory will make us citizens again. While your foes are in confusion and before they have gathered strength, make haste; delay is ever fatal to those who are prepared. The toil and danger are no greater than before, but the prize is higher. Win but two or three battles, and it will be for you that Rome has subdued the world. And remember: Half the world you may not have, but all the world is yours for the taking."

With that, a group of trumpeters broke ranks, gathered around and let loose a majestic call to arms. (Caesar told me later that he saw the apparition of earlier grab a trumpet and blow a thunderous blast.) Caesar stood and said, "Let us accept this as a sign from the gods and follow where they beckon, in vengeance on our double-dealing enemies. The die is cast."

And with that, he mounted his horse, ordered a squad of cavalry to stand fast in the water to hold back the currents (the stream was unusually swift and swollen by this winter's heavy snows), and led us across the Rubicon into Italy.

"Here I leave peace behind me and legality which has been scorned already," Caesar shouted as he reached the Italian bank. "Henceforth I follow Fortune. Hereafter let me hear no more of agreements. In them I have put my trust long enough; now I must seek the arbitrament of war."

Well, we marched ahead and have already captured Ariminum with hardly a drop of blood being shed. The men are tired, but in high spirits. As for myself, I believe this will be Caesar's greatest campaign yet, and I confess to you, Livinius, that I look forward to it. To me the republic has long seemed out of date for our task of ruling the world. But that is just my opinion, the opinion of an army man—and that, by Jupiter, is not always the best opinion to go by.

I am also, and this should cheer you up, keeping an eye on that friend of yours that you missed back in Rome and were so anxious to catch up with. I'm not sure yet what I will do about it—if I do anything at all. And I might add that doing anything at all will be pretty difficult for reasons that I'm sure you can figure out. But he is never too far away, and I am watching him and considering the situation.

That is all for now, my beloved cousin. I wish you well in whatever you choose. Needless to say, your presence here would be most welcome, and a place could soon be found for a man of your quality and intelligence. But naturally I do not expect you to accept such an offer. So, until we meet again, I remain your devoted cousin Avitus Lollianus Fino. And, oh yes, please tell Junius I'm sorry I lost my temper and there are no hard feelings.

And that is the report on the crossing of the Rubicon, the most important event in all history, from my fine friend and cousin Avitus Lollianus Fino.

26

Ah, Cicero! Beloved friend. Inspiring teacher. How much I have loved you. How devoted I have been. How respectful, obedient, worshipful.

But ah, Cicero, you are no soldier. And this is a time of war, and I am young and eager and unafraid. And no doubt I have stayed with you far too long, for so much has happened.

*   *   *

Within weeks after the famous river crossing, Caesar and his legions had swept south across all Italy, and soon afterward I received another letter from my warrior-cousin. A much shorter dispatch, it said simply:

> I have been assigned to a post under Scribonius Curio with a warning from Caesar to "keep an eye on your commander," because, Caesar tells me, he fears what he calls "Curio's natural impetuosity when applied on the battlefield." From what I've seen so far, Caesar is right: your old mentor is no military genius. I can only hope all goes well with us as we cross the sea to much more dangerous ground. Also, I pray to the gods that all is well with you, cousin, and I will write in more detail soon. By the way, as I'm sure you can guess, I won't be anywhere near your friend for a while, so naturally I won't be able to watch him anymore or take any action. I might add that the more I see of him, the more certain I am that he bears careful watching and that forceful action is definitely in order. But there'll be time for that in later days. For now, I remain your fond friend and faithful cousin, Avitus Lollianus Fino.

Ah, Lollianus! Ah, my bosom friend and devoted cousin!

How much I loved you?

How devoted I was?

Well—yes I did, and yes I was. But not enough, I fear. For you were a *soldier!* And as everyone knows, soldiers are crude fellows, lacking in the social graces, perhaps a bit rough and tumble for what good taste allows, and even (may the gods strike me dead for ever having believed this!) a little simple in their thoughts.

And now, having not loved you enough, having failed to properly appreciate you, there is nothing that can ease the ache in my heart each time I think of your convivial, rough-and-tumble, slightly crude and fiercely loyal self.

Two months after receiving Lollianus's brief letter, I learned from other sources of the progress of the military campaign under Gaius Scribonius Curio:

From the start, it's said that Curio thought little of the opposing forces under Attius Varus of Pompey's command. So, in crossing from Sicily to Africa, he took only two of his four legions and just five hundred cavalry.

The campaign began well: the opposing fleet retreated when they saw Curio's more imposing force; several enemy ships were captured. In one early battle, Varus's cavalry was routed and one hundred twenty of his troops were killed in the field. Curio's troops hailed him as Imperator.

Just one day later a cavalry guard at his new encampment saw large reinforcements heading their way. Curio quickly prepared the mass of his army for battle, while boldly dispatching a small troop of cavalry against the much bigger enemy force. Sure enough, the enemy troops were caught by surprise and routed in disarray.

But these were petty skirmishes. Where was the big, decisive battle that all the men wanted? The trouble was that Varus's camp was protected on one side by the town wall of Utica and on the other by the huge substructure of a theater; thus, it was only reachable by a narrow and treacherous passage.

So the petty skirmishes dragged on, boredom set in and, not surprisingly, the camp was soon filled with ugly gossip and complaining. Many of the men were discontented, said one persistent rumor; maybe the whole army was. The rest of the army should have come with them, came another big complaint; as things stood, with less than half their forces available, they had no chance of final victory against a powerful enemy. And finally, it was wrong in any case for Romans to kill Romans; it was wrong to fight a civil war.

So Curio held a war council and found his officers were divided. Some blamed idleness for the bad mood of the troops and called for a swift new attack. Others urged withdrawal to safer ground to give the men time to come to their senses.

Curio, witnesses say, shook his head in dismay at both ideas. "You know how well fortified their camp is," he said, "and I am not so sanguine as to call for a hopeless attack. But to suggest we give up and withdraw to some safe and distant point—well, I'm too young to be that timid."

So he summoned all his troops to assembly and pleaded his case: "Have you forgotten the great victories you just won in Italy? Don't you know of the great victories Caesar has won in Spain? So is it me then, that is making you so dissatisfied? Is that it? I remind you that I brought you all here safely without the loss of a single ship. I scattered the enemy fleet at our first encounter; I chased two hundred supply ships out of the harbor to keep them and their cargo from the enemy; I won two cavalry battles in two days. You hailed me as Imperator.

"Have I committed some grievous offense against you since then? Have you changed your minds? If so, I return your gift, and you can return my name."

Witnesses say the men were deeply moved by the speech and interrupted many times to shout their indignation. "How can you think we'd be disloyal to you?" one man yelled, and a hundred others echoed it.

"Then I pledge to take you into the great battle that you so eagerly await at the earliest possible moment," Curio said with a smile.

The troops cheered wildly, and the very next day Curio led them out to fight.

The first battle was a triumph for Curio's forces. They met the enemy in a narrow valley between two sets of steep and treacherous hillsides. Witnesses say the troops on both sides held off attacking as long as possible to keep the obvious advantages of high ground.

Finally, Attius Varus made the first move, sending down a mixed force of cavalry and light infantry. Curio responded with cavalry and two cohorts. Varus's horsemen, my sources tell me, could not withstand the assault and fled. Left unprotected, the infantry were surrounded by Curio's troops and killed.

Curio then quickly led a massive charge at Varus's lines. And having seen the earlier retreat and slaughter, I am reliably informed that Varus's entire army turned tail and fled back to camp. As a matter of fact, reports say that the retreating forces were so panicked that more of them were killed in the crush of men trying to reenter the gates of the encampment than had been killed in the battle itself. A total of six hundred died and a thousand were wounded, while Curio's army suffered just one casualty.

The next day, Curio began his siege of Utica. I'm told there had been talk of surrender in the city, but word that reinforcements were coming from Pompey's ally, King Juba of Numidia, boosted their spirits and changed their minds.

Curio, they say, also heard news of the reinforcements, but did not believe it at first. When he finally got reliable word that Juba was indeed just twenty-five miles away, he withdrew to Castra Cornelia, a few miles west, immediately sent to Sicily for his two other legions and began gathering stores of food and other supplies.

Soon after that, however, Curio heard from deserters that Juba had been recalled by a border war and other troubles, and had turned back. My sources say Curio accepted this story without question, changed his plans and decided to give battle at once. A small group of his cavalry, moving by night, swiftly attacked a much larger force of Numidian soldiers as they slept in their camp and sent them running in retreat.

A short time later, just as Curio was leaving his camp with nearly all his troops, he met the returning cavalry, heard the good news and sped on with more resolve than ever—even though many of his men, especially the cavalry, were exhausted.

But disaster was waiting: Curio had been deceived; the story about Juba's recall was false. The king was actually just six miles away, and when he learned of the battle during the night, he sent his personal bodyguard of two thousand Spanish and Gallic cavalry, along with the best of his regular infantry, to reinforce the retreating troops.

Meantime, the Numidian commander, assuming that the earlier cavalry had been only a small advance party, told his troops to expect Curio with the rest of his army. And he instructed them to pretend to be frightened, give some ground and retreat slowly.

Well, Curio and his men marched sixteen miles after them, and when they finally did battle they were too tired to fight well. When his troops met the enemy, they prevailed, but then had no strength left to pursue them. The cavalry, straggling behind with worn-out horses, was especially ineffective.

Curio, they say, rose to the occasion. He exhorted his men; he pleaded with them. He told them to rely on their own skill and courage. But slowly the opposing troops began to outflank him and move in from behind. At one point, Curio tried to move the entire force to a nearby hillside, but the opposing cavalry cut them off.

It was a massacre! Nearly the entire two legions were surrounded and killed. Curio's own officers urged him to flee to the safety of the camp, but he refused. "Having lost the army which Caesar entrusted to me, I could never return to look him in the face," he said. With that, he died fighting.

Fighting beside him to the very last, so I am told, was a certain junior officer, late of Caesar's personal staff and newly promoted to the rank of legionary captain: my cousin, Avitus Lollianus Fino, killed on the beaches of the African coast for the cause in which he so fervently believed.

*　　*　　*

So, Cicero, old friend: Ten more months have passed, I have toiled relentlessly in the service of your cause, and now we have word that Pompey himself has been killed—not far, in fact, from the very spot where Scribonius Curio and Lollianus Fino battled their last.

And all this time I have stayed with you here in this house in the countryside not far from Rome, working for what *you* believe.

What was it you said so many times? Compromise, you said. This can all be worked out, you said. We'll bring the republic back, you said, and avoid the bloody horrors of civil war.

215

And even as I sat one fine morning in the little orchard of Cicero's country house under a soft Italian sun thinking all that over and beginning to set it down, I felt his hand touch my shoulder.

"What's this you're writing?" he asked. And though he looked pale with rage, he did not once raise his voice during the lecture he gave me.

"So it's goodbye then, is it?" he insisted. "So you would *write* your farewells to me when all day long we are not more than fifty feet apart? You cannot look me in the face and tell me what you feel? Has your respect for me so completely left you? Has your love for me turned to such contempt? Why, I'd no more suggest you stay here in a cause you no longer believe in than I'd keep you here by restraints or force of arms. Don't you know that? By the gods, what would be the point? If you now believe the time has come for you to do battle for your beliefs, then go with all my love and respect. But if you stay here, going through the motions just for my sake, then you are far less wise than I had imagined."

Red-faced with embarrassment and crying a little, a plaintive "Oh master" was all I could manage—though in truth I'd been hinting for a long while that I might want a change, and I'd tried to coax him into telling me how he felt about it. Now, at long last, I asked him outright: "But what's *your* opinion, master? What do *you* think I should do?"

"I think mostly now about what *I* should do," he said with a shake of his head. "And I think that, alas, you're right: I am no soldier. But I still believe someone should continue to make the effort, however feebly, to avoid the dictatorship that everyone else has for so long considered inevitable. So that is what I will do: I will continue.

"As for you," Cicero went on, "I've already told you: do what you think best. Goodness knows, you've done your utmost in my behalf. Scribonius Curio is dead, and there's surely no more owed on that account. As for my present endeavor, my stubborn quest for peace, there's no doubt that events so far have proved me wrong. So it's hardly to be held against you if you decide that enough is enough—that it's time to pursue some other course."

I studied him a moment, still slightly teary-eyed but feeling exceptionally clearheaded. "Well . . . I'm all packed, dear Cicero," I said with savage abruptness and stood to embrace him.

"I know," he answered. "And where will you—"

"To Cato—if he'll have me."

"Oh, he'll have you. He'll be delighted," Cicero said. "He's a bit blockheaded, of course, but he's essentially a good man and capable of surprisingly sound judgments. So he'll be thrilled with a fellow of your fine qualities. Believe me, he won't hesitate."

"I'm not so sure," I said smiling. "After Curio . . ."

"That won't matter. I'll even give you a letter. I'll explain everything."

"Hmmm." I scratched my head. "A letter from you is fine, of course. But don't say anything about . . . well, nothing about Curio and all that. I'll explain that myself if I have to, all right?"

"Whatever you say, my boy."

We embraced again, and then I left him standing there in the little orchard of his rented country villa, sad but smiling, bent but unbroken, defeated but more determined than ever to carry on his struggle.

★   ★   ★

Well, it was a lost cause from the start. That's obvious now, of course, but I think I knew it even then. If I did, it did nothing to deter me; in some strange way, it may even have encouraged me.

With Pompey's death his son, Sextus Pompeius, continued to lead scattered fighting in Spain, while Cato took command of what was left of the republican forces in northern Africa. And that's where I caught up with him—at the city of Cyrene just after he'd been formally received there.

"So you want to join our ragged remnants, eh?" he said, greeting me at the entranceway of some rich man's house that he'd converted to his headquarters. He took me into a spare little room that he'd set up as an office, sat me down on a hard wooden bench and looked me over with typical disdain. "Weren't you Curio's friend?"

I looked up at him—he was still standing—and shook my head. "I was taken in, my lord, like so many others."

"Mmm," he said. He nodded and finally sat down beside me. "We all were, yes. At least for a time." He stared off a moment, seemingly lost in thought. "Well, I know of your family, of course. And I know Cicero speaks well of you. Is that where you've been all this time? With him?"

I nodded silently.

"Well, goodness knows we don't get much in the way of new people these days." He allowed a brief upward turning of the corners of his mouth—what passed for a smile on his dour countenance—and turned away. He was nearly out the door when he stopped, turned around, glanced back at me and said, "Fine."

It was his one-word acceptance of my application to join his beleaguered troop.

★   ★   ★

"I know, I know," Cato was saying. "You think I'm a prig and a blockhead, and . . . well, who knows what else? I know Cicero thinks that. Other people, too. And I suppose I am, at certain times in certain ways. I know all the mistakes I made during those years in Rome; I've heard them all repeated to my face often enough. But what I want to ask you is, What choice did I have? What else could I have done?"

He stopped, as if actually expecting an answer, but when I said nothing, he went on. "My problem was I had no agenda. Well, I shouldn't say 'no agenda.' I had an agenda, all right, which was to save the republic. But that kind of thing stands no chance against the much simpler, much more single-minded agenda of those who seek only to expand their own power.

"Caesar, for example," he said, pulling his heavy cape tight around him against a wintry breeze. "He's despicable. I thought that then; I think it now." He shook his head and took a heavy breath, talking as we walked—or, to put it more accurately, as we marched—to join the newly unified anti-Caesarean forces of King Juba, Attius Varus (now the provincial governor), and Pompey's father-in-law, Cornelius Scipio. It took us seven days to reach them with Cato marching the whole time at the head of the troop, and always on foot; not once did he use a carriage, litter, horse, or any other beast to ease his burden. And many times, such as now, I marched right beside him.

"But Pompey was no better," he suddenly blurted out, and I stared at him in amazement. He stole a glance at me, shrugged and went on. "I know, I know. I joined him at the start, and now I mourn him and even march in his name. But the truth is he started his career in fraud and violence, and basically he never changed. Indeed, he was far inferior to our ancestors in recognizing the limits of what is lawful. He backed that wretched Lepidus for the consulship some years ago—you may not remember it. And when Lepidus showed his true colors—his ambition to subvert the state, which Pompey had certainly known of all along—Pompey turned on his old friend and made a great show of 'saving' Rome. And that near famine we had a few years back? That was Pompey's doing; by Jupiter if the old prick wasn't trying to corner the grain market—for his personal gain, of course. And . . . what else? Oh, yes: he supported Clodius against Cicero—did you know that? Oh, it was all hush-hush, but I swear that's the truth of it. Why? Well, apparently he never forgave Cicero for successfully putting down that Catiline business. He, Pompey, wanted to be the one to do it. Only he was worthy of the role of savior of the republic. So he quietly gave that Clodius creature his support to send Cicero into exile. Then, a year or so later, he reversed himself again and made a great display of bringing Cicero back.

"I tell you that man was a horror—and, needless to say, no republican. And the point is, in an age when personality and naked power are the ruling forces, where is a republican to turn? Who is left that is worthy of governing a state dedicated to the rule of law? Or at least one that's supposed to be dedicated to that. And that's what I tried to do—save the republic and the rule of law. At first I felt Pompey could be ensnared and then controlled. I know, I know: it was clumsily handled, and it was always a gamble anyway. But there was no chance that we could handle Caesar in that way. I knew that; everyone did. So where else to turn? Reject them both and watch the Senate turn into a powerless joke? Or try to play the game, try to pick one side with power—try to pick, if not a good man, at least the lesser of two evils. As I once said, 'A man who can raise up great evils is perhaps the best man to allay them.' So Pompey was certainly a man of value. And as I remarked at his funeral, 'Sincere belief in Rome's freedom died long ago. Now, with Pompey gone, even the sham belief is dead.' "

"But—"

"I know; you're thinking, But here we are, marching in Pompey's name across the chilly plains of northern Africa."

He looked at me, shook his head and almost smiled. "I'm not sure I understand it either," he said.

★　★　★

The military exploits of both Scipio and Varus went so badly that winter that by springtime they were begging Cato to take charge. But he adamantly refused, inexplicably deferring to Scipio, who was then named overall commander.

Scipio was angry at Utica for its flip-flopping during the war, and his first demand was that all its people be slaughtered and the city be burned to the ground.

"Outrageous! Impossible! Insane!" Cato retorted, insisting that he would in no way be party to such an act.

Scipio finally gave in, but only on condition that Cato himself assume personal command of the city and its government. Cato agreed.

Utica was a major prize for either side in the war, and Cato vowed to hold it. He greatly improved and strengthened the city's already extensive fortifications, repairing walls, building towers, and digging trenches and palisades around the town. He also laid in huge amounts of corn and other supplies, as well as large stores of weapons. In effect, he turned the town into a gigantic supply depot for the Pompeyan army. Even so, he gave strict orders that Romans were to treat Utican citizens with all courtesy and respect.

Cato and Scipio quickly began to have other major disagreements. Cato urged caution, but Scipio, a strutting ass with no real talent to back up his unending torrent of boasting and threats, called Cato a coward and insisted on taking the fight to Caesar.

Sure enough, the campaign soon ended in disaster. In a major battle at Thapsus, the whole army was lost to Caesar's troops. Scipio and Juba narrowly escaped with their lives, along with a handful of aides and other officers.

After the news arrived, it fell to Cato to calm the hysterical city. Word was that Caesar's army was on the move and headed their way, and the people were in a frenzy. But with no bodyguard or even a weapon of his own, Cato went out among the crowds and somehow quieted them down.

"The report is surely exaggerated; early reports always are," he said again and again all over the city. "Most likely, things are not so bad."

He summoned a war council the next morning of all the Roman patricians in the city, the so-called "three hundred." Among them were several senators and their sons, a great many businessmen, and Cato's own party of advisers including his own son and several teachers and philosophers. He told them he would respect whatever decision they made—to battle Caesar, to surrender, or to flee to safe ground, probably in Italy.

Cato happened to be at another of their meetings the day after when word arrived that the city's garrison of Roman horse-guard cavalry had just left through the main gate.

I rode with Cato as he raced after them. Weeping, he begged them to return, if only for another day, to give safe passage to the Roman senators in the town. To my considerable amazement, they finally agreed.

★　★　★

If, in life, Cato was frequently priggish, if he lacked humor and imagination, he was, in preparing for death, nothing less than magnificent. For it was clear enough to everybody in those final days that he had decided, once the affairs of the city were in order, to take his own life. Thus, it was plain enough that all his tireless efforts were without secret motives or intrigues—that he was only trying to spare others any pain or indignity.

"We cannot be like you, so please forgive our weaknesses, Cato," said one old banker at a later meeting of the "three hundred." He was referring to a plan devised by the businessmen to dispatch a deputation begging Caesar for pardon—and for their lives.

"Your intentions are good," Cato said, "so there is nothing to forgive. In fact, I recommend that you act quickly for your own safety. But whatever else you do, do not ask for anything on my behalf. For those who are conquered, entreat; for those who have done wrong, beg pardon. For myself, I do not admit to any defeat in all my life. In truth, I consider Caesar to be vanquished. For he now stands convicted of those subversive designs against his country which he had so long attempted and so constantly denied."

Right after the meeting, Cato was told that Caesar and his entire army were not far off. "Ah, he expects to find us brave men," I heard him say.

Events then began to move at dizzying speed: Cato sadly went about arranging for all the senators to leave; he ordered all the city gates shut, except for one facing the sea, assigned the ships to carry them away and gave money and provisions to all that needed them. I was the only senator who stayed behind.

Later that day, word came that a Pompeyan commander, Marcus Octavius, was encamped near the city with two legions and wanted to "arrange about the chief command of Utica"—in other words, to take personal charge of the city.

Cato shook his head, smiled at me and said, "Can we wonder that everything has gone so badly for us when our love of high office survives even our very ruin?"

He was right in a sense, but it occurred to me that the interest of the commander Octavius was primarily to extract all the plunder he could from the city before Caesar arrived and took it for himself. Of course Cato being Cato, that idea probably never entered his mind.

Then word came that as the cavalrymen were finally leaving the city for good, they were robbing the local people. Cato found the troop, ran up to the nearest man, snatched away what he could and tossed the goods to the ground. I know what happened next will sound unbelievable (I wouldn't believe it either if I hadn't seen it with my own eyes), but the others actually gasped with humiliation and threw down whatever they had stolen.

Cato then returned to the port, flew into a rage when he realized I had stayed behind, then quickly calmed himself and turned to the Stoic philosopher Apollonides, who was there with us. "It belongs to you, sir," he said, "to cool the fever of this young man's spirit, and to make him know what is good for him."

I still refused to go, and Cato finally acquiesced. But he spent much of that afternoon and evening going among all his other friends and urging them to depart. Most did, but there were a few of us who remained.

That night we had a wonderful dinner. There were about a dozen of us, including Cato, Cato's son Marcus, the Stoic Apollonides, the famous peripatetic Demetrius, a few other old friends of Cato's, and the magistrates of the city.

Everybody drank a great deal of wine, myself included of course, and questions of philosophy became the main topics of conversation, with special attention to the Stoic dogma of paradoxes. Only the good man is free, Apollonides argued; all wicked men are slaves. Naturally Demetrius disagreed, and they went on about that and a great many other esoteric points. But when the issue of suicide was raised, Cato argued the Stoic viewpoint—that it is at least acceptable, if not preferable, when one clearly feels that one is no longer able to lead a reasonable and moral life—at such length and with such passion that it was clear he planned to take his own life and "put himself at liberty."

"Nobody's at liberty who's dead," I said somewhat drunkenly and much too bluntly. They all looked at me in horror, but Cato simply smiled and changed the subject. "I only hope our departing friends make it to safety, whether by land or by sea," he said with utmost grace. Then he raised a glass to that.

"May we all reach safety, one way or another," I said, as everyone joined in the toast.

"We will," Cato said. "I'm sure of it."

*   *   *

As was his custom, Cato walked after dinner with his son and a few close friends, myself among them. Then, ending the stroll just outside his private quarters, he gave the necessary orders to the officers of the watch. Inside, he embraced us all with what could be described as unusual warmth and affection. Then, as we were leaving, he lay down on a sofa, picked up one of Plato's dialogues concerning the soul (the one from the *Phaedo,* I believe) and quietly began to read.

The servants said later that after a while Cato noticed his sword was missing and asked a slave who had taken it. He read a bit longer and, getting no answer, irritably summoned all his servants and loudly demanded its return. When there was still no response, he angrily denounced the servants and his son for "betraying me and delivering me naked to the enemy." For, as most of us knew, his son had taken Cato's sword during dinner and hidden it. Then, with a few of us right behind him, his son ran into the room and fell at his father's feet, weeping and begging him not to harm himself.

"When and how," Cato answered with a growl, "did I become deranged and out of my senses? Must I be disarmed and hindered from using my own reason? And you, young man," he said, looking straight at his son, "why do you not bind your father's hands behind him so when Caesar comes I will be unable to defend myself?"

We all walked sadly and slowly from the room, except for the philosopher Apollonides. "And you," Cato told him sternly (or so the old Stoic told us later on), "do you also think to keep a man of my age alive by force? Or do you bring me some good reason why it would not be utterly base and unworthy for me to seek safety from my enemy, Caesar, when I plainly have no alternative. You are silent, I see; you have none. Well, in that case, you will please allow me to follow the doctrines clearly taught by *your* philosophy. And tell my son that he should not compel his father to do by force what he cannot persuade him to do by reason."

The two men left in tears and soon after a slave was at last sent in with the sword. The slave said later that Cato immediately drew it from its sheath, looked at it carefully and, seeing the point was good, said, "Now I am master of myself."

There was no more noise from the chamber that night. In the morning we found him in his bath, his arms and wrists cut open, the bathwater red with his blood.

When Caesar learned of his death, I'm told that he said, "Cato, I grudge you your death as you have grudged me the preservation of your life."

Indeed, it was generally agreed later that Caesar was sincere about this, for he had already shown unusual clemency to his adversaries—as long as they were Roman. Cato's motives also seemed clear enough. For if he had spared himself and then been kept alive thanks to Caesar, his own reputation would not have been damaged much, but Caesar's might have been greatly improved.

Caesar entered the city a few days later and that evening summoned me to dinner at his headquarters.

"Gaius Livinius Severus," he said coolly, and indeed he did not

224

stand or shake my hand or show any other form of greeting. "You're not thinking of suicide also, are you?"

"No, Caesar," I said. I sat down opposite him, grabbed a large chunk of pork and began to bite off big pieces. "If I'd wanted to," I said, obnoxiously chewing a mouthful of food as I spoke, "I would certainly have had ample opportunity to do so these past few days."

"Hmm," Caesar said, eyeing me distastefully. "Just see that you don't. You're one young man who's going to live through this, no matter what."

With that, I stopped my loud chewing and studied him a moment. It was no use, of course, trying to figure out what he meant by that: he was famous for his implacable, unrevealing visage. We ate the rest of our dinner in silence, and I left the instant we were finished.

★　★　★

A few weeks later Caesar sent me back to Rome, and I found myself back at my house with Fulvia and her parents, and all our families intact, except for Lucius Flavius and Avitus Lollianus, of course.

It had been three years since Caesar crossed the Rubicon, and even now much of Rome remained in turmoil. But for a while, at least, life in the capital was all so much the same that one could easily be made to doubt that anything of any importance at all had taken place.

27

Ah, Cicero. So silent for so long: indeed, you were no soldier. The very thought of violence made you shudder with fear, and for so long you hid in your suburban home and busied yourself with teaching—if it can be called teaching to teach the spoiled, stupid children of the rich.

But now two more years have passed, Caesar himself has been murdered, and Cicero, old friend, you have at last awakened from your torpor.

The *Philippics!* Wonderful title, old friend—named (jokingly?) for Demosthenes' attacks on King Philip of Macedon about four hundred years ago.

Actually, your first was mild in tone, very conciliatory. But for some reason the object of your moderation struck back with unexpected harshness. So now you have responded with your Second Philippic. And what a tonic it is to my soul! I have read my copy through a dozen times until the papyrus itself has become torn and frayed. And oh Cicero, old friend and master, while I have no idea if it will help to loosen the grip of tyranny upon our tired country—for if Caesar's death did not do that, I cannot imagine what will—it has made my spirits soar to read your attack upon my most bitter enemy, that swine and murderer of my kin:

> Mark Antony [you told him], you squandered vast amounts of public funds to support a degrading traffic at your house, including every sort of indecency and drunkenness, and anything and everything within your reach was put up for sale.

And now [you reminded him], here in this great temple, in which the most noble senators once consulted about affairs of the world, your chief contribution has been to station your armed desperadoes right here upon the Senate floor. Does this surprise us, my lords? Is there anything beyond Mark Antony's daring? Clearly, Antony, you have no sense at all, for what can more surely indicate insanity than to resort to arms in a manner so destructive of the state?

And now, laughable though it may be, now you have charged that *I* instigated the long-ago murder of Clodius. Well, sir, I remind you that you yourself, with sword drawn, once chased that man through the Forum in sight of half of Rome and would probably have done him in if the wretch had not barricaded himself beneath the staircase of a book shop. Does that lead me to conclude that you instigated his murder? Not really. So what in all the world would lead you to believe that of me? Perhaps I rejoiced at Clodius's death? Is that the basis of this idiotic accusation? What if I did? Should I (of all people) and I alone, have shown grief when everyone else in Rome was rejoicing?

You accuse me of dividing Caesar from Pompey and thereby causing our civil war. What rot! Caesar needed no help from me in that. Once he felt strong enough, once he had no more need or use for Pompey, he simply walked away from their alliance. I didn't like that friendship, but once it was made . . . well, even you, Antony, must have heard my famous saying: "Ah! Pompey, I wish your compact with Caesar had either never been made, or else never been broken. In refusing to make it you would have shown your sound principle; in refusing to break it, your common sense." That was always my advice to Pompey, for once the agreement was made, to break it could only lead to disaster. And quite clearly I've been proven correct in that regard.

And now I come to the outrage from your lips that *I* instigated the murder of Caesar. Well, as a matter of fact, my name has never even been mentioned in connection with that deed—glorious though it was. But did anyone who took part try to conceal it? Hardly! To the contrary there were some who boasted of taking part even though they did not.

But it is your stupidity in making such a charge that is so upsetting, though how can I expect otherwise when you clearly have no more wits about you than some beast of the forest. For I ask you, my lords, to recall the exact form in which this clever fellow convicted me. "When Caesar had been dispatched," goes Antony's version, "Brutus, whom I mention with all respect, at once brandished aloft the reeking dagger, called on Cicero by name and asked him to rejoice with them at the restoration of liberty."

Well, so what! Yet from that alone, "it ought," as you put it, "to be understood that Cicero was privy to the plot." Which is an absurd conclusion in itself from such scanty evidence. But notice, Senate Fathers, that he terms me a vile criminal merely because he suspects that I suspected something. But the man who waved the dagger, Brutus, is mentioned "with all respect."

Mark Antony, sleep off your drunken lethargy; let the fumes of wine evaporate; for a single moment try to follow a sober line of thought. Or must one bring flaring torchlights to awaken this man who snores over such a question?

But let me also warn you, sir: Beware the ancient interrogatory, "Who profits by the crime?" and take care that you do not find yourself implicated in Caesar's death. For wasn't it you who said right afterward that it was a gain to all who did not wish to be slaves? Yet now it is you who are more likely to be tyrant than slave; yet to you Caesar's death is a special gain. For what was there but Caesar's death that could possibly have relieved your poverty and paid your mass of debts? Indeed, you have sold off most of the valuables from his house, and you have turned it into a virtual factory for forged papers and signatures, and a market in which whole towns, territories, and exemptions from taxes and tributes are scandalously bought and sold.

And now you demented man, now that I have answered your moronic charges against me, let us survey some of your past life. Barely out of boyhood, barely of age, and on your shoulders the toga of a man soon became that of a certain kind of woman. At first you were a public prostitute, and a high-priced one at that. But very soon Gaius Scribonius Curio intervened, took you off the streets and promoted you, it might be said, to the status of a wife: he made a married woman of you. Well, no slave purchased to be the victim of lust was ever so completely in his master's power as you were in

228

Curio's. How often did his father eject you from his house? How often did he post guards to keep you out? Still, by night, compelled by passion and greedy for your fee, you time and again crawled across the rooftop tiles—until finally the family could not endure the scandal any longer.

Well, young Curio said he loved you with such passion that he would follow you into exile because he could not bear to be kept apart from you. Throwing himself at my feet, Curio begged my intervention and protection, and so, to redeem that young man of such brilliant promise, I successfully urged a quiet settlement of the affair, and Curio's family was spared a foul and degrading scandal.

But enough about Antony's sex crimes; that is as far as I will go. For there are some things which a gentleman cannot mention. Thus you have the advantage of me, sir, for your crimes are so awful that no respectable opponent can speak of them.

So what of *your* role in fomenting civil war? You blatantly abused your tribunician powers, using your veto to block the entire Senate's demand that Caesar put down his arms—a veto that needless to say had been bought and paid for.

Senate Fathers, we mourn for three Roman armies slain in the war; they were slain by Mark Antony. We weep for the loss of our most illustrious fellow citizens; they were torn from us by Mark Antony. The authority of this very body has been trampled upon; it was trampled upon by Mark Antony. Everything that we have seen since—and what calamity have we not seen?—if we reckon correctly we shall find part of our debt to Mark Antony. In short, Antony, you have been our Helen of Troy: You have brought upon our country war, pestilence and annihilation.

You fought in the war; you drank deep of the blood of other, far more honorable Romans. So be it; I shall not dwell on it. You returned—only to travel about Italy in the atrociously scandalous fashion of a royal pimp. You yourself rode in a lady's carriage, while a certain actress was carried before you on a litter attended by dozens of servants. At each town, the local citizens coming out to greet you were met with this horrifying spectacle. And as you went you forcibly billeted your soldiers wherever you saw fit, driving countless citizens from their rightful homes.

Back in Rome, with Caesar still at Alexandria and unaware of your doings, you were made master of the horse, in charge of public business. And as such, how many illegal decrees did you issue granting to yourself the outright robbery of inheritances, or the plunder of the heirs themselves? Poor man, you were desperate. You had not yet received the huge estates supposedly "left" to you by Rubrius and Turselius. You had not yet started up your unexpected role of "heir" to Pompey. You had nothing except what you could steal; you were obliged to live like a bandit.

Well, now comes an episode that might be considered frivolous by some, at least in comparison to all the rest. You had been at a wedding where you had drunk so much wine that the next day you could not help being sick in sight of the Roman people. What a filthy performance, as filthy to describe as to witness. If it had happened at the dinner table in the midst of your bestial potations anyone would have thought it disgraceful enough. But this was at an assembly of the people, and it was by the master of the horse, in charge of public business, for whom it would have been shameful enough even to hiccup. And there you were, horse-master Mark Antony, actually sick, covering your clothes—indeed, flooding the entire platform—with scraps of food that reeked of wine.

Now Caesar returns, and soon after a public auction is held where the goods of Pompey—alas! I have spent my tears, but the thought will never cease to pain me—the goods, I say, of Pompey the Great were put up and sold by the cold, uncaring voice of the public auctioneer. And for that one moment Rome forgot her bonds and groaned aloud. And though all minds were enslaved by a pervasive fear of the new dictator's government, still the Roman people were free—to groan.

And while all were waiting and wondering who would be so profane, so mad, so hateful as to dare to take part as a buyer in that abominable confiscation and sale, no one could be found except Mark Antony. And that, even though the place was crowded with men who had audacity for just about anything short of that. Antony alone was wicked enough to do what all those others recoiled from in horror. Did you forget what hatred this action would provoke among the Roman people?

Well, your greedy hands closed insolently over that great man's belongings, and then you strutted with joy like a character in a bad

230

comedy, as if down and out one day and rich as Crassus the next. But as the poet Naevius once wrote, "Ill-gotten gains are swiftly squandered." And it is nothing short of incredible to relate how quickly you spent those vast accumulations.

There was an immense stock of wine, a large quantity of the best plate, costly tapestry, much handsome and splendid furniture in several places: of all this there was nothing left in a few days! I think the ocean itself could hardly have so swiftly engulfed such a large amount of property—and at that scattered among several distant locales!

Nothing was sealed up or secured, no inventories were taken. The wine cellars were abandoned to the raids of the vilest criminals; here actors and there actresses were looting the house; the rooms were crammed with gamblers and choked with drunken men; the drinking bouts went on for days at a time.

You gambled away a great deal of it—my lords, you may have seen the beds in the slaves' bedrooms covered with Pompey's rich purple draperies. Indeed, whole towns and kingdoms could have been swallowed up by such iniquitous excesses.

And then, the most brutal insult of all, Mark Antony: then you also seized Pompey's house and gardens. Did you dare even to cross the threshold of that hallowed place? Did you dare to intrude your lust-stained features into the presence of the gods of that hearth and house? Well, of course you did, you wicked man. Perhaps when you saw the memorials in the forecourt of Pompey's naval victories, you imagined you were entering your own house. But wait. No. That is impossible. For entirely brainless and without feeling as you are, you still must surely have some acquaintance with yourself and your belongings and your kin.

And so within that house, which had never seen anything not modest and pious and of high character, the bedrooms became brothels and the living apartments taprooms.

Now let us briefly touch upon your relationship with Caesar: As is well known, you fought many brave battles by his side. So why then did you not accompany him to Africa? And after he returned, what rank did he give you? Well, when he was governor you had been his quaestor. When dictator, you were the master of his horse. You had been the prime cause of the war, instigator of his barbarities, the sharer of the spoils. By your own account you were adopted his son by his will.

Yet what action did Caesar now take? I'll tell you what: He dunned you for the money still owed for the house, the gardens and most of the confiscated property which you had acquired!

Your temperamental reaction was comical: "To think that Caesar should demand payment from *me!* Why he from me rather than I from him? Did he win his victories without me? No. And besides, I gave him the pretext for the war. Why shouldn't the spoils be shared by those who shared the adventure?" But Caesar turned a deaf ear to your silly whining and sent soldiers to collect the debt.

And then you suddenly published that wonderful catalogue! What ridicule it provoked. Such a long catalogue of so many pieces of property, out of which there was absolutely nothing you could call your own. And when the auction took place, how pitiful was the sight. A few soiled pieces of tapestry, a few battered silver cups, a few shabby slaves—till we felt sorry there was anything at all of Pompey's left for us to see.

Mark Antony, you scoundrel, you were in a fix; you didn't know where to turn. And then an assassin sent by you was arrested with a dagger on his person at Caesar's house, and Caesar complained of it to the Senate and made an undisguised attack on you.

Well, time passed by and somehow (I don't even want to think how!) you wormed your way back into Caesar's good graces. And that brings us to one of your most genuinely shocking exploits. Caesar was seated on the rostrum, draped in a purple toga, sitting in a chair of gold, wearing a wreath of laurel. You climbed up, approached his chair and displayed a royal crown. The people groaned. You tried to put the crown on Caesar's head, but he rejected it and kept doing so amid loud applause.

You threw yourself at Caesar's feet. You begged and pleaded, you admonished and coaxed the crowd, and all this—by the gods, could anything be more disgraceful?—without your clothes! That's right, you repulsive villain. You were naked and on your knees before Caesar and all the people in the Forum of Rome.

Well, now Caesar is dead, and for a short time after his death some thought that constitutional government had been restored, but I did not, since with you at the helm I feared every sort of disaster. Was I wrong? All Rome has seen your lists posted every-where of immunities for sale not only to individuals but to whole communities. Indeed, my lords, the whole sovereignty of the Roman people has been frittered away over the counter at Mark Antony's house.

Where are the seven hundred million sesterces, the total amount of the accounts at the Temple of Plenty? If it was not to be given to its rightful owners, at least it might have saved us from the property tax. And the forty million sesterces that you owed on the Ides of March: how was it you no longer owed it on the first of April?

You recently posted a notice that the richest cities in Crete are exempt from the tribute, and that in short order Crete will no longer be a province. Are you really sane? Ought you to be at large? By the sale of this decree, you have lost an entire province! Has there ever been anyone wanting to purchase anything who has not found Antony willing to sell it?

You have illegally established new settlements in Italy, and in one of them your doctor got three thousand acres. What would he have gotten if he cured you? And your rhetoric master got two thousand, and I ask: What would have been his gift if he could have made you an able speaker?

More recently you moved into Varro's house. Ah, my lords, can you remember the words, thoughts and literary pursuits for which that house was once so famous? But while you were the tenant, Mark Antony, every part of the house echoed with drunken yells, the floors were swimming and the walls dripping with wine. Boys of noble birth were mixed up with men of infamous life, and common prostitutes were entangled with noble women.

And now we come to this very moment, and I ask you again, Mark Antony: Why have you brought down to the Forum these armed men, these bowmen from Ituraea, the most uncivilized country in the world? You say it is for your personal safety, but isn't it better to die a thousand deaths than to require the protection of armed men in order to remain alive in one's own country? And what sort of existence is it for a man to fear his own friends day and night?

Caesar perhaps had swords at his command, but they were concealed and at any rate not very numerous. But your despotism—how un-Roman it all is! Your mercenaries follow you in close order; we see litters full of shields borne along. And it is no new thing, my lords; we have become hardened by the frequent recurrence of the spectacle.

Mark Antony, you ought to be entrenched in the affection and goodwill of your fellow citizens, not behind your armed men. In the long run, they cannot protect you. The Roman people will wrest and wring your weapons from you. And may we survive to see it!

If we have learned anything from Caesar, it is how much to trust this man or that, on whom to rely and of whom to beware. Haven't you grasped that yet, Mark Antony? Don't you understand that brave men have only to learn the lesson once how essentially noble and deserving of thanks is the act of tyrannicide?

I have but two desires now: that my dying eyes may see the Roman people still enjoying their freedom, and that every man receives just what he deserves based on his own conduct toward his country.

★　　★　　★

Ah Cicero! What music to my ears. And yet . . . it is Mark Antony who rules here now, along with Augustus. And it is you whose very life may be in danger.

I cringe to think of it: Mark Antony as head of state. A drunkard and a thief. And also a murderer. He murdered Lucius Flavius Severus, the finest of my family, and all those others. But why? That is what I always wondered. And having read your words, now I know: because of petty lust and madness. Nothing more. For I believe now that he is insane—though it is an insanity born mostly from stupidity. He is a stupid man. And a stupid man thinks all other men are as stupid as he, and so he believes that it is easy to get away with . . . well, to get away with murder. And, in a sense, isn't that insanity?

But, oh Cicero, as bright and biting and true as your words were, they were also brittle—like you and like so many of the rest of us, I suppose. Certainly, like Rome turned out to be: delicate as a flower and so easily shattered. For it is Mark Antony who rules here now, and I am powerless to avenge the death of my cousin.

And even as I wrote my own sorry sentences while seated in the garden of Cicero's suburban villa, I felt his hand reach out and touch my shoulder.

"Oh master," I said, turning to greet him. He tried to speak, but no words came. And then I looked into his face and saw the tears cascading from his eyes. They were crinkly eyes now, old man's eyes, a little like Pompey's when I saw them in the Senate all those years ago.

I recalled those days and that parade of men: Pompey, Cato, Caesar, Lucius Flavius, Lollianus Fino. And I felt the loss of them like a great pain tearing through my heart.

Will Cicero be next? I wondered. And then I asked myself: How much more of this can Rome or any nation stand—this government by desperado? And I took Cicero's outstretched hand in mine, held it to my face and wept.

28

Night has fallen and I am curled up on a hard marble bench in a drafty anteroom of what used to be Cicero's town house in Rome, waiting for Augustus to finish reading my report.

It is cool and crisp out, a cool, crisp December evening, and through a small window just above me I can see a star or two shining in the black Roman sky. I shiver in the nighttime chill and pull my toga tightly around me.

Suddenly, just beyond the doorway to the little room, I hear voices and the scraping of iron boots on the soft clay tile floor. There is something about the noise, something about it that carries a curious importance of its own. Almost certainly, I tell myself, it would be a good idea to get up and take a look, but after so many hours of waiting I am too cold and tired to move quickly.

The voices, never soft to begin with, grow louder and a bit angry, and at last I am curious enough to get up and find out what's going on. But then I don't have to because suddenly I can see the angry men from my place on the bench, and I see one of them is Augustus and the other . . . Well, I'll be boiled broccoli if the other man isn't Mark Antony. They are arguing—that much is obvious, but I can't tell what about.

"Just shut up, Antony," Augustus snarls, and I can hardly believe my ears.

Then they actually start shoving each other, though of course it would be no contest: Mark Antony is far heavier and taller than Augustus and much more powerfully built. But then some of

Augustus's guards come up and separate them—two sweaty, red-faced men now in charge of this once splendid ship of state, quibbling over who knows what trifle.

"Wait here, Antony," Augustus says with weary exasperation. Then he turns and walks slowly toward me.

Even as he does so, however, I get a brief glimpse of another man stepping up right beside Mark Antony, and now there is something about *him* that gets my attention. Something about the way the light from a flickering lamp glints off his head. I sit up and lean far to my right until just for an instant I get a better look: It is my uncle's long-lost doorkeeper Telephus, his great bald dome gleaming in the pale yellow light.

"Recognize him, eh?" Augustus says with a smile. He sits down beside me and taps me on the left shoulder with the final scroll of my report, which he is holding in his right hand.

"Outstanding job, Livinius," he says. "Fine work. And incredibly enough, you *almost* got it right."

I stare at him a moment, not quite certain if I've heard him correctly. "Almost?" I gasp, and with that I open my eyes wide with annoyance and disbelief.

Augustus nods with a sigh, reaches into an inner fold of his toga, pulls out a scroll and hands it to me. The papyrus is old and worn, and the seal is broken—although pretty much intact on either side of the split. I hold the two halves together and immediately realize it is the seal once used by my cousin, Avitus Lollianus Fino.

I stare at Augustus again, this time with what I hope is a mixture of wonderment and anger. I open the scroll and immediately see that it is addressed to me. The next thing I notice is the date at the top: it is nearly six years old.

"A little late delivering this, eh?" I say.

"Just read it," the boy ruler tells me quietly and walks lazily out of the room. With no small amount of dread, I open the scroll and begin:

My fine and faithful friend and cousin, Gaius Livinius Severus: What a story I have for you! In fact, you'd better be sitting down to read this or it might just knock you over.

I write this from across the seas—I don't want to say where

exactly, for obvious military reasons, though I can tell you we'll be heading into battle very soon. As I've already told you, I've been assigned to serve under Scribonius Curio, with orders to give a bit of guidance to what Caesar worries is "my impetuous commander."

Well, Curio and I have become quite well acquainted, and he seems to trust me completely. You'll notice, Livinius, that I don't say we're friends. If he had told me anything except what I'm about to tell you, I would have believed that we were, and that's how I would have described him—as a good friend, not just someone I'm well acquainted with.

In any case, as we wait with the troops to begin our first major attack, and with most of our supplies already bought and ready, we've had a bit of idle time lately and I find that Curio is no stranger to the tavern life and a jug of wine now and then.

Actually, for the last week or so it's been more like every night. And a few nights ago, already quite tipsy, he made a not too flattering reference to what he called "the silly fellows who worked for me in Rome," or something like that. I realized right away he was probably talking about you and the Barnabas brothers, and maybe even Lucius. I was about to tell him a thing or two, but then I realized that he probably didn't even know that I'm your cousin, and I thought: How would Livinius or Lucius handle this? So for once I kept my mouth shut, and then the next night I brought it up again and coaxed him into telling me more.

Well, it took three or four drinking sessions over several nights, and an absolutely enormous amount of wine, but I finally got it all out of him. I'll do my best to reconstruct his words, and I'll leave out most of what *I* said, which consisted mostly of silly questions anyway—though I have put in little bits of description here and there when I thought they might help. I've also taken out all the usual little interruptions and combined all the nights into one long talk; it's just simpler to explain that way. So, in Curio's own words, I report this amazing story:

"Let me tell you what I meant by silly fellows in Rome, Lollianus, by asking this rhetorical question: Do I believe Caesar will be triumphant? Well, of course I do. And I have many reasons for believing that. In fact, every day I wake up and repeat them to myself—the reasons why I'm certain that our side will win. But I must tell you, Lollianus: every night after the lamps are out and at just that moment when I pull the covers up and I'm ready at last to pass from waking to sleeping, the same doubts creep over me, much, I suppose, like the darkness itself. What if the people rise up against us? I ask myself. What if our army defects? What if Pompey turns out to be the better general?

"And then, on most nights, an odd thing happens. After a moment or so, or on bad nights a little longer, I find myself smiling and telling myself: How silly to worry about such nonsense! Of course we'll be victorious. And the next thing I know it's morning, and I awake refreshed and confident.

"What I'm trying to say, Lollianus, is that people for the most part believe what they want to believe. They get an idea in their heads, and it's surprisingly hard to shake loose without very powerful evidence to the contrary. I think I've always known that, Lollianus; I think I was born with that knowledge. It's certainly true that I've made use of the idea with remarkable success.

"For example, the fellows I mentioned, the ones you're asking about: I had them working for me in Rome a year or so ago. Rich, well-born young fellows—some of the brightest we have. One of them's even in the Senate already, has been for some time. Well, as I say, they were very smart and eager and hard-working. And they believed whatever I told them. They were in close contact with me every day for a year or more; they handled my appointments, even helped write my speeches and pamphlets. And the silly fellows never suspected what I was up to. Not once did they question me in any serious way. And of course they never did figure out that I was working for Caesar all along.

"They *wanted* to be believe me, Lollianus. Indeed, people can be convinced of anything—but only by themselves. If you understand that about the other fellow—that you have to get him to convince *himself* of what you want to convince him of—then you probably can convince him of just about anything, yes?

"For example, these fellows that worked for me—as I say, they never once realized that I'd been on Caesar's side the entire time. And how that came about is quite a story in itself: It all goes back nearly ten years, Lollianus, when I was supposedly the fiery young man of the people. I played that role for quite a while, and that should have made me a natural ally of Caesar's, but when I tried to forge a real association with him he brutally snubbed me. I was rejected, treated with contempt and therefore driven into the arms of the senatorial party and an alliance with the old aristocrats.

"Or at least that was the idea that got around. And with a rare exception or two everybody swallowed it. Later, I subtly shifted away from the old aristos, carving out a useful niche for myself as an upright, honest, independent Roman politician trusted by all sides.

"Of course what really happened was that the entire thing was a hoax starting with Caesar's snub, which was entirely contrived. The truth was that from that moment on I was Caesar's loyal and devoted agent, moving in Rome's highest social and political circles and using my not inconsiderable powers of observation and analysis to keep my master impeccably well informed.

"And all the while, I worked—we all did, though some without knowing it, heh-heh—toward our final goal. It was quite a plan, Lollianus. It took a long time to put into effect, and if I say so myself it required enormous patience and discipline on my part. The waiting was the hardest—waiting for the day when I could strip away my veil of lies and tell the truth to everybody—that I was Caesar's man. So when I finally set the trap, they all fell into it like so many stampeding wild boars. Let me see . . . more wine, Lollianus? By Jove I feel giddy tonight. Well . . . oh yes, I'd been in office just a short time when, as you may recall, the Senate rejected Caesar's proposed law, the one that would have given land to Pompey's veterans. That was a tricky one, my friend, tricky because behind the scenes I worked fervently for that rejection, even while in public I was very strongly in favor of the bill. And those old-line idiots loved me for it, because naturally they hated that bill, and of course it only fanned the fires against them.

"Later on, I wanted passage of a road repair bill, but nobody wanted to pay for it, so the Senate just naturally turned that down. That gave me my first good excuse to display real anger toward those aristo blockheads. I mean, who votes down a road repair bill? Then I proposed the standard intercalation bill, the one passed every other year to insert the extra month in the calendar. Suddenly

240

all the old-liners were saying, Oh no, you can't do that, that just delays putting an end to Caesar's command. Well of course it did that, too, but opposing it still put those old farts completely in the wrong—and in an extremely unpopular position. Well, the old fools defeated it! Can you imagine? I mean, the whole calendar gets fucked up because they're worried that Caesar might keep power an extra few weeks. After that I started letting it be known that I was really fed up, and that's when Cato and a few of the sharper ones started to smell a rat. Aaagh . . .''

At that point, Livinius, Curio stopped, belched, turned his head away from me and threw up on the floor. Then he turned back, put his face (puke smell and all) very close to mine and stumbled on: "You're a charming and attractive young man, Lollianus, you know that? You apply yourself, keep your head . . . you'll do well. Appealing, attractive young fellow like yourself . . . God, there was one fellow, one of the ones that worked for me . . . beautiful young man, just . . . perfect. God, I wanted him . . . it would have been so sweet. Never quite managed it, though. But Mark Antony did: he got him. He gets 'em all, sooner or later—that slime!

"Anyway . . . where was I? Oh yes: Cato smells a rat—me, of course, heh-heh. And that was all right because it depended on a few of them starting to catch on. But I was still sending mixed signals, keeping them confused, in public professing to be unswervingly dedicated to keeping a perfect balance between Caesar and Pompey. And it didn't hurt that the special elections that summer actually went against Caesar, with the consulships going to two hard-line conservatives, Lentulus and Marcellus.

"Well, finally it all came down to this business of who kept their armies and who gave up their armies . . . like some goddam parlor game, eh, Lollianus? Of course the Senate wanted Caesar to give up his—he was the one they were scared of. And then somebody, just for show, proposed that Pompey give up his. Well both of those failed, of course, and then came my stroke of genius: I proposed combining them. I said, Let's make them both do it. Well, of course it was irresistible. They had to approve it or the mob would have burned half the city down. And so it passed, 370 votes in favor and just 22 against.

"Then came Lentulus's famous words: 'Enjoy your victory and

have Caesar for a master!' He dashed out of the Senate chamber, and he, Marcellus, Cato and a few others raced out to Pompey's house and appointed him to a whole new command with powers to raise armies all over Italy. No Senate approval; no appeal to the people. Completely and totally illegal and unconstitutional! Like I say, they fell into it like stampeding cattle. And so, faced with that, why shouldn't Caesar cross into Italy! And so he did, and now it's all working out perfectly!"

Livinius, here I must warn you—I'm still not sure if I'm glad that Curio told me the rest. But one thing's certain, dear cousin: If I could stand listening to it, coming straight from him, you can stand reading it. So just keep going—all the way to the bitter end:

"It's all so perfect, Lollianus, you stick with me and you won't be sorry. You'll see: when the war's over, I'll be the one to become Caesar's second-in-command. You don't believe me? I'm telling you, Lollianus: I'm the fair-haired boy in this man's army. What about . . . who? Mark Antony? He's out, finished—a walking dead man. Even now, Caesar's so fed up with him, and with what's going to be revealed later . . . well, you wait and see. What is it? Well, it's quite scandalous, I can tell you that much, Lollianus, and by the gods it'll finish that rotter for good, and I'll be so happy." (At this point, he pounded his right fist into the palm of his left hand.) "Mark Antony! Always the bravest, the fastest, the strongest, the cleverest. Well he's an idiot, goddamit! And it'll take more than broad shoulders and a barrel chest and a big dick to run the Roman Empire, I can tell you. I'll see to it that it takes more; I've already seen to it. How? Well . . . Ah, more wine, eh? You trying to get me drunk, Lollianus? Yes, yes, I know: I'm already drunk. Stinko, actually. So . . . I can see you're a fellow of my own stripe, Lollianus, but I'm trusting you with my life when I tell you the rest:

"You see, when the war is over, Mark Antony will be accused of murder. Five murders, to be exact. Five very scandalous murders; three of them, of Fabius Vibulanus, Flaccus Valerius, and Lucius Flavius Severus, involved acts of sodomy, and the other two, of Fabius's girlfriend, Avidia Crispina, and of a slave named Laertes, more or less resulted from the first three.

"Anyway, the scandal will finish him—and all thanks to yours truly, your clever commander, Gaius Scribonius Curio. Will what?

242

Will Antony be put to death? Oh, I doubt that. After all, except for a piece of a doorkeeper's silver sash and a lot of circumstances that are frequently intriguing and even convincing on occasion, there's really very little evidence. But then why should there be evidence, Lollianus? Mark Antony didn't commit the murders.

"I did.

"Or, more accurately put, I arranged to *have* them committed, for of course I touched no weapons nor committed any act of actual violence myself. I simply hired a man to do it, and he did his work quite expertly, I must say. Quick thrusting stab wounds or neatly broken necks, a touch of . . . What did the doctors call it? Oh yes: an 'inflammation about the aperture of the buttocks.' Funny way of putting it, eh?

"Anyway, remarkably enough he was just a slave, this killer, an ex-doorkeeper named Telephus—quite a character, really: this great big bald ugly son of a bitch. But as I say he did excellent work.

"Why did I do it, Lollianus? Because Mark Antony has to go. Because Rome cannot afford such degenerates in high positions of power. Besides that, Antony is stupid and I'm brilliant, so I'm the better man." (Curio leaned back, glassy-eyed, looking lost in thought for a while. Then, once again he pounded his fist into his palm.) "And besides *that,* I told the dumb bastard to keep away from that beautiful boy, that Livinius Severus. I told him: he's mine, keep off him. But of course he wouldn't listen; he had to have him for himself. And now he'll see what happens to people who ignore the wishes of Gaius Scribonius Curio." (He drained yet another full goblet, slumped forward again, though this time propping his head in his left hand, and began to cry.) "Ah, Livinius." Curio said, "I'll always remember you: you're the one that got away."

Well, dear cousin, needless to say, I was shocked almost beyond words, but you'll be happy to know I remained composed throughout. Luckily, that's about all your old mentor had to say, and I'm sure you'll agree it's more than enough. I did ask him, as slyly as I could, one more question: "What ever happened to that slave, that . . . what was his name again? Telephus?" But Curio just shook his head and smiled drunkenly.

It also goes without saying, but I'll say it anyway: that I am now especially close to this new friend and I will definitely take appropriate action very soon. But I plan to think it over a while because I want it to be a grand punishment. Perhaps I'll deceive him about some battle or other; perhaps I'll tamper with some intelligence reports—though if I do that there's always the possibility I might find myself going to my own death right alongside him. But if that's what is needed, then so be it, for my little life is well worth the price to rid the world of the likes of Curio.

For now, Livinius, I wish you as always good fortune in everything you pursue, and I remain your devoted friend and faithful cousin, Avitus Lollianus Fino.

I put the letter aside and realize that once again this long and awful day my face is wet with tears. Ah, Lollianus, I think. Ah, Lucius Flavius.

Again, I hear rough noises just outside the little anteroom. This time I get up and walk to the doorway. Mark Antony is throwing another tantrum, but Augustus is somehow winning the argument.

". . . it has to be done . . ." I hear Antony say.

". . . not a chance in hell . . ." Augustus answers.

Still standing next to them is that man Telephus with a blank expression on his face, his bald head as shiny as ever in the flickering lamplight.

I watch him—watch them all—with an odd feeling of numbness within me, as if the few yards between them and me might as well be the length of the world and I am powerless to act against any of them in any way.

So it is with that feeling, or lack of feeling, that I first see what *might* be the clear and simple solution to my problem. I first notice this thing without thinking. I look at it and look away, then look back at it and suddenly cannot take my eyes off it. I stare at it for quite a few minutes before I finally come to the realization that it definitely *is* a solution, and then I think it over for only the shortest imaginable portion of time—the briefest instant.

And then I act.

The thing, the object, that I have been staring at is in Augustus's left hand. It is being held there quite carelessly, actually dangling down at his left side where anyone can reach it:

It is Augustus's dagger.

244

I quickly estimate that I can cover the distance between me and Augustus in about five bounding steps. So I do it; I make my move: I dash over there, grab the knife, raise it up, indulge myself in just one brief look into Telephus's numbingly dull eyes. And then I plunge the blade into his stomach as hard as I can. I twist the knife and cut a long slit across his midsection; then I yank out the blade. The skin flaps down and Telephus's insides spill out even as he falls to the floor.

He is screaming and nearly dead, surely beyond understanding, but I cannot resist it. I lean down beside him and yell, "You murdered my cousin." Then, for good measure, I slit his throat.

I stand up and drop the knife. There is blood everywhere, a lot of it on me. Antony and Augustus are staring at me with amazed expressions on their faces. Then I swear I see Antony steal a quick glance at Augustus, and then without another word or gesture he turns on his heels and walks out of the house.

★ ★ ★

The next thing I remember I wake up in a strange bedroom, but I feel vaguely reassured by the light of dawn and the sound of birds singing. Then I even feel safe when I look out the window and realize I am still in Cicero's old house.

And then I remember the night before and the whole day leading up to it, and I suddenly feel a terrible trembling in my stomach, so I lean out the window and throw up. I feel slightly better, but I cannot sit still, for when I do I just start shaking and throwing up again. I walk out into the corridor, and naturally there is a guard posted beside the doorway.

"Morning, my lord; feeling better, I hope," he says.

It is one of the large guards who escorted me to this house yesterday morning, and it strikes me that his amiable greeting is almost comic.

"Oh, well, yes, I—"

"Oh good, sir, very good. Then if it's all right, sir, that is, if you're feeling up to it, Augustus would like to see you now."

I tell myself: there are so many things I could say to that, so many facial expressions I could make. But at this late stage, what's the point, after all?

So I silently nod agreement, and he leads me down the stairs, across the courtyard and into a small rear room which Augustus has set up as a temporary office.

The guard announces me, but the boy ruler, sitting on a high stool beside a worktable with his back to the door, is busily shuffling papers and doesn't bother to look up. He merely grunts and waves his hand, and the guard quietly backs out of the room.

I stand there waiting, but only very briefly. For some reason or other, I am once again feeling strangely safe and secure. Indeed, now it is going beyond that: I feel positively bold. Why is that? I wonder. Is it because I killed a man last night and am still alive this morning? Or am I already resigned to being yet another victim of these ghastly new kings of Rome? Or am I simply too weary to care any longer about what happens to me—or to anyone?

Whatever the reason, I look around the room, spot the most comfortable-looking sofa and without waiting for so much as a sign of recognition from the busy Augustus, I walk over to it, lie down and make quite a little show of stretching out as comfortably as I can.

"You're a terrible man, Augustus," I say, and from my view of his profile I can just see the left corner of his mouth turn up in a brief flicker of a smile.

"Oh come now," I snap. "Doesn't a man you're going to murder deserve a bit of courtesy, a bit of priority treatment? Put those papers aside; let's get this over with."

Augustus stops his writing and shuffling, and slowly lifts his head. "Murder you, Livinius?" he says, his back still to me. Then at last he very slowly turns around to face me. "Whatever in the world gave you that idea? No one's going to murder you, not if I have anything to say about it. In fact, if I have anything to say about it—and I expect to have lots of things to say about nearly everything from now on—you're going to live a long, long time."

I suddenly feel like throwing up again, but I decide that probably would not be such a good idea so I fight off the impulse. I try to look directly at the boy ruler, but at this particular moment I find it extremely difficult to do so.

"Please, Augustus, I think I've been through enough, so spare me this ridiculous conversation!" I finally blurt out. Then, with an exasperated shake of my head, I take hold of myself and begin

246

speaking in a much softer tone. "You murdered my cousin Junius Barnabas right in front of me, then gouged out his eyes for good measure. And now that I think about it you probably had my cousin Claudius Barnabas killed as well—is that right?"

"Yes, I did that."

"So then what am I supposed to think? Why should I believe that you plan anything less dreadful for me? So please, Augustus: let me have a last moment with my wife, promise me she'll come to no harm and I'll even save you a bit of trouble. I'll take the dagger to myself. But don't toy with me any longer—I really can't stand it!"

Augustus leans back, smiles and lets loose a snort of laughter. "I'm not, Livinius; I promise you: I'm *not* going to kill you; I'm not going to have anyone else kill you. I'm not going to allow anyone to kill you even if they want to kill you, and there is someone who does, you know. Mark Antony does; he wants to very much. Or at least he did until last night. But now . . . well, it seems he's changed his mind."

Augustus stands up, walks to a small cabinet at the far end of the room and pulls out a jug of wine and two goblets. Then he walks over, sits down beside me on the edge of the sofa and offers me a taste.

I shake my head. "No, thanks—" I start to say, then abruptly change my mind. "Oh, why not?" I say, and think: Everything else has gone crazy, so why make a big thing about wine before breakfast, eh?

He pours off enough to fill each of our goblets about halfway and takes a small sip; I do the same at first, but a minute later change my mind again and swallow most of the rest in one gulp.

"Look, Livinius. I know you've seen some terrible things here. I know you've suffered. I know I seem . . . well . . ."

"Like a monster," I say. "Like a fucking monster."

My voice is suddenly so loud that two guards rush in, but Augustus waves them off. "It's all right," he tells them, but they still glare at me and take a careful look around before they walk slowly out of the room.

"Yes, all right: like a monster," Augustus says with a heavy sigh. "I know that." He stops, takes a deep breath and drains his own

247

goblet. Then he pours us each another, this time filling the containers to the brim.

"I know it seems like that," he says. "I know you're thinking . . . well . . . how terrible things are . . ." He stops again and stares off into space. "But even you said it, that I 'seem' that way. And I do; I admit it: I *seem* like a monster. But I'm not, I promise you; not really." He pauses, shakes his head and smiles. "God, that sounds pathetic, doesn't it?" And he laughs out loud.

"Listen to me . . ." He stops, clears his throat and starts again: "Look, I know a lot of terrible things have happened. And, truth be told, I'm afraid there'll be a lot more of them. But . . . eventually, it *will* get better. I promise you that.

"And you . . . well, you'll be here to see it. I know you'll be here because you'll be working for me. And you'll be working for me because I'm going to need you, Livinius—you and people like you. After all, we can't kill off all the good men and expect to do the job the gods have given us—the job of running the world.

"I will need—Rome will need—men such as yourself, of intelligence, courage, integrity and spirit. We'll need men who can challenge and innovate and improve, and then be willing and able to improve on the improvements.

"Of course as I say it won't be right away. And . . . well, you'll probably have to lie low for a while . . ."

"W-h-a-a-"

"Oh, there are several alternatives. I have a pleasant enough estate down at Capri, if that appeals to you. I can get you whatever you need: a different girl for every hour of the day, if you like. Or boys, if that's your preference: I'm broad-minded."

"Don't be ridiculous, I wouldn't—"

"All right, don't have a fit over it. Take your wife, if you want. That's fine with me. I'm only presenting the options. And then, a year or so down the road, I'll quietly bring you back, give you a minor post in the treasury or in road building. Whatever can be arranged. It's all so flexible, so . . . exciting. All the possibilities stretching out before us, Livinius. A whole new world to build and run, a world ruled by a just and powerful Rome, a world where . . . well, where there'll be no place for the sorts of things that you've seen—that we've all seen—too much of lately."

248

He stops at last and stares off, and I look at him with a feeling of amazement: this butcher, this cruel, power-grabbing boy, suddenly talking about some grand new world of fairness and justice. A world in which *I* will work for *him*. It is, I think, all too absurd to credit with any serious chance of success.

Or is it?

I study him: his brown eyes are wide and intense, his jaw set, his whole face animated with . . . what? Determination? Sincerity? Is it possible that he means what he says? Odd, but I gradually realize that at some deep inner level I want to believe him. And then I realize with a start that I am beginning to believe him, because the things he is saying and the way he is saying them *make* me want to believe him.

"Well, it all sounds fine, Augustus, but with all that's happened here . . . And now you're telling me I have to go into exile for a year? Am I confused about something? Is there something you still haven't told me?"

Augustus groans softly, pours us each more wine, then stands up and paces small circles around the room. "It's all . . . part of the price, Livinius," he says, looking straight at me. He gulps down yet another full goblet, then props himself up on his work stool.

"The price?"

"Yes, Livinius. For keeping you alive." He smiles, though without any apparent pleasure, and wearily shakes his head. "You see, Mark Antony wanted you dead. Actually, he wanted everyone dead who had anything to do with, or knew anything about, that report of yours. That meant the Barnabas brothers, of course. And it meant you. But you could not be murdered."

"Why not?"

"Just wait," he says, holding up a quieting hand. "So the price kept getting higher. 'Get Livinius over here,' Antony insisted. So I agreed. 'Well, have his cousin Claudius Barnabas killed and put his body out on the street for him to see on his way here,' Antony says, and he laughs when he says this. And I agree to that. Then he says, 'Augustus, you personally, with your own hands, have to murder Junius Barnabas, and you have to do it right in front of him,' meaning you. Well, I argued about that awhile, as you might imagine. But I'm no stranger to this sort of thing, Livinius, and I won't pretend otherwise; I'm sure you've heard the stories. So finally I went along with that, as well. And then he says, 'Well, what about Telephus? He must have known about the report. Besides, he really did do all those murders, and he's only an ex-slave anyway.' Mind you, Livinius, I could hardly believe Antony was saying this, because of course it was Telephus who helped save his neck by buying back your father's copy of that other report— the one from your cousin Lucius. Also, I doubt poor Telephus even knew what was in the report—in either of them, or that he ever realized the murders he was doing for Curio were to be used against Antony. In any case, I said all right about Telephus, but then Antony came up with this insane bit of theatrics that you carried out so splendidly for his benefit last night."

I blink my eyes in confusion, then, watching him closely, I realize what he means. "You deliberately held your dagger that way. You wanted me to grab it." He tilts his head slightly forward, a confirming nod, and I numbly shake my head. "Amazing," I say. "You both looked so . . . shocked."

"Well, I don't think you ever really get used to seeing a man killed like that. Besides, I suppose I was amazed that his idiotic plan worked; I didn't think you'd take the bait. As for Antony, I think that for a moment he was afraid you might turn the knife on him. As soon as you dropped it, his business was over for the day, and he simply went out for the evening to wherever Mark Antony goes to on his evenings out."

I shake my head again and actually manage a smile. "By Jove, you're both so disgusting," I say.

"I *have* to go along, I have to do these things—all right!" he snaps. It is the first time I've been able to provoke a bit of real anger from him. "And it will get even worse before it gets better," he goes on. "But I swear to you, it *will* get better—better than you've ever dreamed it could get, better than anything the old republic could ever have imagined."

"So the republic won't be back," I say.

He casts his eyes downward a moment, then looks directly at me again. "That's right," he says very softly. "That old man is gone for good."

"Hmm," I say, staring off. "But you still haven't told me—"

"Why you can't be murdered? I know. Well, it's very simple, really. It's a promise my great-uncle Julius Caesar made to your father-in-law—"

"Avidius?" I say with a gasp, and I suddenly recall seeing him that long, dark night all those years ago as Lollianus and I hid in Caesar's tent outside Ravenna.

"Yes, Victorinus Avidius himself. He was afraid of the murder case you were investigating. He understood how tricky Curio could be. He didn't want you . . . entangled. So he provided my uncle with one hundred million sesterces, and the bribe to Curio was paid directly from that. And by the way it wasn't ten million. It was sixty."

"By the gods!" I gasp again.

"In return, Julius Caesar gave his solemn word that no harm would ever come to you or your immediate family. He even made it a codicil in his will to me, so I intend to keep that promise, especially as I am legally bound to do so. And by the way he made it clear exactly who he meant: you, your wife, your parents, and any children you might have. Your cousins, I'm sad to say, were not protected."

I stare off thoughtfully, wistfully. So does Augustus, from what I can tell. After a while, he orders breakfast of boiled eggs, spinach and diced oysters; I ask for the same. As we eat, we quietly go back over some of the same ground:

Are you sure it was sixty million? I ask. Definitely, he assures me.

But why would he need so much? I wonder aloud. What would he do with it all?

"Well," Augustus patiently explains, "a lot of it was debts from that lavish funeral he gave his father some years back. But it was also the whole way he lived, that high and handsome life. Costs plenty to do that, you know."

We finish eating and stroll out into the courtyard. It is an overcast morning—typical for December, with a wintry bite to the air that sets me shivering. It doesn't bother Augustus, though; he seems quite comfortable as we walk lazily through the little garden together, until a few minutes later when the old timekeeper and his helper come out and head for the hourglass.

Suddenly, Augustus stops dead in his tracks and stares at the old man, and I see him shudder from the cold.

"Third hour, my lords," the timekeeper says.

A moment after that a doorkeeper appears at the far side of the courtyard and rushes toward us. Breathlessly, he announces the arrival of urgent dispatches; indeed, the courier, not having waited to be ushered in, is hot on the doorman's heels. He is also no ordinary courier, I notice: his face is deeply creased, his eyes are cool, metallic and grimly determined. He is very tall and very muscular, and wearing iron-toed combat boots that scrape noisily over the tiles; also, he is armed with a soldier's sword that clanks imposingly at his side. He approaches Augustus, salutes smartly and hands him a papyrus scroll.

Augustus returns the salute, then waves him off, and the courier-soldier turns and quicksteps away. Augustus waits a moment, eyes closed, as if trying to solve a puzzle in his head. Then he shrugs, tears open the dispatch, looks at it and instantly bursts into tears.

These are no light tears of happiness, either; these are great, wrenching sobs that seem to come from someplace deep inside him. Then, to my amazement, he hands the letter to me. I pull it open and read it. There are three words in large block letters on the paper. They say:

"CICERO IS DEAD."

"By the gods," I murmur, and with that Augustus begins to sob more loudly than ever.

"The hourglass, Livinius, it was never for you," he manages to choke out. Then he turns and walks back into the house.

There are no tears from me right off, and I realize that I am more angry than sorrowful. And then it occurs to me that I am only angry at Augustus. He has no right to cry over Cicero, I tell myself. He didn't really know him, didn't even like him much, probably helped bring about his death.

I look at the scroll again. Down at the bottom, in much smaller letters, is written: "The Roman proconsul Marcus Tullius Cicero expired by violence at the second hour on the seventh day of December in this Roman year 707." At that, finding myself alone in the garden of what used to be Cicero's house in Rome, my anger quickly fades and soon enough I am crying my eyes out.

252

"Where did it happen?" I ask.

It is nearly midday, and we are back in Augustus's little office drinking yet another round of wine.

"Near Brundisium, I believe." He stops and shakes his head in frustration. "Such a fool; so unnecessary. I had agents of my own with him—though he didn't know it, of course. And they kept telling him: Take the boat, escape to Africa or Spain, get out of Italy. But he wavered and delayed until finally they hunted him down and killed him." He pauses and his eyes start to mist over again. "Goddam it," he yells, and pounds his fist on the table beside him.

"I gather this was Mark Antony's idea," I say.

"Oh well, you know. I approved it. I can't escape the guilt. Or the shame. But . . . well . . . yes, of course it was Antony's idea."

"Because of the report?"

"The report; the *Philippics;* everything: Cicero's whole life. You understand, Livinius: It's like when Curio told your cousin Lollianus that Antony 'had to go.' It's the same idea. Cicero, at least in the opinion of the powers that be, had simply run out his string. He could no longer remain a living person—not in the Rome of Mark Antony and his estimable colleague, yours truly."

For the first time I feel as though I am getting a glimmer of Augustus's remarkable personality—a personality of such complexity and guile and craftiness as to be almost unfathomable. For some reason, I suddenly think about the scroll again, about the message in small letters announcing the time of Cicero's death. And it occurs to me: that was yesterday morning, at exactly the hour I first saw Augustus watch with such interest as the timekeeper turned the glass. So he knew the moment of Cicero's death that precisely, I think. Yet now he sheds his tears of shock and grief. Was it yesterday that he was acting, when he fairly spat out Cicero's name? Or is it now, with his indignation and weeping?

And then I realize: I don't know, and as a matter of fact I'll never know—not for sure. No one will—not now, not ever—be able to tell for certain the true feelings of this astonishing young man, even though there are of course so many moments of this sort inevitably to come. Right now, for instance, to be able to speak and weep with such genuine anguish over a man whom you have, at least indirectly, helped to murder, and moreover to admit to this complicity—and still be able to live with yourself. Now that to me is truly beyond comprehension!

Then again, I tell myself, perhaps this is simpler than I think: perhaps Augustus merely possesses the personality of the perfect politician. Or does it require something even less than a politician's craftiness to turn an event so completely on its head? Is it something that most anyone might be capable of under certain circumstances—as, for example, a situation in which one might actually find one's self amiably chatting with the very man who just one day earlier had murdered one's own cousin before one's very eyes?

In any case, I decide, he has opened up a subject that I wish to pursue. "Speaking of Lollianus," I say, "you never did tell me how you got hold of his letter."

"I don't know," Augustus says almost dreamily.

"Excuse me?" I say. My tone is sharply demanding, and I immediately get his attention.

"Forgive me, Livinius; that was thoughtless," he says. "What I mean is, I found the letter in my uncle's private files, but I have no idea how it got there. Obviously, it was intercepted in some way, but I have no idea when, or how, or by whom "

"In your uncle's files. You mean, in the private files of Julius Caesar?"

"That's right."

"You don't think Mark Antony had it before that, do you?" I ask. "That is, you do think it's authentic."

"Well, of cour— That is . . . what do you mean? That Antony could have forged it to get out from under his own crimes? By Jupiter, I never thought . . . that is, you think it's authentic, don't you, Livinius?"

"Well . . . I suppose so," I say. At that point, I can't help smiling a little, but I go on anyway. "It certainly sounds like my cousin, and it is written in his hand, but . . ." I shrug and let my voice trail off. I look over to see Augustus studying me, though with a slight smile of his own.

"Ah! I see. You're toying with me a little," he says with an oddly forced little snort of laughter. "Good. Very good. Shows you're learning, Livinius."

I nod agreeably. "Yes, Augustus. I'm learning. I've always learned quickly, once I know there's something new afoot that's worth the effort."

★ ★ ★

It is midafternoon before we say our goodbyes. We have been strolling through the house and right now we are standing near the front of the atrium, just inside the front door.

"I took the liberty of having your wife brought around," Augustus tells me with a smile. "She's outside waiting for you now."

Ah, Fulvia: how wonderful to think of her! And what a pleasant surprise that she's here.

"Remember," Augustus tells me, "you leave for Capri day after tomorrow. And don't worry so much, Livinius. Trust me. It will all be all right in the end."

I turn my palms up in a gesture of resignation, as if to say: Whatever occurs, I'm ready for it. Then I walk out into the hazy sunshine of a December afternoon in Rome and climb onto the *litter where my wife is ready and waiting with a kiss and a tear and a beautiful smile.*

EPILOGUE

More than forty years have passed since that day I left Augustus standing in the entranceway to Cicero's old house in Rome. And while I cannot say that he has been absolutely right about absolutely everything, he has been nearly right about almost everything. And it would be hard to pinpoint even one thing about which he has been proved significantly mistaken.

Fulvia and I stayed at Capri nearly two years before Augustus kept the first part of his promise and brought us back to Rome. Even then, we languished in the background for several more years until the disputes between Augustus and Mark Antony became more and more serious, and finally spilled into the open.

That was when my star really began to rise. Augustus placed me at his side in the most prominent positions of authority, until I ultimately joined him at the battle of Actium where we drove Mark Antony and Cleopatra from the seas. We raced after them to Alexandria, but as all the world knows we were just hours late: the lovely couple had committed suicide before we could reach them and get the pleasure of assisting them with their plan to expire.

By then it had been twelve years since the death of Julius Caesar. It had taken his clever great-nephew that long to consolidate his hold over the Roman world, during which time, to put it politely, a considerable number of atrocities had been committed by all involved. It was one more promise that Augustus had kept. But then he kept another:

Once he achieved sole command, all the horrors ended. The vengeful and snarling boy ruler who had terrified the world with his cruelties for so long now gave way to the remarkable young man whom I was privileged to glimpse on that long-ago day in Cicero's garden. Indeed, within five years he was known far and wide as "Augustus the Great and the Good."

I don't know that Cicero would have approved of that title. I doubt he would ever have called him a "good" man, not in the truly Stoic sense, for at heart Augustus remained a crafty, guileful and ultimately tyrannical politician. But his instincts were good. He knew how to survive, and he understood with astonishing clarity that for him to survive and avoid the bloody end of most despots, Rome had not only to survive but to flourish. And for Rome to flourish, Rome, he knew, needed a lasting and stable government.

And that he has provided; that is what he has worked for all his days: a whole new legal and constitutional system. The republic would not come back—that was another promise he kept. But Rome, he decided, could live without it. And I must confess it seems to be doing that rather nicely at the moment.

★ ★ ★

As for myself, just as I kept my promise to Lucius Flavius, Augustus kept his promise to me: I have lived a long time, and what's more I've spent all my years in the service of the state—and like it or not that has meant in the service of Augustus. In light of all that happened, who would have believed it possible? But survival, I've learned, frequently requires a profound acceptance of the unbelievable.

Well, needless to say I am very old now. Fulvia has remained my devoted wife and helpmate all these years, and to this day cares for me with a special tenderness that leaves me speechless with love and gratitude. I never went off wine again (thank the gods). Nevertheless (or perhaps because of that), she and I ultimately had seven children, three of whom, a son and two daughters, have, praise the gods, survived to adulthood. In fact, there are several grandchildren scurrying about these days, though I admit I sometimes forget just how many. Yes, yes, I have become forgetful, and that's why a year or so ago I finally retired from public life—though I still may have a trick or two up my sleeve and a story or two to tell. Like the one about a certain famous poet sent into exile because he knew too much. But of course all that's for another time.

257

And . . . well, let me see: my father and I eventually reconciled, and he lived out his days in a relatively peaceful haze of wine and warm mead. My amazing father-in-law lived another twenty years after all the troubles were over to the grand old age of seventy-seven. In all that time, he and I never spoke about his extraordinary "protection payment" to Julius Caesar—the payment that saved my life.

What of Augustus? He has also gotten on in years, of course, though not quite so far as I. As a matter of fact, he still rules here, is still very much in charge, and they tell me he shows no signs whatever of slowing down in the slightest.

As for Gaius Scribonius Curio, I still remember him vividly, still think about him from time to time. If he'd lived, what would he have become? I wonder. He had, after all, as much brilliance and promise as any young Roman of his day, and, mellowing through the years, I can look back now and say that the horrors he committed were no worse than those done by so many others.

But what would have been his ultimate place in Rome? Would he have been another Antony, cruel and degenerate with no real sense of how to govern? Or would he have been more like Augustus, with enough of the true statesman deep inside him to overpower his baser ideas?

Then again, aren't comparisons of that sort futile in the end? Shouldn't Curio be judged on his own merits? And if that's the case, one might ask, if he didn't always rely too much on sheer cleverness for his own good? And wouldn't he sooner or later have outsmarted himself in some other way on some other field of battle, military or otherwise (with or without the help of my cousin), and found himself fatally trapped by his own deadly brilliance? If that is correct, then Rome has been better off without him, for as smart and clever as he was, he might very well have taken the rest of us with him to our doom.

That did not happen very simply because it could not happen. For this is Rome, and, just like the men who built it, Rome was designed for survival, above all.

AFTERWORD

Approximately forty years after the end of our story (about thirty years after Augustus's death), the Roman poet Lucan published his history of the Roman Civil Wars. In it he extolled the personal charm, the obvious brilliance, and the undoubted battlefield bravery of one Gaius Scribonius Curio. But in concluding his account, Lucan could not overlook the overriding dominance of his terrible defects:

> Rome never bore a citizen of such high promise, nor one to whom the constitution owed more while he trod the right path. But then the corruption of the age proved fatal to the state, when desire for office, pomp, and the power of wealth, ever to be dreaded, swept away Curio's wavering mind with sidelong flood. And the change of Curio, snared by the spoils and gold of Caesar, was that which turned the tide of history. Although mighty Sulla, fierce Marius, and all the blood-bespattered line of Caesar's house secured the power to use the sword against our throats, yet to none of them was granted so high a privilege. For they all bought their country; Curio *sold* the state!

AUTHOR'S NOTE

The major political events described in *Roman Shadows* are historically accurate, though in one or two cases I have either juggled the chronology or compressed the time involved for the purposes of heightening the drama.

The narrator of the novel, Gaius Livinius Severus, and all the members of his family, are fictional. But the other notable characters, their actions, and the political situations surrounding those actions are based on well-documented accounts.

Caesar, Augustus, Mark Antony, Cato, and Cicero are, of course, real-life figures from the past. The early brutality and later transformation of Augustus, the excesses of Mark Antony, the occasional foolishness and frequent wisdom of Cicero are well documented. All of Cicero's philosophical remarks, as well as his diatribe, or "philippic," against Antony, are adapted from his own writings.

Cicero really was sent into exile in a plot by Clodius (who actually did die a year or so afterward in a gang war on the streets of Rome), and Cicero was, in truth, brutally murdered as part of the mass proscriptions that took place in those early days of rule by Antony and Augustus.

As for Gaius Scribonius Curio, though I have embellished (for with the exception of that famous speech exhorting Caesar to cross the Rubicon, we have very little of Curio's actual writings or speeches), I believe I have done so well within the bounds of his flamboyant personality. Suffice it to say that after more than two thousand years, Curio's acceptance of Caesar's enormous bribe and his connivance in the plot to overthrow the Roman republic remain among the great scandals of human history.

★   ★   ★

A note about the name Augustus: The real-life Augustus was born Gaius Octavius, and he did not actually begin using the name Augustus until a year or more after his final defeat of Mark Antony.

Augustus, however, stopped using the name Octavius soon after Julius Caesar's death, and began calling himself Caesar. But virtually all historians have chosen to ignore that fact. Instead, when speaking of Augustus during those years between Caesar's death and Antony's defeat at Actium, they have chosen to use his boyhood name of Octavius—simply to avoid confusing Augustus with his late uncle.

Since the name Augustus is so much better known, I simply decided in this book to reverse the historian's traditional conceit and pull that name back in time rather than push the other one forward. Thus, I have referred to him throughout by the name he chose for himself in later life.